Spanish Romance

Apostolos Pappas Ph.D.

ISBN: 1456575724
ISBN-13: 9781456575724

Preface and Dedication

This book is dedicated to my grandmother Maria, the best person I ever met in my life. An additional dedication goes to a celebrated English major author, who inspired me to proceed with this project by listening to his wonderful, inspiring and moving writer's almanac.

This book was written between Thanksgiving of 2007 and Easter of 2009. However, the main theme had been spinning in my head for the last twenty-five or so years.

I am not an English major or an author with full command of the English language. I never thought that I could ever be a published author. As a non-native speaker I couldn't easily break this barrier to write a novel in English. As a result the book is written in the form of a gospel where the events, characters and their acts are the important points and are described in a simple vocabulary. The text, in its majority, avoids describing whether the balmy air of the morning reanimated the main character or whether the cloudless sky and the warm rays of the sun, partially intercepted by the tall chimneys, traced brilliant angles of light on the high and somber walls of the room; where on the sill of the window a graceful plant, illuminated by sunshine, played in the breeze.

The reader may find characters that are not fully developed or questions that remain unanswered in this novel, which is intentional to have just enough information to retain independence, yet stand alone as a complete piece of work. God willing, some of the characters will return, some of the questions will be answered, and some of the gaps will be filled. As the secondary title of this book proclaims, this is a prelude to a trilogy that I would like to find the strength and inspiration to complete. This prologue to the trilogy is fundamentally important as it is meant to revive feelings, characters and emotional qualities that have been forgotten, faded and surpassed in our technological, individualistic and money-driven society of the last few decades. The prologue itself has autonomy and sets the emotional pace and milieu for the trilogy to follow.

Apostolos Pappas, Ph. D.
August 7th 2009

To my grandmother Maria (1907 or 1908 - 1997)
and
to Mr. Garisson Keillor.

Spanish Romance
<u>A prelude</u>
Copyright © 2009. All rights reserved

Light! Pure ample light!
How could it be so bright?
The sun is now out of sight.
White clouds cover the sky.
All of a sudden, fast, but why?
Oh! Please God bless, oh my. . .!

Almost dark, but it looks like a game between the clouds and the sun… or better yet…war! Which will win? Darkness or light?
Two people both dressed in white, stand on the roof of the cathedral. They look down below onto the streets, the square and the people. The city feels agitated, yet quiet enough to hear the whispers.
Voices, from different people, are heard in the air:
"Lord, please help him",
"God, please do not abandon him",
"Please, Jesus, do not let him die",
"Please, Lord, help my brother, my fellow man."
"My God, please save him. Please! Please!"
The elder man on the top of the cathedral whispers, "It's a wonderful life."
The younger man asks the older: "Master, why are there all these voices in the air? What is happening?"
The Master replies: "Someone needs help."
Younger: "But who could that be? Someone everyone knows?"
Master: "   A young but old friend."
Young: "What kind of friend?"
Master: "The kind you do not find any more in this world."
Young: "Explain to me, who is he?"
Master: "Someone who is in jail."
Young: "In jail? For what??? What has he done?"
Master: "What hasn't he…?"

Inside a dark cell, where the only window sheds some bundle light, a younger, but nearly middle-aged man, sits at the edge of his bed, bending forward and holding his head. The atmosphere is heavily charged with a heavy pain and the evoked desperation is diffused everywhere. Running tears have left marks everywhere in his face. He remains silent with his eyes filled with pain, while he is staring at the floor without any focus or movement. A face made of pure pain and sorrow, evoking the ultimate loss, the ultimate catastrophe ... however, somehow, once in a while, a question mark sparks from his eyes ... wondering why?

Younger (voice): "Who is he?"
Master (voice): "Well... listen to me. He is one of a kind, but I would rather tell you about his past first."

Queens, NY, the beginning of the 50s – end of 1950.

The arrival of new immigrants from the old countries is an everyday routine. They are tired, but have happy and hopeful faces. The hope is everywhere, in every wrinkled or tired face and the gaze proclaims the hope, for a better future in the Promised Land. The shirts and jackets are old and dusty, but well crafted, evoking care and attention to look as good as possible. People are welcoming people and relatives are embracing each other.
In the middle of the crowd there is a twelve-year-old boy. Shy and humble, he is meeting his uncles and cousins who arrived together with the rest of the extended family. The grandma, slower than all and last, gave the warmest embrace, as her tears joined the peach-colored cheeks of the young man. A very emotional scene, filled with joy on the one hand, but dumbfounded and heart wrenching feelings, on the other for the ones that are missing. The whole family is not all together. Some are still left behind wondering, "Where are they?" What would they become with the passing of the years? Unbridled is the soul of human beings when the memories take over.
Over the years, the boy learned English by watching films every evening after his morning shift at a neighborhood store, and after school in the evening. Late at night, while everyone was in bed sleeping, he kept the light on and studied, till he felt asleep.

A 13-year-old dreamer – working class and poor immigrants but happy

His relatives and family friends employed him as a delivery boy at the local pharmacy. He became the boy for every job: delivering, cleaning, fixing, and just a little bit of everything. He greeted everyone in the streets with a wide happy smile.

Every day he rode his bike to pick up supplies from a warehouse a few blocks down the avenue. On the way to the warehouse, he did a favor for an old lady who was unable to walk to any store and bought her food. He bought yogurt and a soft biscuit for her every day, as most of her teeth were missing and she could not bite on anything else. Every day she would give him a quarter and Dimitri delivered her the food. Her son had left her three years ago. He left her behind in the small studio they used to occupy, when he moved away to San Diego with a girl that he had fallen in love with. She sat in her chair facing west everyday and waited for his return. She spent the whole day knitting and looking west, even during the summer time when the afternoon sun burned her face. She used to sing traditional lamentations and folk songs from her native land and knit for hours facing west waiting for her only son to return and visit her. Her only companions were the street traffic and a pocket-sized radio that she could barely understand, as her English never got to any advanced level. Her pension was only enough to cover the rent and the daily yogurt with biscuit. Dimitri felt a lot of compassion for her since she had no one to help her and she had a gentle, wholesome soul. She once told him the folk story of the mother who was left behind by her son for a girl, something similar to her situation. One day, the girl asked the young son to prove his love to her. The son promised her that he would do anything for her. She asked for the heart of his mother because she wanted to make sure he had love for no one else. The young man, blinded by his passion for her, executed her desire. While he was running fast to return to his love, he stumbled and fell down to the ground. He suffered a sharp pain, while his mother's heart kept rolling from his hands to the ground. While he was crying from his sharp pain, a voice called out from the heart, weeping for him, "Did you hurt yourself, my son?" The story touched him as he felt the heartache

and drama of the old lady, which made him think about his mother and father who did not have the money to join him and had been left behind.
On that same way, he also passed in front of the residence of the Garcia's, who recently arrived from Mexico with their eight kids. The three oldest ones had to wake up early and follow their father to the warehouse to work and earn their daily bread. Dimitri helped the five- and seven-year-old Garcia boys to get to school safely every day, while the other three siblings stayed at home with their mother. He escorted them to the school door and every time he looked at the school building, the flag waving in the wind and the steps, he thought that one day he may become a teacher or a professor or a scientist.

But deep in his heart he was a dreamer! Could it be because he watched too many films? During the daybreaks he would focus on his homework, always hoping to enroll in high school. He also spent a lot of time studying the dictionary. He played with words and their rhymes all the time. Rhyming and the sound of the new vocabulary words fascinated him. He memorized at least twenty-four words a day. Late in the afternoon, he went to the prep school for immigrants and almost every other evening he snuck into the movie theater through the back door.
His family gathered for dinner after everyone finished their jobs and Dimitri returned from school. Uncle Bill arrived last from his bus-driving job, and grandma had the whole meal ready and laid out on the table.
They always smiled during the evening gatherings. They never had a lot on the table or much variety, and it was common for Uncle Bill to remind them that they had to save money; they had to pay the bills; but also increase the savings so they could buy an apartment at some point. Last, but not least, the head of the family and the most respected man, the grandfather, reminded everyone that they also had to send money back to their home country for the rest of the family members, as well as save extra money to bring them to Queens.
Dimitri's parents sent him to the US after the war. There was never enough bread to feed the three kids that survived and their orphan cousins. Everyone had to be considerate with expenses and savings. However, they still looked happy at the dinner table, smiling and treasuring the moment of being together and always hoping for the best. They were grateful to be in the land

of promise, and the warmth of their everyday life was always apparent in the room.

Jewish, Italian and Greek together

In the early fifties, Queens was the place for newcomers and fresh immigrants. Dimitri could have survived there only speaking Greek, as numerous older Greek immigrants surrounded him daily. However, he loved to cross the line and pass to the nearby neighborhoods to meet other children and practice his English skills. The Italians were on one side and the Jewish neighborhood was on the other. He quickly made two good friends, Giovanni and Josef, who wanted to be called John and Joe, so they could feel more like Americans since their parents were fresh immigrants. Both were native speakers, as their families arrived before the war in Europe had started. Joe was born in Queens and John, who became Giovanni again later on, was only a year old when he arrived. They both helped Dimitri perfect his English day by day. They became friends right away, since they all had the same passion, the cinema. The three of them used to sneak through the back door of the nearby theater together to watch movies. They all cherished cinema and John had aspirations to become an actor, while Joe desired to become a director or producer. They were passionate about movies and snuck into Mr. Smith's Odeon Theater together every other day, since they could not afford to pay or get permission to see more than one movie per week. They were so passionate about Hollywood and longed to watch heroic films with John Wayne and Gary Cooper. They never missed a Western or a heroic movie, and also admired Gregory Peck and Tyron Power. They spent hours every weekend talking about the movies they had watched and the ones they were planning to see the following week. High Noon was their favorite, and Joe practiced the theme song on his guitar, which they all sang together in a humorous way.

Outside the theater, forbidden games, 1953- the guitar, the melody- Queens

1953 - Dimitri and his friends exited the Odeon theater, where the marquee featured the movie title "*Forbidden Games*".

Giovanni, who loved foreign films and didn't want to be called John anymore, teased Dimitri, "Why did we watch a French film today? We wasted our time."

"Well, I managed to learn English already, right? … So why not? Aren't you happy to see that a great foreign film?"

G: "Well, it did not have any great-looking girls."

D: "Hmmm… Yes it did!"

"Who?"

"Well, she was all over the screen. Whenever the guitar was playing that melody."

"What are you talking about? Did you see another film? Who are you referring to? Who was there? Explain!"

"That music was as good as any other star we usually watch in a film … with the difference that now you can imagine her as you would like her to be."

"Ahh? You don't make sense and you sound like a lunatic! No music can replace the image of a woman!!"

"You would think so, but right now my brain is playing that melody… over and over again … I do not want to forget it. Let's go get Joe, so I can whistle it to him – he will play it right away for us, he has a good ear."

"So what's the point? I still think we wasted our time today with this Frenchy-film."

"No we didn't!"

His talented in music friend.

Minutes later, Joe was playing the guitar while Dimitri was whistling the tune: "The Spanish Romance". Giovanni later begged him to stop whistling, as he preferred to listen to the guitar alone. Dimitri stopped, but once in a while he still whistled, but quietly.

J: You know I can look for the music sheet at the bookstore and give it to you for your birthday as a gift!

D: What would I do with it? I can't read music.

Dimitri took the guitar from Joe's hands and started scratching it, imitating what Joe played previously.

J: You are getting better and better Dimitri. One day you will learn how to read music.

D: I have to learn how to properly read English first!

J: Oh come on, you are so talented! Three years ago, you didn't know a word of English and now you are fluent. Learning music is easier than learning English. You already have such a talent to put the words together and write lyrics that rhyme.

D: Oh those are just exercises that help me play with words. They have no value.

J: That's not true! The other day you made me cry with your limericks! I am a native speaker and I can't do the same! You need talent for that and you certainly have it!

D: Ah yeah, you are always overestimating me, because I can play and sing without any lessons, but that does not make me a Sinatra.

J: Of course not! But look at me; I can't compete with you in playing with words and putting limericks together!

D: Well, I am learning from my old papou (a Greek word for grandpa), who is so obsessed with these "dictionary games"! Oh you know the greatest Greek poet ever, who wrote the national anthem, he did not know the language very well upon his return to his homeland! He got his education in Italy and had to learn from a dictionary as well; Greek words were all new to him at that time!

J: Really?

D: Oh yes indeed, and his anthem is so beautiful and consists of 158 stangas all beautifully put together. That's from someone who was educated in Italy and did not speak Greek well enough.

J: "That is amazing! Are you related to him?" he asked with a big smile.

D: "No, I do not think so!"

J: I bet you are! Why don't you take it as an assignment, to write lyrics to this wonderful piece of music that has been wordless so far?

D: Do you know the composer?

J: No, I don't think anyone does.

D: Well are you sure there are no lyrics?

J: I am pretty sure this has been anonymous and wordless. Well, in "Blood and Sand", someone added lyrics, but I could not tell you what they are, as they weren't in English.

D: Spanish?

J: I think so, but no one really has written serious lyrics for this composition that has been wordless forever.

D: Maybe this is how it is meant to be?

J: What do you mean?

D: Well, you know it is such a perfect piece of music that once you add lyrics to it you "restrict" it.

J: "Restrict it?"

D: Right! You know, once you put words … they have a meaning … for a specific instance, a specific love, a specific girl, a specific romance….

J: I know English is your second language, but what do you really mean?

D: A wordless melody allows everyone to dress it with whatever dreams, words and faces one wishes to…. If you know what I mean.

J: I think I get it. You could be right…

D: I will never attempt to add lyrics to such a piece of music, which is meant to let you imagine any kind of love, passion and romance.

Romantic guitar, music passion but no lyrics! Love at first site

Dimitri attempted to slowly learn how to play the melody on Joe's guitar on a daily basis. He was not as good as his friend at playing the guitar. However, he played it as much as he could, since it always gave him great pleasure. The melody made him dream about the girl he fell in love with at first site! Dimitri, up to that point had never mentioned her to Giovanni and Joe. He kept it secret. He would dream about her every night and was clearly, deeply in love with her.

Every Sunday he would wait at the corner of the boulevard to see her going out with her family, for what seemed like a usual Sunday excursion to the City; to the glamourous heart of the city, the island, its center, which Dimitri could not yet go to on his own. He could not follow them because he had no money for a cab or even the train. He did not care to know where they were headed, since deep inside him he sensed that his love was destined to be unrequited. The big house at the end of the Boulevard looked too lavish for an immigrant boy to ever think that he could infiltrate such a wealthy family. But of course, other times, he forgot about it as he was such a dreamer and always had a hopeful soul.

Many times he saw the gates of that mansion open as the expensive car was driven out by a chauffeur to take her father to the City. Her father was always nicely groomed and impeccably dressed, which revealed and reminded Dimitri of the many social layers that separated him from the girl. However, that never made him stop playing the guitar or stop dreaming about her. He was a dreamer after all. He borrowed Joe's guitar all the time. He only played that one tune as he could not play any other ones, since he had no training and had to memorize the tunes by heart.

Grandfather and Kipling

One Sunday, the day that everyone in his family was off and rested, he started playing again. Everyone, except for his grandfather, was away from home at a baptism. Grandpa, who happened to hear him play for the first time, immediately realized that Dimitri was in love. He followed the music and once he spotted Dimitri, he looked at him with his eyes - eyes that know and could deeply penetrate the soul of a young man.

Grandpa was not just someone ordinary, but rather a very exceptional person, who held a special place in Dimitri's heart, especially for his intellect. He had only graduated from elementary school and was a man of few words, but words of wisdom. Life taught him a lot in the last fifty-five years of hard work; hard work for survival and about a dozen different jobs, where he encountered all kinds of people, in all kinds of places, before he was able to bring part of his family to Queens. Every time he spoke, everyone held their breath to listen to him with reverence. His dense white hair represented the many experiences he had and the numerous medals of honors he deserved to be awarded throughout his rich and eventful life. How he came to America was a miracle, as he did not even have a ticket but managed to sneak onto a big boat, when he was only thirteen years old. His life was full of hard work, but also full of regret for never being able to achieve any higher education than elementary school. He spent every night reading, not just the newspaper as everyone else did in the home, but literature, poetry and history. No immigrant in the broader neighborhood had his thirst for knowledge and no one else took so many trips to the local library at the end of every working day as he did.

Grandpa never showed off his vast knowledge on things, but he had always been Dimitri's idol who wanted very much to become as wise as Grandpa one day. It was Grandpa with whom he played with words and their rhyme and crafted poems in English. Dimitri found it fascinating, and it was Grandpa who passed onto him the zeal and interest to follow his example. That is why Grandpa spent time with Dimitri, to teach him what fifty or more years of playing with words in his new country had taught him so far.

It was Grandpa who gave Dimitri, Kipling's "If",which was the first English poem that he had ever memorized and became his life's motto. In the meantime, he infused Dimitri with a strong belief in dreams. He knew that if Dimitri could focus and utterly believe in achieving his dreams, he could make anything happen.

Grandpa was the one who insisted on talking to Dimitri in English only. For the first two years, he encouraged him every single night to read books from the library together with the help of a dictionary. The first limerick that Dimitri had crafted as an exercise made Grandpa very proud and since that day he encouraged him to play with words and learn how to use them.

Grandpa, " When did you learn how to play the guitar?"

D: "Joe showed me how – I am not good – I just memorized a couple of tunes."

G: "Well, you could be a Segovia one day."

D: "Who is he? One of your Greek friends?"

G: "No, his name sounds Greek, but he is a Spaniard."

D: "Hey, wait a second, this piece of music that I am playing is also Spanish. That is why they call it a Spanish Romance."

G: "I know."

D: "Well, you always do, Grandpa – People like you should have gone to university"

G: "We can not do everything in this life, son."

D: "Yes, but you should not have cared so much to work around the clock to bring everyone here. You should have let more stay back home and focused on getting a degree. Once you had gotten that degree and a nice job, you could have brought everyone else, right? Perhaps, just a bit later…"

G: "In theory, it is easy to say that, son. But you know, when you have no home and no neighborhood and your family is far away and hungry, you do not think about choices. You don't know what it is like to raise your hands to the sky so they can get warm from the stars in the night… But hey listen, do me a favor and go to university on my behalf – do it for me. I will always live this part of your life with you. It would feel as if it were mine, do not forget that."

D: "You think I can do it? I spent two years in the same class to learn the language and I am behind with …"

Grandpa interrupted him by waving his hands. It does not matter – it is never too late and you may go to the University perhaps two or three years later than the average kid born in this country, but it still is very insignificant in the end".

D: "Yes Grandpa, I promise. Even if I ever loose the burning desire to study, I would still do it only for you."

Grandpa bent down and kissed his forehead.

D: "You know, it is not like you are twisting my arm! You know very well how much I want to study everything from geography to history and math?"

G: "I know and I am very proud of you since no one else cares as much as you do about my books and the poems."

D: "Please let me read all the things that you constantly write Grandpa."

G: "It is not the time yet – it has to be the right time, wait a little bit longer."

D: "What's the problem?"

G: "It's all about timing son, and being able to be in the right place at the right moment."

D: "You think I will not appreciate them that much?"

G: "Something like that."

D: "What makes you think about it? I am almost 15 and already enrolled in high school."

G: "Well, let me give you an example… let me speak in your language. … hmm…Didn't you come out of the theater the other day after you watched "Casablanca" and I asked you, "How had you liked the movie?"

D: "Yes! So?"

G: "Well, you told me that it was good."

D: "Yes, it was OK, really good."

G: "Mark my words, when you watch it a second time, maybe five to ten years from now, you will see more and discover so many more layers in this movie. Then you will feel you did not really watch the same film the first time! ... and you will not say it was just good, but a masterpiece!"

D: "hmm ... interesting.... If you say so."

G: "Well, so tell me about the Spanish Romance. What is in your eyes or better, your mind, when you play it?"

D: "Oh ... nothing ..."

G: "Son?"

D: "Don't ask."

G: "Well, is it bad? At your age, everyone is in love with someone – who is the lucky girl?"

D: "Nahhh nobody... I just play it because it is a beautiful piece of music."

G: "OK, if you say so..."

A different social class

A moment later, Dimitri held his breath for a moment, ran his hand over his head and asked,

D: "Grandpa, can you keep a secret?"

G: "Of course. You know that I have many already ... don't you see how everyone complains that I do not talk much?"

D: "Well, there is this girl that comes out of the mansion at the top of the Boulevard."

Grandpa looked at him with penetrating eyes and scratched his head. He took a deep breath and asked him:

G: "You do not mean the Paulmerts' mansion?"

D: "Hmm... why not?"

G: "Well son... you know ..." he paused to take another breath.

D: "I guess you want to say that they belong to a different class."

G: "Well, this is obvious son, but you know it is more than that?"

D: "Like what?"

G: "Well, they are different people."

D: "Wha…"

Grandpa interrupted him. "You see, they are not the type of people that they would have fun hanging out with us."

D: "Bu…"

Grandpa again cut him off, "Listen, I am not criticizing them, but Laurent Paulmerts owns the whole area and he is *a very focused business man*." The last five words were intonated louder and accompanied by an intense facial expression, which Dimitri could not interpret the meaning of. His voice didn't get louder ,but slower as there was something that irritated him.

D: "Well…"

G: "Look you are at the age that you fall in love, and you will keep falling in love till (pauses)…. till you get sick and tired of it – so no worries, have his daughter in your dreams, but you know my son, the dreams are not reality."

D: "You never had any dreams come true? You are the one who believes in dreams right?"

G: "Oh sure I had, but not all of them can come true as you know – Some are more realistic…"

D: "So, what makes my dream impossible?"

G: "I did not say that. But you know son, at your age, everyone falls in love so easily, so I would not worry too much about it; sure go ahead and play the tune for her or even try to talk to her … but the reality is, as you know, that she will slide out of your hands like a live trout does when you try to catch it with bare hands in a stream.

D: "Bu…"

G: "Listen, I do not want to disappoint you, but you are young and some things cannot be explained."

D: "I do not need that much of an explanation Grandpa, when I know that every cell of my body resonates in her sight… (sighs) such a wonderful and divine creature."

G: "Are there other girls you like? From your school perhaps? Or friends of your friends? Or from this neighborhood?"

D: "What a question? There is only space for her! How should I fit others?"

Grandpa leaned his head back and took a deep breath, looked Dimitri in the eyes and then he took another breath.

G: "I am sorry son, it has been long time since I was 15 and I have to give you a lot of credit. I can't believe I sound so disappointing, forgive me, it's all right I am such a fool"

D: "It's all right Grandpa – I know what I want."

G: "Sure you do, and I wish I could see the world through your eyes again. Oh, how nice it is to see the world through such eyes." He smiled, took another breath and continued, "You see son, life sometimes makes you too cynical ... what am I talking about?" He paused and turned to face his grandson – "Tell me more about her."

D: "Well, she is an angel. Have you seen these types of people that look so unreal, so extraterrestrial? Like they jumped out of an 18th century fresco? How can I ever explain? You know, the type of girl that no one can ever ignore. I have never seen such a beauty. Even Gene Tierney can stand next to her and she will not look as beautiful... Oh you know Grandpa, I am not good with describing perfection."

G: "Nonsense! You almost did." He leaned towards his grandson with a childish smile, which no one could ever tell that his cynical face was ever there. Now enthusiasm and dreams have taken that away. "Tell me more about her, whatever you know".

D: " I do not know much... other than she comes from a wealthy family. She looks very educated and she is absolutely beautiful". He paused briefly and continued, "I have only seen her from a distance."

G: "But when was the first time you saw her?"

D: "It was that Sunday when Giovanni and I went to see a French film. I was standing by the corner of the Odeon, while Giovanni was getting the matinee tickets. All of a sudden, from across the street, I almost got blinded by the light; pure ample light and it wasn't just the sunlight. All of a sudden I see a divine creature ... reflecting light ... so bright, how could it have been that bright? The sun was almost out of sight and she was reflecting the light. Just a moment later, even when white clouds covered the sky, it seemed to be that light was still everywhere around her. All of a sudden, she walked so fast and disappeared from my sight as other people walked in front of me hindering my view. For a second, I thought that I could not live without seeing her again. I never had that feeling before and I wondered why? I started praying, *"Oh please God bless, oh my....!"* I said this for a second... because I wanted her to appear again. I started moving in the direction she had headed but Giovanni was calling me to return back, since the movie was about to start. I quickly waved at him to let him know that I was going to return. I was constantly praying and then I saw her! Beautiful! So beautiful! She was outside the department store with her dad. I could tell right away that he had to be her father, as she had his features and she was looking at him with such a love and respect, that it could have only have been her Dad. I don't know why, but I ended up frozen for a second, as I thought about my Dad, and how many miles away he was. Suddenly, I felt my heart break into a million pieces and felt an overwhelming thunder hit me, when I looked up and saw her big blue eyes staring at me.... I could not move! I was staring at her and she could feel this as I was completely frozen. She greeted me with a smile and then turned around the corner and disappeared. That lasted may be just a second, but it was the kind of second that changes a life. That was, the kind of moment you always know will last a lifetime. In that second, I could feel that from now on life is different – a turning point – a hallmark – an amazing eternal moment, when energy freezes and where you understand that there is a whole new dimension in this world, where you see how life can open horizons that weren't known to you previously... I simply cannot describe it... how that moment felt, in which everything is so ethereal! Including myself! How my mind or soul or my being could move up outside of my head and high enough **to** see myself from above. I turned around the corner as well and saw her father pulling her into this very expensive car and disappear seconds later from my sight....

All of a sudden life became three dimensional again when Giovanni slapped my back and scared me immensely.

G: "Hey, what are you doing?"

D: "Heee ... what? Am I?" I paused... and looked totally puzzled and a moment later became hyperactive. "Giovanni look at this very expensive car!!! What a car?????? I mean who has this kind of car? Take a look, isn't it amazing?"

G: "In Queens only one person has this type of car."

D: "Who is he?"

G: "Mr. Paulmerts"

D: "Who is he?"

G: "Well, an industrialist from a family that has that factory down the river and owns half of the real estate in this part of our world, Queens. That's why I guess; they do not live in Manhattan and are still on this side of the river since they have for years owned the beautiful mansion by the water, at the end of the Boulevard."

D: "Hmm... Tell me more about him."

Gio: "Why are you so interested in him all of a sudden? The movie starts in few minutes. Stop being weird and let's go back".

G: "I guess you learned all about him afterward."

D: "Pretty much! At least whatever everyone knows here in the neighborhood."

G: "And what do you think about them?"

D: "Well, who am I to judge?"

G: "Hey listen, that is what everyone keeps telling me these days.... but I am *old school* and I know that you have a brain and you can choose to use it and think — usually people come up with sophisticated ways to measure things and characterize them, besides they establish laws, courts and a system to keep order in this society. Based on common sense, that I believe that still exists, what do you think about the Paulmerts?"

D: "I guess they are rich and part of a different social circle... but they are human beings as well."

G: "They are, but Mr. Paulmerts is perhaps very focused in being a good businessman and having a good life these days... and he does not know or care about how his "lieutenants" treat and terrorize people if they do not pay the rent or their dues on time."

D: "I know Giovanni and Joe told me about it, but is he really a bad person?"

G : "Maybe he isn't but his "Lieutenants" are, and he should be aware of it and do something. I know he is busy running the business and the factory, but getting a bit closer to the people and the working class wouldn't hurt him. I am sure he has important business to take care of, but he should not lose touch with the people below him and only care about his empire and fueling his powerhouse. Honestly, I heard that he is not a bad person, but he should not just focus on business and success and have these heartless people work for him. Even though he has the mansion on this side of the river, he still spends the whole day running around in members clubs on the other side of the river. If that mansion wasn't built here at the beginning of the century, they would not even live on this side of the river. You see they do not belong here; he always takes his family to the other side, where they have their pleasure place and leisure time. He does not mingle with us, the common people, anymore. And you know sometimes I hear the factory is in trouble, they aren't selling as much as they used to and would like to every year. But the money they collect from rents and from the people here is always feeding their machine and their estate – therefore they should respect all these people here. I know he is not a man of bad character, but he has disassociated himself from the common man, his fellow man, his brother. Hemingway said it clearly, *"that every time the bell tolls it tolls for each one of us."*

D: "You are right Grandpa, but you know… could it be normal for a man of his standing?"

G: "Listen son and absorb it deeply into your mind. No matter your standing, never, NEVER, I said **never** forget, where we all came from. Standing and kolokithia (Greek argo word for nonsense) it does not matter, kid!" He paused for a breath. "You know, son, I have dreams about you! You are different, you know. You will become a great man one day. You will! And you should! But you should always look back, not just forward, and see again and again where you have come from. The same applies to Mr. Paulmerts. His father suffered so much to keep and grow what his grandfather built as a pauper with his own hands! It does not matter how high up you find yourself one day, never forget how the rest of us survived, how the rest of us lived, how the rest of us kept working for this better future, for this day, that we would be blessed to see the light. For a day, on which we would be able to stand up and dance like never before. And if I could not make it happen – it does not matter – it would be the same to me if I could see at least my son make it happen. He couldn't do it. The war did not let him, but he has another chance and that is YOU! And if you make it, it would feel as if he had made it as well! And if my eyes were still open on that blessed day, it would feel as if I DID it myself. Each one of us is a pot that contains part of our ancestors. And son, I am pretty sure that the day that will separate you from the rest of us, will come. But mark my words here son – do not become oblivious to where we all came from, the poverty – the state where the only thing that matters is to be healthy enough and have the bare essentials to survive. These are the only things that matter to a poor, but honest man.

D: "But how can I ever forget this?"

G: "Well, as I have already implied, a lot of people do forget. And I do not mean just Laurent Paulmerts. Look around you in this big island in front of us. Everyone there is getting wealthy and everyone has a good life, but each one of them has relatives here and/or in the old world where they are starving. And they let them starve....

You know son, I wish to see the day when you are getting your higher education. I know you will make it happen and the doors will open up for you."

D: "... Oh come on Grandpa, you know that this will not be easy for me."

G: "I have more than a feeling that you will become a wise man and you will be successful."

D: ".... Oh Gran..."

G: "Listen to me! Once you succeed never forget that all the wisdom and privileges you deserve to get, do not belong just to you. Your father sacrificed his life for you to get you on that boat and send you here, leaving him and your mother and your siblings behind. He lost part of himself to remain behind, without you.... and where in the depths of poverty. You know we help them, but that is not enough.

Everyone who came to this country, especially this neighborhood – including Grandpa Paulmerts, suffered to have a better future. Many of us in this land of opportunity make the dream come true one way or another. But there are also many who are left behind or do not make it."

Hemingway's quote

He took a step ahead and continued, "Once you make it, my son, never forget this day! Never forget my words... it will be harder for you, since you have to start from almost zero and try again and again. I know one day you will make it and you will catch the fish. But son never forget that once you get that big fish, it won't be good enough... unless you bring it back. Like Hemingway's fish at his newest novel, "The Old Man and the Sea". They just gave him the Pulitzer and they may even give him the Nobel Prize. You read every newspaper and they say this and that about his novel ... that it is a hymn of a fight, it is all about the "man versus nature", "the fisherman and his loneliness" and this and that. You know son, forget all these critics and the wise men who talk in the papers about his mastery of English and his meticulous use of the language in the manuscript etc..etc..etc... for me the novel is only ONE thing, "that it is not worth catching the fish, unless you can bring it back, back to your people, so you can share that with them". You see son ... the old man did not catch any fish for eighty some or more days, and he is so exhausted, so humiliated, in his waning years without love and glory... and then comes the day when he catches a big one – such a big one that compensates for all the time loss – such a big one, son, that would make everyone forget about his bad luck and bad days ... and what happens son? The fish is too big and takes him away from his home, his port, and his people. Eventually he loses his orientation and way. You know son, he has the option to let it go and return back home, but realizes ... what good is it to catch a fish if you cannot bring it back..."

D: "So what happens at the end? Or maybe it's better not to tell me, as I would love to read the book. I heard so many things about it, all the praise and awards that it has received."

G: "Well, most of them were given by people who missed the essence of the book, in my humble opinion, son". " Read any paper, any critique, they are all about the language, the emotions, the nature and this and that. At the end Hemingway, in his prophetic nature jokes and alludes about the same complaint that I have, about having these tourists in Cuba who see the remaining cartilage of the fish eaten by the sharks. They are just laying on the beach while completely missing the point, asking the waiter what that cartilage is? The waiter, thinking that they will get it, tells them something like, "Well Sharks" implying that the fish was eaten by the sharks but the tourists once again, miss the point, solely thinking that the waiter implies that the skeleton lying out there is that of a shark."

The city's luxury, the bread and not the cake.

D: " I see papou, it sounds like a story that I need to read."

G: "Absolutely! I just finished it and will return it to the library, but I am planning to buy a copy and will give it to you son, so you can remember this day. I thought of giving you this on your birthday, but can't wait till that day."

D: "Oh please, do not spend a penny for gifts and for me."
G: "I will not do that as it will not be a gift, but one of the bricks for your future that you will have to put together son. I do not buy many books, but when something is necessary, I will not think twice whether I can afford it or not. In fact, let's go take a walk, return this to the library and then go to the bookstore."

They got up, picked up the book and strolled out of the living room to the street. It was such a sunny, clear day and as they walked along the path by the river, they could see right across the city's impressive skyline.
G: "Son, you see the city across the river?" he paused and looked down to the ground. He stopped, turned towards the city and pointed to his grandson, "This is too much luxury for us. Maybe this is true only for this moment. Who knows, one day you may be able to afford this luxury, but for now, we are in a different world across the river, where people simply focus on their every day bread."
D: "But Grandpa, are you worried about me? Worried that I will go there and leave everyone behind? You sound as if I will become like the son of Mrs. Poulas, who escaped to San Diego and left his mother helpless and alone here… and all I guess, for the eyes of a beautiful girl."
G: "Well, not really. But you know, right now you are still idealistic. Later on, life can lead you into a never-ending race … for more and more. You may forget this side of the river and it could be for the better. Not that I want you to live here for the rest of your life… My wish is for you to study, spread your wings and fly, and see the world. Just make sure you never forget your people back home. This side is your "bread" my son, and the city across the river is the "padespani" (Greek word for a Greek cake dipped in syrup). Too sweet, with loads of sugar and that sugar will travel to your brain cells my son, but in my opinion you cannot have "padespani" every day. People do it on the other side, but you know they may become diabetic one day and incabable of seeing. You see, the sweetness and the sugar can lead to an addiction like a drug does and as the need for higher amounts and intensity increases, the sickness progresses. Once it reaches a later stage, it makes people blind. Some may end up with amputated extremities son or open wounds. Then, what good is that? They won't be able to run or walk forward and if they do so, they may have no idea where they would be heading."

D: "Papou you should have studied and become a philosopher!"

G: "Yes, sure, go ahead and make fun of me… I deserve it right? Since I was unable to put my act together and do it. But a philosopher, now? I thought you always envisioned me as a poet? A philosopher today? Ha! And I have not even mentioned any of my vicious cycle arguements yet!"

D: "Why? Was there any room for such?"

G: "Oh sure! I just told you that you might as well forget this side of the river for the better."

D: "So what? I think I got the point but … in any case we should always strive for the better … do I understand you or have I lost you again?"

G: "Well … you know the philosophical argument is that: The better is the worst enemy of the good."

D: "Oh, wow again!"

G: "Once you look for the better, you may lose what you already have, you may lose the good. Its value would depreciate, it would be ignored and lost forever … and after all, it is good my son – It is GOOD!"

D: "OK I got it – but there is no vicious circle here."

G: "Yes there is! Because Good is the worst enemy of the better!"

D: "Oh come on again… but I see"

G: "Exactly! Once you sit back and relax, just because you have the GOOD, you may miss out on probably deserving the BETTER. You do not want to miss out on it and have someone who does not deserve it, get it instead. You should look for it, regardless, because it will bring progress and wisdom to your life."

D: "Now you sound like a real philosopher but of course, you have confused me again and you have messed up my orientation, is there a solution to this philosophical argument of yours? Sounds so Greek to me!"

G: "Well, you should find out for yourself son."

D: "All right you have once again made it easy for me, Socrates!"

G: "Well, there is something that we call balance and another thing that we call a brain, Mr. Plato. Use your brain to find out whether it is better for you to settle for the good or pursue the better. I am a simple and uneducated man – what do you expect me to tell you?

A safe thing would be to pray to God as your grandma has taught you. He would help you choose the right way in life. But I know many people discount it. My advice to you is "do not"! Try to concentrate on your beliefs and use your brain and always balance your life in such a way that it cannot be tilted and thrown off balance with a single blow of the wind!"

D: "Well, it may sound easy now, but hard to do once the wind becomes a tornado!"

G: "You see you are already wise. You may lose control in a tornado as it happens to many men son, but most of the people lose control in a soft wind and are gone – "Gone with the Wind" as the movie you like, son.

D: "And why do you think that happens to most of them?"

G: "I do not know son! But there are captains who have God to guide them through the tempests and there are others who have no compass and get lost. I am not everywhere to see and examine every case, but as you grow up, start to observe why. Look at the facts and look at how many of them have lost their roots. So they fly away like the empty bags in the streets on a windy day. Are the roots, their family, their tradition, their culture, their education, personality, being? Just open your eyes and look. Look, but stick only to the facts."

D: "So once the wind takes them away, they may end up at a better place?"

G: "Oh yes, this is my boy, you are becoming better and better, so you look like the apple that fell down from the apple tree", and he laughed out loud ... "Well, in this case we need some wind son! Because you know below the apple tree there is not much sun and space for the new tree to grow. There won't be, because there is no space to grow roots down in the ground. So, hopefully, one day some apples will fall a bit further from the tree or be moved with the wind. That is how we end up with orchards you know! Once the apples move out of the shadow of their parents, then you have a forest."

D: "I remember the hill back home, I would think that the slope helped the fruits roll down and not just the wind... then the whole hill or mountain ends up with the same kind of tree, either pine, or olive, or walnut, right? The crops will fall and roll away from the shadow of the parent and the mountain will end up full of trees... but I like your wind idea, at least for places that are flat! But grandpa, how did the first tree on the top of the mountain end up there? If the fruits roll downward and not upwards, how did we have this very first tree on the top of the hill?

G: "You see son that was the reason I just told you, that you are becoming better and better! I did not tell you that because you came up with a nice conclusion, and because you keep coming up with the right questions! That is what matters; once you find the right questions, that is when you become wiser."

D: "What happens if you aren't next to me to give me the answer? Like you always do?"

G: "Not always, son, and most of the answers you can get yourself without my help. Life will bring you to the proper conclusions. Do not rush to become a wise old man. The course of that process will take time and you really need to enjoy the whole process."

What is happiness?

As they approached the bookstore and were ready to cross to the other side of the street, the very expensive limo of Paulmerts parked right outside the bookstore. Dimitri suddenly felt his heart pumping with an intensity and speed he had never experienced before. He tried to hide it, as he was with his grandfather. The old man knew exactly what was going on, but he tried not to pay attention to it and masterfully ignored the significance this confrontation had on his grandson.

G: "Come on, let's cross the street," he told his grandson who looked into his eyes and realized that he was aware of the Paulmerts in the limo.

Dimitri was petrified, but continued to walk slowly. He crossed the side street and by the time he reached the corner of the bookstore, Mr. Paulmerts had already opened the door and stepped out of his luxurious car. Dimitri again turned his head slowly right and noticed that Grandpa was looking at Mr. Paulmerts and immediately turned his head on to his left side to see that Mr. Paulmerts started to walk towards the bookstore. Dazzled enough he could feel a vigorous tremor run through his whole body as he noticed that Mr. Paulmerts' daughter was inside the car.

Mr. Paulmerts' tall and impressive figure moved towards them as they approached the door. His chauffer, wife and daughter remained inside the limo. As he approached them in a light colored suit, impeccably dressed, with his impressive tie around his neck, Dimitri all of a sudden sensed an energy coming from Mr. Paulmerts and to his direction manifested in a wide smile just a moment later. Not knowing if this was for him or for his Grandpa, he smiled at him bashfully and whispered, "Good afternoon Sir".

Mr. Paulmerts delivered a loud *"Good afternoon"*, while smiling at Grandpa.

Mr. P: "Hello! Mr. Giovas, is that you?"

G: "Good afternoon, Mr. Paulmerts. How do you do?"

Mr. P: "Mr. Giovas, what a pleasure to see you", and gave him a firm handshake. "Have not seen you in a long time, Sir."

G: "I am here as always, Mr. Paulmerts."

Mr. P: "So nice to see you Mr. Giovas, it reminds me of my childhood and not to forget, all the divine baked goods I ate growing up!"

G: "Thank you for the compliment. I am glad you liked them."

Mr. P: "It seems like yesterday Mr. Giovas, when my Grandpa took me to your bakery for the first time! Ah, the honey walnut cookies! Remember? I got addicted to them. I was raised on them and your bread. Too bad your bakery is not around anymore. I miss it so much."

G: "Well, all good things in life come to an end. I miss it as well. I also miss my customers and your Grandfather. God rest his soul."

Mr. P: "Oh Mr. Giovas that is why I am so glad to see you," he paused and swallowed... Because you know, the first thing that came to my mind when I saw you was him. I miss my father so much." He took another breath and continued, "I do know that my Grandfather was not just fond of your bread. He adored you as a person for all your passion and philosophical discussions. He used to tell me about what good of a person you are and how you helped so many people. It's a pity that you do not have the bakery and we do not see you anymore."

G : "Mr. Paulmerts, I have been here for the last 40 years. Maybe you do not stop by this neighborhood that often anymore. With all do respect, I am not trying to criticize you here, but your Grandpa loved this neighborhood and once he harvested his life's hard work, he decided not to leave this place. He could have, but he didn't, and that is why he built everything here, right? That is why you ended up in my bakery and not in those fancy ones across the river. I miss the bakery as well, but I had to sell it, so I could bring my grandson and my wife's nephew here and buy a place for all of them to live. Life is full of tough decisions as you know."

Mr. P: "I know and I did not forget the many times I heard that you sacrificed everything for your family. I know I have been an absentee from here, but you know, the business is in trouble at the moment … "
G: "Don't your tenants pay rent anymore?"
Mr. P: "Oh no … I mean the factory, but of course the real estate is fine."
G: "Well, if it is fine and with all the respect I have for you, Mr. Paulmerts, try to help and understand these people who live in your properties. I know it is not my business and I do not have the right to talk to you this way", he paused for a while. "Pardon me for this, but your employees sometimes are disrespectful to your tenants and you know who I am talking about?"
Mr. P: "I am sorry to hear that, but I do not think I have an idea what this is about?"
G: " I believe you know that your rent collectors deliberately abuse people that cannot come up with the full rent amount on the first day of the month. Some of them are merchants and they do not have a steady cash flow, others move and bring families here from every part of the world and sometimes they are short a month or so. I am sorry to talk this way, but some of your employees are a little too cruel to innocent and hard-working people; the immigrants who have moved here."
Mr. P: "I am sorry to hear that from you, Mr. Giovas, but I am aware of the people who do not come up with their dues on time. They violate their contract and they could rent other properties in other neighborhoods for less money."
G: "Contract…? I am not one who has the power to teach you these things Mr. Paulmerts but sometimes this is not possible. You see, they work at this place and do not have the means to commute, or they need to be closer to their relatives, to watch the children of multiple families when the rest of the families have to be at work, sometimes working two shifts a day. It is expensive to support a family in this place, Mr. Paulmerts, and I am encouraging you to walk around in this neighborhood, so you can see with your own eyes what is going on."
Mr. Paulmerts seemed to realize that his good mood had passed and as he looked at the young Dimitri, he found an excuse to divert the topic and asked:

"Is this your grandson?" It was indeed a smart and quick way to change the subject and avoid more comments.

G: " Yes, indeed."

Mr. P: "How do you do?" Laurent Paulmerts asked, and extended his hand for a handshake to Dimitri.

D: "Dimitrios Giovas, pleasure to meet you sir."

At that moment, the sound of a shutting car door was heard and everyone drew their attention to Mr. Paulmerts' daughter, who had stepped out of the car.

All this time Dimitri's attention was torn between the conversation and the car, as his eyes always turned left towards the limo. The car was to his left and ahead from the point that he was standing, so he could only see the back of her head. His heart never stopped the fast paced beat and he was constantly sweating from the top to the bottom. He was so dumfounded and he could not stand straight. He constantly moved a tiny step to the left and the next minute a tiny step to the right. He sensed that Mr. Paulmerts and his Grandpa got engaged in a dialogue that could last forever and that someone in the car would jump out to see what was going on. His intuition was absolutely right, as Lauren Paulmerts turned her head twice to see if her dad was still talking to the "strangers". Until that moment Dimitri was not sure if she remembered who he was. Since the first time he had seen her, he kept watching her from a distance as she would come and go every weekend, while she was driven in the car. He followed the car all the way to the mansion and often climbed the fence to see her walking from the car to the door. How many dreams and thoughts that view had generated. How many books had he read during that period and because of her, he felt and understood what love and passion were all about, at least in literature. "Romeo and Juliet" was his favorite of all.

And now here she was stepping out from the limo while Dimitri's eyes were wide open, observing every move of hers and while the sweat was running down from his thick hair all the way to his jaw line and finally dropping down on his shirt like thick drops of rain. He had been absolutely petrified since the moment he got to know her father and then just a moment later he could not lift his eyes anymore to look at him as they were turned towards her. Indeed, she looked like an angel to him with an incredible grace in her face and such magnetic and irresistible big blue eyes.

Mr. Paulmerts immediately understood from Dimitri's move and the sound of the slamming door that his daughter was coming towards him.

Mr. P: "Hey, Lauren. Sorry. I met some old friends, come over!"

He turned towards Grandpa and Dimitri, and with a proud smile after a deep breath that inflated his wide chest, he introduced her to them. "This is my daughter Lauren."

Lauren's face shone grace and class while she smiled in the most polite way first at grandpa and then at Dimitri.

LP: "How do you do?"

G: "Good afternoon, lady. Dimitrios Giovas, friend of your great-grandfather and your grandfather as well!" He turned towards his grandson. "And this is my grandson Dimitri, named after me, according to the Greek tradition"

Lauren turned her eyes to Dimitri and smiled while she sensed that he was looking deeply into her big blue eyes. She sensed that this look was not just a "how do you do look"…

Dimitri suddenly felt an instant electric pulse deep inside him which empowered him enough to say with a clear pronunciation, "Nice to meet you, Miss Paulmerts."

Lauren smiled at him again, admiring his clear and honest face, and then turned to her dad,

"Dad, Mom is waiting."

Mr. P: " I know, but I have not seen Mr. Giovas in such a long time. You know when I was your age, I stopped by at his bakery every day with my Grandpa. Too bad it is not around anymore. It was open when you were very little and we used to have their bread and honey walnut cookies delivered to our house every day."

LP: "Of course, I remember this. I know how much you also loved them and I remember the bread, but that was years ago."

G: "How old are you, Ms. Paulmerts?"

LP: "Almost fourteen."

G: "Ah, you are almost as old as my grandson Dimitri, who is fifteen. You see, I had to sell the business five years ago so I could bring this little chap from Greece here, along with some other relatives."

LP: "I have seen your grandson before!"

At this point the petrified Dimitri opened his eyes wide and suddenly felt his hair stand up on his neck in a sudden burst, a sign that the drops of sweat would again run down his face.

LP: "I did not know that you were Greek."

D: "Hmm... yeah, I am ...."

At that point the only one who was losing control was Dimitri, but he sensed that the rest were standing upright and steady. However, he felt the ground beneath him was like quick sand.....

Grandpa realized that and rapidly turned the attention to him. "Yes, he came almost three years ago and he is doing great! He's reading and studying to preparing himself for a higher education. We had enough bakers, drivers and mechanics in our family."

LP: "My great-grandpa was a mechanic and built machines in our factory with his own hands."

G: "I know and he was a great man, you should be proud of him."

All of a sudden the horn from the limo interrupted Grandpa and everyone turned their heads towards the limo where a rather anxious Mrs. Paulmerts was waving her hands, signaling to her husband to move on.

Mr. P: "Oh, I am sorry, nice to talk to you but I am afraid my wife has been waiting long enough and is getting a little impatient."

G: "Oh, I am sorry to keep you waitin..."

Mr. Paulmerts interrupted him with a gentle slap on his shoulder. "Not at all, I wish I had more time to talk to you, Mr. Giovas, as you have awoken many memories."

In the meantime, Lauren turned her eyes to Dimitri again but she was not surprised to still see him staring at her dumfounded. He was so shy that he turned his eyes away as soon as she made eye contact with him.

G: "I wish you had more time for the whole neighborhood, son – and pardon me for calling you like this Mr. Paulmerts – but I feel the goodness of your grandfather deep inside you and I know he would have liked me to say that to you, as he was always very close and good to the people that he worked with and helped him build his empire. He always honored them and you know that very well."

Mr. Paulmerts squinted his eyes, and tried to see deep into the old man's eyes to identify the deep root of his last complaint, because at that point he was sure it was a pure complaint.

G: "Do not mind an old man complaining, son."

Mr. P: " I do not mind, Mr. Giovas, but you know no one tells me that something is wrong."

G: "I do not expect that from Mr. Fein and his crew, with all do respect."

Mr. P: "Hmm….?"

G: "As I told you, they should give some tenants a break and understand them. They are not criminals, but honest people who work to feed their families and make sure they have bread for everyone; that they shelter in your buildings. No need for one to abuse and terrorize them."

Mr. P: "Terrorize?" he asked with a surprised tone in his voice, which made him turn and look at his daughter, who was listening to the old man and paying close attention to the slightly accented, colorful way in which he talked. Immediately, he felt stressed and embarrassed and looked for a way to move away from this unpleasant discussion.

G: "I am sorry to use these harsh words, Mr. Paulmerts, but if you are not aware of it, then please come one day and ask your tenants about it. They would love to see you."

Lauren watched her father's reaction and saw the stress that was so obviously displayed on his face. At the same time she also felt perplexed, because the gravity of Mr. Giovas' figure and presence evoked nothing but respect. Somehow her internal compass guided her to the conclusion that the old man in front of her could only be honest. Dimitri on the other hand, was embarrassed that his grandpa made Mr. Paulmerts, feel stressed, as all he had in his mind was to find a way to possibly get connected with Mr. Paulmerts' daughter. However, as the aftertaste emerges, after the ingestion of strong and flavorful liquor, he later concluded that his Grandpa had only been right to act this way. He could not forget how Larry Fein abused the Garcias, humiliated Mrs. Poulas and so many other tenants, every time they could not come up with the whole rent at the very beginning of the month.

The memories ran through his head. He remembered how Mr. Fein yelled at Mr. Garcia that sunny day in March when he did not have the rent money. He had spent all of his cash to pay the hospital for his wife's devastating illness that persisted after the birth of his last child. It was a disease that kept her in bed for weeks. Mr. Garcia was always such a nice and polite man with a round face and gentle smile, the widest smile one could actually find in the streets of Queens. Mr. Fein slapped him and hit him in the head in front of his children. He yelled at him in a humiliating way and told him he would do him a favor and grant him five more days.

Mr. Paulmerts had left the management of his real estate property to Mr. Fein and his group. He trusted them and didn't supervise them. He knew the amount of money he should get from his properties, but he didn't know that Mr. Fein did not always offer a lease agreement to the tenants. That's how Mr. Fein gave apartments to immigrants like Mr. Garcia who did not have all the legal paperwork to proceed with a regular lease. Immigrants like him were getting charged a 10% or 20% per month "convenience fee". Mr. Fein would keep this commission from Mr. Paulmerts' monthly income and would never report the extra cash from tenants who could not sign a lease. Mr. Fein was not that tall or impressive and he always carried a wooden stick with him. He would not have been able to fight Mr. Garcia's wide frame, but he was able to strike him with his stick. His crew consisted of his two young and cruel nephews who always ensured that he would never get attacked. Mr. Garcia could not fight back or else his whole family would end up in the streets. Instead, he accepted the strikes and humiliation in front of his children, who were crying. His pride was ruined, his embarrassment was obvious, but he was helpless. He would do anything so his children had food and a roof above their heads. That March, Mr. Garcia ended up working three shifts a day during the five-day grace period. He could not sleep and his health suffered without a good night's rest. He ended up faint with yellow pale skin which replaced his sun-drenched complexion. His eyes were full of pain and humiliation. His children begged him to stand up and hit Mr. Fein, but that day all he cared about was to hold them back from getting any strikes from Mr. Fein's wooden stick. He could not find peace or think of anything other than his humiliation. He was wordless for days. His second son and his older daughter cried and comforted him by embrassing his pain-drenched body and soul. But his first son was very angry with him. He did not want his father to be a coward. He did not like that his father had accepted the strikes. His angry eyes were full of disappointment, as his father betrayed his own image. He remembered his early years in Mexico, where his Father was his idol and used to tame horses. He even moved carriages with his own hands when they needed to be fixed. The portrait of the strong man, who had built his own house with his own bare hands and protected his family, was all of a sudden gone. In the past, he always thought his father could make anything happen, as he had seen him successfully move his family from the Mexican borders all the way to Queens. Mr. Garcia sensed all these feelings as he looked in into his son's big dark eyes, while enduring Mr. Fein's blows. Since he was Mexican, he was afraid of the police. He was afraid to strike back as he would be imprisoned and would never get a fair shake in the court. His family could not survive without him. Mr. Fein knew that and therefore wasn't afraid to deliver menace and set an example for the whole neighborhood.

All these memories flashed back in Dimitri's brain for a few seconds, together with the other instances of humiliation Mr. Fein and his crew perpetrated on many other tenants in the neighborhood. He could not forget scenes of brutality on Mr. Rooney (his uncle's friend, who was a bus driver as well) or to family members of Giovanni and Joe who got slapped by Mr. Fein's right-hand men, Jeremy Marks and "Shorty" (no one really knew his real name). But the greatest atrocity took place in front of Mrs. Poulas, who was almost unable to move. She always sat in her chair with her daily cup of yogurt on a tiny table next to her. She spent day and night either outside on her doorstep or by the front window during winter. She always faced west as she waited for her son to return. Mr. Fein and his crew took no pity on her. Mrs. Poulas's pension from her late husband was barely enough for her rent and food. That month she had sent a sweater to her son by mail and with the rest of the wool she made a small blanket that she needed for her feet. She ended up a few dollars short on rent. She could not explain to Mr. Fein what happened because of her poor English that she was going to pay extra the following month, as she was willing to stop buying the biscuits. Mr. Fein was not a patient person and while the old lady pointed to her small table to show she only had yogurt, Mr. Fein kicked it towards her and spilled the yogurt on her clothes. He yelled at her and she cried since she did not have many clothes and was not able to wash them by herself. She was very embarrassed, and very concerned about how much she would inconvenience people to help her wash the clothes.

She cried helplessly, as she had no other means to find money. She lowered her head which gravitated heavily from the embarrassment and pain. She knew that her neighbors would not leave her alone and would chip in again to help her out. But deep inside her, she felt the pain because she knew well that this money represented the daily hard work, pain and austere saving attempts of everyone in the neightborhood. Her neighbors were people with good hearts who would never let anyone die alone in the streets; they always looked after her and were compassionate. That care and love kept her alive and hopeful till the day that she would see her son again.

In that instant her neighbors realized what was going on. They immediately yelled at Mr. Fein, telling that he should be ashamed of himself. Some cursed him and immediately felt his wooden stick. Mr. Fein could always threaten them since he had the power to send them to court or back to their countries. He knew that no one would have the guts to raise their hand at him. Somehow, every family he let into Mr. Paulmerts' apartments had a family member without proper papers or a rental property without a legal agreement. Everyone was afraid of him. His vindictive character was felt far more by the most uneducated and simple men. On top of that, he authorized Marks and Shorty to break anyone's neck in case there was a mutiny or any resistance against him.

Dimitri had all these images deeply engraved in his memory. It would take only a few seconds to revive them and understand why his grandpa was so direct and probably even tough towards Mr. Paulmerts. At the first sight of his wide and handsome face, everyone could detect the goodness that this man was hiding in his soul, but at the same time see the ignorance in all matters. Mr. Paulmerts looked frozen, as his complexion lost its vivid red hues and turned pale. Grandpa's last words definitely shook him up and made him think again. He immersed himself into deep thoughts and this was obvious to everyone else present.

After a few moments of silence, Mr. Paulmerts looked Grandpa straight in the eyes and told him with determination, "I will have a talk with Mr. Fein to inquire about the problems in the neighborhood."

Grandpa suddenly became almost twice as red as he acquired the lost redness that was moments ago on Mr. Paulmerts' face. Grandpa got animated and opened his eyes wide.

G: "Sir, I suggest that you talk to the tenants, not to Mr. Fein."

Mr.P: "I will do my best, Mr. Giovas, and thanks for your suggestions."

G: "My pleasure sir and thank you for your time and your attention," and he then turned to his daughter and said with a tender smile,

"Ms. Paulmerts, such a pleasure to meet you and allow me to send you one of these days some of the walnut honey cookies that your family enjoyed when you were little ..."

Mr.P: "Oh ... always the same giving and generous man my grandfather talked about. How can we say no to such an offer? But please do not inconvenience yourself, it is not necessary."

G: "You still talk to me like a good businessman, Mr. Paulmerts; certainly there is no inconvenience, only pleasure to do this for the family of an old friend, who helped me so much in the past. You see, one of the things that your Grandpa never told you is that at the time I opened my bakery there were not many who supported me. I was the new immigrant, besides some other Greek immigrants but when your Grandfather became my customer everyone trusted me. So please, do not feel that there is any inconvenience or trouble."

Mr.P: "Thank you very much, Mr. Giovas."

L: "I thank you, as well, sir."

G: "You are very welcome, Ms. Paulmerts." He turned to his grandson, "I will have Dimitri deliver them to you."

All this time Dimitri could not move as he only observed with reverence the impressive figures of the two men and the beauty of his one and only love. He felt he had no power to move and if he could find the power to do so, it would come across as the artificial movement of a mechanical device. He did not move, but his eyes looked deep inside the souls of the two men as much as he could, with the distraction of Lauren's big blue eyes. He saw the blue gemstones turn towards him numerous times. He knew that she was already aware of his deep love for her.

She glanced at him gracefully several times and his heartbeat kept racing. He knew that he looked like an awkward bird that would spit out an ugly sound, if it opened its mouth. He was fascinated with her and observed the details of her skin, which represented a unique perfection, with an intense peachy color in the center of her high cheekbones. He could not stop looking at her slightly wavy, long hair and her sublime eyebrows that seemed to be a perfect spark for a great painter's untamed inspiration. It was then, that Dimitri understood whom these eyes resembled. He remembered the very first time, about two years ago, when his Grandfather took him to the Metropolitan Museum of Arts. He stopped to stare at the eyes of Lepage's portrait of Jean d'Arc. It was then, when he became fascinated with that portrait and searched in the encyclopedia to find out what kind of saint she was. Indeed, it was the first time he came so close to Lauren. Her beauty astonished him, but at the same time he was curious to find out more about her personality. Her eyes revealed a rather delicate but sincere personality. Dimitri was perplexed by her look, which made her realize that he was staring at her a bit more than he should have.

The slam of the limo door again interrupted his thoughts and the conversation. Everyone turned into the direction of the limo to see a rather upset Mrs. Paulmerts, moving towards them. Again the ethereal connection between the two men of the two families, the two worlds, got lost.

Mrs. Paulmerts did not look as a person with patience and understanding. With her stunning long suit and appearance, she symbolized the big gap between the social classes of the Paulmerts and the Giovas.

Mr. Paulmert immediately sensed her frustration and turned towards her trying with his full heart to break into a wide, *"I am sorry"* smile.

"I am sorry, darling, but I met a good old family friend. I know you've been waiting for a long time."

Mrs. Paulmerts with a bombastic voice and without any hesitation said in a refined but dictating tone, "You know very well that we are very late, Laurent; and please let's get going". She stopped just steps away from her husband, passing onto him the subtle, but obvious message that he should better move toward her and leave.

Mr. Paulmerts immediately turned back to face Mr. Giovas, and with a rather rushed movement shook his hand, "nice talking to you Mr. Giovas". He then turned to his daughter, grasped her left hand and extended a smile to Dimitri, "nice to meet you young man" and immediately rushed towards his wife. Dimitri responded at once with a warm, "nice to meet you Sir", and waved his right hand. His eyes locked with those of Lauren that happened to turn her head and looked at him, in a synchronized way. Both instantly and perfectly aligned looked into the depths of their souls, a moment that felt longer than its actual duration and intense enough to become another unforgettable moment in the life of the young man. The impact of that moment was stronger than the loudest thunder that was ever heard on the planet. It took a moment for him to realize that she returned the greeting to him and his Grandpa. The sound of her voice was very melodic, capturing his full attention so that for another time again he could not feel his existence, the gravity of his body, his muscles, his blood flowing all over his arteries and veins. He became ethereal again and for once he knew that his brain could empower a complete sublimation of his body that could turn matter into air. He was so pleased to see that he caught her attention and that her eyes revealed that she did not just return the greeting out of courtesy, but out of a real respect to the grandfather and out of some sort of affection to Dimitri. Moments later he felt that gravity had returned. He could feel in his body that certain hormones were released but surprisingly he was still functional and standing at the same place, right outside of the bookstore. With that realization he returned a warm smile and greeting to her and said goodbye at the same time his Grandfather did, in a much synchronized way. He turned right and saw him staring at them and then he turned his head back again to see the Paulmerts family walking away. The separation made him think "why?" how nice would it be to spend a whole afternoon together with them. However, he could see Mrs. Paulmerts' frustration, as she grabbed them both with her hands and turned them towards the bookstore. At that moment he also realized that his grandfather had turned his head and was looking directly at him. It was not easy for Dimitri to interpret at this point why his grandfather broke into such a smile. He could not read him well, but he knew that his face was an open book to Grandpa.

G: "So, aren't we going to the bookstore as well?"

D: "Well, yes. Why didn't you tell me that you know his family so well? You never talked to me about it."

G: "It was never that important, but as you see today we talked about them and here they are in front of us, what a coincidence? Right?"

D: "Yes ... wait a moment? I never expected to meet them; especially today ... hmm, I mean especially like ..." he swallowed hard as he realized he externalized his excitement too much and was embarrassed that his Grandpa could detect the magnitude of his affection for Lauren Paulmerts. "I mean, you know, the case is that…"

Grandpa interrupted him, "Hey no worries, you do not have to explain, I understand."

D: "Oh come on … it is not what you think!"

G: "Oh, I am sure it is not." He smiled in a very agreeable way to make his grandson feel comfortable. "Let's go and get the book."

D: "But they are inside?!"

G: "So? They won't care."

Dimitri swallowed deeply again and made a huge effort to speak. "But …"

G: "Why are you afraid? Would you rather want to wait?"

Dimitri looked down; he paused and helplessly continued, "I don't know…"

G: "Come on, let's go. You should not be afraid to face people and you should rather move forward and not wait." Then he waved his hand and extended his arm in the direction of the bookstore in an "after you, sir" way. Dimitri took another breath and moment to think as he looked at Grandpa's eyes and then smiled and decided to proceed.

As they walked a few steps, Dimitri stopped again and felt the hand of grandpa on his back pushing him ahead. Grandpa opened the bookstore door and extended again his arm in the same "après vous" way. Dimitri felt his head get cold and crossed the double doors of the bookstore with hesitation. As they entered, they saw the Paulmerts already standing at the cash register ready to check out. Dimitri immediately turned right in a desperate move to hide, as he was too shy to encounter them again. He realized that his grandfather followed him, disappointed, but also amused. After a few moments they stopped at the end of the aisle where Dimitri could hear and partially feel that the family was leaving. He observed through the shelves that Lauren carried a green hard covered book, which was obviously for her, since it was not even wrapped. Again he could not move as he was fully absorbed in her elastic moves and the ultimate grace of her figure.

In that moment he deeply felt again that he should do his best to win her heart. He had the feeling that she would be the love of his life. He thought, "She is the one and only!" The one that would complete him as a person, the perfect companion, the one and only companion that he would want for his entire life. He was so magnetized by her beauty and was positive that no matter who else he'd meet in his life, she would never be able to match or replace her in his heart. He was convinced that he would have no eyes for any other girl. He was convinced of his loyalty to her. He was convinced that her image would dominate his thoughts daily and for the rest of his life. He also felt that at the end of the day, when he would be really tired and would have to shut off his thoughts so he could sleep, he would still see her in his dreams. That night when he returned home, he couldn't even open the book his grandfather gave him. Even though he loved to read, and always did every night. This book was so special though, because it was a gift from his grandpa, and gifts were a rarity in his family, but he simply could not concentrate on anything else other than the memories of his recent encounter with Lauren.

The next morning, before he headed to work, he felt the need to ask his important pillar of his existence, his Grandfather, a question. He was so overflowing with happiness and joy from that eye-to-eye contact with Lauren, but at the same time he felt pain and sorrow for not being able to be with her or perhaps not being able to approach her in the near future. He could not explain this battle deep inside him. He could not understand what was happening inside of him. He could not understand why he was happy and sad at the same time. He could not even understand if this was good or bad.

He approached his grandfather with reverence and respect and asked him, "Papou, what is happiness?" His Grandpa, slightly surprised, turned his head towards him, looked deep into his eyes and said, "Happiness is what follows a period of sorrow and pain." He patted his hair, pulled him to his side and gave him a warm hug.

Love and sacrifice

Seven days later, the following Sunday, Dimitri was awaken by a very unusual aroma; a fragrant wave that had filled his bedroom. After a few sniffs, he realized that someone was baking. He stood up and left his cousins asleep in the bedroom. He glanced at the clock on the wall and was amazed. It was way too early for someone to be baking on a Sunday, as it was not even close to the time that everyone normally got up to go to church. In the kitchen, he found his grandfather reading the paper. It was apparent that he was the one responsible for this divine smell of cardamom, cinnamon and baked honey.

G: "Good morning! Isn't this early for you on a Sunday?"

D: "Sure is! But you got me out of bed with this excellent cookie smell."

G: "I know, but I can not sleep much as you know, and once a baker always a baker. For a lifetime, I had bread ready before the rooster woke up everyone else."

D: "Right. But what did you make? It smells like the honey walnut cookies?"

G: "You are good! I wrote your Dad the other day that you are the only one here who should become a wine-maker, since your taste buds and nose are the best in this house."

D: "Exaggerating again, as always."

G: "Listen, they have to sit to absorb a bit more of the honey syrup, but they should be ready on time."

D: "Why this rush? No one should eat them for breakfast? You shouldn't start that early anyway. You know, no one has challenged or reclaimed your bakery license!"

G: "Hey, I think you forgot that last Sunday I promised to have some cookies delivered to the Paulmerts, right?"

Dimitri's eyes did not move at all as his grandpa continued, "I want them to be ready for them soon, so they can either have them after lunch for dessert or with their afternoon coffee."

D: "You really think I forgot about it?"

G: "I am just amazed that you haven't talked about it yet!"

D: "Why should I?"

G: "Well, weren't you looking forward to seeing Lauren again?"

D: "I saw her last night, when she was on her way to Manhattan. The whole family drove together, most likely to attend one of those members' clubs that they belong to or a high society party."

G: "You keep seeing her from a distance and for a few seconds only. Well, it won't take much longer for you to realize … that you should change the direction you are looking at!"

D: "Then why would you send me to deliver the cookies to them today?"

G: "Maybe to expedite this process."

D: "Oxymoron and philosophical again?"

G: "Witty and humorous as always?"

D: "Come on Grandpa, why do you like to tease me like this?

G: "Because I like you. I only tease people I love and like. The ones I do not care for …. I simply ignore or I do not bother with them."

D: "Why then, have you been telling me that anything can happen? You are the one who taught me that in this country the horizon is wide open. In this country, anything can happen as long as you believe in it? In this country, you have to dream big and you will live big, right? You are my mentor, isn't that what you have been repeating since that I arrived in this foreign country? Right? Since the very first day? Look at all the other Greeks around us. They try to teach their children that one day they should take whatever fortune they make and return to their homeland. You are the only one here in this neighborhood that does not bother to say that."

G: "Oh sure, I do not take any of that back."

D: "So why aren't you hopeful for me?"

G: "It's complicated! Don't ask me; I don't have all the answers."

D: "OK, no worries, what time should I deliver the cookies?"

G: "Let them sit to cool down a bit and get moist. Maybe after church we can try one or two and then we can decide."

D: "OK, papou, but please help me out and let me know how I should present myself to them."

G: "You should be yourself. You may not even get in the house, the servants may pick up the cookies on their behalf. I don't know how they usually deal with such instances." Grandpa looked a bit dumbfounded and full of questions himself.

D: "Maybe I will find my way in and deliver them myself."

G: "If that is what you want, do it."

Dimitri rushed back to his room to get a few more moments of rest, since he thought that he should look well rested. He thought that during the whole week, between the pharmacy store and the deliveries, his evening school and constant studying, he never had enough time to rest and take care of himself. Deep inside him, he was not fond of the fact that on the one day that he could rest, Sunday, he would still have to wake up relatively early to go to church. He always loved to sleep in on Sunday mornings, but his love for his grandmother was so strong that he didn't think about it twice. His Grandma was a very religious and loving person and since she was so devoted to the church, she wanted her children and all of her family to attend church every Sunday as well. Pretty much everyone followed her, not because they were very religious, but because they all loved her and respected her will and desire. Even grandpa would go to church every Sunday in order to avoid her remarks and see her sad. But he was the first to walk out of the church a few minutes before the conclusion of the service.

That Sunday, Dimitri prayed a lot and asked for help and guidance during the Sunday service. He was afraid that he would not find the strength to talk to Lauren and would have to think twice to formulate his sentences, as the words would not flow easily and he might stutter during the most important moment. He was so scared that he would faint or not find the power to say a single word in front of her. He was also worried he may not even see the Paulmerts, as the servants may not allow him to disturb them. Therefore he had many reasons to pray. Not only to find the strength to talk to her, but primarily to find a way to see her and somehow make his presence noticeable to her. He did not want to think of the possibility that they may not meet that Sunday. That day he had many reasons to pray, but at the same time he was aware that all the help that he was asking for was not a spiritual matter, but rather something materialistic and perhaps filled with lust... as he thought at some point. He always asked for forgiveness when his thoughts were perhaps inappropriate, but he could never tell if what he was doing was the right thing. He knew, of course, that he was far from sinful and hedonistic thoughts and his whole attraction to Lauren was far more platonic and romantic. He prayed with all his strength to be courageous and lucky at the same time. He wanted so much to face his one and only love and converse with her with fluency and wit. All of a sudden he felt uncomfortable and concerned that he was behind in his class year, because of his transition from overseas. Later on, the thought that he belonged to such a different social class made him forget about his school class status.

While he was deep in his thoughts, he sensed that his Grandpa stood up and left; a sign that church was going to be over in five or ten minutes. He slowly moved towards the wall and a minute later was outside running to catch up with his Grandpa who was just around the corner. This time grandpa thought it was crucial to leave early, as he was afraid that once church concluded his family members would gobble up all the cookies.

Dimitri followed his Grandpa unnoticed. His pace was unexpectedly fast for an old man in his late sixties, but he looked determined to get there ahead of time. He entered the door and as he closed it, glanced through the window to make sure his grandson was following him as he had sensed. Dimitri entered the kitchen two minutes later and with a shy face asked Grandpa, "Are they OK?"

G: "Indeed they are! I have not forgotten my art, but please, have one and let me know what you think."

D: "But they are for them?"

G: "Nonsense, I told you to just try one!" He said, and his voice growing louder and imperative.

D: "OK papou." He picked up a rather blonde cookie as he preferred the softer over the well roasted ones, which could not soak as much honey syrup. "Really good! Hm… great job papou; you are the master!"

G: "Good to know, from you son, as my taste buds seem to be fading day by day and I don't fully trust myself anymore. You see, getting old … is something that comes with many issues and problems."

D: "Are you seeking compliments again? You know that no one else looks as good as you do at your age; and you are strong too, you know that!"

G: "Nonsense! Why don't you pick up one of these carton boxes from over there and make a nice box, since I am too old to lift them."

D: "Sure, I believe that is the case," and smiled over his grandpa's attitude to joke.

Grandpa folded the sides of the carton box with such care and precision, which demonstrated an old habit and zeal. He picked up the spatula and carefully chose with care the best looking cookies and placed them in the box, one by one. Once he was done, he wrapped a ribbon around the box and made a very artful knot with the help of sharp scissors. He took another careful look at the box, another deep breath and turned to Dimitri to tell him. "Look, it is almost lunch time so you better hurry up."

Dimitri moved towards his Grandpa, gave him a warm hug and took the box and tried to rush out of the kitchen. His Grandpa yelled at once with his deep bass voice, "Do not rush! They are nicely packed and make sure they are delivered properly and in the best way."

D: "OK, grandpa, and do not forget to pray for me."

Grandpa whispered silently, "I will, but for what, exactly I am not sure."

As soon as Dimitri got out and closed the door of the house, he saw across the street and diagonally at the corner the whole family returning from church, escorting the grandmother who was in the middle surrounded by the crowd. She could not walk fast, so everyone always arrived at home much later than Grandpa, which in this instance provided enough time for the cookie issue to get settled without everyone inquiring about it. However, it wasn't enough time to avoid them completely. Dimitri was sure that grandpa never told anyone about the Paulmerts and no one really knew why grandpa decided to bake the honey walnut cookies that Sunday. At this point he did not care what excuse Grandpa came up with, when they discovered that thirty from the forty-five were missing. Dimitri turned left to avoid them and rushed around the corner. His cousins saw him and called him, but he accelerated his pace yelling back at them: "I will be back soon; have a delivery to make, see you all at lunch".

"Hey, stop and come here for a second," his cousin Chris yelled.

"I really can't; will talk to you later, sooooorry , he turned his back to them, feeling guilty but also fearing that one or more of his three cousins would follow him to the Paulmerts' mansion. He did not look back but sensed that his younger cousin was following him, so he accelerated his pace, but then instantly remembered that his Grandpa dictated him not to rush. He was frustrated that he would have to explain the situation to his cousin, who was definitely unaware of it is, as he was sure that Grandpa never talked about it. Giovanni and Joe knew everything about Lauren, but none of his cousins did. When he turned at the boulevard's corner he realized that his cousin Chris had left him alone as his grandmother or father probably had called him back. He realized he had taken a detour and had gone to the wrong side of the square, in order to avoid his cousins, and any possible explanations. He turned again to continue on the right path. The neighborhood was very quiet as usual on Sundays. Most of his neighbors were at home enjoying their time with family and, of course, the Sunday meal that commenced early in the afternoon. The Sunday meal was the best of the week, as most of the housewives cooked their favorite recipes.

The Paulmerts mansion was further away and Dimitri had to walk another ten to fifteen minutes. So he had time for some final thoughts on how to better approach Lauren and ask her out; or better yet to see her again and build a friendship. But of course, the question was where could he meet her, as they were both too young to go on a date and Lauren was never alone in the neighborhood. He also had no idea where she spent her time in Manhattan. He alternatively thought that he could ask her out to see a movie, but that was too much of a stretch, then again, it was the only solution in his mind. Unless he proposed to go to the local ice cream store for a cone or an ice float. He thought that he would be sixteen soon enough, so it could be OK to propose a date like that. Deep in his mind he did not know what the best option was, and was very puzzled. He felt helpless. Half way to his destination he felt that he was not ready for the encounter. His pace got slower and all of a sudden he had a desire to prolong the seven minute walk that remained. He walked slowly and stared left and right. All of a sudden he heard the sound of the bells ringing; it was noon already. Twelve o'clock! He counted all the rings one by one and decided to change course and go directly to the church to light a candle and ask for help one more time. Dimitri, after all, had a religious soul. His grandmother was the kindest and most respectful person in the whole neighborhood. She was known for her great generosity and personality. She never taught him anything about religion, but just the fact that she was such a strong believer made Dimitri religious and he deeply believed in God, prayed faithfully and read the Bible chapter by chapter.

He reached the church and looked around to see if there were any familiar faces around him. He soon felt embarrassed being there! He thought that if someone saw him and asked him why he returned, he would feel awkward and could offer no valid explanation. He thought that everyone would laugh at him if they found out about his possibly, inappropriate and unrealistic desires and dreams to date Lauren Paulmert. However, he was convinced that she was the woman and love of his life. His heart felt like it was bleeding, when he realized that this was somewhat unrealistic. He trembled once again since he was very modest and shy by nature. He stepped inside after he ensured himself that no one had followed him; no friends and family and simply no one else saw him entering the church. He went ahead and dropped a nickel into the collection box and lit a candle. He didn't care that a nickel was a big amount from his savings. He prayed deeply and with complete concentration in his own words, after carefully placing the box with the cookies on a chair nearby. A minute later he felt much better; he picked up the box and continued on his way to the Paulmerts' mansion. Once he had left the church he turned back one more time to see the church's bell tower and felt confident that God would help him.

About ten minutes later he was in front of the impressive steel doors of the Paulmerts' mansion. He rang the doorbell with hesitation. He took a step back and saw that someone was already walking towards him from the garden. The Paulmerts had a small army of employees besides the chauffer, who was also responsible for the maintenance of their luxurious limo. There was a gardener, a cook and several servants. The cook was Giovanni's uncle, so Dimitri knew a lot of things about the Paulmerts, because Giovanni listened to a lot of stories from his uncle.

The servant was almost at the door and looked Dimitri in the eyes as he delivered a formal greeting.

"Good afternoon, how can I help you?"

D: "Good afternoon, sir. I have something to deliver to Mr. Paulmerts from my Grandfather."

Servant: "I can do that for you young fellow."

D: "I am sorry sir, but please announce to Mr. Paulmerts, that Mr. Giovas' grandson is here and has something to deliver in person."

Servant: "Well young man, Mr. Paulmerts is a very busy man, … but I will do it… I can tell though that you would insist."

D: "Thank you sir."

Dimitri was immediately happy, as he realized that his posture and voice were decisive and effective enough to get his point across and achieve his goal. His happiness was an oasis at this point, as he relaxed and felt liberated; his brain did not go through the same round of thoughts that had previously made him nervous. Slowly he realized this and that awareness made him nervous again, as he was good at making himself nervous. He tried to distract himself by thinking of his glorious posture and presence in front of the servant. He thought that he was not that young anymore and besides he was 6 feet tall; so he should not be afraid and shy, and should be able to make a good impression. That gave him courage and conquered once again his fears and inferiority complex, which mainly stemmed from his thoughts that he belonged to a poor family of immigrants and a different social class. His mind meandered in his love for science, poetry, art and his firm belief that he could be successful in life, as hard work could make him achieve anything he wished for. "It is just a matter of time", he thought. After all being idealistic was not a bad thing, as he and Lauren were too young to have a relationship and by the time they would be ready for that, he would be in a university and his horizons would be wide open; for anything he wishes for, he thought again. The arrival of the servant interrupted his thoughts. He opened the door and waved to Dimitri to follow him: "This way young man", he said, with an extremely polite voice and smile as he could see that the boy was from his social class and radiated goodness.

Dimitri finally made his first steps into the property that he had only seen from a distance. He crossed the gardens and followed the servant towards the main door. The servant led him in and took him through the hall to a living room, a library and finally to another living room, which faced the backyard and the garden. He could see that the Paulmerts had been there a few minutes ago, since the newspaper was lying on the big armchair and there were teacups on the coffee table along with some porcelain dishes and a pair of reading glasses.

"Wait here young man, Mr. and Mrs. Paulmerts are finishing up their brunch and will be with you in a few minutes."

Dimitri felt that he was not ready to encounter all the luxurious setting and art; and perhaps digest everything he saw on his way to that final destination. He looked around with his mouth wide open as he was deeply astonished. When he crossed the library, he saw a thick green hard covered book lying on a desk. He was almost sure that it was the exact one that Lauren had picked up the previous week from the bookstore. He was also sure that one of the paintings was a Monet. Everything around him indicated a luscious lifestyle, the precise antithesis to what he was used to. There were four people to a room in his house and certainly not four rooms per person; he thought. Suddenly, he spotted a book by Homer in front of him, next to the pile of the newspapers. He took a few steps and he saw that indeed it was the Odyssey! Wow, he whispered for a second. He had studied that himself as a student in Greece, right before his departure and immediately became very happy, since he thought that this was a great topic to talk about with Lauren. He was certain, that she was the one who was studying the book and that her parents had read the newspapers.

In the next moment the door opened and his head turned quickly into that direction. Again and suddenly his eye pupils instantly aligned with Lauren's. The goosebumps he felt right away made him unable to move his pupils away from hers and she rested her gaze on him by doing the same. His hair felt as if it stood up, spiked like pine needles in a cold draft. He had a full head of thick hair, always combed and no matter if it was styled enough, his hair always made him look handsome. It never occurred to Dimitri that he might represent the handsome southern European male to a girl like Lauren, who was used to socializing with a different style high-class, Anglo-Saxon community kids at Manhattan's Upper East Side. It never occurred to him or perhaps never had time, to consider that he could ever look attractive to a girl like Lauren. The last three years since his arrival, were only focused on how he could help his family pay the extra expenses they had incurred due to him, as well as all the other fees and debts that the family previously had. During his free time, he was very much focused on learning English and educating himself, and he was scattered between his work, the language school, the high school that immigrant and poor kids attended in the afternoon and all the rest of the books that he loved to read during work, breaks or late at night after the cinema. He daydreamed a lot, and the movies were his escape from reality and he never really had time to think about dating or socializing with girls. During the movies he dreamed one day he could be like his idols: Cary Grant, Clark Gable and Tyrone Power, but he really never knew that he could look as attractive as them.

Therefore, life consisted of work and studying; the cinema was his only escape; a brief escape that never led him to brainstorm if he could realistically be a handsome boy for a girl like Lauren. Lauren's eyes were an absolute spectacle and her pupils at that moment were only a tiny dark dot in the vast deep lake of blue, which constituted a potent gaze that could make anyone feel intoxicated or dizzy. Dimitri was solely concentrated on her eyes, since he found the power and will to look straight into them. Her light brown hair and fair complexion also radiated light and care as did her whole existence, dressed in a white polo tennis shirt and skirt. Even though she was in a closed space, she radiated as much light as on that sunny day when their paths crossed outside of the bookstore.

A few seconds later she broke into a smile and gave him a warm greeting, "Good afternoon Dimitri."

Dimitri's face changed expression and his eyes lit up. "Oh... you remember ... Good afternoon, Lauren."

L: "Of course, how are you?"

D: "Fine, thank you! And you?"

L: "Good, thanks. My dad sent me to let you know that he will be here in a minute since we are just wrapping up brunch."

D: "I am sorry to interrupt your brunch, Ms. Paulmerts..." he swallowed when he had addressed her by her last name and this came naturally to him. Was it out of respect? Or was it due to the formal and upper class environment he was immersed in....? He could not figure that out at that moment, but immediately heard Lauren's voice. "I am Lauren", and then it occurred to him that it was based on unfamiliarity.

D: "I am sorry ... just ... am not ... I mean in Europe, when we don't know someone well, we address them by their family name. But I am sorry to forget that this is not the case here; Thanks! I appreciate it."

L: "So, when did you leave Europe? Greece, right?

D: "Right! At the end of 1950, during Christmas."

L: "Wow! Not long ago and your English is so good."

D: "Thank you Ms. ... I mean Lauren. Thank you for the compliment, but I still have a thick accent."

L: "Not at all! Sometimes I cannot even hear it and it sounds nice and charming."

D: "Really? I don't sound "handicapped" when I speak?"

Lauren interrupted him. "Do not say that again, be proud of yourself!"

D: "Thank you ... Lauren."

L: "You know we have this Mexican boy here working in the garden and he still has a much stronger accent than you do and he has been with us for more than five years. Or my piano teacher, she has such a thick accent and she has been here for more than ten years, I can cite more examples for if you want me to."

Dimitri realized for the first time that Lauren was not the typical spoiled brat that she could have been, being raised in such a luxurious environment. However, he was not quite sure if she fully respected the Mexican boy or the piano teacher. But for the moment he was so happy since he had engaged himself in an unexpected and positive dialogue. So much better than he imagined, since he originally worried that he would only get to see Mr. Paulmerts. Now he had the courage and the power to even ask her questions.

D: "Have you ever been to Europe or abroad?"

Lauren smiled and said intrigued, "Many times."

Dimitri could hear traces in her answer that alluded to other layers of meanings, so he continued by asking, "Where about?"

L: "Wherever Hollywood has taken me, from the Incas trails to South African farms and the streets of Rome."

D: "You mean being escorted by Charlton Heston, Tyrone Power and Gregory Peck?"

Lauren seemed impressed and bent her head forward with wide eyes open and said, "Oh you are good!" "How did you figure this out so quick?"

D: "Cinema is one of my life's passions and I try not to miss a single movie... I wish I had more time to watch more of them, but my family always tells at me that I am not using my time wisely and my head is getting filled with dreams, etc... but I do read a lot of books as well."

L: "You impress me; I thought you only worked as a delivery boy in the pharmacy store across the street from the post office."

D: "How do you know this?" Dimitri asked completely astonished.

L: "Well, I have seen you many times riding the bike or sitting by the window reading, since I go to the post office almost every week."

D: "You do?" He could not believe that and was totally surprised; he had never noticed her? It was hard for him to realize it. At this point his puzzled excitement was so deep that he was worried that his face looked very dumb in front of his one and only love.

L: "I have pen pals all over the world, so every week I take a walk to go through the neighborhood to buy my magazines and mail my letters.

D: "But I have never seen the limo."

Lauren said lauging, "Oh yes, that gets me into a lot of trouble with my parents, since they are worried when I walk in this part of the city," she smiled and continued, "They have one of our staff members follow me all the time, just in case."

D: "But the neighborhood is very safe, there is nothing to be afraid of. There are lots of poor people out there but there is no crime."

L: "I know! I feel the same way, but my parents still think that I am twelve years old."

At that point she was interrupted by her father who entered the room dressed in an impeccable casual outfit, stylish as always, posing an impressive posture. "Oh, good afternoon young man, nice to see you again." Mr. Paulmerts moved fast towards Dimitri and extended his hand for a handshake. Dimitri promptly shook his hand and delivered a warm handshake with pleasure and happiness in his face. "Good afternoon Mr. Paulmerts, how do you do?"

Mr. P: "Excellent and yourself?"

D: "Very good thanks, and sorry to bother you with …"

Mr. P: "No wait, it is no bother to us, we just finished our Sunday brunch. Has Lauren already offered you something to drink or a treat?"

L: "Sorry father, I didn't find the time yet?"

Mr. P: "Not yet? What do you mean? What have you been doing all this time?"

L: "Well you know, it looks like Dimitri is a movie buff like me. He was able to guess at once what movies I have seen, from my quotes."

Mr. P: "Oh I see, so what kind of movies do you like Dimitri? American movies?"

D: "Of course, sir. I love adventures, westerns, love stories, musicals… everything!"

Mr. P: "Really? Which one is your favorite?"

D: "Oh, I have many but …"

Mr. P: "Don't bother, I see you are like my daughter, I get the same answers from her. So how is your grandfather?"

D: "Very well, sir, he sent me here to deliver this box to you with what used to be your favorite cookies"

Mr. Paulmerts with a surprised but serious gaze, exclaimed, "Really? I was not expecting this… please have a seat." Dimitri grabbed a chair to his right and Mr. Paulmerts sat down across from him on the coach and Lauren moved slowly to sit on the sofa's armrest.

D: "Sir, I was present when he promised you these. Remember? We were outside of bookstore, last Sunday."

Mr. P: "Really? You know how many people promise me things Dimitri? I guess promises have no meaning to me anymore. But your grandfather is such an honest man. I wish you would always use him as an example Dimitri." He took a deep breath and looked Dimitri deeply in the eyes.

Mr. P: "Your Grandfather is a great man; you know how he started his business, right?"

D: "I guess so, he rented the establishment from your father or grandfather, I guess, pardon me as I am not sure."

Mr. P: "That is what he told you son?"

D: "Yes of course! He told me that without the help of your family he would not have been able to have the business. He always talks with admiration and respect especially for your grandfather."

Mr. P: "Really? So what do you know exactly?"

D: "I do not know much sir, except that somehow he rented the place from your grandfather. I guess that was during the time your grandfather bought most of the real estate in the neighborhood and was really successful."

Mr. P: "Yes, and what else did he tell you?"

D: "Nothing much, you now he does not reveal many details when it comes to his achievements and his artistry. He never elevates himself to the level that he really deserves. He is a very modest man."

Mr. P: "That I know, and I rather say, I heard about it many times, but why is that?"

D: "Well... I think it's because my grandmother is very religious and he is trying to make her happy by living up to what's in the Bible; he best likes the phrase that, "the one who is trying to raise himself without being humble he would be humiliated but the one who lives and endorses humility would be elevated" and pardon me sir, if I do not know the exact translation, as the one I read is in the original Greek version."

(Who exalts himself will be humbled, but he who humbles himself will be exalted.)

Mr. P: "Of course there are so many great books and scripts written in Greek. Lauren is reading Homer for her schoolwork right now. It seems that your grandfather never told you how he really started his bakery..."

D: "What do you mean, Mr. Paulmerts?"

Mr. P: "He never told you about the fire and my grandfather's loss?"

D: "I don't think I know what you are talking about?"

Mr. P: "Hmm... perhaps he would rather tell you one day, instead of me..."

D: "But he hasn't done that so far, sir?

Mr. P: "You are right ... you know, young man, your grandfather tried so hard to make a living here and send money to feed his children and family back home ... I guess your father is one of them. The beginning of the century was tough for every immigrant. He was the same age as my father and obviously junior than my grandfather, who at that time was already successful in the industry and bought a lot of real estate as an investment. I think your grandfather had to change his job ten or more times and from what I remember, work in more than ten states. He worked day and night like everyone else and sent all his money to his wife and three children back home. He still could not afford to have them come over to America. He also could not get the papers; I don't know many details but he eventually successed, after years of hard work, at bringing his wife and one of his children. However, the point is that he was making a buck here, a buck there. In the summer of 1918, there was a devastating fire in the neighborhood and my grandfather lost a lot of money from some real estate developments. One of the establishments he had, a bakery, was completely burnt from the fire. Your grandfather and everyone else used to buy their daily bread from Mr. Schneider, who watched his investment disappear with the fire and left New York; not sure where to, as he was unable to restore his business. My grandfather didn't know what to do with the building and wanted to empty it and sell it. At that point, your grandpa went to him with a proposal. He suggested letting him restore the bakery, paint it, fix it up and operate it for one year. In exchange, he would have his daily bread for that year and at the end of the year he would get a job at my grandfather's factory. I guess once a factory worker he then would be able to have a steady salary and send money to his family back home. So my grandfather gave his crew access to all the paint, cleaning materials and tools he needed, so he could restore the building and repair the machines and the oven. My grandfather, who always passed by the neighborhood, watched the progress and soon enough the bakery was reshaped, painted and up and running. The machines and oven were repaired and my grandfather had no clue how your grandpa did it without any specialized knowledge, but he did it. Months past and my grandfather always had bread delivered during his working hours at the factory, so he never bothered to check on how the bakery was doing. At that time, Queens was not the Jewish, Greek and Italian community it is now, but somehow your grandfather had a few customers who trusted the newly arrived Greek. One time my grandfather stopped by to buy bread, as he was happy with all the work your Grandpa had done with the building, and he complimented him. My grandfather though was a busy man and he didn't have the time to stop by all the time. However, a year later your grandpa showed up at his doorstep. My grandfather immediately thought that there was some short of trouble; he asked him "what was the matter?" Your grandpa reminded him that exactly a year ago; he had convinced my grandpa to repair the bakery and brought to him all the profits from the year. You can imagine how dumbfounded my grandfather was as he had forgotten about the profits from the bakery; he figured that your grandpa repaired everything in the building, painted, repaired the machinery and oven and whatever he earned would be for an exchange of services. He totally forgot about the details of the agreement; what the exact deal was, and why the profits of the bakery should go to him, while Mr. Giovas got the building back to its original shape. He could not believe that there was so much money in the bag that Mr. Giovas handed him. He asked your grandpa if he had spent any money during the last year. Your grandfather answered that he only bought tomatoes from the local farmers market or vegetables to eat with his bread and nothing else. Whatever was left, he thought, was the profit for my grandfather, as Mr. Giovas had only asked for his daily bread. When my grandfather counted the money, he realized that your Grandfather could not possibly have sent not even a penny to Greece. That whole year, Mr. Giovas had told his family and relatives to be patient and to wait until the following year when he would have a permanent job at the factory and a normal salary. My grandfather was amazed at his honesty and he refused to take the money from him and told him that he could keep the bakery as his own business. You see until that moment, my grandfather had been betrayed many times by partners, colleagues, coworkers and greedy people. He didn't trust much the common man and your grandfather's honesty made him sincerely cry. All the disappointments and everything he had endured, had made him a tough and resilient man. That, young man, in few words, is how your grandfather entered the bakery business, and was eventually able to pay for his oldest son to come to America. I guess after the stock market crash, it took him many years to bring his wife and cousin over and then with the war he could not bring all of his children, but eventually he brought you, the next generation.

D: "I was not aware of that story and maybe nobody else in our family knows, maybe except for my grandmother," he said with a low voice, full of emotion as his eyes teared up.

L: "I could see the other day, Dimitri that your grandfather looks like a great and wonderful man."

D: "He is, but why has he never told me that story?"

Mr. P: "I guess in a way you know, he is too modest."

D: "Indeed he is, and I am so glad to know that you, Mr. Paulmerts, you have a good heart. I can see that from the way you told me the story. So really, Mr. Paulmerts, my grandfather was right to have asked you to come to our neighborhood more often and to reconnect with the working class, the one that pays rent to you and struggles with the daily bread and suffers when Mr. Fein is twisting their arms."

Mr. P: "Look Dimitri, I talked to Mr. Fein and I did not detect that anything was wrong. Besides right now the competition and stress in the factory is fierce and my estate needs all these rental income. I cannot run a charity when the government is after me for taxes and everything else. We used to be the only factory, but since the war things have changed drastically. Mr. Fein has my sympathy in his tough job to collect the dues."

D: "I understand that sir and forgive me for my comments. I do not intend to be disrespectful and pardon me if I came across as such. I also do not wish to be unpleasant, but if you ever think that something could be wrong or detect that something is not right, please, let me or my Grandfather talk to you."

Mr. Paulmerts could see how smart Dimitri was at this point, as this was an excellent move and very diplomatic. On the one hand, he avoided getting into an extended argument with him, but on the other hand he made him feel that something was really wrong with Mr. Fein, and even he himself chooses not to take a closer look. He took a deep breath and a facial expression that let Dimitri know that he understood him and when the right time would come he would talk to them. He was confident that the boy across from him would understand his facial expression and agreement. However, he over-looked the fact that his daughter detected this as well and got the idea that something was really wrong with Mr. Fein, who was a really good employee and devoted servant to her father till that moment.

L: "Dad are you really sure about this? Why would Dimitri and his grandfa-ther ever lie to you? Maybe you should listen to what he has to tell you."

Mr. Paulmerts at that point realized his mistake and became serious, looked Lauren into the eyes and said, "Can we talk about something else? Why don't you tell Dimitri about Homer and this book over there, or the rest of the Greek literature that you have already read?"

The heavy tone of his voice made it clear that he was in no mood to argue and left no room for additional arguements. All of a sudden he realized how important all the income from his real estate in Queens was to him. That income, especially in the last few years, has been vital to his survival, since the factory was in trouble. In addition, he instantly thought about all the expenses that Mrs. Paulmert's incurred with her fascination to conform to the upper class of Manhattan and all of the rest of the expenses associated with the maintenance of his status and estate. The last thing he ever wanted at that point was to have to give up any of the steady income that Mr. Fein and his crew constantly added to his estate.

On the other hand, Lauren was a daughter who really loved her father. Maybe she didn't have the same affection for her mother, who was impossible to please, as it seemed like she inherited the open and good heart from her great-grandfather, an industrialist, but also a good man. A self-made mil-lionaire, who never forgot that he had started out as a poor man early in life. Dimitri didn't feel the strength to bring up any more arguments against Mr. Paulmert and believed he saw the same feeling in Lauren's eyes. He instantly thought that it was a pity that most mistakes in life could stem from the inability of people to act at the right moment and the right time. However, deep inside him he knew that this might not be the right moment. The voice of his grandfather entered his mind subconsciously, saying that there is always a right time, and the wise man is the man who understands when that time is. He did not have another moment to think as Lauren said respectfully, "OK Dad, I guess we can postpone this for the moment and instead talk about my favorite book the Odyssey", she turned to Dimitri, "Have you ever read this book?"

D: "Of course I did, and in fact when I was a pupil back in Greece, I also loved this book."

L: "It is such a great adventure with so many interesting characters and situations and tests that Ulysses has to go through. I wonder how much of it is reality and how much of it is fiction?"

D: "Well, there are some things that make it fascinating enough, no matter how much is true or not."

Mr. P: "Like what Dimitri?"

D: "Like the persistence of the main character to return to his country, to find the right path in his life's journey, and to reach his final destination."

Mr. P: "Indeed, what a fascinating journey and determination, as well." "I read a lot of Greek literature myself when I was young, but indeed, Homer fascinated me more than anyone else. I probably got more interested in Plato later, and got fascinated with how two and a half thousand years ago, he could lay out a master plan on what a Republic should look like. Later, as a student at the university, I had the desire to learn how to read the original scripts, since the original version of the New Testament was also written in Greek. I took two semesters of classics and started to study classic Greek, but that was when I met my wife and fell in love. I guess I got distracted by too many things that were going on in my life and dropped any extracurricular activities."

L: "What do you mean? Mom was the reason you stopped studying?"

Mr. P: "No, of course not, I continued my studies but I didn't have as much free time for extracurricular activities, since I had to spend time with your mom. The studies I mentioned were more or less my hobby."

L: "Oh, so mom was demanding even when you were young and at university?"

Mr. Paulmerts did not think that the last comment was appropriate, especially in front of Dimitri, who was unaware of Mrs. Paulmerts' personality. Again, he thought that the best strategy was to distract everyone from any unpleasant conversation and change the subject while he disregarded anything that may become unpleasant for him and his wife. After all, he always protected every family member regardless how burdensome Mrs. Paulmerts' demands were. Deep inside him he was always a loyal husband who was attracted to her everlasting beauty. He found the strength to curb all of the unnecessary expenses that her lifestyle constantly incurred. Mrs. Paulmerts was, after all, a very elegant socialite, offspring of another very well established family. Her father, Mr. Herve DuPont, was one of the main heirs to a late magnate and pioneer in the steel industry that moved to New York City early in the century to enjoy the city life, away from the industrial and rural settings of Western Pennsylvania. The DuPonts never revealed the real magnitude of their estate, but they were practically living off their wealth, exploiting the assets that they had inherited. However, rumor had it that their wealth was steadily declining to alarming levels. Perhaps, her roots in the aristocracy made Mrs. Paulmerts demanding and hard to please. Mr. Paulmerts was so much in love with her during their relationship that he never cared to ask for any of her fortune prior to their wedding. He only wanted to get married to her and did not care if she brought anything from her father's fortune to his estate, as he always felt like a very wealthy man. He was certain, that in time of crisis she could save the family and support him, but on the other hand he was confident enough that he would never reach that point. He always felt sturdy enough to manage what he had inherited from his family, plus he had plenty of wealth and fortune to not make him fear he would ever reach an alarming point. So he had always allowed her to be capricious and did not care about her extravagances and need to impress and to spend. He was mature enough and felt that her demands were part of her being and not something that Lauren should ever criticize.

Then Mr. Paulmerts remembered the point of Dimitri's visit and pointed to the box of the cookies that he had brought to his house. "So are these the famous walnut honey cookies that your granddad used to make in the good old days?" he asked with a pleasant voice completely ignoring Lauren's comment.

D: "Indeed sir, they are and they are made especially for you and your family. My granddad wanted me to bring them to you today so you could have them for dessert or with your afternoon tea."

Mr. P: "That is so kind of him and thank you so much for bringing them all the way here, thank you very much and please extend my sincere gratitude to your grandpa as well."

D: "With my pleasure, sir."

Mr. Paulmerts moved his hand into his pocket and pulled his wallet out. He didn't have a moment to glance at it as he was interrupted right away by Dimitri, "Sir, I hope that you understand that this is a gift?"

Mr. Paulmerts looked him deep in his eyes, "Well, but he spent some money on the ingredients and you delivered them all the way to my house?"

D: "I do not think he would accept money in return and neither would I, with all do respect Sir, please, you know him so well, and this is from the depth of his heart."

Mr. P: "So here's some money and please consider it a small gift from me to you. You like books, movies and other things I suppose, so spend it as you please," and extended to him a five dollar bill.

Dimitri almost fainted and immediately stepped back shocked with wide opened eyes. "Please sir, I cannot accept this as it is our gift to you and should not be associated with any monetary value in return."

Mr. Paulmerts could see his stubbornness in his facial expression, along with the fear that his Grandpa would yell at him if he ever accepted money for the cookies. He pulled his arm back and tried to think of what he could possibly offer Dimitri in return instead of money. Dimitri in the meantime, thought about how angry his Grandpa would get once he heard that he received money for the cookies or the delivery. Grandpa was a very proud man and a very giving person; one that would never accept any money as a gift.

For a moment it looked as if Mr. Paulmerts would not insist further and Dimitri would not say anything unless Mr. Paulmerts would say something. Mr. Paulmerts turned to the side and asked him, "I know you like books, or am I wrong? Or anything else?"

Dimitri totally dumfounded answered, "Well... movies."

Mr. Paulmert: "Oh that's right, you are like my daughter," he said as he turned towards Lauren who had been carefully observing the interaction of the two men.

Mr. P: "What about Manhattan? What do you like over there, son?"

D: "I do not know the city very well Sir, we do not go there very often," and after few moments of silence he said, "I have been to the Metropolitan museum and the park a few times with my grandpa, but that is all. We can hardly find the time to go there."

Mr. Paulmerts turned his back to Dimitri. Perhaps he did not want him to see his face and possibly detect his thoughts. He immediately remembered that the young man in front of him was the grandson of a baker and an immigrant who had to work around the clock to earn his living and educate himself. He took a few steps away from Dimitri and put himself into deep thought to find something that would be a reasonable gift that would bring joy to the poor boy. He obviously did not think it would be appropriate to offer him and his daughter movie tickets. Suddenly he thought of this possibility again, but rejected it once more since he had no desire to offer something that could possibly be perceived as a date. He liked Dimitri but of course, he was not the right person for his daughter. He was fascinated by his grandfather and did not mind if perhaps, once in a while he met with Lauren to talk about Homer or the movies, but definitely not to take his daughter out on a date. Suddenly like a spark, he had an idea; How about if he offered him his help. Perhaps to help him find a better job where he would earn more money? That's it! He thought at once and turned 180 degrees to face him.

Mr. P: "Dimitri how much do you like the work at that pharmacy, by the post office?"

D: "Very much Sir."

Mr. P: "Well, can you tell me why?"

D: "Oh, I have learned so much about what everyone needs for life; what makes them happy; what makes them healthy. Everyone stops at that pharmacy to talk and chat and I hear their stories and problems and learn something new every day. I also like that they give me the bicycle to deliver everything in the neighborhood. I pretty much know everyone in the neighborhood. I go to everyone's house; I greet everyone; I smile at everyone and they smile back at me. Mr. Paulmerts, it's great to know everyone in the neighborhood and their problems and sometimes I can help them."

Mr. Paulmerts again looked deep into his eyes. He could see the uncurbed enthusiasm of an idealistic young man and a major excitement, but he could not understand how the things Dimitri just listed could be so important. He thought that he was a young and inexperienced man who does not yet know the power of money, or how much education and specialization could one day improve his life. Mr. Paulmerts now recognized that Dimitri was a very social person and that his interactions with unimportant workers and common people, meant a lot to him.

The fact was that Dimitri didn't have such interactions in his early years while he grew up in Greece, and Mr. Paulmerts could not understand why all these things that Dimitri listed had an important value. Therefore, he concluded that it was some kind of a superficial pleasure for someone who lived in the streets of busy neighborhoods; something that people raised in such an environment could feel. Mr. Paulmerts thought again, "How important can it be to know what kind of candy or medicine someone needs? And knowing everyone is not as exciting as knowing the right people". Mr. Paulmerts felt that the youngster across from him had a good soul and thought that he could maybe guide him through life and perhaps one day offer him a job, since he always complained about how many of his people were insincere and not trustworthy. All of these thoughts lead him to ask Dimitri

Mr. P: "So, do you enjoy all these social interactions and biking around in the neighborhood?"

Dimitri without realizing what use this seemingly information could be for Mr. Paulmerts enthusiastically said, "Absolutely Mr. Paulmerts! I get to meet and to know a lot of people. That is how I met a lot of non-Greek people, like my friends Giovanni and Joe and the Murphy's, the Garcias and so many more. Of course, I love to bike around, as I owned a bicycle when I was back home in Greece Sir."

Mr. Paulmerts bit his lips by the time Dimitri finished his last sentence, as for him the name Garcias reminded him of something... a few moments later he thought , oh yes it was Mr. Fein's' complaints about incompetent workers who were always late with the rent. Mr. Fein had talked to him many times about evicting certain families from his establishments, as there was always demand from others to move in. The Garcias were definitely on the top of Mr. Fein's eviction list, as they always paid the rent late. For another time he thought that the boy across from him was very intelligent but did not use his intelligence and potential the right way, as he had most likely been misdirected. He felt that this was the right time to offer an opportunity to this honest young man.

Mr. P: "Have you ever thought of doing another job? Something different from what you do now?"

D: "Like what Sir?"

Mr. P: "Look, I have a lot of workers in the factory, plus many people who help me here with the maintenance of my estate and I keep hiring people for all kinds of jobs."

Dimitri was shocked! At this point he could not believe that Lauren's father was considering him for a job. The first thing that crossed his mind was that he would be close to Lauren. Maybe he could become a frequent visitor at the Paulmerts? And he could get to know better, the person he wanted to be with for the rest of his life. That idea was so tantalizing that he immediately felt a certain intensity; an intensity that usually could become an obsession. Suddenly all kinds of different scenarios unfolded in his mind; especially on how he could socialize with Lauren. It was quite unbelievable to be at the Paulmerts' home, in the first place, and now Mr. Paulmerts was about to offer him a job; or a better an opportunity. Perhaps this was a great chance to help his dream with Lauren become real. He became so hopeful that there would come a day when he would be close to Lauren and could possibly convince her that they are both meant to be together. He instantly dreamed that her powerful and beautiful eyes would one day stare at him with love and care … Oh what a dream! He wasn't shy anymore and to Mr. Paulmert's amazement, moments later asked with sparkling eyes:

D: "What are you implying, Sir?"

Mr. P: "Well Dimitri, if you ever get tired of your current job and wish to earn more money, you should talk to me as I always need people like you."

D: "For the factory Sir?"

Mr. P: "Not necessarily young man. Since you know the neighborhood so well, you can work over there, perhaps with Mr. Fein."

Dimitri's eyes widened again, as any reference to that name was associated with pain and sorrow. His family did not have any major interaction or argument with Mr. Fein as they were not Paulmerts' tenants, but almost everyone else around them had. He was somehow disgusted at the way people were treated in front of his eyes. Even scarier were the stories that he heard from people in the streets. He never imagined that he and a person like Mr. Fein would ever get along. Everyone had problems with him even his best friends.

Joe's family had problems with Mr. Fein and even Giovanni had once been kicked by him once in the street. Mr. Fein was the kind of guy who saw everyone in the neighborhood as a pest. He probably did not like his job that much and everyone who was poor was a nuisance to him, a kind of problem and an additional thing to worry for his job and life.

D: "Well Mr. Paulmerts, I think I told you about my feelings for Mr. Fein and his work."

Mr. P: "Well young man, don't you think that this could be the best reason for me to have you work with him?"

Dimitri's eyes widened again as he looked at Mr. Paulmerts' intrigued gaze. He was amazed and surprised to understand that Mr. Paulmerts was much more intelligent and foretelling than he previously thought. Dimitri was smart enough to understand that as a good businessman, Mr. Paulmerts wanted to resolve any possible issues with Mr. Fein in a very sophisticated and diplomatic way. On the one hand, he was protecting his employee, since somehow he did not want to believe any rumors and he really had no time to monitor his activity and authority. On the other hand, by allowing Dimitri to infiltrate his organization, he would give him an opportunity to correct any injustices towards the tenants. Dimitri immediately understood that this was the real point behind Mr. Paulmert's proposition. He wondered for few moments if he should confirm that his thoughts were correct. However, he was not sure if engaging Mr. Paulmerts in this kind of dialogue would be for the better or for worse. He was taking so much time to decide on how to proceed, that Mr. Paulmerts voice interrupted his thoughts: "so do you want me to explain why?"

D: "I think I understand Sir and pardon me ... but do you think that Mr. Fein will ever agree to work with me? One of the insiders from the neighborhood and especially an inexperienced person like me?"

Mr.P: "Mr. Fein is a very good employee, he is always doing what needs to be done and what I tell him to do." He paused for a second to glance at Lauren, who was following the discussion with extreme interest, before turning his gaze back at Dimitri and then he continued, "He is one of my most loyal employees."

This definitely, worried Dimitri as Mr. Paulmerts' positive perception of Mr. Fein's loyalty and devotion, was most likely extended to his personality and not his professionalism. He questioned his feelings for a moment in case he was wrong about Mr. Fein's personality, but of course he could not really change his mind that easily, when all the memories of cruelty were so present and emerged again and again in his mind. However, he thought that this might be a great opportunity for him to make things better for the people he loved and everyone who had suffered from Mr. Fein's practices. He pictured himself one day having the authority to replace Mr. Fein and make deals with the neighborhood's residents to better handle the problems of the monthly payments. He thought for a moment that it could be the best solution to alleviate the problems. He could be useful to everyone he loved in the neighborhood and offer them help.

All these thoughts flooded his mind and he was convinced that he had nothing to lose and that he should accept the offer.

D: "Mr. Paulmerts it really honors me that you are considering me to be one of your employees and I would love to accept your offer right away, but..." he paused for a second.

Mr. P: "But? Shall we discuss the details of the offer so you can see if this would be better than your current job?"

D: "Oh, no.. no.. no.. Mr. Paulmerts not at all, that is not the reason I'm hesitating Sir." He paused and glanced sideways at Lauren who was looking at him, "No, I just thought for a second that I may need to discuss this with my grandfather and check first if I can really leave the pharmacy, my current job?"

Mr. P: "Oh, absolutely son! Take your time to think about it and let me know whenever you are ready. You don't have to let me know right away. Take your time and if you want to work for me, please come and visit me any Sunday around this time and I will make the proper arrangements for you."

D: "Mr. Paulmerts, how can I ever thank you for this great honor Sir ... I am really very thankful that you are considering me for such an opportunity and pardon my hesitation as I am not eighteen years old yet, and I cannot make decisions without consulting my family. You know, I need three more years to finish school and then my dream is to make some money and try to go to college. It might be better if I waited and worked for you later when I would be in college or ... I do not know Sir, but I'm so excited to know that you are considering me and I cannot thank you enough for this."

Mr. P: "You are very welcome, young man, and for the time being, just thank your Grandpa for being such a great man and for sending me these exceptional sweets; which by the way we had all forgotten about." He grabbed the box, unwrapped it and carefully opened the top while staring at it with admiration. He held the box up to his nose and took a whiff and said "Ah... what a smell ... as it comes from the good old days!" He turned to his daughter, "Lauren, please come and have one of them, I grew up with them."
Lauren moved, as always with the grace and style of a ballet dancer and with a posture that indicated her aristocratic roots, to her father's right and reached for one of the cookies. Mr. Paulmerts then held and turned the box towards Dimitri who was immediately ready to object, as his facial expression took an obvious no.
D: "No, thank you Sir, these are for you."
Mr. P: "So what? Can't you have one?
D: "No, please Sir my grandpa made more for us, so these are all for you."
Mr. P: "Come on, just have one? There are so many more in this box."
D: "I insist Sir, these are only for you and your family."
Mr. P: "This is very Greek to me, I guess," he said with a smile. "Well, I won't wait till you change your mind and will have one myself. Can we offer you something else? Perhaps a cup of tea or some orange juice? I am so embarrassed that we kept talking all this time and haven't offered you anything!"
D: "Do not worry Sir, I am OK."
Mr. P: "I can see that young man, however, we broke every "savoir vivre" rule, since I have been consumed in a discussion without a break to rest and drink, I certainly have to apologize to you."
D: "Oh, no need to do that Sir. I am quite OK with it and maybe it is time for me to go."
Mr. P: "As you wish, but please feel free to stay longer. I am sure Lauren may have questions for you about her Greek studies. But allow me to wrap something quickly and have you deliver it to your grandpa." He tried to move to his right, but immediately bumped into Lauren who had the cookie in her hand and was waiting for him to take one so she could start eating it. "Oh you see what happens, I forgot that I also need to try them," and without hesitation, he bit into one and immediately closed his eyes as if he were

dreaming of heaven. Lauren did almost the same and both turned to Dimitri and said in unison, *"These are so good!"* Lauren adding, "Really amazing!" Dimitri was so happy and he felt that this moment was one of the happiest moments in his life. He had a huge smile, not only because of the praise for his grandpa's cookies, but also because he could definitely face the love of his life, a face full of grace, beauty and happiness, which he would now felt was connected to him for life. She was right in front of him and happy being in his presence, *"what else do I need in life?"* he thought and then broke into another wide happy smile. Besides that, he was constantly thinking about Mr. Paulmerts' job offer, which would open the door to lots of future opportunities, including chances to share time with Lauren. He never fell in love with another girl in his tough and full of hard work life and he knew at that moment that he would only have eyes for her. His imagination was full of fantasies and projections that included him and Lauren talking and walking by the water, having picnics at the park, holding hands and being very much in love.

Mr. Paulmerts interrupted these images and fantasies that were running through his head by again offering him a cookie. Dimitri could not say no again and this time he extended his arm and grabbed one.

Mr. P: "Very good son. You see eventually I convinced you, and as you can see it takes time for things to happen in life. I guess one of the lessons here is that if you are persistent enough anything can happen."

Dimitri at once shifted his eyes to Lauren's eyes, as he registered Mr. Paulmerts' advice literally for what he cared for most. His eyes turned back to face Mr. Paulmerts, who was observing him carefully and he said, "You are right, Sir."

Mr. P: "Right about what?"

Dimitri quickly said, "Oh, about the cookies Sir, they are amazing!"

Mr. P: "Well, I guess Lauren said this, but I also agree with her."

Dimitri sensed that Mr. Paulmerts' penetrating gaze could have gotten a sense of what was going on in his mind. He felt awkward and that made him become shy and look a bit uncomfortable. "Oh ... indeed, Sir ... but you liked them as well as your facial expression revealed."

Mr. P: "Indeed Dimitri, and I'm glad that you recognize that a facial expression is good enough to understand many things, which do not have to be talked about."

Dimitri did not feel any better at this point and nervously repeated, "Maybe I should go and let you enjoy the rest of the afternoon, Sir."

Mr.P: "As you wish Dimitri. Lauren could you please escort Dimitri to the door please?"

L: "Yes Papa, I will."

D: "Well… thank you so much for the hospitality and the conversation Sir… and most of all for the job offer, Sir. You know it could be important to my family as well, since we still have siblings and cousins to bring over here."

Mr. P: "I wish we could have offered you more of our hospitality, Dimitri, but we were too passionate and talked too much, but feel free to stop by again when have your answer to my offer."

D: "I will, with pleasure Sir" and moved his head delivering thanks and respect. As he turned his eyes to Lauren he saw for another time her big blue eyes looking deep into his eyes and he froze for a second, "Enjoy your Sunday, Miss Paulmerts."

L: "I am Lauren, enjoy your Sunday Dimitri."

Mr. Paulmerts with a smile on his face asked Lauren to escort Dimitri to James' desk.

Lauren said softly, "yes father", with sweetness in her voice. This somehow gave Dimitri the idea that she probably enjoyed being around him. She was definitely not the spoiled girl that everyone else thought she probably was. Most likely, since she never socialized with the children in Queens, everyone assumed that she was a social snob and had been raised as a princess. This was the first time Dimitri was assured that she was not as spoiled as people thought, but she was a rather genuine person with a friendly and welcoming personality.

Lauren walked towards the door, signaling Dimitri to follow her, as he did after a last glance at Mr. Paulmerts' enigmatic face. He could not tell what this facial expression was all about and thought that for a second it was the expression of a father who worries about his daughter, getting involved with the wrong person, someone who could not make her happy and satisfy the lifestyle that she was accustomed to and perhaps deserved. Dimitri did not want to think for another second what that face was about and turned his head towards Lauren and looked deep into her eyes as he followed her. As they crossed the library silently he felt shy again and glanced one more time at the big green hardcover book that was open in the study, the book that Lauren had gotten at the bookstore last Sunday. He was so tempted to ask about it, but he could not find the courage to talk to Lauren. He could feel that once he opened his mouth he would start stuttering. A few steps later he was at the entrance hall where the service manager James, sat at his desk writing. Dimitri realized that his time with Lauren was almost over so he found the power to ask, "Lauren, would it be possible to see you again?"

L: "What do you mean? I do not go out without my parents."

D: "Right. And even when you go to Manhattan you never hang out with people our age?"

L: "Oh, sure I do, at the club, but they are all friends of the family."

D: "And when you go to the movies?"

L: "Well, do you think they let me go alone? Whenever my Mom cannot come they have Esther or James escort me and watch the film with me."

D: "Hmm... I see ... I just wanted to let you know that it would be great to see a movie together, but perhaps I should first ask your dad for permission" he immediately smiled as he realized this was a brilliant idea or at least a feasible move for him.

L: "We'll see, ... but I guess if I wanted to see you, I could cross the street at the post office and drop by to say hi at the pharmacy. You are there almost every day, aren't you?"

Dimitri's face got even brighter, noticeably illuminated from excitement, "Yes, that's right! Please do so!"

"Hello Miss Paulmerts, I suppose the young man is done with his visit?" James said, who had become invisible to Dimitri.

Lauren smiled and gave James an, "I don't know look?"

Dimitri's excitement was interrupted but not depleted, and after a good look into Lauren's eyes he said, "Sure! But..." he paused for a while, and again looked at her deep blue eyes, and continued, "Sure, I will see you soon again, I suppose, thank you for everything Miss ... I mean Lauren and enjoy the rest of your Sunday". He extended his hand and gave her a firm handshake, which left Lauren dumfounded and in pain, since it was too firm of a handshake for a girl.

D: "Mr. James, I am all yours now."
L: "Bye Dimitri."
Dimitri turned back, "See you soon Lauren." He turned his back to her because he did not want to read what was on Lauren's mind and James escorted him to the front door.

Convinced that they were right

Dimitri was back in the streets alone again. For a second he thought he was immersed in a totally different world. The same streets, same paths and same neighborhood were so much brighter now; same, but somehow different, and he felt that he was seeing them with completely different eyes. Indeed they were simply not the same, but soon enough he was convinced that his perception had changed and not the streets. The world was the same but his mind was different now. His mood was great whistling happily and care-free. As time passed, he realized more and more how significant the last few hours were in his life. The past hour he had spent with the Paulmerts felt like months, even years. He knew he would never forget these moments. He didn't notice the people around him and the world had taken on a brighter hue; everything had a brighter reflection, which he could have easily attributed to the beautiful weather. He felt like yelling and screaming, he was so happy. He was able to spend a few important moments with her, in her intense pres-ence, which was like a major part of his previous dream world. Her face, was the face that would replace every beautiful actress's face on the silver screen. He was now even more in love with Lauren. He even thought that he might have a chance to be with her some times during his life. He suddenly stopped his carefree pace as he decided he needed to see his friends in order to get a reality check. He was looking forward to sharing his recent experience with Joe and Giovanni.
As he approached the neighborhood, where his beloved extended family and friends lived, he suddenly envisioned himself wearing clean and fashionable clothes and greeting people and collecting rent with professionalism, emit-ting care and kindness. He thought he could orchestrate a scheme in which he could cover up the failure of families to pay rent on time. He had no idea how, but he felt confident that there would be a way and he'd find a solution.

All of a sudden it was apparent to him that he really had to take that job offer from Mr. Paulmerts. He was convinced that this was the right thing to do and that Mr. Paulmerts was right to invite him to work for him. Such a win-win situation; he thought for a moment... it would only help his people and friends, but also get him closer to Lauren and be part of the family in the way he had always dreamed of. Oh ... what a dream? He slowed down for a moment; his steps got heavier and paused; a sigh came out of him. He was almost across the street from his home and just realized that he hadn't thought of what he was going to tell his grandpa!? Should I tell him everything he thought? How would he react to Mr. Paulmerts' offer? The last thing he wanted at this point was a negative remark from his family. What would he write to his brothers back in Greece? To his mother and father? It was Sunday after all and every Sunday since his arrival to the States, he has spent hours writing to his family and friends... but he was puzzled now. He did not know how he could explain what had happened to him on this day in a single letter. Suddenly, he felt tired from this emotional confusion and brainstorming. He took a deep breath and proceeded toward his Grandpa's house.

It was almost three in the afternoon and everyone was gathered in the living room. His uncle Bill sat in the big armchair reading the newspaper and sipping coffee, which he and his brother brewed at least twice a day. His other uncle, Kosta, had a cigarette in his mouth while he played backgammon with his cousin and the rest of the children played some card game in front of the fireplace. His aunts were ironing and sorting out the week's laundry, while his elder cousin Stella was knitting a pullover for one of the young ones. Grandpa was not in the living room.

His uncle Kosta asked him about the visit, and Dimitri said everything was OK and that the Paulmerts were nice to him and very hospitable. His aunt interrupted the conversation and reminded him that he should be hungry and that bread and food were waiting for him in the kitchen. Dimitri rushed to the kitchen, since he had really forgotten about his hunger and figured that grandpa would probably be there. He did not see him in the kitchen, but spotted the bowl of chicken soup and slices of bread on the table. He sat down and gobbled up his lunch fast but with an intense pleasure. When he finished he looked for the honey walnut cookies that his grandfather had saved for the family. He could not find them, which reminded him that he better find his grandfather first. His cousin Chris stopped him on his way out of the kitchen to inquire more about the visit at the Paulmerts, but Dimitri was not in the mood to tell him much as he wanted to talk to his Grandpa. He got the impression that the whole family had talked about this over lunch, but Grandpa was the only family member who knew details that no one else did. Dimitri rushed upstairs to his Grandpa's room, but stopped right at the door, as he thought that his Grandpa was probably taking a nap. He stepped back for a moment. However, he could not resist and slightly pushed the door open to see if grandpa was really inside sleeping. Suddenly he saw that he wasn't there. He pushed the door all the way open and saw that all the beds were made and there was no sign of anyone sleeping there. He went inside slowly and spotted a book from the library on grandpa's nightstand. He took it and saw that it was a book written by Victor Hugo, a book with a strange title, nothing he had ever heard before. As he was putting it back on the nightstand, a piece of paper fell out. Dimitri picked it up from the floor and he wanted to place it back to the book, but he was not sure which page the paper came from. After some hesitation he decided to look for grandpa, and let him know about it, as he was sure that grandpa used the piece of paper to mark the page he read last. As he turned and moved towards the stairs, he realized that the paper was full of words written in blue ink. He could immediately tell that it was grandpa's handwriting. He unfolded the paper and read it slowly and with a slow pace.

Distressed but ordained
his existence pertains
Diffused and confused
His emotion refrains
Perplexed but vexed
his tears sustain
Bewildered and wicked
His enemies' stain
Perceived but deceived
His constant complain
Caressed and seduced
his emotional drain
Inspired but hallucinated
His mind insane
Derailed and disillusioned
His favorite pain
Illuminated but enslaved
His vision again
Obsessed and blessed
His spirit maintains
Abused but amused
His fears detains
Betrayed and embittered
His will abstains
Portrayed but escaped
His heart unchains
Alleged and alerted
His kingdom reigns
Empowered but exhausted
His life regains
Amalgamated and dissolved
His soul retains
Revealed but sealed
His dream remains

The last line was underlined and pressed harder than any other one, indicating that this could be the title of what seemed to be to him, an incomprehensible poem. However, when he flipped the page, he realized there was another short verse

Repented and enlightened
Redeemed is again

Puzzled as he was, he continued down the stairs when he it occurred to him that the last place to look for his Grandpa was down in the basement, where there was a small room next to the cellar, where Grandpa sat sometimes so as to be away from the crowded house and relax. In that room he had placed a desk by the window, which was almost at ground level facing the courtyard with a small garden, where his grandma planted vegetables and flowers. As Dimitri stepped downstairs and crossed the cellar, he could smell and feel the presence of his Grandpa in the small room on the backside of the house. He often spent time alone there meditating, thinking or writing on his diary and his poems. "Well, I found him", Dimitri thought for just a second, however suddenly he felt reserved to disturb his Grandpa, as he had the feeling that he could be in the middle of his meditation or in the middle of a creative moment. He thought for a second that maybe he should read the poem again, but as he paused to do it, he changed his mind. His steps became slower, reluctant and almost silent. As he reached the back of the cellar, he saw the small opening to the back room and his grandpa's shadow in the ample light that shun through the window. He started walking on his tip toes so he wouldn't disturb him as he clearly saw that his Grandpa was in his chair looking high above the window, meditating and fully immersed in his thoughts and day-dreams. He stepped back again but nothing happened. A moment later, his Grandpa turned parallel to the window and started looking at the other side of the room down below to the floor. Next to him was a small desk with a notepad and a pen on the top. His eyes were sad and the face had a rather frozen expression, clearly in the middle of very deep thoughts.
Dimitri realized that he should leave him alone and return back later. As he turned around to leave, his Grandpa's voice immensely surprised him, since it gave an end to the previous deep silence.

G: "So, you won't tell me what happened?"

D: "Oh Grandpa! I did not want to disturb you."

G: "You aren't, it is a pleasure to see you and I thought you'd come back earlier."

D: "Oh. Well, I first had lunch upstairs and then came looking for you ..."

G: "I know that; indeed I noticed it, but I meant earlier in reference to your return home. I heard your steps as soon as you arrived and clearly you stayed longer at the Paulmerts than I had expected."

D: "Right Umm.."

G: "So what happened?"

D: "They really liked the desserts and enjoyed my visit."

G: "Of course! And what else?"

D: "You know, grandpa, they are not as complicated as you may think. They were simple and welcoming and were interested in engaging me in a conversation."

G: "Really? You mean Mrs. Paulmerts, as well?"

D: "Well no. But", he raised his eyebrows and immediately realized that his Grandpa again examined all the different aspects, as he did with any issue.

G: "But ... don't you wonder why I am asking you son?"

D: "I am trying hard, but why do you always go into all these different levels and layers of thought?"

G: "Because she is one of the two pillars of that house, and we know very well that it does not matter how much the rest accept and welcome you."

D: "Well Grandpa, where are you heading? I did not even start telling you what happened over there and how good I felt and all sorts of things... I mean the nice things that happened; why, after all are you so focused on Mrs. Paulmerts?"

G: "Because I'd rather get straight to the point."

D: "What is the point Grandpa?" he asked very perplexed and with some frustration in his voice.

G: "Don't worry about it son, you are not ready for it. I'll stop being negative right now and please go ahead and tell me what happened."

D: "Grandpa you know how much I appreciate your thoughts, but please do not bring me down today, when I am so happy about my encounter with them."

G: "You are right my son, go ahead tell me more."

D: "I guess you want me to keep dreaming, but deep inside I see that you do not believe that I will ever find the true love that I seek, is that what it is Grandpa?"

G: "Son, do not worry about an old man who has lost his wings and cannot fly anymore to discover whatever he dreamed of in this world, the world he left behind many years ago. I am cynical sometimes, because I cannot have everything that I dreamed of in this life. I don't have all my children and none of my childhood friends around me. And yes, I don't have most of the things I once dreamed of, which I had hoped to have around me one day. I learned to drink from a half empty glass and listen to music from a gramophone that got stuck every other minute. Don't think the same will happen to you! Sometimes, I let myself be that way, but never and I repeat *NEVER*, think that you will have the same life as mine. You will be so much better off and will make everything happen as long as you keep holding onto your dreams in your heart and brain at all times." He paused for a second, turned his eyes to the light coming from the window above and started again: "You know the other day I read this book *"The Duino Elegies"*, which is about the difference between angels and people, the meaning of death, and the author's idea that human beings are put on earth in order to experience the beauty of ordinary things. I am in the fall or more accurately the winter of my life and regardless of how down to earth I want to be, I know that one day I will go up there, and perhaps the wings will come back to me again as I will be leaving this earth. I am happy to know son, that I will be up there, looking at you and all the great things that you will achieve one day. You are different my son and you will achieve greater things than you can imagine now." Dimitri as always a modest soul, tried to interrupt him, but Grandpa without even turning his eyes to him, sensed that and lifted his head in a *"do not interrupt me"* way and continued, "I am not saying all this to make you feel good or to put a lot of pressure on you son, but my eyes are too old by now and can see things clearly. Never forget Kipling's "If" which I first read to you in this country and also, most importantly, where you came from. You will be able to charm Lauren Paulmerts, but so will many other people on this earth. Never forget though, that in the difficult times... you do not want to compromise the beauty of your soul and the beauty of the ordinary things."

D: "Grandpa be more specific! And please do not tell me once again that right now I am not ready to discuss the real essence of "Casablanca" with you, or Mrs. Paulmerts or the ordinary things."

G: "That's right my son. That is what I would tell you exactly at this point, because some things in life are for you to discover….. when the time is right. Besides, I want to hear what happened at the Paulmerts."

D: "Oh come on, this is unfair as always; you started something and you do not want to finish it!" He then remembered that he was carrying the Hugo book and the piece of paper with Grandpa's incomprehensive writing. "So, wait a second, I found this upstairs and this piece of paper fell out and I apologize, but I am not sure where it should be?"

Grandpa looked very surprised, turned to Dimitri and said with a mellow voice, "Please give it to me!" He took it and glanced at it and then looked at his grandson.

D: "What is it? A new poem that you wrote?"

G: "Oh nothing. Do not bother."

D: "You are repeating yourself here. What is the meaning of _his dream remains_?"

G: "I have no idea." and turned his eyes toward the window.

D: "Let me guess… hm… I am not ready to comprehend this poem at this point in my life?"

Grandpa looked at Dimitri with love and care. "Precisely! and I understand your frustration son, but yia yia … later in life; no worries though if you don't comprehend it, since what you have read is only half of the poem."

D: "Where is the other half? Can I read it?"

G: "Not now, but later for sure!"

Dimitri said with an anxious voice, "is it ready or have you not finished it yet?"

G: "I am not so sure son, but wouldn't you rather tell me about your day?"

D: "If it is ready, I want to read it Grandpa. Where are the next 17 verses?"

G: "Who told you there are 17 more?"

D: "You told me it is half, so there are 17 more."

G: "Not necessarily, it could be that you have 17 half verses."

D: "Oh I see, so two more lines are missing from each one."

G: "I am not sure yet son, but please go ahead and tell me about your visit."

Dimitri knew very well that his grandfather didn't want to talk about it anymore and gave up. He started talking about his experiences from a few hours ago. He went into detail when he described Lauren, but not that much when he talked about Mr. Paulmerts. At some point he realized that he had to talk about Mr. Paulmerts job offer. He hesitated enough, but his grandfather could read him well.

G: "And what else? Is there something else that you want to talk to me about?"

D: "Well I am not sure if this is the right moment, Grandpa."

G: "As you wish Dimitri. This is something that only you know. If you need a pair of ears, my head happens to have a couple of them."

D: "So there is the right time for this as well?"

G: "Absolutely and if you feel this is not the right moment, do not worry about it and let me know whenever the right time is."

D: "I definitely think this is something that I will definitely need your help with".

G: "I plan to be around for some time, so anytime."

D: "What would you think about … me getting a job from Mr. Paulmerts?"

G: "Doing what for him?" He paused and looked at his grandson in the eyes. "You already have a job and you really need to study a lot on the side and make sure you will go to college one day. Not to forget that you should rather get a scholarship so you can alleviate the burdens on this family."

D: "Oh of course Grandpa, I would only start working for him in a couple of years and when I will be at college, perhaps part-time." He paused for a moment and continued. "He wants me to help Mr. Fein collect the rent in his properties here at Queens."

Grandpa's face took a dramatic look and looked alarmed in Dimitri's eyes. "What can you possibly do for Mr. Fein, be specific please?"

D: "It will only be for the better Grandpa. You know Grandpa, I complained to Mr. Paulmerts about Mr. Fein and I tried hard to describe what is going on in this neighborhood. He did not want to believe me, but I think his intentions are genuine you know. I mean he has good intentions by offering me that job. It will be a win-win situation since the people will not have to face Fein anymore and I will certainly give them a break, but at the same time, will find the right balance between the people who rent his properties and the required returns to Mr. Paulmerts. I know that working next to

Mr. Fein is not great at all, and he would be a big burden on me, but maybe it would be worth it to give it a shot."

G: "I am not thrilled by this idea son and I would rather see you work somewhere else or better yet, get a scholarship from a school so you can just study and nothing more."

D: "Oh Grandpa, I would love to work for Mr. Paulmerts!"

G: "And see Lauren all the time, right?

D: "Why not?"

G: "You will be just one of the many employees he has. Do you think they all share time with her?"

D: "I know I will be different, besides just let me dream about it, it is so important to me."

G: "Sure son, I understand and who knows what will happen in the next two to three years, until you get accepted at a college and where" pauses "You may end up going to the West coast, have you thought about that?"

D: "No! You know I will not leave the family behind. I will stay around and help as much as I can, no matter if I have money for a scholarship or not. I won't go that far."

G: "Well, Lauren may choose another college far away."

D: "It does not matter. She will always be coming back on holidays and to see her family."

G: "As you say son, and my blessings to you."

D: "Grandpa, there is something else that came up in the discussion."

G: "What?"

D: "You never told me the story, about how you started the bakery business after the fire and fixed up everything and saved for…"

Grandpa turned and looked into Dimitri's eyes and interrupted him with his potent gaze. "Son, some people I guess know what happened and some others don't. Sometimes in life it's not good to wonder around telling stories about how good you are and make people believe that you are this and that. Remember, what I always say about being humble? In fact I didn't say it, as you very well know … but if one day you want to feel good and useful, try to keep a few of the good things you do in life only for yourself. The more you talk about yourself, the less you will end up doing, son. And sometimes the ones that brag a lot about themselves end up humiliated. Do everything in life without expecting returns and you will be glorified." He paused for a second and continued, "I didn't say this, someone else did way before my time," he paused again and took another good look at the innocent and altruistic eyes of his grandson. "If returns come to you for every great thing you did, it will be God's will. If nothing comes back to you for all your brave and great acts, you will still be happy, because you know that you did the right thing." Grandpa took a few moments to think, squinted his eyes and said, "I am not sure what version of the story Mr. Paulmerts told you, but no matter what happened son, I still do not have all my children and grandchildren around me", grandpa's facial expression revealed how much he was immersed in his memories and thoughts; and this was simply fascinating to Dimitri, therefore he could not interrupt him. Grandpa continued after his long pause, "I can only tell you one thing that whatever Mr. Paulmerts told you, is only what he knows; perhaps what he heard about at that time and nothing more. Just a version of what many others will propagate one day and others will distort another day. Only very few people and God know what really happened." After another long pause he said, "forgive me for not telling you more about that story but let this be my little secret," his face at that point resembled the head of a marble statue, adamant and rigid; however to Dimitri's surprise a thick tear ran down his cheek; without a single move of any facial muscle. Dimitri looked down and pretended to be unaware of it and whispered to his grandpa, "it's OK Grandpa, you can tell me whatever you wish." He paused, "and whenever you wish; do not worry about it, I just thought that the story that I heard from Mr. Paulmerts was so great and made me very proud of you. I just wanted to hear more about it, but do not worry … maybe you will tell me another day."

G: "May be son, and know that you make me proud every day! You will always remember this day, as many things happened today for the first time and many things were discussed. It is good son. This is good. Make sure you do not forget this day."

Dimitri leaned to his Grandpa and gave him a firm hug full of love.

Grandpa pleased and with a proud smile said, "And of course there are things that you did not learn today, like this unfinished riddle that I have on this piece of paper, there is always the right time for that too, do not forget that!"

D: "Sure Papou."

The day passed with the family together in the living room by the fireplace; some reading the papers, others studied homework, or knitted while others wrote their regular Sunday correspondence. But Dimitri could not do anything except think, daydream and brainstorm about the future. He thought about what happened, his grandpa's words and how he would come up with a plan with Joe and Giovanni in school the following day, to orchestrate his future approach and friendship with Lauren. He could not wait. They usually snuck into the movie theater together every Sunday afternoon, but he did not join his friends that Sunday. It was worth missing the last John Wayne flick, he thought, since he spent his afternoon with the Paulmerts and his grandpa. It was so worth it for him that the rest of the day he stayed inside writing to his parents and brothers and thinking about Lauren, but also about the words he exchanged with his grandpa during their encounter in the basement.

The following day, Monday, while at work, he was full of anticipation that Lauren was going to stop by the post office. She didn't and he was disappointed that an encounter did not happen. He convinced himself that she probably stopped by the post office while he was doing a delivery. He was curious to know and asked the post office clerk that day if a girl with Lauren's features had stopped by that day. The clerk gave him a hostile look implying that this was none of his business. Dimitri got the point and he convinced himself even more that he had missed her, while he was not at the pharmacy. He felt so sure that she had stopped by the store at some point that day. After all, he did not know her daily schedule, when her classes started and ended, as she did not attend a nearby school. He was sure that she most likely attended a private school, perhaps in Manhattan. It would be normal to miss her all the time, as she could be in Manhattan any time of the day. Usually he crossed her path with the limo over the weekend. The next few afternoons and evenings he spent hours with his two friends talking about her, his time at the mansion and the job offer. Neither Giovanni nor Joe was thrilled about that job offer. They were concerned and warned Dimitri that he should never work with characters like Mr. Fein and his crew. On the other hand, they could see the benefit of that job, which was the only one. He would be much closer to Lauren and perhaps there would be the days when he would share more than just a chat with her. They could although, not believe that his presence in Paulmerts' workforce would make Mr. Fein become nicer to the tenants.

Dimitri's passion for Lauren was growing day-by-day and month-by-month. His disappointment was apparent, since over the next few months he saw the limo only a dozen times and he could only wave at Lauren from a distance. One Sunday, about four months after their last encounter, in his desperation he did not join Joe and Giovanni for their Sunday film excursion. He passed the whole day around the corner of Lauren's mansion. He stayed away enough in order to avoid being seen by the Paulmerts' personnel. He had his bike next to him always ready to pedal in the direction of the limo, so it would seem more like a random encounter. He spent hours reading his book but the limo did not leave the house that day. The next Sunday he did the same and at about 2pm the door opened. Dimitri quickly jumped onto his bike and by the time the limousine was visible he was biking fast towards the avenue. As soon as he reached the avenue he made a quick turn and started biking back. The limo appeared and it was only a hundred feet away from his turning point. Excited he broke into a big smile and got ready to greet Lauren again, but then his enthusiasm diminished when he realized that the whole family was inside the car. He stopped the bike and waved his hand respectfully and to his disappointment no one from the Paulmerts noticed his greeting, as they were involved in a discussion. But when the limo passed him he instantly turned his head back and noticed that Lauren had spotted him and he saw for just an instant Lauren's eyes looking at him. He was very sure that she waved at him right before the limo turned onto the avenue. His original plan had failed because he wanted to believe that the limo would stop and he would have been able to talk to her. But this was not possible as the whole family was inside and they were probably heading to some function or to an appointment.

Dimitri waited and waited for another encounter every weekend and the months were going by fast. One day his dream became true and it was when he least expected it. He was waiting for Joe to come and join him to sneak into the movie theater as always. Giovanni was already there with him and deeply absorbed in reading some comics. All of a sudden, to Dimitri's amazement, Lauren and her chauffer walked out of the movie theater. There were two other girls with her and they were all escorted by the Paulmerts' chauffer. Dimitri was shocked and dumfounded. Instantly he knew it was now or never. He ran towards the group of girls who had obviously attended the matinee performance and Giovanni, without realizing what was going on yelled at him to come back and wait for Joe. That annoyed Dimitri and made him feel fragile and by the time he was face to face with Lauren, he did not have a happy face as he was annoyed and stressed at the same time. When he realized the girls had noticed him he felt a cold wave of fear and stress run through his body. He tried not to feel nervous, but at this point he was embarrassed because Lauren's girlfriends were also looking at him. They were all dapperly dressed with bright colored elegant dresses that reflected the ample sunlight, which made him feel unattractive in his old unfashionable clothes. Up to that point he had never cared that much about his appearance, but now it was obvious to him that he did not fit in Lauren's social circle. That realization added stress to him as he felt the sweat beads forming on his face; it was so apparent, that he became tongue twisted to the point that Lauren was the first one to say hi and smile. Dimitri delivered a "Good Afternoon" and by the time he smiled the girls had already passed him heading in the opposite direction. Dimitri felt helpless and stupid, but he knew very well that he did not have many opportunities to talk to Lauren. When they were already ten feet away from him, he turned and called Lauren. Lauren heard him and turned her head, she smiled apologetically declaring with her facial expression that she had to continue walking with her friends and most importantly the chauffer who was escorting them. Dimitri did not have the power or strength to follow them and felt heavy and empty. By that time Joe, had arrived and together with Giovanni who was already at the scene, realized what had happened and ran towards Dimitri. When they reached him, they tried to revive him from the coma-like state and deep hibernation he had fallen into. They tried to get him to run after Lauren, but somehow Dimitri did not have the courage. He was too reserved and very humble as always. He didn't have an aggressive personality, which would not have let an opportunity pass by.

The years flew by quickly and the Giovas family was working hard to keep their relative daily prosperity of having a meal and the comfort of a big house, which hosted many family members. They gathered every Sunday and enjoyed the fortune of being together. However, there was never any luxury, as they had to send money back home to the other family members and additionally save money for more relatives to come to America in the near future. Every two to three years they managed to bring over new family members.

In the two and a half years that passed by, Dimitri saw Lauren a handful of times. The emotional connection that he thought he had established that Sunday in the fall of 1953 at the Paulmerts faded and sublimed with time. However, he had an enduring nature and he knew that the right time would come later on when he was older and more mature. His friends also had no time for romance, as they had to study and work around the clock. He was not alone during that long and torturing sentimental deprivation. They spent hours talking about their dreams and their future. They had the maturity to realize though that all these dreams were heavily infused and influenced by the movies that they watched every week. They could see their life being very adventurous and filled with excitement, but not until later on – when they could leave their neighborhood to go to college. Dimitri did not care much for the present time as he felt helpless and had to wait for the time that he would be ready to attend college and could also work for Mr. Paulmerts. During that time he always looked for the limousine in the streets. In a few rare instances he got to talk to Lauren, but only for a minute or so at a time, since Mr. Paulmerts' personnel, which made their encounter difficult, were always escorting her. He met her three times, when she dropped letters at the post office. He had a couple more random encounters in the neighborhood between her mansion and the bookstore, but someone was always escorting her. Besides that, she did not seem very open to him and in addition he was always very shy and reserved, as he did not want her to ever feel that he was being inappropriate. He sensed that she appreciated the distance and deep in her eyes detected sympathy or perhaps a good feeling that she harbored for him. Perhaps not the open love that he would have liked to see, maybe only as much as his eyes revealed to her, however he definitely saw a rather affectionate feeling. Many other girls from his school were interested in him, but he had no eyes for any of them. His love for Lauren was deep and uncompromised.

Dimitri worked hard and with zeal and finally excelled in school. Eventually he was only a year behind in school as he quickly caught up with many of the school's requirements.

In 1957, he was nineteen and just a year older than his classmates and ready to go to college. His friends Joe and Giovanni were already in Law school, while he was still a senior in high school. Joe was one of a kind, sharp and more energetic than any other student in his class. With the help of his uncle he got accepted at the Columbia Law School. Giovanni was almost as good as Joe and he was able to secure a position at NYU. They were both poor enough not to leave for far away colleges, and had to stay local, as their families could not afford to pay for room and board. The same was the case for Dimitri who had to try and succeed in getting into a local school. For him it was not just because he had to live and eat at the Giovas's home, but also because he wanted to be close to the Paulmerts, so as to work for them.

That same year, was the year Lauren also graduated and entered college. She was a year younger than Dimitri, and he was happy that he was able to catch up with her class. When he arrived in the States after his twelfth birthday, he was behind in his language skills and fell behind more than a year in school. But due to his diligence, intelligence and commitment he caught up with English and with all the other classes.

Of course for Lauren, the doors to any university were open. Dimitri figured that her father and her private school that had a great reputation would be instrumental in helping her enter an Ivy League school like Harvard, Yale or Princeton. He was hoping that she would choose Columbia University. He saw that choice as the best-case scenario, since she would still be in NYC. Dimitri thought she would be in Queens a lot and she potentially would become connected to Joe. Lauren was a very good student and her preferences were art and literature. That's all he knew about her. Dimitri wanted to become either a doctor or a scientist. He thought that he should start with something in science, which he could later use for his pre-doctoral degree. He excelled in math, chemistry and physics.

He was nineteen years old, full of hope and dreams as he received very high grades in math and science. He had average grades in English, which he had never studied in depth, as he focused more in science. Naturally, he was at a disadvantage compared to the native speakers, since he lived in a bilingual environment for seven years. His family did not spare enough money to pay for the college application fees and invest in finding the right university. Both of his friends had secured tuition waivers and financial aid from their respective schools. This was imperative for Dimitri as well and was the only way for him to enter a private school, like his friends did. But by not being a native speaker, his grades in language were not as good as those of his friends. However, his science and math grades were higher than those of his friends. Finally, he had only enough money to apply to three schools. Two private schools accepted him but he could only get financial aid from the local state school. He had no choice, as he could not risk accepting the offer of a private school without any aid and with just hope that he could get financial aid later. He was a bit bitter about it, as he knew that he could do well in a private school, but he was content with what he had achieved so far. He did not want to risk his family support in such matters. Besides, he knew that he had started from zero nearly seven years ago, so he was content with what he had been able to achieve. He initially enrolled in a general science curriculum and later developed an inclination for physics and engineering, as he was a stellar student in math.

Lauren got accepted at Brown University, an Ivy League school and very prestigious, where her father was on the board of trustees. Dimitri was very unhappy with the news. He wished that she had stayed at a not so distant Ivy League school. Therefore, he knew that she would not be in NYC much aside from the major holidays for the next four years. For someone like him, going to Providence, RI, was quite a trip. He was wondering why life created all these hurdles and why the Paulmerts didn't try to help her get in to enter Columbia University perhaps, where it would have been just across the river. Or at least she could join Princeton, which was just a bit over an hour away. He was terribly disappointed, as he had planned to go and knock on the Paulmerts' door and ask for the job he was offered four years ago.

Dimitri spent weeks thinking about it, wondering why he should do that, when Lauren wouldn't be around much during the year. Obviously he thought that she would be back for Christmas, perhaps spring break and summer, but not most likely every other weekend. However, sometimes he thought that it would be easy for her to visit often since the Paulmerts had numerous cars and a chauffer who could transport her back and forth with no sweat. In time, he decided that he should rather be looking into something long term. He thought that the summer break, especially, was long and she might not enroll in any classes and therefore would spend her time in Queens. He would rather be an employee at that point. After all, if things went well, he could end up going to Providence once in a while and keep in touch with her through letters and perhaps sometimes by phone.

The summer of 1957 had almost come to an end, and the time to enroll and start college was approaching. Dimitri was full of curiosity and anticipation to see his transition from a delivery boy and a pharmacy clerk to one of Mr. Paulmerts's employee. He saw this as a huge improvement in his life, given that the new job would not have regular business hours and he would be flexible to freely attend his classes. His life was on the rim of a major change. He would not spend money on tuition and would work flexible hours and perhaps live off of what he imagined to be a better stipend. His schedule would still be loaded with work, classes, study at the library and homework, but he felt an air of freedom now to dominate his life, since he would have more freedom to choose movies, concerts and art events, if he found the time. Giovanni and Joe were still his movie companions, as they had no luck getting dates with any girls at college. They both had to return to Queens in the evening and work hard to contribute to their families' needs. They also had to return to work after classes because there were plenty of younger siblings and grandparents that could not work. They still gathered around the local square after work and talked about women, adventures and music over an ice cream, a float or a soda. Giovanni was hoping he would soon get a job close to NYU, as he was anxious to live in Manhattan and be amongst more women that were studying on campus. After all, he was successful getting attention from women, but was too shy to talk to them or did not have enough time to go out with them. Now that he was older than eighteen, he could think about having a girlfriend since he spent most of his time away from his conservative Roman-Catholic family. Joe was more into art and into playing his guitar, but that is how he attracted women. He always played music and when Dimitri was present they both hummed over his tunes and melodies. Once in a while, he taught Dimitri how to play some chords and accompany him with a second guitar. Sometimes he played some foreign songs or improvised by playing chords and Dimitri made up lyrics and placed his own word improvisations. Joe was always impressed with Dimitri's word-smith abilities, but could not convince him of his great talent.

The summer was coming to an end and everyone was getting ready to start the new college year. Dimitri decided to go knock on the Paulmerts' door the last Sunday of that summer. Indeed, it seemed to be a quite a "heavy" decision. Too much water had passed under the bridge and times that he had not encountered his love or her father; perhaps Mr. Paulmerts would not even remember the conversation they had almost four years ago. He also never understood why the encounters he once dreamt, he would have with Lauren, never took place. More than three and a half years have passed since that day and it was very normal for him to be hesitant. His internal flame and passion for Lauren though never faded. They were kept unaltered deep inside him; the type of deep and strong passion that was rather getting invigorating in the absence of contact. He was idealist and ultimately romantic and knew that people like him persisted in the utopia they created in their minds.

In the mean time, during those three and a half years nothing had changed with Mr. Fein. He still insulted people and he always instilled fear in every new tenant and immigrant who was trying to make a living in their new country and in the world, of that wonderful by all means neighborhood. Mr. Fein and his pals insulted the poor Garcias' son and his old man, as well as several other people who could not pay on time multiple times in the neighborhood. To the amazement of the neighbors Mr. Paulmerts was never around, especially when they evicted the Barley family, an honest and hard working father and son company, which went bankrupt a year ago. For two generations they tried to establish a family fund and loan to help new Irish immigrants move to America. In fact, grandpa Barley was a schoolmate and close friend of Mr. Paulmerts' grandfather. Their sons were also friends. But the family connection was not enough to generate any respect from Mr. Fein and apparently Mr. Paulmerts was either tremendously ignorant or indifferent to their situation. His unresponsiveness was sometimes the topic of discussion between Joe and Dimitri and additionally reminded Dimitri that perhaps he should not get involved in that operation.

Dimitri, though, had the gut feeling that his time would come, and it would be part of his life and part of an experience that he had to acquire. He was convinced that he should ask his Grandpa to bake the famous honey walnut cookies once more. After all, Dimitri thought that a visit with them in hand, would refresh Mr. Paulmerts' memory of the discussion that they had years ago. His Grandpa was still in a great mood and mostly in good spirits. His age did not diminish his constant zeal for reading and philosophizing about almost everything in this life. He was also very excited ever since the day Dimitri told him the great news about his successful acceptance into college and the potential bright future ahead of him. He already had several grandchildren that had stayed away from the academic life to work and support the family by opening up new businesses. He was additionally pleased because Dimitri succeeded even in getting a tuition waiver and some financial assistance. Grandpa Giovas was very proud of his grandson, since he had a big gap to close by not speaking a word in English when he first came to America. Mr. Giovas was almost rejuvenated and always looked robust and much younger than his advanced age. When Dimitri asked for the cookies, he knew exactly what was going on in the mind of his grandson. They both tried to understand each other and at this point grandpa would do anything to please his grandson, but also to show him that from now on he would be responsible for his actions and therefore Dimitri's decisions had more value and gravity. Despite that, grandpa still tried to convince him to negotiate for a part-time job at the pharmacy where he worked for the past six years or another job somewhere else. But deep down inside his grandson's eyes, he could see that he would never give up.

He therefore baked the cookies and the following Sunday out of superstition, Dimitri tried to replicate every act and the timing with the first visit at the Paulmerts' house. He arrived again with the freshly baked cookies a bit after Sunday's lunch at the Paulmerts' mansion and was pleased to see that the new limo was parked at the house. He rang the bell and after the typical formalities he was on his way to the family room. He was sweating due to the weather and stress, but he knew that there was nothing he could possibly do about it at that point.

He could not believe it, as it almost seemed like a metaphysical moment to him. Something he had seen over and over again in his dreams and more precisely in his daydreams. Here he was once again, in the same room facing the same deep blue eyes of a more mature, almost adult, and not teenager anymore, Lauren. Everything seemed a type of a déjà vu experience that had run through in his mind again and again. She was so beautiful and time had been gracious in preserving all her freshness and the beauty that he had encountered years ago with an even more delicate appearance, indicative of a healthy lifestyle that she surely had. She looked happy and very welcoming and was even friendlier than he had expected. She accommodated him with a lot of respect and interest that left him dumfounded. He was trembling slightly and knew that she noticed it, but of course she was so seasoned in her manners and had such extraordinary grace that he would eventually feel comfortable. Apart from exchanging the regular greetings, Dimitri at once jumped to his favorite subject, which he very well remembered was her favorite as well.

D: "So, which one is your favorite movie so far this year?"

L: "Hm... that is always a tough question for movie maniacs, don't you agree? Many! But I saw, "The sun also rises" last week, have you seen it yet?"

D: "Oh indeed!!! I saw it the other day – of course, it is not as good as the book, but it is fun to see one of my favorite dramas animated, and with great actors."

L: "Really, I have not read the book, so I guess I liked it more than you did."

D: "Well, it does not matter, it's wonderful to see places like Paris and Pamplona and people who have such eventful lives ... ha! Apparently with a lot of wine and fun."

L: "Indeed it is sad at the end and without the absolute fulfillment. Are the lives of the wealthy people supposed to be like this?"

D: "Why do you say that? Do you feel that way? And pardon me for making a safe assumption here?"

L: "Oh no worries at all but ... know that does not apply to me, I am pretty happy it's just that my parents..."

Mr.P: "Hello Dimitri, welcome once again," he interrupted Lauren, who was surprised, with an enthusiastic and rather unusually loud voice. "Wow, don't tell me these are cookies over there?" he pointed to the box that Dimitri had placed on the coffee table. None of the two young adults had any idea that he had already entered the room and was so close to them.

D: "Indeed Mr. Paulmerts, these are the honey walnut cookies that you like, my Grandpa baked them for you."

Mr.P: "How come? Are you celebrating something? Is something special going on?"

D: "Well, I guess he is extremely happy these days as I will be attending college in a few days."

Mr.P: "Oh congratulations Dimitri I had no idea. That is so great that you were able to catch up with everything so quickly; where are you going, if I may ask?"

D: "To the state college around the corner sir...you know... I had to take an offer accompanied by some financial assistance and ... well, I chose that."

Mr.P: "That is fantastic that you got financial assistance, you know Lauren got accepted into Brown."

D: "Oh yes! I heard about it and congratulations Lauren that is a great achievement."

L: "Thanks, and good luck with your studies, do you know what you will be majoring in?"

D: "I think science or engineering. And you?"

L: "I am not sure, but maybe arts or ... who knows it is too early."

D: "I wish you the best Lauren ... but you will really have to live in RI away from home?"

Mr.P: "We are going up to Brown next weekend to get her settled in a proper house with our friend's daughters, who are also over in Providence studying."

D: "That is wonderful. So she won't be alone."

Mr.P: "Oh absolutely, I cannot leave her alone and I will even rent an extra room for us to go there periodically."

L: "Oh Dad ... "

Mr.P: "Absolutely! I will even go by myself in case your mother cannot make it." He turned to Dimitri, "And you Dimitri? Are you getting room and board or will you have to stay with your folks?"

D: "Well... I will be staying with them. I have no choice Mr. Paulmerts. The situation is not that easy, as we plan to bring my whole family over here in the near future."

Mr.P: "My best wishes to you Dimitri and let me know if I can help with anything."

D: "In fact sir, that is the reason I came here today?"

Mr. Paulmerts looked as if he hadn't expected that, as he probably said that last sentence out of custom and without really meaning it or expecting a comment in return.

D: "Oh, sir, I am referring to the conversation we had three and a half or so years ago, when you offered me to work with Mr. Fein and help out on the rental collection... and of course at the same time make things a little better for the neighborhood ... but also for you, I mean, better for everybody," he said the last few words after swallowing really hard as he was not relaxed and felt uneasy asking him for this job.

Mr. Paulmerts : " I see ... hm... indeed I think I remember our conversation, right!"

He fell into deep thoughts and stepped away in the opposite direction, turning his back to Dimitri whou could not see his facial expression.

Mr. Paulmerts was moving distracted and somehow disconnected from the environment. As soon as he turned to the side, Dimitri could see something in his eyes conveying the message that this was not a very good idea. Dimitri kept staring at his profile and felt that he should not have said it in that way, however he was ready to take on the challenge. He knew it was something that he wanted to do, so he could finally encounter this heartless and resentful employee of Mr. Paulmerts.

Mr.P: "So Dimitri I guess you are old and mature enough to take on this job. I will think a little more about it and discuss it with Mr. Fein. I guess it would be the perfect job for you as you can do this part time and could help out as needed, since there are not really any office hours. Do you really want to be out there knocking on doors and asking for money?"

D: "Of course, Mr. Paulmerts, and as you said, this is the perfect job for me, I can help out here and there, as my schedule permits. Of course, whenever Mr. Fein needs me I will make myself available and I can ensure you that things will work out for everyone involved."

Mr.P: "OK young man! I think I will confirm everything with him and notify you tomorrow afternoon."

D: "Oh Mr. Paulmerts, you are so gracious and I am deeply grateful for this," and as he finished, he extended his arm for a firm handshake.

Mr.P: "No worries, Dimitri, as you know it is not a big deal and we always have young men in that office to do jobs here and there. They all work part-time or do it as their second job. I am sure we will find some time slots for you as well."

D: "Thank you Mr. Paulmerts, I can't thank you enough sir, words are not enough."

Paulmerts: "Of course! That is why you brought these delicious cookies, which I will devour momentarily," and extended his hand and grabbed the box. "Would you like to have one with us?"

D: "Oh these are for you, Mr. Paulmerts, we have plenty more in the house. But would you mind me asking you for something else...?"

Mr.P: "What is it?"

D: "Would you mind if I could ask Lauren and see if she would like to join me one evening at the square?" his face turned red and sweaty but determined as well and he continued, "maybe for a walk and some food or ice cream or a movie, if that is OK with you?"

Mr. Paulmerts was shocked again, but full of admiration for the courage that this young man had to ask that question. However, he broke into a smile that revealed, that he did not quite understand the question, and at the same time showed his surprise about this young man across from him who had the courage to ask him something like that.

Mr.P: "Well, have you asked her? Have you done it already?"

Dimitri quickly interrupted him as he rushed to say, "not at all, she does not know about it and may very well reject the idea, but what I am asking is the permission to ... I guess, to ask her..."

Mr.P: "Oh that is very respectful, but why do you think you should take my daughter out to the square? Maybe you should go and meet some of her friends in Manhattan, I think that would be better, and what do you think Lauren?"

Lauren with her eyes wide open, who did not expect this kind of dialogue around her, revealed her surprise with her body language and the upward lifting of her shoulders. She looked unsure on how to react and feel about it or even what to say so she replied, "Oh, I don't know let me think about it... you know the square is around the corner from where I have lived my whole life and I have never been there, but maybe it would be better to join my friends in Manhattan as Dad suggested". She had turned to face Dimitri, who did not know what to expect and he could only accept her decision and any possible outcome from that dialogue. Lauren sensed that Dimitri was about to agree with everything and would not argue so she continued, "Look this is the last weekend before we all go to college, so we have some interesting parties in the city these days, why don't you join me next Saturday night,

before Labor Day Monday and before we all head off to different colleges?"
Dimitri moved his shoulders up and said, "Sure and thank you so much, it
really sounds wonderful". He turned to Mr. Paulmerts, "Thank you so much
Sir for suggesting this to me and accepting me … I mean … what I want to
say is that…".

"Sure I understand young man," Mr. Paulmerts said with a smile full of satisfaction, as he probably preferred that his daughter was not alone with Dimitri
in his neighborhood, but rather in her familiar surrounding and together with
friends.

D: "Then, what time shall I be ready next Saturday Lauren? And where shall
I meet you?"

L: "Come over here at 6pm and Robert will drive us together," she then
looked at her father's eyes, who waved with his head in agreement.

After he observed Mr. Paulmerts' face Dimitri said, "OK I will be here at
6pm next Saturday and will wait for your news tomorrow sir."

Mr.P: "All right. I will have someone talk to you tomorrow and see you soon
Dimitri."

Dimitri left that day from the Paulmerts' mansion full of happiness as he
did more than three years ago. The "flame" burning in his heart was too
strong as always. That evening he did not talk to his Grandpa though, as he
had done that Sunday evening in the basement of the Giovas' residence. He
slept and his sleep was full of dreams. The next day he was full of joy when
a Paulmerts' employee met him at the pharmacy and told him that he could
start working for Mr. Paulmerts' agency the following Tuesday. "What a
change in my life?" thought at once as he was about to start a totally new life,
a totally new part time job, but also college, which was his dream. But there
was of course the weekend ahead of him before that great new start. The first
evening in his life that he would share with the girl of his dreams. However,
it was the last time, before she went away for her studies. It was also the very
first time that he would face Lauren's social circle and friends, which somehow additionally stressed him. But he thought that this was the last thing
that he had to worry about, as he needed to focus only on her and ensure
continuity in their relationship. He could not believe that his first date with
her was going to take place in Manhattan, and not Queens. The last time
he was on the island was with his friends Joe and Giovanni, when they were

checking out the campuses and the new territories where they would be going to school. That was a long time ago for Dimitri who was always excited whenever an opportunity came up to go to the center of the Big Apple. The days passed by quickly and Dimitri asked his Grandma to have his Sunday shirt, the only formal outfit he had and wore to church, ready, washed and ironed on Saturday afternoon this time. That was an unusual sign for Mr. Giovas who was following the strange moves of his grandson during the week without saying a word, waiting for the time Dimitri would talk to him. He was not happy that his grandson was going to work with Mr. Fein soon. However, he was the kind of man who believed that everything happens for a reason and every hurdle in life would bring about something better in the very end.

On Saturday at 6pm sharp, Dimitri was outside the Paulmerts's residence dressed in his Sunday clothes, wearing his well-ironed white shirt and dark blue pants and impeccably polished black shoes. He feared that this was not probably the most fashionable outfit for the wealthy and hip society of Manhattan, but he did not have any other nice formal clothes. However, Dimitri's figure was impressive as he was tall, slim with wide shoulders and nicely combed rich dark hair that harmoniously paired his suntanned yet still relatively fair complexion. Lauren had an impeccable and beautiful summer dress resembling the glamorous Marilyn Monroe dress in the famous seven-year itch scene. Dimitri was totally impressed with her look and couldn't hide his admiration for her elegant and flawless figure. In his eyes, she was the most beautiful girl in the world, and he had been in love with her for the past 4 years; so in love with Lauren! He was convinced that Lauren knew that and prayed that he would not make any wrong moves that would compromise her and her family's trust in him.

The ride in the limo was rather subdued as the right words did not come to his mind and he was rather uncomfortable, in that huge leathery limo seat coming from such a different social class. The start represented the interactions throughout the whole night, as he did not have the chance to talk to Lauren as much as he wanted, since her friends always left him out and away from their conversations, interests and company. At one point he stood frozen in a corner of the luxurious clubroom engrossed in his memories of the poor but beautiful sites where he grew up in Greece; all places and faces from his childhood suddenly ran through his mind. Many places, landscapes and farms filled with people who worked around the clock for a piece of their daily bread. Their faces burnt by the sun and full of grooves from the hard work, the troubles and worries of surviving in a beautiful, but harsh land. His father and mother constantly came into his visions and many times he saw himself as the outsider, as the person who did not belong in all these rich and spectacular settings, dressed unfashionably without a jacket and with an outdated and rather ridiculous pair of shoes which did not follow fashion. These thoughts constantly ran through and stormed his mind and had such an impact on him that it impaired his ability to get Lauren's attention or even to substantially engage himself in any discussion. He tried to talk about Henry King and Frank Capra or how he had been following the transition from Mitropoulos to Bernstein or how he would have loved to see some of his favorite books played on stage, but no one cared about his words and made him feel like he and his themes were boring. Several of Lauren's friends made fun of him, his outfit and his slight accent that stereotyped him with people from Queens. Lots of them wondered how he infiltrated their prestigious club and how was he Lauren's friend?

Dimitri felt out of place; a rough situation as it was clear to him that he was not a part of that society. He could not speak their slang; talk with a naughty accent and style that some could do very well; and he could not relate to the discussions about their travel experiences or family fights. Then he felt that he should run away as he was making a fool of himself in front of Lauren. "But what a pair of eyes?" he thought and instantly got inspired to pick up his pen and write a few lines in a piece of paper that hopefully would become a poem one day. Moments later he had the whole poem completed and he saved the piece of paper in his pocket to share it later with Joe. He was heart-broken as he saw that Lauren was always distracted by all her friends and clearly the pair of eyes that fascinated Dimitri had many other fans. They were all preppy school kids who talked in a manner that was foreign to him. Suddenly he decided that he should pull Lauren away from everybody and talk to her. Moments later he asked her to follow him to the huge balcony where some of her friends stood to look at the skyscrapers and the park in front of them. He tried to be as direct as he could possibly be and told her that he wanted to see her more often and to be able to meet her whenever she was back home visiting her parents. Lauren looked a bit uneasy, but already knew and could feel that Dimitri was deeply in love with her. It also seemed that she liked him, maybe because he was a bit different than the average person she knew. She was attracted to him, his features seemed always attractive to her and she could feel a connection, but she was reserved because he was not one of her kind. She did not feel like shutting him out, or shutting a door to his face, and told him to be patient. Dimitri was nervous and he couldn't think of what to say and do at that point, but didn't feel that he could stay at that "members" club all night, since most of the guys made him feel uncomfortable and Lauren was going to be busy talking to others. He said goodnight to Lauren, which made her feel uncomfortable, as she thought that they would leave together and she would have liked to have her chauffer take him back to Queens. Dimitri did not accept her offer and told her that he would take a taxi instead. Lauren went back to her friends and Dimitri of course did not consider the taxi as a solution. He crossed the Upper East Side, the bridge and walked all the way back to his home that starry summer night; a very long walk that gave Dimitri the opportunity to think a lot about the future.

The following Sunday he went back to Paulmerts' mansion and asked to see Lauren who came out to the garden. Standing behind the iron bars, Dimitri told her that he would wait for her to come back on Columbus Day weekend to see her again. After all, he emphasized, it would be easy for her to contact him, since he would now be one of her father's employees. There was some sadness in his face, but he saw that Lauren looked at him with sympathy and felt encouraged that there was still some hope. Indeed Lauren's eyes had some sublime sadness as well but he could not tell why. He asked her if something was wrong, but she left without answering. Dimitri yelled, "see you in October" and wished her the best of luck.

The next day he went to Mr. Fein's office. It was a much more spacious place than the store that he had worked in for the past seven years. He was only three blocks away from his old place and closer to the Paulmerts' mansion. Indeed, Mr. Fein lived up to his reputation of making him feel uncomfortable for being a poor immigrant in their first meeting. It was obvious to Dimitri that Mr. Fein was blatantly opposed to his hiring, but most likely Mr. Paulmerts had given him no choice. He most likely thought that he would make

Dimitri's life miserable and eventually force him to quit. Mr. Fein's figure looked scary at the very first look, revealing a very tough man with his penetrating eyes, which looked deep into Dimitri's soul, carefully searching to find a weakness. Mr. Fein explained his rules and gave him a lecture on how dumb and lazy the people in the neighborhood were since they have a hard time coming up with the rent on time. Dimitri, after his last statement tried to correct Mr. Fein, that this happened periodically and perhaps once a year, but Mr. Fein told him to shut up and remember that he was only an employee who had to do his job and not talk. He continued his derogatory comments about all the families who struggled to survive and Dimitri again tried to point out that they were immigrants who were trying hard to bring more of their family members over to this country. Mr. Fein got outraged at that moment and told him that he had no right to talk back and argue with him in this job and was only allowed to listen. Listen and then execute, according to Mr. Fein's rules.

The same day he gave him some paperwork to familiarize him with the bookkeeping part of the business. After he explained the basics to him, he told him that he had to work in at least twenty hours a week and could fix his schedule every Friday. Dimitri was pleased with the flexibility that the job offered and could after all envision how he could really help a lot of people by showing up at their doorstep instead of Mr. Fein. The rent collection initially started with Dimitri being only the spectator of the process. He knew that he had to wait until he gained Mr. Fein's trust and could do the rent collection alone in the future.

At the same time he worked hard to organize the bookkeeping and the files in a more efficient way. Mr. Fein could see that Dimitri's work was making a difference but he always resisted in complementing him. Dimitri was also delighted by his new life on campus. His life was filled with new exciting material to study and he felt great being part of an academic community. He was enthusiastic about the new knowledge he acquired and his subjects. He studied hard every night at home. After all he only had time to socialize with Joe and Giovanni and had no need to meet any girls.

October was coming soon and the collection of rent became painful for Dimitri as he had to deal with all of Mr. Fein's cursing that he amply distributed to the neighbors. There were no serious mishaps as most of the tenants had the rent ready on time. Columbus Day was around the corner and only one thought was on Dimitri's mind: Lauren. He looked forward to seeing her again. He had so many questions about her new life. The time came and it was the Saturday before Columbus Day. He saw the limo leaving the mansion and ran to get in front of the car. The chauffer stopped and Lauren opened the window, "Hey, you crazy; what are you doing?"

D: "Welcome back Lauren, I did it so I can catch up with you. "

L: "Well I have to be in the city in fifteen minutes to meet my friends, why don't you jump in and join me?"

Dimitri got into the limo, but he told Lauren that he could not join her group, as he saw her in an impeccable outfit and he was not dressed up. Besides, he did not want to encounter the same characters he saw a month and a half ago. Lauren looked at Dimitri's eyes; she had a happy smile in her face and a flirtatious look about her. Of course Dimitri did not miss that and was encouraged to continue the discussion. He asked her about Brown University and Providence, RI. She enthusiastically told him about the great and stimulating environment that surrounded her. The time passed quickly and they were already on the Upper East Side at the doorstep of the club. Dimitri asked her if he could meet her tomorrow and Lauren was hesitant.

"Monday perhaps? My schedule is filled with friends and family activities tomorrow". Dimitri agreed to meet her on Monday at noon and told her that he would wait outside of her home. He returned to Queens again by foot but he did not care about walking alone for more than five miles. It was a long walk but he thought it was worth it.

Sunday was a quiet day for him as he watched a movie with his friends and talked about their girlfriends. Late at night, he spent time with his family. His grandpa kept asking about Lauren but Dimitri was superstitious and did not want to talk about it as he thought that it might end up in disaster.

On Monday, Dimitri waited outside of Lauren's place from 11.30am till 1.30pm, but Lauren did not come out. The limo wasn't there. Disappointed he returned to his home and to his studies. He knew that he had no chance of seeing her that day as Monday evening she had to be back in Providence. Disappointed like never before, he realized that he would have to wait till the end of November for the Thanksgiving holiday.

Thanksgiving arrived but to his disappointment he found out that the Paulmerts decided to spend Thanksgiving with Lauren in New England, as they
had family in the Boston area. Deeply disappointed again, he realized he had
to wait for another month till Christmas. At least at that time the Paulmerts
would be in New York as always. In the meantime, he had regular conflicts
with Mr. Fein, who had nothing sacred inside him as he was constantly yelling at tenants. He never took mercy on them and even warned them not
to dare spend too much during the holiday season, to make sure they could
all have the rent ready on the 2nd of January. Mr. Fein couldn't tolerate any
comments from Dimitri and warned him several times that he would talk to
Mr. Paulmerts to get him fired, as he could not take it anymore; Dimitri was
described to be simply "too much noise in his ears". Dimitri tried hard to
convince him, to let him go on his own to the various tenants and do the collection. Certainly that amused Mr. Fein, as he could not believe that Dimitri
alone could make them pay. The neighborhood had too many people that
were not even waiters at restaurants, but rather busboys or maids and their
income was solely from washing clothes at the homes of middle class citizens.
Their income was not high or steady and they had many children and elderly
parents to take care of. Surviving in that part of Queens in the 50s was not
easy. Many of them had two shifts or two jobs like Mr. Garcias.
Dimitri had an idea to make things smoother. He knew that some of the
people with better jobs could spare some money so he wanted to suggest to
them the idea of putting money into a mutual fund. When someone was
unable to pay the rent right away, the fund would loan the money to them and
that person would then return the money within one or two weeks or in general within the month of the loan. After all, they were all very hard-working
and honest people. They did not have a constant cash flow, nor could they
get any credit from the bank due to the lack of a credit history, or incomplete
immigration papers. He did not even discuss this with Mr. Fein as it would
illicit laughter from him, and he would of course find it very unrealistic.
However, the time came when Dimitri talked to a couple of households and
they agreed to give it a try once Dimitri took over for Mr. Fein.
Christmas time was approaching and Dimitri saw that the Paulmerts were
getting ready to welcome Lauren. He felt that he should invite her out as he
had saved some extra money for that. He dreamt of talking to her, about

their lives and future plans, in a romantic coffee shop in Greenwich Village. The day before Christmas Eve, Mr. Paulmerts stopped by Mr. Fein's office to wish him and his employees the best wishes for the season. Dimitri happened to be there and Mr. Paulmerts checked in on him. Dimitri was so grateful but he told him that it would be better to talk privately at some point. Mr. Paulmerts agreed to do so and before he stepped away Dimitri asked about Lauren. Mr. Paulmerts said that she was fine but did not invite Dimitri, to stop by and see her. Dimitri spent enough time watching at the limo come and go during the Christmas days but he could not approach it as the whole family was inside. Suddenly two days after Christmas while he was on his way to the bookstore he saw that Lauren was outside looking at the window. His heart started beating. He started breathing fast as he ran towards her. When he stopped running ten feet away from her, Lauren turned towards him and immediately smiled at him and opened her arms to embrace Dimitri. "Hey, wait a second" he thought… I have never done this before. But immediately he moved forward and gave her a hug.

D: "Lauren, how are you? I haven't seen you in ages!"

L: "I know! Sorry about Columbus Day. My mother messed up my plans."

D: "Oh, I was so distressed that day and I did not see you for Thanksgiving, … I know, I know you have family in Boston, you see… I am working for your father these days, so I am learning more and more about your family."

L: "Is that right? And how do you like that job?"

D: "Hey, Lauren could you please do me a great favor and ask your father to give me more authority? Can you convince him to let me do the collection without Mr. Fein?" It would be great!! I am not sure if you remember any of my comments about him that day …"

L: "I do and do not worry, I will talk to him."

Dimitri felt more comfortable and at this moment he sensed that she was attracted to him, but he could not figure out why. He certainly knew that he did not have the social status that all the boys she met had. He was sure wealthy and promising young men surrounded her through her family or at Ivy League circles. However, while in Brown, she may have met students from different countries, who may have helped her see him in a different light. Besides, he was not fully aware that he was handsome enough to feel confident. He tried to see deep into her eyes but couldn't quite detect anything beyond the safe wholesome trust of a good-hearted person. Her mother, who exited the bookstore holding several calendars and stationary, interrupted his thoughts. She was very surprised to find her daughter talking to someone out on the street. She rushed over with a highly accelerated pace and asked with a rather high-pitched voice, "Who are you, young man?"

L: "Mother?"

D: "Oh Hi, Mrs. Paulmerts, I am Dimitris Giovas and I work for your husband down the road in his real estate offices."

Mrs. Paulmerts: "And how do you know my daughter?"

D: "I have been at your place a couple times and know your husband..."

Mrs. Paulmerts interrupted him and delivered a rather cold statement, "well nice to meet you, but excuse me, we have to run."

L: "Mother, could you please give us two minutes?"

Mrs. Paulmerts was astonished at that point and she reused her previous high-pitched voice, "What is so important that you have to spend two minutes on, when they are waiting for us?"

L: "Mother please don't do this to me, you know very well that two minutes is more than fine."

Mrs. Paulmerts: "I am sorry, but I do not see the reason? What is it that you have to discuss with this young man?"

L: "Ask Dad; he is not just our employee, but a grandson of a family friend and please stop this," while she raised her voice with a distinct anguish tone.

Mrs. Paulmerts: "Oh really? Who are you young man? To me you look like someone from the neighborhood."

D: "Precisely, Mrs. Paulmerts, this is where I grew up and live, but.."

At that point Mrs. Paulmerts again interrupted him. She warned Lauren that she would not tolerate this joke anymore and she ordered Lauren to follow her at once.

Lauren was so embarrassed by her mother's disrespectful and erratic behavior that her eyes teared up while she glanced at Dimitri with sympathy and remorse. Sadly enough she turned to her mother and followed her. But when she was almost thirty feet away from him, she suddenly turned around and rushed back to Dimitri with such a fast pace that she approached him in a couple of seconds. She quickly told him to come and meet her the next day outside her social club at 5pm. At the same time, her mother was storming and yelling at her to come back. It did not take long for Lauren to deliver the message to Dimitri, so her mother stopped shouting and everyone got relieved soon, however still Mrs. Paulmerts seemed very upset. Even when her daughter returned, Dimitri could feel the tremendous tension.

Dimitri had no choice other than to take the train to Manhattan the following day and wait for her outside her social club at 5pm. It was on his winter break after all, so he was relaxed and could spare sometime between his studies, but he had to cancel his original plans to go to Giovanni's place for some homemade Italian food and then later to the movies. Of course, when he explained to his friends why he had to cancel they both told him not to worry and to go. However, they both reiterated that they were way below the social tier the Paulmerts belonged to. Joe told him for the first time not to be naïve, as Dimitri was not part of her social circle, a circle that does not easily accept immigrants, especially second-class citizens, as the social classes that inhabited their neighborhood in Queens. Dimitri of course felt the care and honesty in Joe's words, but he still believed that anything could happen in America, so he distracted them by changing the conversation and subject. Joe realized his move and said, "Dimitri let me tell you once again. I was born in this country and some of the people across the river consider me a second-class citizen. Look at me, at Giovanni and even you. It doesn't even matter that we were born and raised here. The people at that social club that the Paulmerts go to, do not like to mix with the working class. You are almost like a colored guy to them!" Dimitri got upset and told him to stop. Joe tried to comfort him by telling him that he did not mean to upset him and that he was commenting on his people and Giovanni's people as well. Dimitri realized that his friend was looking out for him and saw that Giovanni was in full agreement with Joe. Dimitri always knew that his friends cared for him and they didn't want to hurt him. A couple of minutes later he went home and played the "Spanish Romance" for the whole night. A few months ago Joe had bought a new guitar and gave Dimitri his old one as a gift. Dimitri was not a very good guitar player, but he had a good ear and could "scratch" a simple melodies here and there. That night he really played the piece with passion and great concentration. After all it was a musical piece that was not that hard for him and it helped that he could also play it with a melodica.

The melodica was a Christmas gift from his aunt and the first piece that he ever played on it was the "Spanish Romance".

The next day Dimitri went to the social club, where Lauren told him to be at 5pm. It was such a cold and windy day but Dimitri managed to stay warm by wearing heavy layers of clothes. He knew that his clothes were not attractive or elegant but they served the purpose. He felt bad that he could not dress better, especially while he observed all the elegant young people who passed in front of him dressed in highly fashionable clothes, right before their entrance to the club. It was 5:15pm and there was no sign of Lauren. He could imagine that she couldn't do as she pleased. Her mother could have slowed her down so Dimitri decided that he should be patient. At this point he was glad and satisfied that he chose the warm clothes to wear as he could hardly stand the cold and the wind. It was 5:30pm and there was still no sign of Lauren. He started to panic, as he did not know how he could ever approach her again without knocking at the Paulmerts' door in a formal and direct way and perhaps having to deal with Mrs. Paulmerts. He imagined her always strict and storming at him. He remembered the day in the basement when his grandfather questioned if he had ever met Mrs. Paulmerts; and indeed that was one of his first questions that day; he thought and realized for a second that Mrs. Paulmerts could be the biggest obstacle in his path. He started walking back and forth thinking about his encounter with Lauren and trying to stay warm. He smelled the chestnuts roasting on an open fire by a street vendor right across the street from him. He did not want to spend even a penny, since he had to take the train to Manhattan. He thought most likely he would have to repeat that on his return, as it was too cold. He loved chestnuts but he was there for something more superior and divine, his one and only love. At 5:45 pm he realized he could not wait any longer, as he was freezing out in the cold and did not have the guts to ask the doorman in the lobby to let him wait inside. He thought that the doorman would have to ask him a lot of questions and he also realized that his shoes were in really bad shape. He saw from the people's faces that they perceived him as a peasant. He had no choice at that point other than to do his regular routine, walk back and forth on the sidewalk. Suddenly he realized the guy across the street was waving at him to come over. Dimitri crossed the street and realized that this was the man who was selling the chestnuts.

"Hey, could you please do me a big favor?" the man asked.

Dimitri asked, "like what?"

"I need to take a bathroom break, so could you please keep an eye on my cart?" He looked deep into Dimitri's eyes and added, "Please don't take any nuts, I will give you some when I get back."

"Oh don't worry sir, I won't do that," Dimitri replied.

"OK, you look trustworthy and I know you will not do it. You know I paid for every nut on this cart and need to make a living."

"Oh please don't worry, it's OK sir, I am not hungry and do not worry at all, I will do this for you," Dimitri replied.

"If a customer comes, tell him to wait for just for a minute, I will be back", the man added.

Dimitri gave him his word and the man took another good look at him and said, "Young man, I know I can trust you, even though you look as poor, and hungry as I am".

Dimitri replied, "No, it is the cold that makes me look tired. I know you are suffering here to make a penny and I will not take it away from you".

The man turned his back and crossed 5th Avenue and ran towards Central Park leaving Dimitri alone. Dimitri took a good look at the big well roasted, cracked on the top, chestnuts and could immediately imagine and almost feel their sweetness and taste. At exactly that moment he lifted up his eyes and saw Lauren's limousine. It seemed that while he spoke with the chestnut vendor the limo arrived to drop off Lauren and two friends in front of the club door. Dimitri at once jumped a little to the left and called as loud as he could Lauren's name. He saw that she was with another girl and a boy her age. Lauren heard him and immediately waved at him to cross the street, but Dimitri waved back to her to cross the street and come to his side. Lauren waved at him again and Dimitri signaled with his hands, "to wait a minute, I can't now". Lauren was perplexed, as she could not understand what was going on and why he did not want to cross the street.

"Please come over," he yelled and she eventually realized that he was not coming to her side. At that moment, two customers showed up and asked for chestnuts. Dimitri immediately tried to explain to them that they had to wait for a minute, but at the same time he juggled to keep them waiting so the man could earn his money; he did not want them to run away instead.

Lauren was getting impatient with him, as she could not understand what he was doing on the other side of the street. What could be that important, for Dimitri to have her wait outside in the cold? Eventually she decided to cross the street, but then her friends asked her what she was doing. She stepped back and Dimitri saw that, but he was determined to keep his promise and the customers at the chestnut stand. He knew that if he crossed the street, the tourists would grab the chestnuts and perhaps leave without paying. His frustration with waiting outside in the cold for almost an hour, along with the stressful moment in which he could not explain to Lauren what was going on, and making her wait out in the cold made him look and feel confused. He wondered why was this happening to him at this point... however he had to stick to his promise. Lauren was about a hundred feet away and suddenly she looked as if she was giving up on him as she was way too cold. Her dress under her coat looked elegant, but light enough to make her feel very uncomfortable being out in the cold. Dimitri kept yelling, "one minute, just a minute I will be there", while the tourists also looked puzzled. Lauren, who also had a confused look, decided to cross the street and find out what was going on. By the time she arrived at the chestnut stand, the vendor appeared from the park and Dimitri shouted, "You see he is coming. I am keeping an eye on his cart as he had to take a break."

L: "Come on, you are not supposed to do that and have me wait out in the cold." At the same time her friends across the street were obnoxiously yelling at her, "What is going on?"

D: "I am really sorry Lauren, I profusely apologize, but it was just for a minute or two, the man I guess has been here the whole day and he saw me waiting across the street and just asked me for a favor. He needed help."

At that moment Lauren turned her back to him and started walking towards her friends who were yelling at her in a somewhat angry way about the whole situation and for being out in the cold. She turned to Dimitri and said, "Please follow me, you either come at once or stay here, I can't have them wait out in the cold!"

D: "Oh of course I am coming. You see him, he is almost here, he is coming." Lauren turned her back again and continued crossing the street towards her friends. The man was almost a hundred feet away and Dimitri yelled at him, "Come on, run, run" as he saw that the tourists were making fun of him and the whole scene. They saw that the man wasn't running, but walking slowly so they turned to Dimitri and said, "This is ridiculous, we can get chestnuts two blocks down the street. There is another cart".

Dimitri was almost loosing Lauren out of sight and turned to the tourists to tell them that they should not leave now after what happened. The tourists laughed at him, turned their back to him and left. Dimitri was frustrated and devastated; and the man who was now about fifty meters away but still not running, waved to him, "Make them stay, I am coming". But Dimitri could not make them return as they were even making fun of him. He then turned to the man telling him, "Why don't you run and get them?"

D: "I am sorry I have to run to her," he said pointing Lauren who was already at the gate of the club, with her friends.

Man: "Hey wait, don't go! Wait for me!"

D: "Are you crazy? Everything is OK, your cart is as you left it, I have to run," and he started running towards Lauren, yelling her name.

Dimitri was almost at the gate when Lauren and her friends were at the door. Lauren heard his voice and signaled to the doorman to let him in. Dimitri begged her to wait for him at the door. So she did and had her two friends proceeded ahead without her.

D: "Hey Lauren, I am really sorry about what happened, but I just wanted to help this man."

Lauren looked into his eyes and she could not understand him, she said, "Weren't you supposed to wait at the door and not just chat with random strangers across the street?"

D: "Oh no, I was waiting in front of the door, but I had to get warm and I started walking but…"

L: "But, when you see me across the street you can make an effort to terminate these talks of yours with all these people that have nothing to offer to you … other than waste your time!"

D: "Lauren, let me explain, I was waiting outside the gate and this man.."

Lauren interrupted him, "Listen, do not worry now and please you do not have to continue, it was mostly my cousins who were totally impatient with the whole scene and the cold."

D: "But Lauren, I did not realize that you wanted me to go inside with you," he whispered that to her as the doorman was only nine feet away. "I thought

you told me to meet you at the door and we would just chat with you outside."

L: "What is wrong with you today? In such cold weather?"

D: "Well, yesterday I had no idea that this should be the case … I mean that
it would be this cold today… and as you see I had to dress warm," he turned
his head down as he could not face her eyes, and continued "…everyone here
can see that I do not belong here,… you know what I mean."

Lauren took a good look at him from top to bottom, resting her eyes on
Dimitri's shoes for more than few second. Then looked at him in his eyes
and said, "And you couldn't get anything warm that is more appropriate? Or
what was your idea? Just chatting outside?" Lauren delivered the last question
with obvious angst.

Dimitri almost faded and became pale at the first question as he realized that
Lauren had no idea that he does not own anything more appropriate that was
warm, "Well Lauren, I am sorry I thought it was going to be a short talk,
otherwise I would have suggested something else. I am free these days and
what I had in mind was to propose to meet another day and go for tea or to
the cinema and chat at some more convenient place. I have so many things
to share with you about the great cinematic year of 1957 and my predictions
for the Academy Awards. What a year? Wow! I have also discovered a lot
of new recordings that got recently released and I wanted to tell you all about
my studies, the books I have read, my dreams and perhaps hear yours as well.
I am so curious to hear about your life in Providence? Can you please take
the time one afternoon before you go back to Brown and chat with me?"

L: "You surprise me… but why can't we have all these discussions here?
Tonight? Come on let's do this!"

Dimitri took a deep breath, "Well… I do not feel that comfortable here.
But of course I don't mind … as long as I can talk to you and you won't get
distracted by all your friends here that come and talk to you all the time.
Remember the last time?"

L:" Why are you so uptight? This is a social place, be social to everyone as
well and talk to people, we can certainly catch up with each other s while we
are here."

Dimitri was so magnetized by Lauren's eyes that he would have done anything she wanted him to do, especially at that specific point. He agreed and

followed her to the reception hall. He took another look at his clothes and
again felt uncomfortable. He compared them to the well-dressed young men
that he could see at the end of the hall and right before the dinning halls.
Half way to the reception hall Lauren's cousins were waiting for her and they
looked at him astonished. Dimitri immediately felt their eyes staring his old
and worn, but comfortable clothes. As he proceeded, his pace became slower
and slower. Lauren was ahead of him and suddenly she realized that he was
staying behind. She turned to him and asked him if something was wrong.
He hesitated for a few moments, and told her that it would be better if they
could see each other later at some other place. Lauren reiterated not to worry
about his clothes, as she did not care herself, "I invited you here because you
are a nice person and you deserve something better than your neighborhood
Dimitri."

D: "But Lauren, I like my neighborhood… which is your neighborhood as
well…? Do you forget?"

Lauren looked deep into his full of goodness eyes and felt sorry for him as
she sensed that her cousins were ready to yell at her again.

L: "OK Dimitri, I understand and do not think I blame you."

She paused and told him, "Do not worry, go back if you want and I will find
a way to send you a message and meet you another day."

Dimitri's heart pounded with unpredictable intensity, as he realized that
Lauren deep inside her was very understanding and could feel his pain and
read his mind well. However, at that moment his desire to be with her grew
again and he did not want to leave her alone with all the other people, who
probably wanted her full attention. But, it did not take a long for him to
change his mind when Lauren's cousins approached her again asking annoy-
ing questions about him and his clothes and the reason why he was at the
club. Dimitri turned around and walked towards the exit and as he turned
back to glance at Lauren again and say goodbye, he saw a teardrop in one of
her gorgeous eyes as she waved at him.

"Wow! What a confirmation that she is different and that she cares about
me," he thought. Dimitri was so happy to realize this and for the first time
in his life he had two completely opposite feelings that harbored his heart.
On the one hand, was his disappointment and deep sorrow for not being
comfortable and appropriately dressed in such a club and on the other hand,

his happiness about the confirmation that Lauren was probably harboring feelings for him.

He did not turn back as he saw the resentment in the annoyed faces of Lauren's cousins along with the mocking smiles of the young gentlemen passing by. He was out in the cold again and thought for a second that it was definitely a good idea that he left all his savings at home, because if he had more money on him than the train ticket money, he would have used it to buy a hot drink to warm him up. He had to keep his entire savings at home, as he was not sure how much a night out with Lauren would cost him. He put his hand in his pocket to make sure his coin was still there, as this was the only one that ensured his subway ride home. This time he could not really walk back home like the last time, since it was too cold. As he crossed the street he saw in the dark the man with the chestnut cart wrapped up in a blanket all the way to his top, trying to stay warm by leaning his body against the warm cart. He said a good night, but when the man realized who he was he asked him, "Hey, why didn't you wait for me to return?

D: "What do you mean I didn't wait? By the time I started running, you were only 30 feet away!"

Man: "So what? I cannot run young chap, I have bad knees. Did you think I was not running because I wanted to have you wait longer and torture you in the cold? ... Oh well! You should have waited for me, someone could have run fast and grabbed anything he wanted from the cart."

D: "Oh come on! There was nobody that close and the tourists went the other way."

Man: "I know, but I still wanted to thank you young chap, for helping me out."

D: "No worries, it is OK."

Man: "In any case, thank you and allow me to offer you a chestnut to extend my gratitude if you do not mind."

D: "Oh it is not necessary Sir. No worries."

Man: "What? You don't like my chestnuts?"

D: "Oh no Sir. I love chestnuts, but you don't have to thank me by offering me one."

Man: "Please, it is my pleasure and you should enjoy it, I paid way too much to get the best quality and now look at them, nobody is buying them and they are getting dry."

D: "Don't worry, you still have few more hours left, not the end of the day yet. People will buy them before or after dinner."

Man: "You know it is already late and I did not sell any today, such a strange day. Everyone is afraid of this cold weather and have stayed inside with their families, in their warm home while mine is cold and my family is starving. Can you believe that no one bought a single chestnut today? I'm here freezing the whole day and no one wanted to help me." The man burst into tears and looked to the ground.

D: "Yes, but you may sell them now. People are out in Manhattan even after midnight, there are so many tourists for the holiday season."

Man: "Not in this neighborhood young man, people are never out after dinner and I do not have a license to sell them anywhere else. You know what this means? A whole day without selling one!! How can I buy more tomorrow? I will feed my family with these tonight but will have to buy more tomorrow and …Oh, why do I bother you with this young pal, please have your chestnut tonight and thank you again for helping a helpless man tonight."

D: "Oh well, can I suggest to buy the chestnuts tonight and you can treat me another day?"

The man looked at him incredulous in the eyes, as this was unexpected to him and said, "I was not whining here to have you buy my chestnuts? Thank you! You are a very kind person," and as he paused briefly he thought for another moment and he continued, "but wait a second, what is a nickel or a dime to you since you can get into such a prestigious club?"

D: "Right! You are right! A coin is just as much as a subway ticket, nothing to worry about it."

Man: "But you are not dressed like all the chaps who go to the club, are you an employee? You look like you are from Brooklyn or Queens or … where are you from?"

D: "Well, what does it matter, give me these wonderful chestnuts, take my coin and promise that you will treat me another time, next time you see me, deal? Here it is and it may it bring you luck!"

Dimitri gave him his coin, took the paper funnel filled with the chestnuts and continued in the cold. He fully enjoyed every single one of them! Indeed they were delicious chestnuts, the best the man had and so carefully placed in the paper funnel for Dimitri to enjoy. He did it slowly, as slowly as he could to keep himself warm on this long, and awfully cold trip back to Queens. It seemed too long, much longer than the past trips, especially when he crossed the cold and windy bridge, his bones started aching and he thought about how stupid he was moments ago to have bought these chestnuts. Unfortunately, the next day he awoke sick in bed and was not able to do to his regular routine in the neighborhood or meet Joe and Giovanni. He thought that he was not lucky enough these days and was tortured by the thought that perhaps Lauren might be looking for him in the neighborhood to give him a message about their next meeting. New Year's Eve came and he still had no news from Lauren. There was no way to know if that was because she could not find him or if she did not care to leave a message for him. By New Year's Day, he had recovered from the illness and brainstormed on his next moves with his friends.

He did not want to approach her through Mr. Paulmerts' employees and compromise his professionalism. He was an employee after all. The days passed and he still had no word from her. Suddenly, one of the very first beautiful spring days, at the end of March, he found a letter on his desk. Mr. Fein probably left it for him, but the writing was artful and the calligraphy wasn't Mr. Fein's. He opened it at once and found a single piece of paper with the same artful writing:

"I hope you are well. Write me at: 121 Thayer Street, Apt. G, Providence, RI. Best, L."

The "L" itself was a piece of art! It was exquisite as well as the feelings that Dimitri had as soon as he read that letter, from his one and only love, Lauren. Did she drop it off herself or did someone else do it for her? It didn't matter… what was important was that he could now communicate with her. Or at least write her. She wanted him to at least be her pen pal. That somehow felt nice for the romantic heart that Dimitri had. He was so happy that he immediately left the office, went home, grabbed his guitar and played the Spanish Romance. But this time he also played another tune, he wasn't sure what it was, but he just improvised. He wrote a few short poems and decided to send one to Lauren in his first letter. He chose the one that was far less flirtatious and then he composed a three-page letter telling her how happy he was to receive her letter and then he wrote his news.

The following days, he did not wait for a reply and he kept writing to her about his classes, the interesting things he learned in his engineering courses, his dreams and of course about the movies he had seen. He received a response from Lauren and they kept writing each other till the summer semesters were over. The summer of 1958 was half way through. Dimitri was getting as many credits as he could during the summer since he wanted to finish school as soon as possible. He had already secured a full scholarship for the next years, as he was stellar in science and engineering. However, he knew that this summer was going to be very important for him and Lauren, especially when she would return to New York from Rhode Island.

He did not receive any news from her the whole month of July and figured she probably was not at Brown that month. He heard in the office that the Paulmerts were supposed to travel to Europe in August, but of course he could never imagine that the whole summer would go by without seeing Lauren around. However, Lauren did spent the entire summer on vacation touring Europe with her family. Dimitri never stopped writing her letters and mailed them at least one a week. In September, after the semester had started, he received her first one filled with postcards that she collected from Venice, Vienna and Paris for him. He was happy for her that she could travel so much. He then realized that he would have rather had a photo of her instead of the postcards. He asked her to include one in her next letter to him along with an answer to when they could possibly meet.

Two weeks later Lauren sent him one, which gave him the most pleasure since the day he saw her teardrop in the club. He immediately placed it across his bed and played his favorite melody with his guitar. In the letter Lauren wrote that she would be home for Thanksgiving. Dimitri was so pleased to read this and he knew that there was nothing that could make him happier. He constantly ignored every girl who flirted with him in college and always focused on writing the best letters to Lauren.

The situation in the office was getting harder and harder as Mr. Fein was an impossible character to work with. Dimitri asked Lauren several times to do him the great favor he had asked her once in the past. Right before Thanksgiving, Lauren wrote him that she would do it when she got back for the holiday. She also wrote him to be ready to see her the Friday after Thanksgiving. Undoubtedly, he would plan nothing else that day and as his savings grew more and more, month by month. He decided he could even propose dinner and a movie to her.

That Friday was cloudy and cold. A gray Friday reminiscent of the cold winter night they saw each other last time. Lauren told Dimitri to wait for her outside the bookstore in Queens. Dimitri arrived early enough and browsed the books while keeping an eye toward the window above the curtain, for the limo. All of a sudden, he saw Lauren's face looking at him through the window. He was astonished and felt like he was hit by lightning, as Lauren's eyes were even more pronounced and bigger. He realized that it was part of the effect her new hairstyle had on her appearance. Her hair was pulled back and did not hide any part of the forehead. In addition, she had a much lighter and blonder color than what Dimitri remembered, which made her eyes bigger and brighter. She was elegantly dressed and so irresistible that Dimitri felt he was about to make a rather big mistake and reveal his absolute five-year devotion to her.

Lauren entered the bookstore and greeted him with a big smile and spoke first, as he was speechless. She suggested that they should go somewhere in the neighborhood, wherever he wanted. Dimitri was amazed to hear that, since he had put on his Sunday clothes under his thick jacket, which were the best he had, but not the warmest, as he thought that they would go to Manhattan. Lauren understood this and as soon as they got into the limo she told the chauffer to take them to Rockefeller Center. Dimitri was pleased about it and started talking to her full of excitement about his studies and the books that he had read in the past year. They had a nice chat, but as soon as they arrived at Rockefeller Plaza, Lauren suggested to go watch a movie, as they both loved the movies.

They entered the huge mid-town theater and watched "Vertigo" which impressed them, but at the end Dimitri was more affected by the vertigo that Lauren's presence induced. He suggested going for dinner, but Lauren asked him to take her home as she was recovering from a cold. Dimitri immediately asked when they would meet again and Lauren asked him to give her some time to reply. At the end of the night, the hug was full of tension and Dimitri was dissatisfied because he could not read Lauren very well. Before he stepped out of the limo, he reminded Lauren about the favor that he kept asking for in his last letters. Lauren reassured him that she hadn't forgotten.

This was the only thing in his mind that would distract him from his total devotion to her eyes, hair and genuine figure. It was important because Christmas and New Year's were close. December and January were the most difficult months for the rent collection. Mr. Fein never cared about the need for expenses that families had during the holiday season. Dimitri wanted to help them all and knew that he would find a way to be successful.

He did not see Lauren again that weekend as she left earlier than expected but the next Monday he received a letter authorizing him to do the rent collection in the area of his choice and in one fifth of the households that Mr. Fein was previously responsible for. The letter indicated that Mr. Fein had been copied. It was then obvious to Dimitri that the next time he would face Mr. Fein, he would most probably have a wicked and vindictive look on his face revealing his disapproval and opposition to Mr. Paulmerts' decision. Dimitri felt a deep fear rising in his body, as he sensed that it was going to be much more trouble than he originally anticipated. Mr. Fein after all, was a master at hurting people and he never missed a chance to make his life miserable.

Dimitri looked forward to meeting Lauren over Christmas to extend his immense thanks for her help. A few days later, he unexpectedly received a letter from Lauren stating that she planned to spend Christmas with family and friends in Vermont. For the first time he realized that he was not very happy about her travels and her extravagant lifestyle anymore. He could not think of an easy way to approach her. He thought of visiting Brown, but he could not be spending money on a regular basis for that, since his savings were important to his family. He could never imagine spending them on trips, hotels and meals. He could not forget that till he finished college and got a real job, he would still live in one of the poorest part of Queens. Not only live in perhaps the poorest part, but also experience the poorest lifestyle, without any money to spend besides a ticket to the movie theater.

He thought many times about going to Providence during his spring break, but Lauren also had spring break that same week and he hoped that she would return to New York ... or maybe she would go away to an exotic and extravagant location. Dimitri was desperate for contact and decided to open up more to her in the following letters to her. He decided to declare his love for her or at least to reveal more of his real feelings for her in every consecutive letter.

In the mean time he used his new authority with passion, love and zeal and promised Mr. Fein that he would always have all the rents collected within the first five days of the month. Mr. Fein cursed him out in front of everybody in the office for being such an idiot and warned him that he was not going to have any mercy on him if he failed. Dimitri already had a diagram and list of all the tenants under his authority. He classified them in four tiers: the ones that had no problem paying rent, the ones that always came up with the money in the first five days, the ones that sometimes didn't have the money by the first five days of the month and the ones that most likely did not have the money by the deadline. The latter group consisted of street vendors and people who made a penny one day, a dollar another day, or simply nothing for the next ten days. It included people like Mr. Garcia, who no matter how many jobs he had, just had too many kids, a sick wife and enormous responsibilities and bills. During his first collection he tried to persuade people in the first tier to put some money into a common mutual fund for the people who needed it most. He personally guaranteed that the people in need would repay the money by the middle of the month; and that the money in the fund would never get lost and would be accounted for. As an incentive he offered the people in the first tier free services or products from the people in the fourth tier. He talked to all the families, but the majority did not want to participate in what they perceived was a naïve project, as some of them termed it. However, many people in the fourth tier were willing to provide services for free to any of their first tier benefactors. Dimitri started with a couple of these benefactors in the first month and he slowly built up the fund month by month. Everyone was responsible for his or her neighbor and all were trying to be good citizens as much as they could. Mr. Fein suspected that something different was going on as he saw that the young man didn't have any problems with the collection. Nevertheless, he did not miss the opportunity to offer derogatory comments about Dimitri, by assuming that the money was stolen from banks. Dimitri was always calm and patient and never fired back at him; at the very end he felt compassion for Mr. Fein's evil and arrogant character and wanted to believe that one day he would repent and discover the light in his dark path.

During the following years Dimitri's job was not smooth as he sweated out numerous times to ensure the proper payment of rent and avoid arguments between the benefactors in the first tier and the tenants in the fourth tier. Unfortunately, these arguments continued all the time, as Mr. Paulmerts increased the rent significantly in two consecutive years. His manufacturing facility was not doing that well since the competition from overseas stressed the production's high cost to a level that would minimize the profit margins. It was well known that the Paulmerts' factory was not doing well at all; however, their lifestyle never seemed to be affected. Lauren was almost never at home the following two summers as she traveled to Europe for exchange programs between her university and European colleges. The Paulmerts visited her and toured Europe with her and continued to live a very extravagant lifestyle. Dimitri externalized his passion for Lauren more and more in numerous letters, but Lauren did not write as frequently anymore. She wrote one letter every season and always avoided answering Dimitri's specific points about their future meetings or plans. Time flew by and Dimitri got closer and closer to the realization that his love would be a not corresponded one. Unfortunately, there was nothing he could do about this, especially from a distance. He also had no idea and could not find out if Lauren had a boyfriend or someone significant in her life. They had no mutual friends that he could ask. He sensed that his letters proclaiming his love to her made her more distant. He did not know what the best path was for him to follow. Since the summer of 1958 and after the evening at the movies, two years had passed and he was getting ready for his senior year. In his lonely times, he played the guitar alone in his room thinking about the next time he would face Lauren.

It was 1960 and he was getting ready to graduate in the summer of 1961. He constantly dreamed about the day that he would eventually be free to get a job. He thought it was worth waiting another year because he would then be free to pursue Lauren and would start making more money on his own. He dreamed of his ideal life in which he was independent from the rest of the family as they now had enough money saved up to bring over his older brother and another cousin of his. He would soon be able to travel and explore the world outside of Queens and New York. He had seen a lot of European Art in the museums of New York and he dreamed of the day he could tour all the places in Europe that Lauren had visited. He also dreamed of the day he could go back to Greece and see his best friends from elementary school and all the children he grew up with. He had left right before starting high school and still had many friends from school who lived in his neighborhood. There were many of his relatives back in Greece who he was also missing a lot. Of course, he continued his correspondence with most of his friends and relatives over these years, but he had such a strong desire to see them all again, besides his father and mother, whom he missed dearly; such a part of his constant daily pain, the pain that only an immigrant who left his family behind could feel. These could have all been additional reasons why he did not have any more space in his heart for any other person besides

Lauren, since he cared so much about his parents, friends and relatives. All these people in his life did not just compete for space in his heart but perhaps for some angst and pain as well. How much more could a heart accommodate? He always wondered about this but couldn't find the answer.

He was very much aware that his senior year would define his career path for the rest of his life. Since he did very well in the past three years, he could not stay unfocused during the last and most determining year of his life. He was the best student in all his math classes and excelled in physics and engineering. He knew that a great senior year would assure him a generous scholarship for graduate studies. At this point, he was not sure if he wanted to continue his studies or work. Working for a corporation with a good salary would instantly gratify his need to be away from Mr. Fein's office and the pain of dealing with him every day. However, he knew that once he left the neighborhood the tenants would suffer, especially after the two consecutive rent increases that were enforced during the past two years.

Dimitri worked hard in his first senior semester and he excelled, his grades and performance were outstanding and his professors wanted him to continue to graduate school. Christmas vacation was approaching and he knew that it was about time for Lauren to show up. The Monday after Thanksgiving, he had to attend a meeting with Mr. Paulmerts and Mr. Fein. He was wondering what could be wrong. He had no idea, but he felt that something was really wrong. He did not see anyone leave or enter the Paulmerts' mansion during the whole Thanksgiving weekend, another sign that something was not right since the whole family was away. He did not know how to make sense of all these signs and besides he was not in the best of moods since another holiday passed without having seen his one and only love.

That Monday, after Thanksgiving weekend and right before his morning class, he entered the office and to his amazement he saw everyone sitting around Mr. Paulmerts. He walked softly on his toes to not interrupt the ongoing discussion. Mr. Paulmerts did not notice him right away, as he was talking about numbers, but Mr. Fein saw him immediately and did not miss the opportunity to give him one his most wicked looks, but this time paired with an aftertaste of some short of satisfaction. Dimitri sat down slowly without disturbing the conversation. A couple of minutes later he understood that the talk was about Mr. Paulmert's awkward situation. He was about to face bankruptcy due to the factory's shortage in cash and loss of money that were used to cover paper bills of operational costs. Dimitri was not that proficient in economics so he could not really understand the nature of the problem and all the sophisticated "money" terminology used in the discussion. Later he understood that the factory products could not compete with cheaper foreign products. It was apparent that he was afraid his business may not survive the fierce foreign competition. However, he was determined to save the factory and the business that his grandfather started two generations ago. He did not want to give up. He was very much convinced that the crisis would last a year or two and eventually he would recover. So together with his officers he was assessing which properties in the neighborhood could potentially sell to generate cash for his factory business. There was a group of new immigrants from Europe and they were able and willing to buy property in Queens. Mr. Paulmerts went through the property evaluations with his employees to assess which ones could sell faster and generate optimum profits; plus which ones he should keep. It did not take long for Dimitri to understand that Mr. Fein was trying to convince Mr. Paulmerts to keep all the properties and further increase the rents, and this way collect the extra money he needed. In case the so called "incompetent" and "dirty" creatures, according to Mr. Fein, who were not be able to pay the extra rent, he would then vow to kick them out as soon as their yearly lease was up and subsequently have new tenants move in and pay the higher rent to Mr. Paulmerts. After Mr. Fein presented his financial analysis to Mr. Paulmerts again and again, it started making sense, but Mr. Paulmerts pointed out that they had already increased the rent the last two years. Mr. Fein kept ensuring him that this was not a problem because there were all these new immigrants who were willing to pay higher rent for a place close to Manhattan. Dimitri could not tolerate it anymore and interrupted Mr. Fein telling him that he should be more considerate and humane. Mr. Fein with a fierce full face told him to shut up at once and that this was not his business, but Mr. Paulmerts asked him to calm down. He briefly looked at Dimitri but turned to the opposite direction and told his employees that he had never been in such distress and that he was forced to do things he normally would never consider.

Dimitri did not want to believe that Mr. Fein's suggestion for such an unreasonable rent increase would be approved. He knew that most of the tenants had no cheaper place to go to unless they moved to a far more dangerous neighborhood away from Queens. Besides, each one of them harbored people with incomplete immigration papers or people that did not have a proper rental agreement with Mr. Fein, so he could terrorize them and effectively kick them out when he wanted to, since he could cause them a lot of legal trouble. Dimitri followed their discussion with despair and half an hour later was convinced that Mr. Fein would try to kick some of his "enemies" out of the Paulmerts' properties. Mr. Fein's proposal was calling for a considerable immediate rent increase and for an immediate collection of the extra cash from the tenants.

Dimitri was fully aware on how hard the collections had become right after the two consecutive rent increases and his "mutual neighborhood fund" did not exist anymore. He did not know how to help the neighborhood. He was in distress and thought of talking to Mr. Paulmerts after the meeting was over. That did not become possible as Mr. Fein pushed him aside, while Mr. Paulmerts was on his way to his limo. As soon as Mr. Paulmerts left the office, Mr. Fein pressed his face against Dimitri's forehead and told him that from now on he had to forget his practices and had to go after the tenants that could not pay the rent. He was going to enforce a 30% rent increase immediately on December 1 or a 20% increase if they gave him cash up front for the next two months. Dimitri yelled, "Are you crazy? How can they possibly have extra cash when sometimes they don't have the rent for the month?" Mr. F: "Oh come on, you make me laugh! Don't you know that your friends spend their money to have a good time? Guess what… the good times have come to an end now. They have to help their real benefactor, Mr. Paulmerts, who has let them use his property all these years for peanuts! I do not care where they find the money. They can work around the clock or they can rob a bank. However, if they do not meet my demands and goals they will be kicked out!"

D: "You are so cruel and horrible Mr. Fein. These people already work around the clock and they do not spend money the way you think. They save to bring over more relatives from their countries."

Mr. F: "That is exactly true! I am not an idiot, I know that they all save money and have savings so they can help out now our very "special" situation here."

Dimitri felt that he was about to lose control and attack Mr. Fein, but "Shorty" moved next to him with an attitude that if he did something like that he would pay for it dearly.

Mr. F: "Ha ha, do you think I should be afraid of you little man? You look like you need a lesson ... Ha ha, do you want me to give you one?" He pulled his belt out of his pants while "Shorty" grabbed his stick and stood by anxious to use it.

Mr. F: "By the way stupid little thing, I told you that I will give them options and they can end up paying as little as 15% to 20% if they give me cash upfront in the next few months." He paused and with his wicked smile continued, "besides if they cannot come up with the rent, they are better off moving to another neighborhood or going back to where they came from."

Dimitri knew that it was not fair and he said with an intense voice, "Well, do not count on me then, do your atrocities yourself. I resent you and don't want anything to do with you anymore."

Mr. F: "Hey what is that? Do you really think you can walk out right now? After all the support that you got from Mr. Paulmerts you will abandon him? Now? Smart little piece of nothing? Ha ha ha, you think I will let you do this to him? I will break every bone of yours, if you do not work with me right now since you very well know who has jewelry and who has extra valuables to auction or give them to pawnbrokers and raise money for me."

Dimitri was astonished by Mr. Fein's words; he looked into his eyes and told him that he was a really sick person. He compared his words and acts to the Mafia and said he was disgusted and that things couldn't be done like that, especially in this country and in such modern times. He turned his back and left the office disgusted; he could not believe everything he had to tolerate during these last few minutes. As he was walking away, he knew that Mr. Fein would try to make his life difficult but he did not care, as he needed only six more moths to finish college. He thought that he could always go back to his old job and study in the evening around the clock to finish school. He was so upset and he did not want to talk to anyone for hours. At the end of the day, after leaving the library, he thought of crossing the river and going to talk to Giovanni or Joe. But it was too late to do that and he felt tired from the stress of the day.

The next day a big surprise was in store for Dimitri after his morning classes. He was not sure whether to go to the office and have to run into Mr. Fein. However, he wanted to tell him, right to his face that he had decided to quit his job and was absolutely sure about it, no matter how Mr. Fein would threaten him. "But could I really quit without talking to Mr. Paulmerts?" he thought to himself. And would he be able to quit his job without suffering a serious act of vengeance from Mr. Fein? Or should he stay at that job? The neighborhood would suffer even more without him. These were haunting questions and he was not sure what the right answer was. He thought that he should really talk to his grandfather, to help him make a decision. However, he also felt compelled to talk to Mr. Paulmerts. For some reason that seemed more reasonable at the time. But how could he make this happen? Go to his place later or to his factory right away? "Oh well", he whispered as he realized that the mansion was more or less on the way to the factory and felt that he should walk that way. To his amazement, Mr. Paulmerts's car was right outside the house. "Well, he is home today," Dimitri thought and rang the bell. Just then he immediately felt her presence in the house. He was again in front of something metaphysical and magnetic, which resonated with a wave of goose bumps in various parts of his body. He was right! As the door opened, Lauren stepped out of the door staring directly at him. Dimitri did not know how to explain what was going on, as he was again petrified and astonished since he hadn't seen Lauren in such a long time. "What a glorious figure!" he thought as she posed right in front of his wide-open eyes. Dimitri could not hide his feelings at that moment, which were immediately released with a cataclysmic magnitude. Indeed, she was the one and only girl he would ever love in his entire life time. She was almost two feet away and only the tall steel door separated them.

D: "Lauren it has been such a long time."

L: "Indeed it has been. Are you OK?"

D: "I am fine … and hm… sorry for not asking how are you doing, but you look stunning and very OK."

L: "Well, but I am really not as OK as I look and in fact I was on my way to come and meet you."

D: "What? You mean … you? To come and meet me??? Are you serious?"

L: "Very much so and there is a very serious reason for that Dimitri."

D: "What's the matter Lauren? Speak up, please speak up."

L: "I think you know very well what the matter is. Mr. Fein just explained to me that you were present last night and know very well that my father is in big trouble at the moment. I have never seen him in such bad shape and I know he has never been in such a situation before; nothing like it, in his entire life."

D: "Right, I heard about it… I am not sure if I know all the details but I know that things are tough for your father."

L: "Yes, very much so."

D: "I hope everything will be better soon."

L: "That could be the case if everyone could help, in fact, that is why I wanted to come and talk to you, but it is unbelievable that before I could look for you, you are here in front of me."

D: "Why would you look for me? What for? Why?"

L: "Is it so hard for you to understand why and for what? We just talked about how things are tough and according to Mr. Fein you are the only one who knows the neighborhood well and knows who can pay a little more this month and the following."

D: "Lauren, what do you mean by "extra"? These people out there struggle with their daily bread and feed their families. They don't have anything extra and besides I am not sure what kind of info Mr. Fein uses to brainwash your father but you need to listen to me since I know the neighborhood. I know that these people do not have anything extra and if they did they already gave it to you through all these consecutive rent increases. Do you really think that the people in the neighborhood have savings? Ha! Is that what Mr. Fein says about them? I am sorry to say that I am very surprised." As he said his last sentence, he saw that Lauren looked deep inside of him, which invigorated his full-blown passion for her. He was really so in love with these deep blue eyes.

L: "Dimitri, I know that you care about your neighborhood and all your friends over there. My father has already borrowed money from every bank and besides that there are many new people who are looking for housing and are willing to pay more money than the current residents. I know a little bit about it since Mr. Fein explained that they still have low rent, since they have been living there forever and the raises did not happen until recently." She took a breath and raised up her arm to stop Dimitri who was trying to interrupt her. "Look, I know very much that you want to protect them and I know very much that you will do everything to make them happy. But this time you have to help us as well. Please, do not forget how graceful my father was to let you do everything you wished. Something you don't know though is that... I had to talk to him for a long time to convince him and I hope you did not forget my other intervention to let you work without Mr. Fein. Please, understand that I did everything for you. My father did everything for you. Do not forget that ... do not forget that when you needed some help from me I was there and I did it. Now is the time for you to help us Dimitri." Her raised voice and the emphasis on every word revealed her passionate side, which made her look more impressive and magnetic to Dimitri. "Please consider that now we need your help! If all these people could give 30 or 50% more, for the next two months, they could provide some relief for my father. His creditors are after him and they are trying to take over his factory, and our property, which was built by our ancestors. He needs your help. I need your help. I know that you have power over all these tenants and you can make them give something extra." Dimitri's eyes were full of compassion for Lauren's open heart and pain and he could see again that she was so sensitive and delicate. "Dimitri, don't you think that I also see when I go to the post office or the bookstore that some of them do have valuables and can really help us out temporarily? Just for these next couple of months, please think about this! How many times have I noticed that the ladies down in the neighborhood wear earrings, rings and other jewelry? Please tell me if I am wrong?"

D: "Oh I am sorry ... Well Lauren, I never observe these things. I wouldn't know about it even if they do have..." he felt strange about his ignorance.

L: "I understand you never observe these things, but believe me as I have no reason to lie to you, they wear these all the time. You think they do not have savings, but you and your family know very well that every single one of them is saving money for the next family member to come over, isn't that true?" Dimitri as he waved his head said, "You are right."

L: "So on top of the jewelry and the savings you admit they have, but choose to ignore, you also don't know or better yet you don't want to know what else they own or have, because you choose not to see that. I know they are not wealthy, but your eyes do not want to see how much more they can afford as they choose not to spend and show off to their neighbors since they chose a safer path: savings and security! Am I right or wrong? I heard from people other than Mr. Fein that you created a pool of money from many families several times to secure timely payments for other families".

Dimitri lowered his head, as he did not want Lauren to see his eyes. He was surprised to find out that this information had been propagated to the Paulmerts.

L: "So please Dimitri, remember all the help that you have received from at least my father and please do something for us right now. There are so many tenants out there who can chip in a little bit extra for my father so he can avoid a disaster. Please be considerate and help us in this difficult time." Lauren's voice was so sweet and convincing that once Dimitri lifted up his eyes, he could only express his agreement and compassion about the situation. D:"I understand Lauren."

L: "I hope you do Dimitri because now is the time that we need your help. You need to go out there and convince all of them to either give you extra cash or some valuables. Mr. Fein has already arranged for the pawnbroker by the post office to accept anything valuable for the best price and for the best interest. Please help us now that we need your help. We know from everyone in the office that you are the only person who gets along with them. Everyone likes you and trusts you and you have the grace and the power to convince them. After all, if my father goes bankrupt who knows what is going to happen to the neighborhood. He could be forced to sell most of the properties and the tenants may have more problems than they have now."

Dimitri's eyes got wide open, as he had never thought about that possibility. He was so ignorant about business matters that the last phrase awakened him even more as he thought of the worst. Indeed, he thought, they might end up with more serious problems than the ones that exist at this point.

"Please talk to them as they will do us a big favor, but at the same time it may be a bigger favor to themselves, as this could be much better for them later on … think that they will feel that they will be doing you a big favor as well…" her eyes were flooded with tears and reflected the sunlight in an amazing way. Dimitri suddenly felt the tears in his eyes as well and felt for one more time the need to embrace her; he did, even though the iron bars of the mansion door were between them. Lauren embraced him as well and he felt her warmth and caress of her body. He was immersed in a deep ocean of feelings and he could feel that this moment was significant for the rest of his life. He again felt that Lauren harbored feelings for him.

He was convinced that she was right, as most of the people in the neighborhood lived there for many years. It could be in their best interest for Mr. Paulmerts not to go bankrupt. Dimitri spent a few more minutes with Lauren, asking her about her future, but Lauren was so distressed that she asked him to postpone the conversation for later, perhaps for Christmas. She left him after looking deep into his eyes; an amazing gaze that certainly penetrated his eyes; trying to seal his promise that he would help out the family in these very critical moments. Dimitri starred at his favorite pair of eyes wordlessly till she turned to enter the impressive door of the Paulmerts' residence.

Extra rent collected, the bell tolls and the return.

Dimitri turned around to take the return path to his home, full of thoughts and concerns for one more time. As soon as he turned around the corner he came face-to-face and bumped into a very old blind lady. She sensed that he was a young man, from his pace and breathes. She asked him for help, but not for money, as she wanted to go back to her home. Dimitri didn't have any money in his pocket, but was happy to help her.

Old lady: "Young man, I am so thankful that you lend me your eyes as I need to return to my home."

Dimitri detected a foreign accent since her English wasn't very good, but he was emotionally charged from the meeting with Lauren and he did not want to ask many questions. He escorted the lady back to the address that she had asked for and immediately realized that she was one of the numerous Paulmerts' tenants. Suddenly he found the courage and asked her how she became blind and the lady explained to him that during the war she lost her parents while she was still a baby; it was a day when her home was bombarded. Later her relatives found her between the ruins nearly burnt by the sun, since she was a baby and was unable to turn away from the sunlight. Her burns healed; however, she lost her vision. A few years later she lost her only brother and some of her other relatives, so she ended up a beggar for the rest of her life. She came to America years after the war was over with the help of the Red Cross. However, things did not work out for her at a factory where she had to answer phone calls and she became a beggar again. She ended up living at one of the Paulmerts' property, as a guest of a family that offered her a tiny room in the basement. For her, the absence of pure ample light in the basement was not an issue. She became a great help to the family, as she shared her money with them but most importantly she entertained their own blind and handicapped relative with daily long conversations.

Dimitri returned to his home and immediately felt the need to talk to his grandfather. It had been a long time since they talked the way they did prior to his college years. Dimitri's interest in university and his determination to over perform were unprecedented in the Giovas household. He was constantly busy. Between his work and meetings with Joe and Giovanni, there were very few moments to spare for the family. Besides that, he had to help his little cousin with his school homework. He simply did not have the time to immerse himself in the philosophical conversations he used to have with his grandpa. Plus, his grandpa had returned to work as a cashier at the local diner that belonged to his cousin. There was always a need for an extra pair of hands there as well as extra savings.

The next time they coincided at home he talked to him about the problems that Mr. Paulmerts had. His grandpa was not that keen about discussing them. Dimitri sensed that his grandpa always underestimated the problems that wealthy people like the Paulmerts possibly had. When Dimitri explained to him that the Paulmerts' problems might affect the community his grandpa was still not motivated to talk about them. In the most important moment when Dimitri was about to explain what he was about to do,

Grandpa left the room to take his cousin's phone call. He did not return, as he was apparently needed at the diner. Dimitri did not like the idea that his grandpa felt uneasy. He wanted to talk to his grandpa about what he was about to do and once he decided to do so, he spent too much time getting to the point that time ran out. He had to act immediately though, as he would have to face Mr. Fein and the tenants the following day. He thought of following his grandpa, but sensed that it would not be a productive discussion. He knew that he could not really explain the need to help someone as wealthy as Mr. Paulmerts and partner up with Mr. Fein. During that long night, he also wondered if things were as hard for Mr. Paulmerts as Lauren portrayed them to be. "Why wouldn't Mr. Paulmerts talk to his tenants and explain the situation himself? Or perhaps he was afraid of the impact that this would have on his status?" He was not sure, but he also thought for a second that Mr. Paulmerts could just ask to borrow from them and not impose another significant raise. "And what about his rich relatives or Manhattan friends?" But maybe that was unrealistic for someone with such a social status. There were many questions that Dimitri could not find the answers to. Before falling asleep he thought about the old blind lady with the accent.

The morning came and Mr. Paulmerts was with Mr. Fein in the office. Dimitri sensed the severity of their conversation and did not dare to interrupt. Minutes later Mr. Fein came out and spotted Dimitri. He immediately told him to get ready. Dimitri stood up and waited till Mr. Fein got ready to open the door.

Mr. F: "Well, well, I hope you are ready, just follow me." And exited without any hesitation out onto the street. Dimitri followed him although he wanted to greet Mr. Paulmert who was still in the office.

"Where are we supposed to go now?" he asked Mr. Fein as he exited the office.

Mr. F: "Well, the collection should start now and I will show you how to do it."

D: "I thought I could do it alone."

Mr. F: "You really think you can do this on your own?"

D: "Of course I can."

Mr. F: "Well then here is the list, just grab your pen and mark half of the names — I will do the rest with my crew. Quickly, they are all waiting for me at Ryan's."

D: "I cannot write and walk fast to follow you, wait in the office with me it will only take ten minutes."

Mr. F: "Neither I nor you have the time, just follow me and do this. It is easier than you think take these two pages and I'll take the other two."

D: "I beg your pardon, but I can do all of them and you do not have to get involved, at least in my neighborhood."

Mr. F: "As far as I know, you own neither a neighborhood nor a house so keep walking and stop wasting my time".

D: "You know what I mean, Sir and you can spare the nasty comments," he said while running after Mr. Fein.

Mr. F: "Listen kid, I do not need your help and I can do it on my own. I gave you a choice to do half of them and I am not here to negotiate with you. Either do what I tell you or I can send you to hell at once."

Dimitri looked him in his eyes and pictured how Mr. Fein's crew would be more than happy to harass him once their boss dictated it. He followed him silently, while reading the two pages of the households he would have to visit. At the same time he thought about the ones he wouldn't be able to visit and they would have the unpleasant surprise of seeing Mr. Fein's face.

By the time he finished going through the pages, Mr. Fein was already outside Ryan's residence. His crew was waiting for his arrival, and as soon as Mr. Fein joined them they offered him a fudge-glazed donut. Somehow Mrs. Ryan sensed that something was wrong when she opened the door. Soon after, Mr. Ryan came out looking sharp in his tidy, well-ironed uniform. His job was to deliver appliances from a big department store to households in the city. Mr. Ryan was home since he had an afternoon shift. Out of all the tenants, he was one of the few who was on relatively good terms with Mr. Fein. His daughter and wife also worked and they could easily afford the rent. Mr. Fein got directly to the point, telling them that he would require an extra third in rent for that and the following month. He explained that there was an urgent need and no other way around it. Besides if he did not pay, Mr. Paulmerts would be forced to sell the property and kick the family out since there was no proper lease. Mr. Ryan who had come from Ireland five years ago, did not care about the formalities of a lease, but at that point he regretted it. His face became sad and he asked for some time to think about it. Mr. Fein immediately moved closer to him and wiped his hands on his white spotless shirt, smearing the fudge that was on his fingers. He moved with an extreme comfort having his usual sarcastic look and delivered a friendly but sardonic smile together with some ironic comments about their friendship and Mr. Ryan's greatness which always ensured the best for his family. He reminded him that his extended family was himself and Mr. Paulmerts and that the following morning "Shorty" would be there for the collection. Absolutely the criminal-like looks of "Shorty" and gaze were scary and Mr. Ryan knew that "Shorty" wouldn't leave his daughter untouched either. He smiled and agreed to give them what they needed. Dimitri was so disgusted by the whole scene as he looked at the fudge from the donut on the perfectly clean and ironed shirt of Mr. Ryan. He knew that Mr. Ryan was not rich, but he always looked sharp and classy. He was the kind of person that only had two shirts and Mrs. Ryan timed the spotless appearance of her husband every day so he would not have any problems loosing his job, as he always had to show up at the department store spotless. Dimitri was very angry, but thought that this was the least of the terrible things that could happen between Mr. Fein and the tenants, since Mr. Ryan was the most cooperative and friendly person in the neighborhood. However, he instantly recalled Lauren's distress and desperation and the promise he made to help her father. He was not just in love with Lauren, but also appreciated Mr. Paulmerts influence in his life so far. He really wanted to help, but perhaps not by using Mr. Fein's techniques.

He left the scene and brainstormed about an efficient way to collect the extra money. The Garcias family and Mrs. Poulakos were on his list, "Thank God!" he whispered to himself. How could he ever get more from these people? He thought for a second and promised to himself to take this as a challenge. Perhaps an academic or philosophical project where two sides have to remain happy; a solution that this was up to the manager of the project, obviously himself. Dimitri kept walking and was so deep in thought that he lost his direction. Several times he closed his eyes and did not care what way to follow. He thought about going to the Garcias first, since that was the biggest challenge. He did not have unlimited time to complete the collection, but he thought for a second that he should relax and do it slowly.

Dimitri never stopped thinking about his challenge, but he had faith that God would help him do the right thing. He never had the chance to talk to his grandfather about the challenge, but he prayed a lot instead; a long prayer, but a very honest one. Dimitri felt again the need to pray and started walking to the Garcias with his lips repeating the same prayer. On his way to the Garcias, he passed by Mr. Martini's house and decided to stop by. He knocked on the door and explained to his wife that it was imperative for their future and in their best interest to let him collect the extra amount requested by Mr. Paulmerts. Mrs. Martini told him that this was not going to be easy since they were never able to save anything extra. Dimitri did not argue too much and pointed out to her porcelain statuette, stating it would get her amount needed at the pawnshop and would keep everyone happy. Dimitri always enjoyed the trust of the Martini family and left with a small bag with the Venetian statuette wrapped in a thick layer of paper. After that he stopped at the Periklidis family and got the extra cash after half an hour of arguments and rhetorical declarations. The Periklidis family had been saving money to bring more relatives from Greece to America so they had some extra savings but gave them to Dimitri since they adored him and believed that he had a good reason. The same was the case at the Pearlman's, where Dimitri was able to extract a golden bracelet from Mrs. Pearlman. But his heart was broken in pieces, as he knew that this could have been used to send more clothes and food to their son, a friend of his from high school who was a student in California and had not been back to see his parents during all these years, since he could not afford the trip. He knew that his old high school friend had to share a room at a family's friend house with two other students and had no scholarship. His life was tough, full of struggle and finishing college would make a difference for him and his family.

A few minutes later, he was at the Garcias' house. The children were playing in the street; he entered the tiny courtyard where he witnessed once Mr. Fein torture Mr. Garcia. He entered the house and immediately was welcomed by everyone with laughter and warm hugs. Dimitri alleviated a lot of trouble and pain from the past. He was always welcome and a dear family friend. The Garcias did not have to deal with Mr. Fein and Dimitri's plan had always worked out well for them. They offered him food and some baked goods and Dimitri had to swallow hard for a moment. He explained the situation to them in a very direct way and was particularly repetitive. Mr. Garcia knew that he was not lying and thought that perhaps helping Mr. Paulmerts at this point was also helping themselves and Dimitri. Mr. Garcia felt horrible as he realized that he cannot help since he did not have any savings. Dimitri pointed to some of the crafts that were on the table, which the family had brought with them from their hometown in Mexico. Tears welled up in Mrs. Garcias' eyes when she explained that their price was not significant, but their sentimental value to the family was priceless. Dimitri reiterated that they had to come up with 20 to 30% more one way or another and had no choice but to sell something from their belongings to the pawn shop to generate some extra cash. The Garcias resisted the idea of selling all these figurines and crafts that had so many symbolisms and memories. Dimitri persisted and asked them to reconsider, as he was convinced that at some point the Garcias had to help out as well just like the other families did. Mr. Garcia asked Dimitri if they could have more time to find a solution; and then he turned to ask his wife about some new ideas. His wife talked to him in Spanish, which sparked a conversation that Dimitri could not understand. Dimitri asked them to discuss the matter with him in English. The Garcias told him yes, but five seconds later switched back to Spanish. Dimitri asked them once again and Mr. Garcia told him "of course" but ten seconds later he spoke Spanish and Dimitri started scratching his head. He thought that as the manager of this project he didn't think of the efficiency factor, if there could ever be such a factor with a big family such as the Garcias. Frustrated he begged them again to stop the conversation in Spanish and Mr. Garcia explained that his wife did not understand the relationship between her aunt and her cousin. Dimitri asked what this had to do with his request, and Mr. Garcia pointed out that they have to discuss this because it was important to figure out the sentimental value of the artifacts that they had to sell to the pawnbroker since they wanted to keep the most important ones. Dimitri was definitely stressed and in despair he begged them that they had to hurry and that at some point they would be able to get the artifacts back from the pawnbroker. But the Garcias started arguing in Spanish again. Dimitri was losing his patience, as it seemed like a silly discussion to him. The Garcias continued and Dimitri kept scratching his head and started sweating from the frustration and ran his hands over his face. At some point he burst and screamed, "Please, understand the severity of the situation and do something instead of being so inconsiderate; please do not ignore me, I have to run!" Mrs. Garcia became angry about the erratic behavior of the young man and berated to him in Spanish, which irritated Dimitri even more. He then screamed at them, "Come on people, can you please be considerate and do something at this point and at once! Can you just give me these ... stupid pieces and let me get out of here. Don't be so insensitive. Please, I have helped you so much in the past and you have to remember this! Please do something good at once!" Mrs. Garcia could not understand why he was yelling at them and was so hurt that she started crying and left the room. Mr. Garcia looked very sad, obviously perplexed with Dimitri's last sentence and reluctantly pointed to the crafts and told Dimitri to take one. Dimitri grabbed three of them and put them in the bag that he got from Mrs. Martini and turned to leave. While he was leaving he saw Mr. Garcia crying like a little child, holding his head and yielding to immature age gestures for a man his age. Dimitri left as quickly as he could, as he could not stand his crying and on the way out saw three of the Garcia children that he had not previously noticed. They were watching the scene and they all had tears in their eyes.

Dimitri started running; he ran fast, as fast as he could. He had a feeling that he lost a lot of time. For some reason he felt late. Each visit took him longer than he had anticipated; he had spent more time than his original calculations ... "calculations" he thought for a second and paused... However, he was still confident that what he was doing was for the best of everyone. For Mr. Paulmerts of course, who needed the extra money, for him as well as a devoted employee but even for the Garcias in the very end. "Of course for them as well" he thought! He was convinced that they would rather have Mr. Paulmerts as a landlord. Dimitri of course did not forget that this was also for the promise he gave Lauren. He felt proud that he eventually accomplished his mission, and would enjoy Lauren's admiration in the future, since he was even successful at extracting more from the Garcias. His pace got faster and faster again as these thoughts excited him more and more. His pace was faster and the thoughts as well, they passed back and forth and got filtered again and again: his mission: The belongings. The money. Mr. Paulmerts and Lauren. But Mr. Fein? He could see Lauren treating him as a hero and as the savior of her Dad's crisis. That thought and the imaginary smile on Lauren's face made him more and more excited. His pace got faster and his mood better. He felt good again and the air now was like the sweet air of freedom; he was filled with happiness and confidence that his project would have the best outcome. "What an achievement," he thought repetitively. He again felt extremely proud, but something interrupted his thoughts and pace at once. The bells! The Bells! The BELLS! What a sound! Wow! He was just a block away and almost across the street from the church that he used to go to every Sunday. The bells tolled continuously and very loud but with such an unusual sound. Loud! So loud; without a single break; in a very unusual tempo. One toll after another! Non-stop! Why? He wondered... what kind of sound was that and why? He had never heard them ring like this before. One toll after the other, constant and loud, announcing something special; perhaps joyful? What was going on? He was impressed by the sound of the bells. Dong, dong, dong , dong, dong, dong, dong,.... So loud and repetitive, penetrating his ears, his heart and soul. His pace became slower until he stopped at the corner and diagonally across from the church. He could not move anymore, he looked high at the bells. "What an impressive sound!" he thought. He saw people running towards the church. He asked, "What is going on?" An old lady with a shawl covering her head replied, "They brought the remains of the Saint for us. They will stay here from now on. They just arrived at the church". So he thought that the bells were a joyful invitation for the parishioners to go and welcome and observe that important ritual. Indeed this was very important for the devoted Christians in his parish.

"That is why I never heard this impressive sound of the bells," he thought. Now he knew that it was something very special and the bell sounded different and festive. Dimitri took a deep breath and wondered why this was so significant to the church? He thought he should go inside and find out, so he got ready to proceed. He took a slow step but suddenly felt frozen. He could not move ahead. He felt the heavy loud sound of the bell again and had no idea what was going on deep inside him. He took a few slow steps ahead and stopped again. He looked at the bag with the objects that he had gathered so far. He took a good look inside and then looked at the deep blue sky. It was a bright day. He tried to take another step, but stopped again. He put his hand in his pocket where the extra dollar bills were.

Suddenly he turned his head left and saw the back of a man who was sitting on the top of the steps leading to the entrance of a basement. He was wearing

a hat, but Dimitri could see his dark sun burnt skin and part of his face from behind. The man tilted his head and body forward. He looked like he could be a relative of the Garcias. Dimitri was still frozen by the sound of the bells and in a way he could not understand. They were not ringing anymore but the memory was potent and had changed his pace and mood. As he was unable to move he took another look at the man on his left. The man tried with a lot of effort to take off one of his shoes. Slowly and carefully he took off his sock. Dimitri saw that his foot was seriously inflamed and covered in dark dried-out blood. He could not clearly see the wounds but his foot was seriously hurt. He felt horrible and took another look at the wounded foot. He saw that his blouse had the logo of a moving company on the back. "Hm... that explains it", Dimitri thought for a second. Perhaps, he got hurt while he was moving something heavy. He felt bad for him, but immediately realized that it was getting late. He felt that he should hurry and proceed fast to cover as many households as he could. Then he thought that he should take a break, as he was curious to see how much money the pawnbroker would give him for all the things he had collected. He started moving towards the pawn-shop, but he still felt sorry and deep inside him a pain for the condition of his fellow man. He could not easily erase the wounded foot from his mind, so he started walking without being focused. His gaze, was the gaze of an absent-minded person. Suddenly someone elbowing him interrupted his abstract gaze. He turned around and saw the old blind lady who was trying to make her way in the opposite direction; the exact opposite from the one that Dimitri had chosen. She touched the walls of the houses with one hand and held the cane with the other. Dimitri was embarrassed that he was careless and absent minded enough not to see her, so he profusely apologized. However, instead of seeing her face become angry or show some pain, she gave him a big wide smile. The old lady had recognized his voice. She knew at once that he was the young man who had escorted her to her home a few days ago. "Oh young man, I remember you! You gave me your "light" the other day! You "gave" me your eyes remember? And I could see my way with your eyes. I asked you questions about what you see here and there, remember?" the old blind lady said.
Dimitri recognized her and her unique voice, the English accent, but tried to tell her that she was wrong. The old lady insisted and told him that he had

other things on his mind at that time, as his replies to her were "mechanical". She remembered that well and told him details about many things, but sensed that his answers were abstract, as he was in deep thoughts. Dimitri wondered for a second if she was right? Of course he had Lauren on his mind and since he did not have the time to argue with the old lady he agreed, so to continue his way. He agreed with a dry "right" and was ready to continue and leave. The old lady stopped and asked him, "Is something tantalizing your soul young man? Is there something I can do or help in any way?" Dimitri was dumbfounded and did not know what to say. He was perplexed and didn't know how a blind old lady could be of any help and then he saw that besides the cane she was holding a few coins in her hand. They were probably what she had gathered from a whole day of begging out in the streets. He thought, she was naïve to think that her few coins could make a difference. How could they really make a difference? And what else could she ever offer? Could this be amusing? He thanked her for her offer and reiterated that she should not worry about it and tried to proceed on his way. As he stepped away he remembered that the old lady was also hosted by one of Mr. Paulmerts' tenants. He was perplexed again. He could not leave; he turned back to the old lady and looked at her one more time. The old lady sensed it and told him, "I can only help by talking to you, not that I am wise, but talking may help you". Dimitri took a step closer to her and thanked her again but told her that he had to go. At that moment he remembered her story about how she lost not only her sight but also her beloved relatives. His steps became heavy again. The wounded foot flashed back into his mind and the bells … oh the bells rang so loud inside him again and again. He was not moving and looked at his bag again. He felt the dollar bills into his pocket again. He stepped ahead again with heavy steps. His mind could not think, he had never felt this way before. Something was suffocating him and then he fell into a deep silence. The next step was care-less enough and he tripped on a pothole and fell down with his nose touching the ground. The bag with the collected artifacts rolled away from him to the sidewalk. He felt a sharp pain. Suddenly he heard a voice, "Did you hurt yourself young man?" and distracted him from the pain, which disappeared at once, since he was so concerned about the objects in the bag. He rushed to stand up and examine them one by one. He had them all and they were intact. "THANK GOD!" He yelled at once and again put his hand in his pocket to make sure the money was still there. He placed everything back in the bag and then took a good look at his hands. The right one hurt from his attempt not to hit his head on the curb. He took another good look at his palms. He started starring at them over and over again. He lifted them up in the sky. He put them on to his face. Now his face was covered with his hands and his eyes which saw the old blind lady, the dark skin blended with the dried blood of the moving company worker and heard the bells once again. He realized that the old blind lady had offered him help instead of begging him for a penny. He realized that the middle-aged immigrant mover probably had many children waiting for the daily bread. He realized that his foot was in a condition that would make his working life miserable if not impossible. He realized that his dark sun burnt face was full of grace, goodness and not pain. His face was the face of a fighter. He realized that he went in the opposite direction his fellow Greek immigrants were heading to, when they heard the bells. He realized that a minute ago he was yelling at the Garcias, simple people, honest and poor who never committed any crime other than being very poor. He realized that he was carrying the precious belongings of his fellow men. He realized that he never gave a penny to the blind old lady. He looked at his hands again. They were empty, but his pockets were full. He turned back and started moving toward the old lady. She was busy talking to someone. Dimitri was reluctant to interrupt her conversation and was filled with unprecedented embarrassment. He ran back to the steps where the wounded mover sat but he was not there anymore. He looked for him left and right, but could not find him. His soul was filled with anxiety and all of a sudden he heard the bells ring again and again and again, deep in his mind. He started running to the Garcias' house direction. He ran fast and with all his force. He ran so fast that once the Garcias children who were playing outside the steps saw him, started shouting; their facial expression changed and they were rather scared. The three year old started crying while Dimitri rushed to knock on the door and took the Garcias' crafts out of his bag. When the door opened he handed them to a dumbfounded Senior Garcias while asking him for forgiveness. Mr. Garcia's round and kind face was filled with an immediate happiness and care for the young man in front of him. Dimitri's eyes welled up in tears and the Garcias tried to get him to come inside and treat him to some sweet fried dough that Mrs. Garcias had prepared. Dimitri thanked them, but he told them that he had to finish his work. He immediately ran to the rest of the houses, returning everything he had acquired from all of them.

Once he had returned the last penny, he was relieved and a brave and happy feeling overfilled his heart and soul. But now he was back in the streets alone and without anything to offer to his employer and the Paulmerts who had high hopes and expectations from him. But he was not depressed, as his happiness overtook his feelings of failure to collect what he was supposed to and meet the business expectations. He immediately ran to the office, but he did not see Mr. Fein. He sat down and composed a letter of resignation stating that he was unable to fulfill his duties and asking for understanding and forgiveness. He left the office knowing that this would be good news to Mr. Fein. He was still very satisfied despite the fact that he could imagine how much Lauren would be disappointed by him. He did not even want to think about how he could ever face her again, but he thought that at some point it would become imperative to do so. However, she was away at school, so it would not happen any time soon. He went home and composed a letter explaining his inability to fulfill his mission. The next day he talked to his grandpa who did not say much, but was full of pride for his grandson. He was afraid that Lauren would never respond to his letters anymore. He started looking for another job, as he knew that there was no way he could work for Mr. Paulmerts again especially after what had happened. He only needed six months till the end of college and was willing to start any job after Christmas vacation. He was looking so forward to Christmas vacation. He wanted so much to talk to Lauren in person and explain his weakness to her.

A couple days later Mr. Fein met Dimitri on the street, and cursed him and berated him with a lot of derogatory comments. He heard from the neighbors that Mr. Fein had a hard time collecting the extra money and that he was unsuccessful as well. Some of the tenants who trusted the police and had good immigration papers threatened that they would get the police involved. However, the neighborhood was still under a serious threat, given that the Paulmerts could sell their houses. Nobody knew what would happen at the end. They also knew that as soon as Christmas and New Year's festivities were over, Mr. Fein would knock on their doors again.

It was a few days before Christmas when Dimitri sensed that Lauren was back from Brown. He spent at least half an hour a day outside her home to see if he could find a chance to talk to her. He did not want to ring the bell, as he did not want to encounter anyone else, especially Mr. Paulmerts. He did not know how an encounter with him would be in the future. Dimitri had written him two letters apologizing and explaining why he quit his job. But he did not receive a response. Of course, he also had no idea if Mr. Paulmerts ever read the letters. Dimitri wrote seven letters to Lauren and got no response. He did not know what to conclude from her silence, other than disappointment. He was used to sparse communication all these years. He counted how many letters he had written to her since the time she gave him her address. Sixty-eight letters, and how many did he receive? Only seven. Well, it was just two days before Christmas and he realized that the best way to meet her was to wait for her outside the social club where she would probably spend her free time. Indeed, he dressed the best he could and went to the lobby of the club requesting to see her. "Does Ms. Paulmerts expect you gentleman?" the manager at the lobby asked. "Of course," Dimitri replied, realizing that he was lying, perhaps for the very first time in his life. He immediately felt horrible and since he was not a great actor, the manager noticed it and sent someone to ask her to verify if she really was expecting him. Dimitri waited in the lobby, shy and feeling guilty trying to find the proper excuse to justify why he had to lie. He did something he always detested. "Well," he thought for a moment, "I wrote her all these letters, therefore she should expect that I would make every effort to talk to her." That idea comforted him enough to find the courage to look into her eyes, once she appeared in front of him.

Twelve minutes later Lauren walked into the lobby and once she saw Dimitri sitting down she immediately waved at him to stay where he was. She joined him and sat next to him at the lobby's sofa and asked, "Why are you here?" D: "I wanted to explain to you how I feel and what happened," he replied. L: "You don't have to, I know all about it from your letters. In fact, there were far more details than I needed to know; and about some bells and some colored wounded guy and a beggar and … what else would you really want to tell me?" D: "I think you know how much I adore you and long for your friendship, Lauren."

L: "Why don't you stop right here Dimitri. There is no need to say more. I asked once for your help and precisely for you to help my family. I trusted you!" with a louder voice she continued, "How can you possibly forget that I was in despair and I needed you to live up to the expectations we all had of you! You have the guts to tell me that some strange feeling and some random stranger and your fantasies and all this naïve romanticism that you evoke in all your letters can explain why you chose not to help my father? The one who really believed in you? The one who granted you whatever you wished for? My father did not have to do this, right? What kind of silly arguments do you want to lay out here? I was in tears that day and I never trusted anyone out there, in that silly neighborhood as much as I trusted you."

Dimitri's eyes were wide open proclaiming that her last comment on his fellow men disturbed him a bit and he felt that her comment was totally unnecessary.

"Oh, I know how you feel about all these people; don't we offer them reasonable housing and jobs and a life and whatever else? You think that we owe them on top of all that? You know Dimitri they would not be there if they did not like it and don't get me started."

Dimitri : "Lauren you may be wrong here, everyone is grateful and nobody complains about what they have and what they don't have, it is certainly not the way you think and …".

Lauren interrupted him at this point, "Listen, I am not here to analyze this with you at this moment and I know that you understand them better than me because you are one of them," Dimitri's eyes opened wide again, "but I am here to tell you that I do not want to discuss what happened with you anymore and to tell you again how disappointed I am with you and all your unappreciative friends. I trusted you and you betrayed my father." Dimitri interrupted her in a rather intense way, "Lauren it is not what you think and let me …"

"I do not want any explanation, please leave me alone and stop pretending that you understand us and our situation," Lauren said with a higher intensity in her voice.

Dimitri realized that the club manager noticed their heated conversation. He did not know how to react as he was out of his comfort zone and unsure of what to do; continue arguing or leave at once. His flame for Lauren was still intense and he found her fascinating even when she argued with him. He smiled for a second and took a deep breath.

"Lauren, please understand that you have the most special place in my heart and I would do anything to always be next to you...with you... stand by you! I am sure you were able to deduce that from all my letters ... and from my past acts. I want to believe that I understand you more than you can imagine. Think if the opposite were true, if for example you did not understand people who are like me; or like 'them'."

Lauren stood up, revealing that she was insulted and told Dimitri, "Certainly, I am not one of them and you better pray that my Dad can survive this crisis," she turned her back to Dimitri and left towards the dining halls.

Dimitri stood up and tried following her, "Lauren please don't do this, please let me finish and listen to me."

At the same time the lobby manager who followed what was going on, approached and told Dimitri to leave the club at once. Dimitri looked at him, deep into his eyes and thanked him for looking after Lauren. He lowered his eyes and turned towards the door. He sensed the undesired tears in his eyes and knew that the last few days contributed to the end of his "platonic" relationship with Lauren.

He walked back to the subway station with heavy steps and took the train back to his neighborhood. He was devastated, as he could not believe he ended up in such a fight with the love of his life. He wondered while in the subway, if what he did for his neighborhood was worth it. He ended up helping the neighborhood, but at the very end he ruined all his possibilities with Lauren and possibly alienated himself completely from her. After all, he only wanted this last job to get him closer to Lauren. "How can I possibly reverse this misfortune?" was the only thing on his mind for the rest of the evening. He could not find a solution, but felt and knew that his love for Lauren was still the prime reason for his existence. His strong feelings neither faded nor were tamed. Even over the following few days when Joe and Giovanni tried to calm him down, he could not forget what had happened. Dimitri's pain was not easy to relieve.

Giovanni tried hard to convince him to stay focused on his last semester and on his next step, either getting a job or going to graduate school, which would give him the wings to fly away from his neighborhood, forget about everything and start a new life. Dimitri was still sad and could not think about those options. Joe tried to distract him and offer him relief; he worked hard and within his family's contacts Joe secured him a job offer at a retail store that belonged to one of his wealthy merchant uncle, who offered Dimitri a position the day after New Years. He thought that the news about a new job would relieve his pain. But Dimitri's spirits were still very low. Joe was really upset that Dimitri's mood did not change, so he went together with Giovanni to see him the day after he had told him about the offer.

"Dimitri, do not be so stubborn about Lauren and be happy that your family and friends still care about you. You were never close to her and it was never realistic to think that she could ever be yours," Joe said.

D: "Well, you never were optimistic about it, but it is OK you do not have to understand me."

J: "Understand what? Perhaps you are the one who does not understand. I am sorry my friend, but you could have never been her boyfriend. How could you be so blind? Can't you see that you both are two different kinds of people! From two different worlds! Do you really think that her family would ever accept you? Don't you see that the Paulmerts treat you and your people as second-class citizens? You can never be one of them, wake up!"

D: "Stop this Joe! Please!"

J: "Stop? What do you mean? I say these things because I care about you and someone here has to open your eyes! I know that love is blind, but once you decide to open your eyes you can see the truth. For people like them you and your people, Giovanni and I are like slaves. Don't you see how they treat the tenants? You are not that "upper class" or "white" enough for them, my friend. And it is not just you, all of us here are "colored" in their eyes don't you understand?"

D: "Oh come on, you are exaggerating again!"

J: "I don't think so and I know the day will come when we won't be considered like this anymore. May be the next generation will bring another perspective, but at this point you are banging your head against the wall. Look at them! They still have servants in their home and they spend too much money and then they complain that they don't have enough? What kind of people live like them nowadays?"

D: "Joe, I get your point, but Lauren is not like them. She has a sensitive side and she is far better than the average person in her social class."

J: "That is not good enough, my friend. She could have been hanging out with all the kids in the neighborhood. You should not wait until she considers you her equal. Or better yet, … until they consider their servants equals. Please move on with your life and accept the offer from my uncle. You need the money and you should not have Mr. Fein laughing at you by being unemployed and struggling. My uncle doesn't pay as much as Mr. Paulmerts, since he believes he offers more than just money. Take it as an apprenticeship, since he will open your eyes to the real world and teach you how to run a business. You will gain a lot from it and it will be the best investment no matter what career you follow later in life."
Dimitri appreciated this great offer and Joe's friendship; both of his friends constantly offered him that gift, but he was simply not in the mood for further discussion. He stood up and left them after hugging them and saying good night.

Desperate Love but deep, no luck but water, open eyes and geniuses.

Dimitri was on his way home and grateful for being healthy and surrounded by good friends. His grandfather learned about what had happened and sensed that Dimitri was in distress, but never had the time to talk to him. The holiday season kept him busy at the diner and he worked more than usual. So the two hardly overlapped at home. A couple of times both tried to initiate a discussion but they could never reach any depth, as one or the other was on his way out. Besides, grandpa Giovas wanted to wait till his grandson was ready to talk about it. The fact that Dimitri had no job was another hurdle for him to start a conversation.
That night, Dimitri entered his house and glanced at the living room where some family members were either resting or reading. He went upstairs to look for his grandfather but did not find him. He ended up in his room playing the guitar and writing poems. He could not finish one that night, even though he started seven of them. He left them all unfinished and kept starring at Lauren's picture. His love for Lauren had never been so desperate. He spent the following day studying and solving challenging problems for his upcoming classes but took a break every twenty minutes to think about

his future path to Lauren. She was clearly angry with him and felt that he didn't explain himself very well during their last encounter. Besides, he had always been nervous in front of her. His feelings always hindered his ease to talk and his brain always froze upon an encounter with her. He thought for a moment that he should write another letter to her. He started one but he ripped it apart. Then he went through his poem collection. All the love poems that he wrote for her were in front of him. He thought that he should pick out the best for this circumstance and send it to her. He did not know though, which one was the best. He found every single one mediocre and at the end he thought it was a bad idea to send her a poem from the past. He was devastated and was not sure if it was a good idea to go to her place and talk to her again, or go to the social club in Manhattan.

Since he could not decide on the best way to approach Lauren, he thought that he should not be embarrassed anymore and go talk about it with his grandfather. Over the last four years, he had never asked him for any type of advice regarding Lauren. He decided the best way would be to start a general conversation with him, and see what his grandpa would advise him later about his desperate love. When he heard his steps in the house he got excited and waited for him to go to his private room in the basement where he always meditated. Finally this happened and Dimitri went to the basement to talk to him. His grandfather had turned on the radio and was listening to a classical music concert. He was the only other person in their home who listened with passion to classical music, as everyone else listened to Greek music or rock n roll depending on their age. Dimitri recognized the piece, which was by his favorite composer Beethoven.

"Ah great," he said. "Great piece of music papou!"

"Like every single one he composed," his grandpa replied. "This one changed my life when I first heard it. You know I could not believe that I was on this planet for so many years without knowing this piece of music, hm … so many years and I had never heard this."

D: "Really? How old were you at that time?"

G: "Does it matter? But you know this happens to many people when they listen to a masterpiece like this for the very first time. Others had this feeling with a Bach fugue or Dvorak's cello concerto, a piano composition by Chopin, or a masterpiece by Tchaikovsky, or Rachmaninov, just to name a few. But, indeed, there is not a single piece by Beethoven that is not a masterpiece."

D: "Indeed, every one of his 135 opus pieces."

G: "Well, more than that."

D: "How come? What do you mean?"

G: "Well, many of his works are unlisted in the opus classification. But you are not here to discuss this with me son. What is on your mind?"

D: "Nothing, but oh … you know, … need to decide some major things in life as you know."

G: "Well, I hope you decided to continue your studies?"

D: "Either that or get a great job."

G: "Well, it would be better for you to continue to more advanced studies, don't you think so? Stay longer in academia son. Don't give up, you know that you are talented and your grades are superb. If you start applying for a scholarship now for graduate school, I bet my life that you will get at least ten offers."

D: "Always overestimating me."

G: "Always humble and that's OK, but I hope you will do the right thing."

D: "I hope so too and since I cannot move up the ladder in Paulmerts' workforce anymore, I may as well study longer."

G: "Well, there is nothing great about their workforce, son, especially since you can study to become a great engineer. I don't think they will hire you to run their factory or to build more homes for them or implement modern technologies to their facility and other engineering projects."

D: "Why do you say that? They might."

G: "Well, after what happened? Not really … but hey look, I am happy since you deserve something better than what they could ever offer you. Do not worry, just get out of here and conquer your own world. Their world is small and shrinking. Start your own career. As you know, I heard about their troubles and your troubles and I would not waste another minute worrying about it. Shshhh listen to me! Everything happens for the best!"

D: "I know how you think, but nothing is 'best' between me and Lauren now."

G: "If you had chosen to listen to me, you would have understood that your chances were always slim and I never discussed this in detail with you, since

I wanted you to see that with your own very eyes. They do not belong here. The fact that they happen to live on this side of the river, son, tricked you. But they were never close to this place. They are like everyone else on the other side young man."

D: "I know your theory, but we are all part of the same world."

G: "Oh the world … yes the world! You see son, the world is composed of approximately 70% water. Isn't that the same for our human body? Almost 70% water son! No matter if it is your body or the earth. You see every civilization throughout history flourished wherever there was water, my son… either on the banks of a river, or by the sea, or a lake, or the ocean. Look at all the capitals of the world. Water everywhere! Surrounded by water. You see son, the island on the other side from us, is not just on the banks of a river. It has couple a of rivers and an ocean as well. Too much water flows around it and the waters are competing to see which will wet the sides of that island, spoiling it with pride and greed. Simply, too much water. More than any other place perhaps. Every other center of civilization grew to its zenith and then its citizens spread out and built colonies. The people from this island cannot do that, as there is nowhere else to go, especially nowadays. Yes indeed it's the same world, but parts of it they tend to be more extreme and eccentric. Open your eyes to see a little further than the Paulmerts' residence. It is not the end of the world … definitely not the end of your world. There are so many other corners that will accommodate you and will replenish your thirst for knowledge, pleasure and experience. Just take the steps with open eyes."

D: "You will end up telling me like Joe, that love is blind and I need to open my eyes to see the world."

G: "I am not sure my son, what Joe had told you, but some people indeed tend to close their eyes and refuse to see things. Others keep them wide open, but choose to sleep … hm yes indeed with their eyes wide open. Others choose to dream with open eyes. Others live with their closed. There are all sorts of variations out there, but the eyes do not see. It is the brain that does and chooses what to see, not the eyes. Therefore, think hard and cultivate your intellect, besides looking at the beauty of one girl for the past seven or so years. You may see the same things over and over again, but each time they will look totally different to you after years of experience and studies.

At this point, I only hope that you will do your best in college and I do not give a damn if a preppy wealthy girl does not care about you. I also do not care that you lost your job. We can all be patient for the next five months and everyone in this house will understand that."

D: "Oh do not worry papou, Joe's uncle has offered me a job in the department store at the end of the subway. He wants to train me in business, but I am not really sure how much I should commit myself to this job. Isn't there anything for me at the diner? Or perhaps one of your Greek friends needs help?"

G: "You mean in the construction business or at the restaurants? Forget it, why don't you take Joe's offer? Is it because they are not the Paulmerts or they are not Greeks? They can't be tougher than Fein. Everyone in this house works with Greeks, but you should not be afraid to get out of your comfort zone. Do you expect to have a compatriot to pamper you for the rest of your life? Or will you go down that path only for a pair of beautiful eyes?"

D: "Not really, but I do not know them!

Grandpa : "Well you know Joe, right?

Dimitri : "Yes, but everyone here in the house tells me to ask for a job within our community."

Grandpa : "Nonsense! You should not. End of this discussion! You should not be afraid to work with the Jewish people or the Italians or anyone else.

D: "But no one else around me does so?"

Grandpa : "You better work with the Jewish people," he paused and looked at Dimitri deep in his eyes, "half of them are geniuses."

Dimitri felt that this was the end of the conversation and that he should go back to his homework. As he took a last look at his grandpa's eyes he asked, "And what about the other half?"

Grandpa looked at him with a strange enigmatic smile, took a moment to reply and said "Oh, the other half? ... simply very intelligent people."

Dimitri went back to his room and studied, but at the same time thought about his next step to reapproach Lauren. New Years Eve was around the corner and he figured that because of her family's financial trouble, she would most likely stay in town. He figured that she would most likely spend New Year's Eve with her Manhattan socialites at the social club playing cards. He did not have the guts to knock on her door or wait for her outside of the club in Manhattan. He decided to focus on his studies. After all, it was his last semester and he would have the additional work of applying for a graduate scholarship. He felt pressured to narrow down his professional career in the next six months. That was not easy and at the same time he had to work at the department store.

A few days later rumor had it that some wealthy friends of Mr. Paulmerts lent him enough money, which was instrumental for him, to escape his current crisis. Dimitri was very happy when he heard the news and felt that Lauren would eventually not be that stressed anymore.

He spent every night praying intensely that this was only a break in his communication with Lauren and in time, God would show him the way to reapproach his one and only love.

College and success.

Dimitri spent New Years Eve with his family and he joined his close friends at a local diner after midnight. The New Year was off to an intense start as Dimitri got very busy with his studies, his term papers and his work at the department store. He excelled in all of his classes and was remarkably good in math and science. His professors encouraged him to apply for graduate schools. Dimitri had no idea what Lauren's plans were after her graduation. He wished he knew so he could apply to a nearby college. Since he had no idea, he decided it would make more sense to apply to local schools. Moreover, he did not want to be far away from his family, as they always needed an extra pair of hands and income. Perhaps his grandfather could stop working now, since he was approaching his late seventies. He loved his family and he did not want to go away. Besides in the back of his mind, he always thought that Lauren might return to New York and possibly get a job at her father's business.

His job at the department store was not that difficult and gave him a good crash course on how to be street smart and operate a business. It was a great experience for him. Dimitri and his friends, Giovanni and Joe, were stellar students and all got scholarships to continue their studies. Giovanni and Joe both went on to law school as they had initially planned and Dimitri got a scholarship for a Ph.D at a local state university. He also received a graduate assistantship from better schools in the Midwest and New England, but he did not want to leave his neighborhood and family.

It was already 1963 and Dimitri was 25 years old, and almost half way through his doctorate degree. Joe was almost done with the law school and started looking for an apprenticeship primarily on the West Coast. Giovanni wanted to stay on the East Coast. On Dimitri's birthday, Joe had a surprise for him. For his "quarter of a century" birthday, he played a song that he composed with lyrics that Dimitri had written years ago. Dimitri was impressed and couldn't stop laughing, but also sincerely admired his friend's creativity. It was the first time that Giovanni and Dimitri believed that Joe should head to the west coast, and work in Hollywood, which was also his dream. They did not want to be separated, but were convinced that it was worth it for Joe to pursue his west coast dreams and a career in the entertainment industry. That day Dimitri felt great about his gift, the song, so he handed Joe a few more limericks and short poems that he had put together, during the past three years.

It was also the year that Dimitri and Lauren met again. She spent a few weeks of that summer at the Paulmerts residence. That summer Lauren had written him an unexpected letter, with the news that she had finished Brown in 1962 and had moved to Boston to work in a gallery in as a part-time curator. He wrote her back requesting a meeting with her over the summer. Apparently it was impossible for Dimitri to forget her. He tried to meet some other girls, but could not get Lauren out of his mind and that was a constant problem. They did meet for coffee at an outdoor café near the New York University campus and Lauren talked a lot about her exciting life in Boston. She still avoided commenting on many personal details other than describing her recent trips to Europe for work. Dimitri was curious to know more and when he decided to ask, Lauren told him that she had to run to another meeting and would contact him soon to arrange another coffee meeting. He felt helpless again, but waited for the next letter.

He did not hear from her in the next few weeks, so he sent a letter to her new address. Lauren wrote in early October that she was going to spend Christmas at home and that she would like to invite him to a couple of parties right before New Year's Eve. Dimitri was perplexed at the idea that he would escort Lauren to some aristocratic parties on the Upper East Side of

Manhattan. Of course he loved to go out with Lauren, but on the other hand, he did not feel like he could be a good fit for her bourgeois parties. However, as always he decided to take it on as a challenge. He was twenty-five years old after all and mature enough to handle difficult situations. Besides his intellectual side, and his thirst for art, always made him an interesting person for all kinds of conversations and he thought that this time he could handle any kind of party that she dared to invite him to.

The luck and the return

Christmas of 1963 had already passed and Dimitri was looking forward to taking a rest from his heavy duties and projects at graduate school. Work at the retail store was also busy during the holiday season, but he had off the last week of the year. Deep inside him his now ten-year-old flame had never faded and he constantly longed to see Lauren again. This time he also wanted to take the opportunity to inquire about her parents' opinion of him, especially after he quit his job at Mr. Paulmerts' agency. He had a long list of questions for Lauren and that made him feel a bit overwhelmed. He was not sure if at that point he should fully externalize his absolute devotion and deep love for her. He was still young and without substantial savings. His assistantship was enough to pay his bills and send money to Greece, but not enough to support a family. He thought that he should tell Lauren that in about two years, in 1965, he would finish his doctorate and be able to have a well-paying job and perhaps the following year he could get married. He wanted to discuss all these things with her. He was not sure if he should seek the advice of his grandfather. Both of his close friends thought that Dimitri had become a hopeless romantic again or a lunatic and had lost his sense of reality.

Lauren dropped a card in the mail, which Dimitri received on December 28. It was for a party the following day. She wanted him to escort her at a private party on the Upper East Side, where some of her friends would gather to play cards as it was the custom for them towards the end of the year.

Dimitri again waited one more time in front of the bookstore at 6pm. A new limo arrived at 6pm and Dimitri realized that was a Paulmerts' new car. An amazingly beautiful girl was inside. Dimitri lit up immediately from happiness at the thought of getting a second chance, as soon as he realized that Lauren was smiling at him. He ran to the car and was happy to see her smile at him in such a graceful way showing no signs of being mad at him. Despite that, she was twenty-four years old and incredibly beautiful. Dimitri got the sense that she was not seriously involved with anyone at that point in her life. However, he was not very sure how much she was attracted to him and what his chances were at that point. He was confident that the next few days would clarify everything.

As they approached her friends' apartment, he realized that he would feel and be more confident this time, as the dress code was casual. He was not worried about his clothes, which were more appropriate than a few years ago. He still had no fancy clothes like her friends, but he simply did not care anymore. The party started at about 7pm with drinks and food and a diffused gaiety. Everyone was young and relaxed and enjoying the libations that the host offered. It was almost 9pm and Dimitri observed that there were at least three other guys present who were really interested in Lauren. He noticed that another girl was trying to get his attention and was flirting with him in a sophisticated way; however, he was not interested at all. He only cared about Lauren. At 9:15 pm the host banged on two covers of the kettles that were filled with popcorn and caramelized nuts and announced the beginning of the card game. His brother immediately opened two boxes with cards and another box with what looked to be round plastic coins. Dimitri had no idea what they were. The host gave each of the eighteen participants the colored plastic coins and explained the face value of each colored coin. Dimitri realized that each participant got enough coins equivalent to twenty dollars. Dimitri panicked, as he did not have twenty dollars in his pocket. He only had enough money to return back to Queens by subway and get a snack on the way back. Lauren did not tell him that they will play cards for money or that they would need to bring cash; especially at a private party. Lauren understood what was going on and suggested to give him credit and settle everything later. However, deep inside him, he did not want to gamble twenty dollars, as this was the amount he would spend over several days. He felt uneasy to gamble with money and considered it foreign to his own moral code. It was not part of his world as he played cards with his grandpa, uncle or cousin for fun and never with money. But he felt he could not bail out of this game, as everyone wanted to play. He did not want to isolate himself and have everyone make fun of him. It would be another reason for Lauren's wealthy and preppy friends to make him feel unwelcome. There were a couple of men who were openly jealous of him since he was her escort and at that same time they could not understand why. They looked at him in a strange way and succeeded at making him feel like he did not belong there. Besides, Dimitri was mostly shy and felt naïve due to his innocence and lack of ease and comfort in his manner and moves. Some of the boys who were interested in Lauren were talking to him sarcastically. Dimitri sensed that Lauren picked up on it as well, but did not do anything to stop it. He was already uncomfortable enough from all that, so he did not want to invite any more criticism by not participating in the card game. He thought positive that after all, this could be an escape from all the previous conversations that he could not participate in; like walking the streets of Paris, or going to the jazz clubs in New Orleans and the fancy restaurants downtown. Mentally he had been to all these places through the numerous books he had read and the movies he had watched. But he did not know what they were really like. Every time he talked about an author, or art or anything intellectual, no one was interested in continuing. He was desperate to fit in and the cards seemed like a solution. They started at about 9:30-10 pm and played for the whole night. Dimitri was always lucky and everyone commented that it was beginner's luck. It was almost 1am and the game was still on. He was the winner of his group. He thought that it was about time to stop, but then he realized that the two top winners of the three groups had to continue together in a final round. Dimitri had almost $100 dollars in his possession, and was the winner of his group. It was obvious that everyone who was interested in Lauren was resenting him for this extra luck.

The finals were announced between him and the other winners, but Dimitri expressed his interest to return back home, as it was really late. That was impossible for him though, as everyone else thought that he wanted to leave with his earnings and was not obeying the rules of the game and the deal that they originally had. Dimitri was given no choice and played against the other winners and eventually there were three who still had money to play. A well polished and enthusiastic young man his age, who seemed nice and a greedy and arrogant Upper East Side kid, who was always trying to make sure that Dimitri knew he was an outsider; not one of them. Dimitri was very careful with his moves and rather conservative and the competition was mostly focused on the other two. He did not care too much about the cards and realized that if he played conservatively, he would be able to at least keep his initial twenty dollars. He wanted to return them to Lauren at once. They had been playing for an hour and somehow Dimitri was doing great. He was a bit ahead of the other two contestants. Both saw that he was conservative and sensed he did not care too much so they focused on how to burn the other, but not Dimitri. Finally, an hour later Dimitri was far ahead of the other two and had almost 90% of all the money from the player pool. He had almost $330 dollars and the other two players became frustrated with his luck. Finally, they both called for either doubling what they had or loosing everything. Dimitri had two aces in the final round and won. "What a relief", he thought as he could leave now. However, he sensed a strong resentment against the low-class outsider from Queens, who won all the money. Few of them congratulated him and a few minutes later they brought the pack with the 20-dollar bills for him.

Dimitri was dumbfounded. He realized that this was rather serious and explained to them that he should not take the money. Now everyone else was dumbfounded with the naivety. His words and voice sounded naïve and no one could understand him; and asked him to explain himself. He said that in his opinion playing cards is a game and he did not want to consider himself a gambler. This is what his grandfather taught him and he did not want to infect himself with money from gambling, since playing cards should only be a pastime. No one could understand his reasoning and Dimitri sensed that; again and with a very shy voice he explained to them that he did nothing to earn this money. He did not work for it or provided any service and, went ahead and distributed the round plastic coins to everyone, convincing them that they should keep their money. Some of them laughed at him, but others sensed he had an unspoiled soul and charisma they wish they had as well. Dimitri insisted and stood up to leave.

Lauren told him to his amazement that since it was late she was going to stay over at her friends' in Manhattan, and therefore had sent away the driver. Dimitri was very surprised that she never warned him about this. He looked at his watch and realized that he might miss the last train by a few minutes, as the time was approaching 3 am. Lauren asked him to stay for another drink, but Dimitri was tired and wanted to catch the subway at 3 am, otherwise he would have to wait for the 5am train, which was the first one in the morning. He asked her if he could see her tomorrow and wanted to save his energy for the next day, the day before New Years Eve. Lauren agreed and told him to wait for her at the bookstore at 6pm. Dimitri asked for his coat so he could leave. On his way out, a few of Lauren's friends asked him for his contact information as they liked his genuine character. However, his Lauren's rivals made fun of his naivety after he had left and Lauren tried to make them stop, but there was no success.

When Dimitri stepped out onto the street, he realized that he was in trouble as he had talked too long with Lauren's friends and it was too late to catch the last train to Queens. It was also very cold and he had to cross the whole city, as once again, he did not have enough money for a taxi. He felt good though about giving the money back to everyone at the party. He sensed that not all of them were wealthy and that some of them had restrictions from their parents; twenty dollars was also a lot for a middle-class kid, not only for someone from Queens. He was happy that he found the strength to return the money even though he had a long wish list he could have fulfilled with the money. He thought of the vinyl records, the movie tickets and of course, some treats for the family while freezing out in the cold. The streets were empty and icy. He crossed all the blocks to the bridge without meeting a single person. He tried to walk as fast as he could to get warm. He was tired and cold and after a few miles he felt that he could have spared some money for a taxi, but immediately the vision of his grandfather's disapproval flashed before his eyes and he again felt that he did the right thing. The thought of the few kids that were not that wealthy comforted him again. He walked alone in the cold with only taxis passing by slowly looking to pick up a fare. Several taxi drivers lowered the window and asked him where he was heading. When he told them his address in Queens, they thought he was crazy. He told three taxi drivers that he had some money, but not enough for the ride. Of course, all of them refused to drive him for a lower fee. One after the other, they left him alone shivering in the cold dark streets. More than an hour later, Dimitri arrived almost frozen at the Giovas residence and knew that his grandfather was going to wake up soon. He tip-toed so he didn't wake up anyone and went directly into a deep sleep.

The next day his younger cousins, who were noisy and very animated, were at home as they were off from school, and awakened him early. He was exhausted and started coughing hard. He thought he should get more rest and a hot cup of tea, as he wanted to be ready for Lauren at 6pm. He struggled the whole day with the cough and a heavy headache, as he was not used to staying out that late. At least Lauren had not mentioned any party so he hoped that it would be just the two of them. However, his head felt heavy and he did not feel well. He thought, "why is this happening when I have been waiting for this day for such a long time?" He was always healthy and now that he had a date he was sick. He thought again that he could have returned only half of the money to keep enough to take a taxi home. "I would have treated myself as a lord and a great chap," he thought. But instead he was foolish enough to return everything, especially to some probably wealthy kids. He felt like an idiot; and different thoughts battled again in his mind. He knew that long term he probably did the right thing and could sleep peacefully for the rest of his life … hm… "How much more peaceful? When I ended up sick?" he thought again.

The afternoon went by fast and Dimitri shivered once in a while. He got ready a bit after 5pm and took another short nap before he headed back into the cold to wait for Lauren to pick him up in her limo. As soon as he stepped out he felt really cold and weak, despite his warm clothes. Due to his great anticipation and stress he ended up at the bookstore at 5:45pm. He decided to wait inside in the warmth, but he still didn't feel 100% all right. Lauren arrived, 20 minutes after 6pm, as Dimitri was exhausted. She apologized but it was obvious to her that he was pale and he did not look as handsome as he usually did. She asked him if they should postpone their meeting to the day after New Years Day, but Dimitri did not want to. She took him to a café down the Greenwich Village area and proposed to eat something when she realized that Dimitri ordered only a cup of tea. "I am fine," he said; but Lauren called the waiter and ordered food and told him, " This is my treat."

Dimitri insisted that he should pay for it, but Lauren told him that she was so proud of his act the night before, that she wanted to treat him. Dimitri felt that he had no choice and decided to let her do this. For some unknown reason, he could not concentrate on talking about their future …he could not concentrate at all. They spent over an hour and a half talking about movies, Brown University, his graduate work and the gallery where she worked in Boston. After that, Dimitri was exhausted but tried to concentrate and pull himself together to address what he initially had wanted so much to talk about. He felt uneasy and his moves where not very smooth. He started by going directly to the point that he wanted to spend more time with her and that he cared so much about her well-being and her life. Lauren at first kindly paused him and then asked him if they could talk about something else. Dimitri replied that he had waited a really long time for this and he insisted in talking about it. Lauren interrupted him and pointed out that he looked exhausted and also looked like he was sick and in pain with all his sneezing and coughing; he looked like he had to put a lot of effort and energy just to talk. She paid the bill and led him outside to the limo. Dimitri felt that she was right as he was trembling a lot and had lost his confidence to talk clearly to her. He felt weak and he agreed with one condition to go on another date before she headed back to Boston. Lauren agreed and half an hour later, Dimitri was dropped off at his home almost half asleep. Lauren gave him a rendezvous for January 6, which seemed too late to him, but he had no energy to argue. He fell into his bed and spent the following couple days lying sick at home until the third day of the year.

At least he had something to look forward to. However, he took a lot of sick days from work and Joe's uncle asked him to make up some of the time by doing some extra shifts. He agreed with the only exception that he would be free on January 6 after 5pm. Although Joe's uncle agreed to it, when the day came he was understaffed and asked Dimitri to stay till 8pm. Dimitri explained to him that this was not possible and asked to be let out at the latest at 5.45pm. Joe's uncle really needed his help, but Dimitri was determined to even quit his job to make the rendezvous. Once his manager understood that, he let him go, but to Dimitri's amazement, when he arrived at the bookstore, the Paulmerts' chauffer announced him that Ms. Paulmerts had an emergency and left for Boston early in the morning. The chauffer told him that Lauren would contact him to soon to apologize. He handed Dimitri a small envelope, which contained a card written by Lauren asking for forgiveness, as she had to leave on short notice. She also wrote that she would write him again to make up their appointment.

Dimitri was deeply disappointed and once again filled with desperation. He wrote her a letter and without waiting for a reply, another letter explaining his feelings for her. This time he was more direct than any other time. He waited more than two weeks for a reply, but nothing came along. He decided to write her another letter. He wrote her that he would plan a trip to Boston to see her. He wouldn't cancel unless she told him that she had plans to visit her family. Lauren wrote him a week and a half later saying they should meet on May 1st in Providence, RI, as she would be there for a workshop at her old Alma matter. Dimitri managed to block that day from his working calendar, even though he had to prepare for finals. He decided to use some of his savings for that trip and not spend any more money until the trip. However, a month later Lauren postponed their meeting until summer when she would be back in Queens.

Memories and music throughout the studies

In the meantime, Dimitri focused on his research and graduate school and he got the best reviews for his work. Lauren was constantly on his mind, but finally he knew that he had expressed himself clearly this time, so she was totally aware about his feelings for her. After all, he was approaching twenty-six and after the summer of 1964 and would be starting the final year of his doctorate degree and would start looking for a job. He was confident that by the time he graduated, he would have a good job and would be able to support a family, his own new family. Of course, he would still help his parents and relatives. Dimitri was brought up in an environment where he never had too many choices in life. But he could see that once he finished his degree, the horizon was wide open. By the time that he finished his doctorate, he would have devoted more than twelve years to his love, Lauren. Indeed, Lauren finally met him during the summer of 1964. Their meeting was intense but Lauren refused to engage in the conversation that Dimitri wanted to have. She confirmed she was fully aware of his feelings; however, she was not ready at that point to have the discussion he wanted to have. She told him that they should talk about something else. Dimitri took this as a sign that she was not as interested as much as he was, but vowed not to give up. He thought that he should fight for her and the fact that she did not push him away was a sign that he had to fight harder. He was not happy, but he felt OK with that idea as he had another year full of duties, work and no free time for anything else ahead of him. He had to focus on finishing his dissertation; he knew that it was not easy and thought that whatever happened was for the best. Throughout his last year of studies, he indeed had no free time as he also continued to work for Joe's uncle. The little time he had, he used to see a movie or play the melodica or his guitar. He could not concentrate on writing lyrics anymore. He felt that he should rather spend time helping his cousins with school and writing letters to Lauren, his friends in Greece and his family. He never forgot them, even though it was so long since he had seen everyone. His mother and father were about to join the rest of the Giovas family in Queens the following year. Therefore the next year looked great, as he would have his family together, his degree and a really good job. Hopefully, Lauren would be available for his talk, the most important talk. Summer of 1965 was close enough for him; he learned to be patient all these years and he developed resilience and self-confidence since he was totally assimilated into the culture and of course, excelled in his studies.

Solitude but goodness.

Dimitri had a very lonely year as Lauren was never at her parents' place in Queens. In fact the Paulmerts, were out of town most of the time, spending time between an apartment in Boston and their new summer house in Newport, RI. Joe and Giovanni had girlfriends and jobs in big corporations and could not spend much time with Dimitri. Joe had moved to Los Angeles where he was drafting contracts as a lawyer for major producers and record labels in Hollywood. Giovanni was still in NYC, but in a big corporation as corporate lawyer. He was flirting with the idea of working more on financial contracts and Joe coached him, since he had been more on a fast track and dealt with major corporations in California. Joe was ahead of all the other lawyers in Hollywood and specialized in major productions and intellectual property rights. Both were financially secure already and

Dimitri was dreaming about the summer where he would also get a job. His major achievements were in thermodynamics and engineering, control panel systems to monitor reactors and their activities in industrial plants. He had a very lonely year, but was looking forward to his grandfather's official and final retirement as he had promised to leave his work at the diner and just stay home. Grandpa was also very excited to have Dimitri's parents join them. He retired to pass on his job to his son, Dimitri's father, who would need a job once he arrived. Grandpa was approaching eighty, but he was still strong, full of life and walking tall and proud. For him eighty years old, was not an ultimate milestone as his ancestors lived very long lives in worse conditions. Dimitri was very excited about summer of 1965. He had all these great reasons to be. His doctorate, and Lauren's return to NYC as he envisioned it, but also the arrival of his parents from Greece and finally the retirement of his very beloved grandfather. All these things made him not mind the solitude and devotion to finishing his studies and writing his dissertation. He called it "desertation" since he had to stay away from social activities and pretty much everything else that year. It was a challenging year but also a very spiritual one as in the midst of his loneliness he constantly thought about his future life and work. He often thought how thankful he should be to God for having so much love in his life from his family and friends and success in his studies. His work occupied him a lot and was able to solve most of the difficult problems that his fellow students could not. Prior to the summer, he started applying for jobs and his professors helped him with their contacts outside the university.

The summer of 1965 was glorious, as Dimitri indeed had a very successful Ph.D. defense and just a month later was able to welcome his parents, almost fifteen years since they last saw each other, moments that could never be described with words as there was no way to count all the teardrops of happiness from every single family member. His parents were approaching their mid fifties and had aged features from the hard work and daily struggle of the fifteen years since the moment they said goodbye to their young son on that memorable rainy night in Piraeus. That day the boat did not take just one of their children, but a piece of themselves, their life and their being. A piece of their life that they now encountered in a mature form, filled with good spirits, handsome and a wholesome man who excelled in his studies.

The only issue to be considered at that time was Dimitri's challenging job offer that was by far, the best. His professors tried to persuade him not to pass on this opportunity for anything in the world. He had sacrificed already many years for his family by staying in Queens. Especially for graduate school he could have gone to a far better school and been away from the family but Dimitri did not want that to happen. So the issue was that he had a very prestigious offer to join a project at the National laboratory in Los Alamos and continue developing his engineering systems to monitor the production of gases, or volatiles, or radioactivity. Dimitri was offered a very high salary, much more than he expected. However, the prestige was also far more significant than he ever thought, because after a couple of years of experience at the National laboratories, every door would open up for him. Then he could move close to New York again. His dissertation received a lot of praise, since his publications were presented at major national meetings by his advisor. Everyone could see the usefulness of his knowledge and dissertation, as many of the industrial plants were getting bigger and more automated. Human labor consisted of more and more monitoring of huge consoles with hundreds of buttons and screens that were either fed or got signals from multiple sensors.

He was extremely happy that he got an offer from a company that was serving the National Laboratories in Los Alamos and to become part of something so unique that wasn't researched anywhere else in the world. However, he could not get comfortable with the idea that he would have to move so far away from his family, especially after all his longing to be with them. On the one hand, the change, the desert in New Mexico and the unique environment were fascinating to him, since he loved the idea of exploring the Grand Canyon area and all these places that he knew of from John Ford's films. On the other hand, everything seemed awfully far from New York and his family. He dueled a lot with the choices and everything else that had been offered to him. The pressure from his professor was tremendous and his psychological state was turbulent. The arguments inside him were constant and tantalizing. He had stayed close to his family, but not his parents. However, he was used to living far away from them, so it should not matter if he had to deal with this situation for a few more years. He did not know what to do… he dueled and dueled again with the idea, knowing that he would never know what the best decision for him was, until he had another philosophical debate with his grandpa on what to have and have not... His grandpa favored the idea to move to New Mexico for two to three years, but Dimitri could not understand why his life had to be complicated. His grandpa reminded him that it was not complicated anymore once he accepted the fact that one cannot have everything. Dimitri dueled again and again, but also he asked himself the question, "What about Lauren?" He still had no idea what would ever finally happen between the two of them during the long Fourth of July weekend. His head was heavy again... decisions, decisions and he had no idea what would happen to him.

He decided that the meeting with Lauren would define his future. If Lauren agreed to start a relationship, he would forget New Mexico at once. He knew from the sparse correspondence that this was also a year full of decisions for Lauren. The factory had trouble again and the Paulmerts were spending more and more time in NYC. In fact, Lauren also spent many years away from NY and was thinking of leaving New England and either returning to NYC or living elsewhere. This was all the information that Dimitri had. The Fourth of July weekend came soon and he was ready to find out everything he wanted to know. Lauren also was prepared to face Dimitri, as she knew she could not deny anymore the fact that Dimitri had openly confessed his love for her.

So they met on a great summer night right before the sun was about to set and take his final step behind the Manhattan skyline. The lavender skies made the view from Queens exquisite that night. Dimitri insisted that they meet in Queens and walk along the river and later go to one of the popular Greek restaurants on Broadway for dinner. Lauren was rather easygoing with the idea. Dimitri was well prepared and looked extremely smart with nicely combed thick hair and a new outfit that he had bought with his leftover savings, once his parents arrived in Queens.

Lauren commented on his flawless posture and presence, however she was flawless herself. A couple passing by told them that they were the prettiest couple they had ever seen. Dimitri was so happy since he was not used to these kind of compliments, but at the same time he became red, since he was still a very shy and modest person. Lauren, however, was very used to flattering comments. They walked along the water and Dimitri went straight to the point. They were almost alone since no one was in the warehouse and industrial area that they chose to walk through. He sounded confident and Lauren looked deep into his eyes. Lauren's eyes were pure magic for Dimitri and a few minutes later he burst out to a declaration about how much he has loved her all these years. He declared to her that he had never dared look at another girl. Dimitri knew he was living one of these special moments in life; one of these life-defining moments; a reference point; a moment one waits to experience for a long time. In addition, a day he knew was going to be a turning point in his life. Life after this point in time would never be the same. He did not even want to think about the possibility of failure. He would not be able to imagine life without her. He would not be able to understand a negative decision. In fact, he had never prepared himself for such an outcome. He was sure that there would not be such a moment. Worst-case scenario for him was that Lauren would postpone the serious decision for another time. However, he had a whole arsenal of ideas and plans to confront that. He was determined to find out, as he was about to make a big professional decision. He did not want to go to New Mexico alone or he was ready to drop that offer in a heartbeat in case Lauren told him that they should stay in New York.

Lauren was fully aware of the severity of his situation and looked at him with complete and profound understanding. Lauren suggested taking a break at the closest bench overlooking the Manhattan skyline. They sat on the bench and starred at the skyline in that perfect summer night before the big Independence Day celebration. Lauren took a deep breath and told Dimitri that he should not count on her. Dimitri's face turned pale. Lauren did not let him say anything and explained that a relationship between them would never work out. Dimitri kept asking her questions and Lauren touched upon how different their worlds were and that she would never want to live in New Mexico. Dimitri immediately assured her that he would not take the job. Lauren stopped him and then emphasized that she was already involved in a relationship that her family favored a lot. Dimitri was devastated and his face looked tragic; a face that Lauren had never seen. She seemed to have feelings for him, but also looked like she was thinking a lot; She was a person that never allowed herself to become unrealistic, leaving behind her world and the opinions her family had for Dimitri and his relatives. She knew that it would not just be difficult because of her mother's reaction, but also because everyone else in her circle would never understand why she chose Dimitri instead of all the proper Upper-East Side heirs who were after her. Dimitri was absolutely devastated and a storm of sadness hit him like a hurricane. All of a sudden he could not talk; he could not repeat the lines he had in mind in case Lauren became difficult. He walked Lauren back to her mansion and he did not have the strength to even say a good night. He thought of all the years that he had waited for her. He thought about all the love stories and all the literature he had read and absorbed all these years in America and could not think of a hero who endured the same pain. He remained silent, simply devastated, and mind scattered for the rest of the night; he could not move once he reached his bed. He cried and then remained thunderstruck, frozen for the whole night without sleep. He composed three poems to document the tremendous devastation he was feeling at that moment. There was a revolution in his mind; almost a war and suddenly he realized it was rather a "civil war" as he was fighting it himself, with his own being since he let himself believe in unrealistic dreams. He did not know what to do about his depression. The next day his grandpa noticed at once, that Dimitri had been through an emotional tumultuous time. It took him only few minutes to understand what had happened; what Grandpa had in mind was correct. He knew at that point that his grandson had learned his lesson, but so many years later. He was not that concerned, as he knew that his grandson had a whole lifetime ahead of him. He offered to talk to Dimitri but without success, as his grandson did not want to talk about it. Grandpa talked to his parents and brother, so everyone could help him in a discrete way. Dimitri also felt that his pride was hurt and did not want to talk about anything. The persistence of his family to help him made him more stubborn and he just wanted everyone to leave him alone. Less than 24 hours later Dimitri announced to his family that he would accept the job offer in Los Alamos. No one could really tell if his decision was influenced by the incident with Lauren or not. Everyone guessed that he wanted to escape New York and his neighborhood. For the first time in his life Dimitri had the desire to isolate himself and thought that the Los Alamos labs would be the perfect place for that.

The young in jeans listening to Mahler unnoticed.

He packed some of his belongings the following day and announced that he would spend the day with Giovanni and then the following week he would fly to Los Angeles to meet Joe. He decided to spend a week in Los Angeles prior to his job in Los Alamos. For Dimitri this was a huge decision since it was his first major trip, ever since he arrived in New York as an immigrant. He could not believe it, as the word vacation was foreign to him. That thought kept him out of a depression, since the trip was exciting and unprecedented for him. After calling his friend Joe to tell him about his decision and his desire to visit him, Joe talked to him for hours and somehow relieved him and promised him he'd have an amazing time in Los Angeles.

Dimitri had signed a generous contract. He did not care about expenses, as he was deprived his whole life of any kind of entertainment that cost more than a dollar or two. He had been deprived of any kind of luxury such as trips or entertainment other than the cinema. After he spent the day with Giovanni, he stayed with his family day and night the following week and did not leave the house. His family could not believe that after so many years of being apart they had to say farewell all over again. However, they knew that from now on it would be easier to meet. Dimitri clearly told everyone that he would come home every holiday. Eventually everyone was happy for him and that he was going away to work at a prestigious laboratory. They believed that he would become famous and prominent so and if that was what fate had in store for him, they all had to be content about it. They were convinced that he would excel; and no matter how sad they were about his departure, they were happy for him, as they knew that he also needed time for himself to forget Lauren. They were concerned that he would be isolated but were comforted by the idea that he would visit his dear friend Joe in Los Angeles for a week. They heard about the bon vivant life that Joe was leading so they were assured that he would take care of Dimitri and they would have a very good time together. Joe had a villa in northwest LA and Dimitri was impressed that his childhood friend socialized with celebrities. Joe was not just a lawyer in the entertainment industry; he invested in the production of projects and was already an executive producer for three films.

Dimitri was impressed with his lifestyle. He met many beautiful women, since Joe was party hoping at at least three or four parties every night. Dimitri was way too shy and Joe tried to coach him but without much success. The third day in Los Angeles Joe unveiled a huge surprise to Dimitri. He took him to the studios where he was going to record one of the songs they did together years ago. Dimitri thought that Joe was joking, but he wasn't. They drove in his big limo and pulled into a parking lot right before the big studios, where supposedly famous singers were recording songs that day. As they walked from the parking lot to the studio, he saw that the boulevard was filled with beautiful and handsome young people. "A few actors and many wannabes," Joe whispered to him. He saw crowds mingling at coffee shops on both sides of the street. As they walked in that direction, they came across a car parked in front of a parking meter and Dimitri heard that the person inside was listening to music. Even though the windows were almost closed, he saw a young girl inside in ecstasy listening to a grandiose orchestral piece. Dimitri recognized right away that it was Mahler's 9th symphony and was amazed that a young girl could get so ecstatic and absorbed about it instead of some type of rock music.

During their visit to the studios, Joe introduced Dimitri to many of his colleagues. Dimitri was impressed by his ease to communicate with the big shots in the industry. Joe introduced him as a songwriter, which embarrassed Dimitri, as he never considered himself a songwriter. Half an hour later they went out for lunch with a group of people. As Dimitri was walking outside, he noticed that the person listening to the Mahler symphony was still inside the car. Joe and everyone else crossed the street and headed to the outdoor café. After they had ordered, Dimitri saw that the young woman had opened the door of the car and walked towards the studio. He asked everyone, "is she a famous actress?" Joe and a couple of his friends replied that she was no one famous. Dimitri noticed that she had beautiful features, which resembled Lauren's. She was wearing jeans and a simple top, but had features full of grace. He asked them again to take another look, as he could not believe that she was not a famous young actress or singer. They all made fun of Dimitri's enthusiasm and naivety since to them she was a nobody and simply just another pretty face or "wannabe" as Joe previously said. Dimitri sensed their arrogance and told them that it did not matter if she was a "nobody" at that moment. He thought, "How odd is it that she is so beautiful and young and goes around unnoticed". He started a philosophical dialogue typical of his grandfather with the group about how this unknown person was not getting any attention. How funny and odd is the world? Perhaps in ten years she might get involved in a big production or make a successful record or movie... and will have everyone in the world competing for her time or for a place next to her. Dimitri sounded funny to them, as he was talking like a philosopher and a scientist, by breaking down every problem in measurable dimensions. They all found him amusing and pleasant but only for him was it such a great observation. The figure, posture and memory of that young girl opened up a different chapter in his mind and for the first time there was a new tantalizing debate for him. Previously, he could not answer the question if he could possibly fall in love again with another girl. But deep inside him he knew that this girl in the car fascinated him enough to be hopeful that his soulmate was really out there.

The last day before his departure to Los Alamos, he played music with Joe all night long. In the early morning hours he handed to Joe a few more lyrics from his years as a college student and then left to take the bus to Los Alamos.

Success and career.

Dimitri settled at a residence provided by the national laboratories. It was the first time in his life that he had neither family nor friends around him. He had such a great time with Joe in Los Angeles and felt he could run to him, if he ever felt too lonely. He was alone at the moment, but he did not care much as he saw this moment of his life as a time to heal from the wound of a twelve year devotion to a woman, who most likely would never become his wife. He was feeling rather mature at 27 years of age. He felt that he had a desire to be a husband and a father, but still only to Lauren. Dimitri devoted himself entirely to work with passion and enthusiasm. He did not care too much about the limited options of entertainment in his new environment. The other people in his group were scientists and engineers and did not have much time outside of their work and family. Dimitri spent two and a half years of loneliness, deserted in the desert, trying to analyze how a sensor could monitor specific emissions. He enjoyed his work very much and his supervisors were very impressed with his abilities. He spent hours listening to music and writing to his friends and family.

A year later after his arrival there, in 1966, Joe told him that he would be receiving royalties beginning in 1967, once he agreed to a contract for a release and publication of one of the songs they wrote together. Dimitri read all the relevant contracts regarding the release of the song, but he blindly trusted Joe and did not care too much about the details. He never believed that he would get much out of it. But he was excited and proud that someone was interested in his song. He could not believe that there would be another time this could ever happen again. He thought everything happened because of Joe's tremendous abilities to convince a producer to include it in a record. Once in a while he thought about how famous he could become one day, but he did not get obsessed with the idea. He was uncomfortable with the idea that perhaps more people would read his name on the album cover of a record than his scientific work, writings and achievements. To him it was just a silly song he and Joe crafted together in a moment of craziness one day! It took him some time to digest it, but he had faith in that Joe could make anything happen. His blind trust in Joe was such, that he signed a contract where Joe would always represent him and be his lawyer for any intellectual property rights. Joe tried to convince Dimitri to move to Los Angeles but Dimitri never believed that he could or should. Joe announced to him that he would try to have more of his lyrics published or become songs. Dimitri always joked about it and went back to his regular scientific job. Joe's mastery though made things happen and one day during a telephone conversation he announced that a major artist would record another of his songs.

"Who?" Dimitri asked.

"The greatest artist in America," Joe told him.

Dimitri was dumbfounded and asked Joe "Sachmo?" and Joe laughed. When he told him the artist's name, Dimitri had no idea who he was. However, his royalties went up every time their song aired on any broadcast and any time someone bought the vinyl record. In the beginning of 1967 Dimitri realized how profitable this was as soon as he got his first royalty check. He was amazed, as this extra money would allow him to visit his friend and family more often. He was very happy and thankful that he had a friend like Joe.

Some time later one of the top managers and partners of the firm that collaborated with the Los Alamos laboratories, where Dimitri was an employee, suggested him to leave his current job and join him in the efforts of raising money to found their own firm. Dimitri did not care about this, as he was more interested in science and not entrepreneurship. However, he sensed that it was a very attractive offer, as he would be able to relocate closer to his family, since the plan was to move to New York State. His job at Joe's uncle's business gave him a good sense about the gravity of such an offer. So far he was able to fly to New York every Christmas and Easter. He eventually started missing more and more his life and family back in New York.

So the moment came that he accepted the offer and moved. It was about time for him to do so, as he had spent more than two years in New Mexico. He moved about sixty miles northwest of New York City and started doing research on a new generation of sensors with his new partner. They filed for a patent together which got approved and published in record time. By the end of 1968, in his 30th year, he was an entrepreneur and a scientist. He also succeeded in being close to his family, having his own successful business and becoming financially stable.

On his 30th birthday he felt very alone. It had been three years since the day he decided to forget everything about Lauren and start a new life. He felt that he was ready to meet someone else and start a family, but had not invested the appropriate amount of time in that. At least at that moment, his new job provided him with more freedom and time besides the financial security. He was still receiving royalties from his songs with Joe. Joe was such a capable person that he had even succeeded in having one of the songs on a show that aired for a long time, ensuring royalties for many years. In the meantime, he was trying to publish two more songs that they crafted together. Dimitri's scientific patent was a huge success right away since a big corporation that installed control systems in industrial plants licensed it from his company. So at the beginning of his 30th year, he had the best prospects for a financially secure life. The predictions of his grandfather came true, as no one else in his family was as successful as he was. His grandpa was very happy and proud.

Thirteen years of solitude; Los Alamos away from socialites; devotion to work but prosperity; Social differences; no response.

The older person on the roof of the cathedral sighed, "Something happened then."
The younger man asked the older: "When? What happened?"
The Master replies: "Something that broke his heart."
Younger: "Like what? Something serious?"
Master: "Well, I guess so."
Young: "With his family?"
Master: "Not really..."
Young: "Explain to me; what do you mean not really?"
Master: "With Lauren."
Young: "Again? What? What has he done with her?"
Master: "What hasn't he...?"

"It came as a shock one day at the end of that year and drastically changed him emotionally. The news was out that Lauren Paulmerts got married to a multimillionaire heir from Pennsylvania. He was devastated. He was trying to convince himself that this was rather a relief, but he was very unsuccessful. The news that the newlyweds would reside in New York made him want to escape again.

He talked to his partner and decided to do more research and at the same time to take on huge installation projects in Europe and the west coast. Dimitri suddenly felt like he had to escape and wanted to see and explore the world. The world, he never had a chance to see. His thirst was unrestrained. He knew that the contract he had signed for his patent would bring him loads of money, so he was financially secure and had the power to negotiate his position within the company. No one could stop him. Not even his family that always wanted him to stay as close as possible. Dimitri reiterated that this was the era of traveling and that he had to see the world and return to his roots, to see his friends and relatives he never had the chance to see. The jet era and the airplanes were already popular and all the important people in New York crossed the country and the ocean in a heartbeat, without thinking twice about it.

The time came and Dimitri left New York again to go back to the desert of New Mexico and Arizona to supervise new installations that new nuclear energy and chemical plants had ordered. Three years later he moved to Europe where he found the time to visit his relatives and friends from his childhood. His feelings and experiences were intense and he did not dare describe them to his friends and relatives in New York. After all these years, his childhood friends had become mature men and his middle aged relatives older and weak. He remained emotionally charged for years, which filled his life with emotions that took the place of past emotions and remembrances. He indeed tried hard to forget Lauren.

Younger man: "So where did he settle in Europe?"

Master: "He never did. He moved from one country to another for several years. Perhaps that was the reason he did not have a long-term relationship. In the beginning, he stayed away from socialites and parties. But after a year or two, his friends from Greece helped him a lot to change his mentality. His friend Konstantin and his family were always close to him. Konstantin and Dimitri grew up in the same neighborhood and, were in school together from the very first day. When Dimitri left for America, his friend was devastated and almost fell into a depression. When they met again, they both felt that nothing had changed since their school years. They had exchanged hundreds of letters during the past twenty or so years. Dimitri reconnected with his extended family as well.

Younger: "But for the last thirteen years he did not really meet a girl that he fell as much in love with as with Lauren. He is a handsome man after all, right?"

Master: "Well he did. Maybe he never fell as deeply in love as he did with Lauren. From 1968 until now ... sure, he met quiet a few ... Thirteen years, but they were not easy for him, at least at that front."

Younger: "Why not?"

Master: "First of all, whenever he returned to the US he resided in the southwest desert away from socialites. He was also very much devoted to his work. The royalties from his engineering patents made him feel extremely responsible to deliver the highest quality job to his clients. He had a very successful patent and was still collecting royalties from his songs. He became wealthy,

as the checks came in from all different sources. But he certainly deserved
them."
Younger: "So, how come there was no girl then who was able to seduce him
in all these thirteen years?"
Master: "Apparently there were quite a few who did this successfully... but
they were not quite his taste. Especially right after he moved away from New
York, he fell for a few right away, but they did not inspire him much, ... I
guess, ... especially in his first years. But the problem was that none of the
girls that he had fallen in love with ever felt the same way about him. His
love for so many was never appreciated."
Younger: "That sounds weird... how come?"
Master: "Perhaps some were too pretty and thought that they had better
options, others were from a different social class and others simply did not
care about him."
Younger: "What do you mean? Which kind of difference in social class
are you talking about? Since he was making tons of money. Actually, more
women should be running after him, once they discovered that he was
wealthy and successful."
Master: "Not really! He never advertised it; he never really disclosed this,
or showed it off... Some upper-class girls couldn't see that, as he was just
another engineer to them and not an heir or a banker; Dimitri wouldn't talk
about his lyrics and involvement in the entertainment industry. Besides,
do not forget that he never stayed in one location for more than two years.
Could that be another factor? Perhaps ... who knows? He was in Paris and
randomly met a girl at a street café that inspired him to write poems again.
They dated for a long time. He was in love with her, but she never wanted
to be contained in a marriage and have children. It turned out to another
uncorresponding love ... in the city of light. Dimitri ended up alone again
walking left and right to meet his mate. Another girl that he fell in love with
turned out to be very snobbish, since he did not belong to her social class.
Even another one rejected him because of his modest background. Another
one told him that her parents would hit the roof if she married a Greek.
Someone else got scared at his extreme attention to her; she thought that
he was too intense and ran away. Indeed his passion was sometimes unlimited. Others ignored him completely since he was not into modern or trendy

things. Most of the girls he fell in love with had better choices. However, most of the girls that wanted to be next to him were not his type and this is what made his life such a riddle with all these unmet expectations.

Younger: "Maybe it was so the right one could come along."

Master: "You could be right and that is how he continued to think. You see, he believed in God after all; he always thought that every hurdle was a lesson for him and God was keeping the best for him for the right time and moment."

Younger: "So, I guess that was the one he met last year, the one in the newspapers..."

The Master suddenly interrupted him and pointed far away to the streets that ended at the square by the City Hall.

Younger: "What happened?"

Master: "I think it is the time when everyone is going to pay their dues."

Younger: "Explain, what do you mean?"

Master: "Let me recap, so indeed last year he met his fiancée."

Younger: "Oh! So he fell in love again?"

Master: "He did and ...", tears started rolling down his face even though he did not move his eyelids. "He did pray for that ... oh please God bless; well it happened and it was sudden and so fast; he was wondering about it ... but he knew that it was something important ... very important. He met her at a store while he was in Europe. A cloudy day; lots of white clouds covered the sky with the sun breaking through the clouds once in a while. All of a sudden, he left the store by the central square and for few minutes it was so bright. He wondered how could it be so bright? All of a sudden he observed a young lady with light colored hair and bright clothes across from him. So much light, pure and ample light was emitted in his direction that it dazzled him. He was attracted to her elegant tall figure. He approached her and she turned toward him. The greeting was warm and the smile sincere. He did not miss the chance to ask her if she needed help with her huge shopping bag and ended up helping her. He offered her a coffee at the department store's café and that was the beginning of their romance. Christmas of 1980 was around the corner and they went to a concert together. It took them some time, but they decided to tie the knot. They were almost ready until ... the disaster happened."

Younger: "You mean the accident in the factory?"
Master: "Right!" He took a deep breath and sighed with sorrow.

1981 – Love and success; the children's visit and the incident.

Master: "I wish I knew the exact details, but as you already know, nobody really knows everything, except him, as there were not any witnesses besides him. His partner had asked him to travel back to Arizona and California to check on the maintenance and also supervise the new installation of a new console for a chemical and nuclear plant respectively that were at the borders of the two states. The chemical plant manufactured a variety of petrochemicals, pesticides and had a variety of sensors that monitored the emission of gases and other byproducts from its reactors.
Dimitri had to personally supervise all the monitoring systems and test from the console, the control of every valve and pump from all the deposits and exhausts of gas. The plant's board decided to replace the whole control panel with a more modernized version. The cost was tremendous, but in the long term the company would save a lot from the operating cost of the facility. Dimitri had to supervise and synchronize the control room's computer with every single operating machine. The same morning he had heard that a high school was about to visit the area. High schools visited these plants as part of an educational program that exposed students to industrial settings for their education. Since this was common for schools in the area, the plants had a crew that hosted the students and gave them a tour of the various facilities. Dimitri did not like the idea of having too many spectators around him, while he had to perform his job. But the factory management did not care as it was far less trouble for them to have visitors taking tours while several units were down for maintenance and testing. They thought that that he and his crew would eventually need to stop the operation of the engines once he turned different engines on and off from the control panel.
Apparently he was given no choice by the management of the plant and had to continue everything as planned. All of a sudden while he was in the control room shutting everything down and then back on again, he realized that there was a pressure problem in one of the gas deposits, which apparently did shut off when he shut it down. Dimitri observed suddenly a peak of activity

in one of the monitors, which was completely unexpected. However, at that moment he was operating the back up control panel and not the regular panel. He was on his own in the room that was hosting the robot and the main computer. When he realized that this was a highly explosive and poisonous gas he had to shut everything down at once, since he feared that this part was uncontrolled. Unfortunately, by doing this, he caused damage in the main controlling system and corrosive reagents ran into the pipes of every tank and deposit of the facility. The damage was excessive. Unfortunately he could not control and stop it immediately. The sirens alerted the plant crew and someone rushed the high school students out of the facilities. However, there was nothing dangerous to fear for the spectators, as Dimitri blocked any potentially hazardous material to leave the circulation and leak out to the environment, but instead they circulated within the pipes and deposits of the plant.

The end result was serious damage from the corrosives for the majority of the facility. The manager and everyone there were scratching their heads as they could not believe that their facility would be out of operation for a long time and most of the reactors, pipes and deposits had to either be cleaned thoroughly or worse disposed of and replaced. It was a total catastrophe for the plant and while Dimitri was working at the control panel, there was no record of what really happened because during the test many of the main back-up systems were shut down and blocked by his desperate attempt to restore the system.

The plant manager and members of the board were called into a meeting at once. They could not believe the magnitude of the disaster that had taken place. The director of operations blamed Dimitri saying that he should have released the pressure and let the gas escape into the atmosphere and never allow what happened to take place. Dimitri did not agree with him as he explained that the most important thing was the safety of the high school students and the workers who were still around.

The manager did not care about Dimitri's opinion and asked him to exhibit the records that prove the peak of activity that Dimitri had observed in the monitor and was the cause of the disaster. Dimitri explained that there was no recording when the back-up system went off line and while he was checking "the brain", the central computer and control panel. The members of the board and the manager were enraged, as they could not believe the magnitude of the disaster. The following moment someone entered the room and reported that a worker was found unconscious at the part of the plant where the pressure problem was. As the management rushed him to the emergency room of the local hospital, they called the police to perform an investigation. Their lawyers suggested that the authorities should arrest Dimitri until the investigation clarified what happened. Dimitri perplexed and confused realized that they were trying to charge him with criminal charges. He could not believe it, but he was more than welcome to cooperate with the police, as he was more concerned about the health and life of the worker. He was sure though that he was not unconscious because of any toxic gas leakage as he successfully prevented it.

The plant management filed charges against him including criminal charges for the worker that ended up at the hospital on life support. The charges were many and heavy that would keep Dimitri in jail until the end of the investigation. They charged him heavily as the factory would have to withstand damages in the range of tens of millions of dollars and the management felt that Dimitri was solely responsible for them. According to the state law, Dimitri had to be arrested. Arizona and New Mexico had unique laws that were different from any other state due to the nuclear testing that took place during the past decades. The law was strict especially for accidents in factories and plants due to ignorance or errors. It was an odd situation for Dimitri as this law stemmed from the 1950s. Other States did not have these kind of laws that Arizona did. Dimitri had to spend his time in jail and most likely until the investigation was over. Dimitri was taken to the local police station and was detained. The following day the insurance company could not accept that there was not a single recording of the activity that Dimitri had witnessed by himself. Dimitri's boss apparently did not have the best insurance coverage for such an accident and somehow the only way for Dimitri to get out was to pay his own bail.

To his amazement, the bail amount was related to the cost of the damage and the very old state law had it as a percent of the damage. The bail was set at $100,000 dollars, which was far more than a year's salary of only the very wealthy in Los Angeles or New York City. Giovanni represented Dimitri and rushed from New York City to support him. Dimitri had already been detained for two days at the local police jail and when Giovanni arrived, he assured Dimitri's boss that the company should pay the bail on his behalf. However, minutes later and during a subsequent phone conversation with the president and the board of Dimitri's company, he could not get a firm commitment from them. Giovanni left, as he had to go to New York to fight with them face to face. The next day he called Dimitri to announce that the board was not willing to pay that amount of money on his behalf as the company was in trouble and had been hiding that from him the last few years, while he spent time away in Europe. In fact, it became apparent to Giovanni that a member of the board was responsible for fraud and the company was not able to spend that amount of cash to bail Dimitri out. This sounded very unlikely to happen as $100,000 dollars was not that much for a company, however, Giovanni discovered that the company, due to the fraud that just emerged had a net debt to creditors.

Giovanni however, was optimistic about the case and told Dimitri on the phone to be patient, as there was enough money that he could bring from an alternative source. That day Dimitri begged him to return to Arizona to have a talk with him face to face. Giovanni asked him to be patient for another day or two, so when he returned to Arizona he would definitely have the money. He didn't tell him though, that he had an additional family commitment for one of his daughters the following day. He apologized and suggested to Dimitri on their next phone conversation, to pay his bail from his savings and then he would replenish it within the next day or two.

Dimitri was desperate after the conversation. Giovanni was confident that it was not a big deal for Dimitri to pay the bail initially from his savings, until he had Dimitri's company's board reimburse him. After all, for the past thirteen years, Dimitri had made a lot of money from the royalties besides his generous salary and earnings. He was considered by his friends to be a millionaire. His royalties from Hollywood and his patents brought at least three millions dollars during the past dozen years and his relatives joked that he was a multi-millionaire! Certainly, in the beginning of the eighties there were not many in his financial standing.

Dimitri called Giovanni the next day from jail and begged him to come to Arizona as he was not able to pay the bail and he would need his help immediately. Giovanni tried to convince him not to be stubborn and order the payment from his savings. Dimitri asked Giovanni as his official lawyer to demand again from his bosses to cover that amount of money, as they were far more established than he was. Dimitri could have saved more than a couple of millions of dollars all these years, but his bosses were at least five to ten times wealthier than him.

Unfortunately, they were not responsive and did not want to pay that amount of money to protect him. They were afraid that they would get sued for tens of millions of dollars and they wanted to take a secure path and examine the case; probably get away from their responsibility to pay, since Dimitri had most likely violated some rule, which made him responsible, and not the company. They could also not understand why Dimitri was stubborn and chose to remain detained, instead of paying the bail from his savings and deal with everything else later. Giovanni called him multiple times during the day begging him to stop being so stubborn and just pay his bail. Dimitri always replied that someone else had to pay the bail and not him. He begged Giovanni and Joe to ask the producers of his songs to please lend him the amount of money needed. Giovanni could not understand his behavior. He had been detained for almost a week and the court date was not determined to be close enough. According to the state law it would take normal priority, which was perhaps months later.

Dimitri continuously begged Giovanni to ask the producers of his songs. Giovanni could not understand why he had to do that and not ask others. Instead, Giovanni begged him to authorize the transfer of funds from Dimitri's personal account. Dimitri insisted he wouldn't do that. He was determined that he should not pay out of his pocket. He had worked so hard for his company, which profited way more than he did as well as his producers who made ten dollars for every dollar he made.

Giovanni had no choice and called both of his producers who could not understand either, why they had to lend Dimitri the money for the bail. They knew that Dimitri had made quite a lot of money from his three songs that they had published and he should have no problem financially. Giovanni conveyed the message to Dimitri and asked him again to pay the bail.

It was already a week since Dimitri was detained at the local police station. The trial was going to take place six months later, so the local authorities had to transfer him to the nearby state jail. His family in New York was deeply upset and angry at the authorities and the chemical plant along with his bosses who let him be detained for such an accident. They could not understand why his company was not helping him out and had abandoned him in such a way. His brother, together with his cousin, traveled to Arizona to see him. Dimitri did not want to talk to them much and they could not understand why he did not pay his bail, as they knew he had at least a million dollars or more in savings. Dimitri insisted that he should not pay, but his bosses should. They were begging him to pay and get out as soon as possible and claim the money later, when he was out. Giovanni and Joe talked together on the phone and could not understand why Dimitri was so stubborn and refused to pay his bail and deal with the money issue later.

The day arrived when he would be transferred to the jail and Giovanni could not comprehend what was wrong with him, so he flew to Arizona again. Dimitri met him in the visiting cell and asked him again to go out and ask his bosses or producers for a loan. Giovanni asked him for permission to get money from a specific fund that Dimitri had, which Giovanni oversaw with other lawyers. Dimitri's eyes widened at once and he yelled a loud and intense "NO!" Giovanni begged him again to open his savings account and stop this craziness that brought so much pain to the people who loved him. The guards were ready to take Dimitri and transfer him to the jail.

Giovanni had started sweating and yelled: "So what? Are you going to let them take you to jail? Are you nuts? WHAT IS WRONG WITH YOU? Why do you want to keep $100,000 dollars in your account and put yourself into jail with all the criminals?"

Dimitri very calmly looked at him and almost whispered, "Giovanni, you are my best friend, you are one of the pillars of my life, you are my brother…. Please … please could you please lend me that money?"

Giovanni looked at him with wide-open eyes like he was addressing a crazy person, "I don't understand you at all Dimitri, I cannot understand what is wrong with you! You know very well that as your lawyer I can be authorized to pull the funds from your special secret fund that I manage! And you know very well that you do have this amount of money. Why should I pay for this??? Because your bosses and producers do not want to pay for it! They made millions off of your work? What is wrong with you? Why are you asking me this?"

Dimitri lowered his head and whispered, "Could you please do me a favor?" he opened his eyes looked at Giovanni and asked him again, "Could you please ask Joe to lend me this money?"

Giovanni was dumfounded. "Dimitri, please tell me what is wrong with you? You made sense your whole entire life and I cannot understand how all of a sudden you don't make any sense!" He took a long pause to look at Dimitri straight into his eyes, "Don't you think about your family in Queens? Don't you think about your fiancée? They are all so worried and they cannot understand why you have planted yourself in this desert … and why you are being so stubborn; so stubborn! Christina is really mad at you and does not know why you tolerate this… what is this question now about Joe?"

D: "I just wanted to ask my friends for a favor, I will return the money to you very soon."

Gi: "Are you crazy? And why should we pay for this when you have the money in your savings and at the fund that I am assigned to? What kind of caprice is this? Please, tell me what is going on?"

D: "Giovanni… you and Joe are the last ones I can ask for this money. Everyone who got rich off of me does not want to help me. The question is can you help me?"

Gi: "Are you insane? I have a wife and three kids, who will have to go to college and I am not even making $100,000 a year. How can I have this amount of money in my savings when I have to feed my folks and my own family??? What is wrong with you Dimitri?"

D: "I thought I paid you enough all these years that you have been my lawyer and much more than you claim you earn?" Dimitri's eyes became as innocent as a five year old child's eyes.

Gi: "What kind of test is this? … Are you serious? … You are going to jail and you don't want to pay your bail from your money and you want to test your friends??? You know very well that I will do anything for you, but I don't have that amount in my savings … and even If I had it … I'd have to think about my family, you know… think about my responsibilities, why should I pay on your behalf, especially when you have the money… more than I could ever save, right? What is wrong with you?"

D: "Well then, please do me a favor and ask Joe to do this for me."

Gi: " Here you go again! Is there something that got loose up there in your brain? After being here all these days? Did you stay out in the Arizona sun for a long time? Are you serious? Please, stop this and authorize me to pay the money from your fund, please!"

D: "Please, Giovanni ask Joe, we both know that he has made much more than I have from royalties and gets paid a lot from all these celebrities."

Gi: "Sure, but Joe has an expensive lifestyle and do not forget all the alimonies and summer houses he has ..."

D: "Oh come on! He has hundreds of thousands in his account. I am sure."

Gi: "You too!!!!!! Why do you want Joe to take out all this money for you and not you, for yourself? You are going to jail in few hours don't you understand that???"

D: "I know I will, unless Joe agrees to lend me the money and wire it today so I can get out."

Gi: "You are impossible! So stubborn!"

D: "I did not do anything wrong, you know? Understand please, I was at the console and I had to think about all the lives in the factory that were threatened by these toxic emissions. Between all these lives and the pipes, I chose to contaminate the pipes, the tanks and the deposits, so what? Even the worker that was found unconscious is slowly recovering and nobody knows what happened to him. Why should I go to jail? It was an accident and the main control panel did not understand that one of the gas deposits got out of control. I was operating this from the back up system without any monitoring... Should I go to jail for such a mistake? Shouldn't my insurance pay for that? What kind of liars are they when they claim that this particular case was not covered by the current policy? What kind of liars are my bosses when they say that they don't have the money?"

Gi: "Listen, Dimitri – they messed up the insurance policy and indeed there is fraud in your company, so digest this please! Whether it was your mistake or not, your insurance and bosses will not bail you out. Not even all the other people who made money off of your hard work and inspiration. Please, pay the amount from your savings or let me take it out of the fund and do not twist our arms just because we are your friends and happen to have some money saved up for a rainy day."

D: "What do you mean, for a rainy day? You know that I will give the money back to you, I am only asking for a loan! In nine months I will make a hundred thousand dollars from the royalties alone, so what is the problem?" Gi: "How stubborn you are? You have it already and your fund is almost half a million, besides your personal savings. Why should I pay? Why don't you get the loan from your fund and pay? It does not make sense! I have never seen you like this before in my life! ... So unreasonable! Please, find your sense of reality otherwise go to jail!"

Dimitri looked up, as this felt like a heavy blow to his stomach from Giovanni ... it almost sounded like blasphemy. Giovanni realized this right away; was repentant and took his coat at once, announcing that he would call Joe right away and return as soon as possible.

Half an hour later Giovanni returned with despair in his eyes and told Dimitri that Joe asked to talk to him tomorrow. Dimitri told Giovanni that tomorrow he would be in the jail and may not be able to talk to anyone. Giovanni, with tears in his eyes, sat next to him and embraced him. "Look Dimitri, you know good old Joe. He already has two divorces, he is dating this young actress and has all these crazy expenses left and right. He is not that convinced that you cannot pay by yourself..."

Dimitri told him to stop. He had tears in his eyes and stood up, ready to move towards the guards. He was devastated, but so was Giovanni. "My brother please come to your senses and make a reasonable assessment of the situation, I cannot let you go to jail. I have promised your family and Christina that I will bring you back to New York tomorrow. You only have to sign this paper and transfer the money from your fund to the state of Arizona," and he handed Dimitri a set of papers.

Dimitri did not look at them and slowly moved towards the guards while Giovanni pulled him in his direction. Dimitri turned to him, "You and Joe can take care of me, my brothers and can lend me the money. You are my true friends. Everyone else who got wealthy off of me abandoned me, but you cannot do this."

Gi: "I will not do it, so let me get your signature here and then transfer a hundred thousand dollars from this account."

Dimitri put his face close to Giovanni's face and for the first time yelled out loud, "I need a loan, don't you understand!?"

Giovanni lost his temper and yelled even louder back to him, "Are you crazy? What kind of a stubborn idiot are you! Get the loan from this stupid fund

instead of giving this money to all the impotent and brainless crowds!"
Dimitri looked deep into his eyes and turned towards the guards with an
accelerated pace. Giovanni ran after him and tried to pull him back, but
Dimitri pushed him away, throwing him to the floor. The guards intervened
and took him away.
Giovanni said with tears in his eyes, "You are crazy! You are crazy! What will
you get out of all this stubbornness? Or what do you think that all these beggars that crunch your funds will benefit? You are nuts!"
Dimitri did not turn back and the guards took him to the other room.
Giovanni kept crying and yelled at Dimitri, "I will talk to Mr. Wells to
release the funds immediately!"
Dimitri turned around and told him firmly and with a strict tone in his voice,
"Not only did you sign a contract saying that you cannot do that, but you
also have made a firm promise to me". He turned back to the guards and
continued toward the van that would take him to jail.

The court but no bail; the begging lawyer but no loan; friends from childhood poor but caring.

Dimitri was taken to the jail that day. He left all of his belongings at the
check-in window and got his clothes, blanket and a small bag with a tooth-
brush and towels. As they took him to his cell, his inmates noticed his clean-
cut look and immediately berated him, cursed him and threw some unusual
adjectives to him. He was also hit by a cup, pencils, flying rubber bands and
other objects despite the efforts of the guards to make everyone act civilized.
He was taken to a cell on the middle floor, while his inmates welcomed him
with derogatory comments from every one of the three floors of the jail.
Giovanni very agitated and frustrated, called Joe and every affluent friend he
had, as he had given up on Dimitri's pride. He decided to raise the one hundred thousand dollars from everywhere he could. Dimitri's pride was strong,
as he claimed to be innocent and was disgusted at the way the management
of the plant, his bosses and the insurance treated him. He refused to accept
to pay the bail as he believed he did nothing wrong and was just protecting
the lives of his fellow men at the plant. Giovanni talked to Joe and confirmed
that despite Joe's lucrative pay and occupation, he had too many expenses and

loans to risk a $100,000-dollar loan at this point. Joe could also not under-
stand Dimitri's stubbornness. However, Giovanni did not give up and spent
the day calling every affluent person in Dimitri's industry to pitch in money
for the $100,000-dollar bail. However, to his amazement, not a single per-
son could comprehend why he should pay for the bail of a person who could
easily spare a million or two. The only people who were inclined to give
money were his relatives in Queens, who would never have enough money for
such a bail. His friends from high school and college and his relatives pitched
in about a dozen thousand dollars, according to Giovanni's calculations.
Giovanni figured that he and Joe could add another dozen each, but there
still was a significant amount missing. Giovanni thought again how pathetic
this was and figured he should talk to Dimitri again the following day. He
cancelled his flight and decided to stay in the motel another night and go visit
him in jail the next day. His anger grew even more as he knew how much his
wife would yell at him the next day for his prolonged absence. Besides, he
could not go back and face Dimitri's relatives, especially Christina and tell
them that Dimitri went to jail. Christina did not get any updates from Giovanni in the past week, other than the basic information that they were going
through a typical procedure and would have him released next week. He
knew that there was no way for him to go back without Dimitri.

Giovanni called Mr. Wells, who managed a fund that they had established
together on Dimitri's behalf. The fund had more than half a million dollars
and Giovanni had appointed Mr. Wells as a manager. Giovanni never knew
how much money went in and out of that fund on a monthly basis.

Mr. Wells reminded Giovanni that all the funds were on hold and they could
be released only with Dimitri's signature.

The next day Giovanni visited Dimitri in jail but had no luck again as they
repeated the same agitated conversation. Giovanni got really angry again and
told Dimitri that he could not deal with this situation anymore. Dimitri
asked Giovanni to have Christina visit him.

Giovanni looked at him, "Don't you understand that I cannot go back without
you? Your family will have a heart attack, when they find out that you are in
jail. Why don't you just pay the bail? What is the matter with you spending
all this money that you made all these years here and in Europe? I helped you
open your Swiss bank account. If you do no want to take out money from

your fund with Wells, authorize me to take it from the Swiss account. Don't you understand that I need you to come home with me? How can I work on your defense, if you are not next to me these next six months? You have to educate me on how the valves and the control panels work and how the accident happened and why when the main panel was off, there was no documentation, monitoring and why it was not your fault... Your bosses and partners have alienated themselves from you, since they have defrauded so much money. Who will work with me? They don't want to pay the damages and as far as I can tell, your case is very difficult. Who will believe you? The recorder was off and there is no record of the peak that you claim you observed? Are you serious? You think because you look like a person who can be trusted; the judges will listen to you without proofs? What am I going to do? Travel back and forth between New York and Arizona or rather camp out here? I have other clients as well in NY. Please if you do not have mercy on yourself, have mercy on your family or me. How will they accept the news? How will they react? Your folks are old and cannot take that distress. And Christina? You don't give a damn about her... don't you? She left Europe to come and live with you! What am I supposed to say to her? That you decided to stay in jail till the trial and explain how some beggars out there crunch your fund!"
D: "You are not allowed to say anything like that! Remember? You gave me your oath! Please!"
Gi: "OK! OK! You are right! Keep Wells to continue managing your fund, but let me get something from your Swiss account. It is insane to bring all this distress to your family and your friends, because you do not want anyone to touch your precious Swiss account. How can you possibly be serious and sane when you don't do the obvious thing?"
D: "But why is it so difficult to get a loan?" he paused for a moment and he continued with eyes full of hope, "OK, listen! My friend Konstantin will take care of that. I mean the Swiss account... But why if I may ask again, can't I really get a loan from all these wealthy and affluent friends and colleagues that I have?"
Gi: "Why should you? – Everyone knows that you are wealthy as well and have the money for the bail."
D: "It is a matter of principle – I did not do anything wrong. Besides, my friends and colleagues have to help me, when I ask them for help."

Gi: "Sure for reasonable help, and it looks like your family can only come up with ... maybe five to ten thousand dollars, but they will not have enough, so please sign this paper for me and I will get the money from Wells within a couple of days." he pointed for another time to the same draft of a contract.

Dimitri took a look at the paper and stood up ready to leave the room. "I cannot do this now! Maybe I will in a week. Besides, don't I receive more than $100,000 dollars from royalties, in less than a year? Sooner or later I will have the money."

Gi: "So,... indeed, you are really nuts! Why don't you use the money from Wells'???"

D: "Well, when you talk to him again, he will explain why."

Dimitri turned his back to Giovanni and while he was walking away told him, "Please ask for a loan, someone out there will do it and have Christina visit me."

Giovanni was in tears again and could not get up from his chair. The guards eventually removed him from the visiting room.

The next day Dimitri had to leave his cell and join the other inmates for lunch. Nobody could explain how this happened, but a couple of his inmates hurt him severely, while they were walking to the big dinning hall. They noticed he did not get out of his cell the first day and were waiting to get "introduced" to him. The rumors spread quickly that he was wealthy and perhaps a powerful man, so everyone was trying to show him that they could offer him protection from everyone else. Dimitri got confused so they lost their patience and started beating him. Every time this happened, the guards would arrive too late to rescue him and Dimitri's face was always bruised up. The guards, who understood what was going on, tried to protect him. However, the inmates who wanted to sell him their protection, would get him first and hurt him. Sometimes they could not get to him, and other times the guards protected him from them, but some inmates successfully spit on him, or threw things at him and always called him derogatory names. Dimitri was only there for two days and was terrified at the idea of spending up to six months in that environment. He was partially relieved when Giovanni passed him a message at the end of the night that Joe was on his way for a visit the following day. Dimitri understood that Giovanni could not go back to New

York without him, and felt that his friends were also suffering. He was not alone.

Joe came along with Giovanni to the visiting room the next day. When they saw his bruised face, they got enraged and realized that they could not tolerate this anymore. Joe's frightened eyes examined Dimitri's eyes who could not look straight into his eyes.

"Well, I hope that at least this has taught you that you should rather work with us on getting you out," Joe said to him.

D: "Sure, I want to get out Joe!"

J: "Why don't you do so then?"

D: "I think Giovanni explained this to you."

J: "Yes, he told me something very incomprehensible indeed."

D: "Look Joe, I got a telegraph from Konstantin in Greece, saying that he had gathered about a dozen thousand dollars for me. My relatives in Astoria also have another dozen or more, as Giovanni knows. Can you please lend me seventy five grand?"

J: " I wish I could, but you know how much I struggle with the two alimonies and the kids and oh … come one, man, you know my life has been a mess the last ten years."

D: "Oh! Come on Joe! For every million that I made in the last ten years and thank God, because of you, you made at least three! Why can't you loan me seventy five grand or may be sixty if Giovanni could add another dozen," and he looked at Giovanni who kind of nodded his head, a sign confirming that he would do that sacrifice for him, his dear friend.

J: "Dimitri of course you are right, but I have lost almost half of it to my first wife and then another huge portion to my second and have to keep paying all the stupid bills… non- stop… for the kids, for them, for this and that… what can I tell you? In fact, I am poorer than you or that you may think. Besides you know, we are not that young anymore, I have to save for … and you know that I am dating another beauty … well it takes a lot to maintain that relationship… you heard about her right? The stunning new starlet … we are so in love!"

D: "Oh sure, you mean the one that you told me about the other day, the one who is twenty years younger than you? And is better than me … sorry!"

J: "She is beautiful! You have not seen anyone like her."

D: "Well, Joe what I don't understand about you is that you were the brain, the intelligence powerhouse of every school that you attended; so how come you let yourself slide downhill so fast? And concentrate only on beauty? Your previous wives were extremely beautiful, but you were not a good match and you did not care."

J: "Oh believe me, I am not here to analyze this with you at the moment. Please, do not forget that I am here to solve your more serious problem. I cannot understand why you pick on my obsession about beautiful girls."

D: "Well, … I wonder if it is better to keep your savings for them or to loan them to your childhood friend?"

J: "Come on! Dimitri! And why do you have that incompetent Wells keep your money anyhow?"

"He is right!" Giovanni intervened with passion and continued, "What are you getting from all these beggars?"

Dimitri's face got red at once, "You were never supposed to say this ever again!" he slammed his hand on the table and repeated the same sentence to him again.

J: "I don't understand what is going on here? Giovanni?"

D: "And this is nothing you need to understand! Giovanni has to keep his professional engagement and oath here."

J: "Hey, wait a minute! We have never had secrets between the three of us … what am I missing over here!?"

D: "Nothing! If you could please continue; we were at the point that I wanted to ask you, why should you keep your savings for beautiful girls that you hang out with?"

J: "What is wrong with you? I really don't get it!"

D: "OK guys, let's just drop it. I am done talking."

J: "Well, what does that mean?? What??? Are you going to stay here in jail and let all these vulgar people brutalize you?"

D: "Perhaps not, my friend. I think Konstantin from Greece will gather the appropriate cash."

J: "Konstantin? Well … how? For them one hundred thousand dollars is like a million dollars! You have not spent that much time with him, why should he do this?"

D: "That is not true! All the years I spent in Europe, I reconnected with all of my friends in Greece."

J: "And what makes you confident that he will get the cash for you?"

D: "I cannot tell you or maybe I don't know … but I have faith."

Gi: "Why? Because he has access to your Swiss bank account?"

J: "Be serious! I want this to be real, so let's think for a moment, they only had a dozen grand so far with your family's savings, and with my contribution and Giovanni's we can't even get fifty thousands but Konstantin from Greece will find another fifty?"

D: "Then lend me more than what you estimate now."

J: "You are impossible and this is beyond the point! We talked about Wells and about your money! So you don't need mine and let me spend it on beautiful girls! I had enough of you! How stubborn are you! Why is my life full of people I cannot communicate with?"

D: "That's why you fall for girls who are only pretty; no need to communicate right? Love is blind, right?"

J: "Oh stop it! Even if they are not a good fit for me, I still enjoy my life and I don't care that I have burned through my savings. I don't care if a beautiful girl has more opportunities to be spoiled and consequently mess up my life. I will choose one from that group again, even if they are superficial and fake!"

D: "Doesn't that depress you? When at the very end you again choose another one from this group?

J: "Oh certainly. I am totally depressed. That is why I am prescribing myself with a heavy regimen of beautiful women, so I can get away from that depression."

They all laughed again the way as they used to during the good old times and Dimitri stood up to leave them.

Giovanni stood up as well and reminded him that he cannot go back to New York without him and cannot keep telling lies to Dimitri's family, saying that they were stuck in some bureaucratic procedure.

D: "Believe me my friend, I don't wish to stay here for another hour never mind six more months. But it is impossible for me to come up with the money for the bail!"

J: "Why? Explain to us why you can't? You have the money!"

Dimitri again stated that he had to get the money from somewhere else, from his friends or from people who had benefited from his work and life. And he reiterated that he does not enjoy staying in jail.

The guards took him away and again after he begged Giovanni to ask Christina to come and visit him.

Giovanni and Joe were left alone; they looked at each other and were embarrassed that neither had the money or the power to lend Dimitri that amount. Joe had too many expenses and fronts to fight, and Giovanni would never get his wife's approval given he had three children and not the absolute control of his savings account. After all, Joe was not as wealthy as he was on paper and Giovanni did not make nearly as much as his two friends.

Giovanni and Joe had a talk and decided to take the initiative without Dimitri's approval and go to Wells' office in NYC and put pressure on him to release the one hundred thousand dollars to get Dimitri out of the jail. They also thought about how to break the news to Dimitri's family who were very sensitive people. However, they respected Dimitri's request to have Christina visit him.

They both flew to New York the next day, while Dimitri was constantly being humiliated by his inmates and even beaten when they had the opportunity. Dimitri never reciprocated the curses and eventually told them that he would help them once he got out. Most of them wanted to know specifically how, but the guards or a couple of inmates who sympathized with him and were trying to protect him always interrupted them.

Giovanni and Joe visited the Giovas' residence once they arrived in NYC. They were bombarded with questions while Dimitri's mother wept nonstop. Christina arrived and could not believe the news. Dimitri's mother fell into a delirious state and when the ninety-six-year-old grandfather heard the news, he almost fell into a coma. Christina left immediately to arrange a flight and visit Dimitri. The family was in the worst condition ever, outraged and puzzled. They had no idea why Dimitri did not pay his bail. They were told they needed to collect money for him as a loan because supposedly he could not liquefy his own funds. Everyone was very puzzled and shaken. Nobody could understand what was the exact problem was, but they had some hope that Dimitri's two-childhood friends would find a solution, which was linked with to a visit to Mr. Wells.

Christina in the meantime arranged her trip for the next day. On her way to Arizona, she was very puzzled about what would happen and what she would discuss with him. She could not believe that her fiancé was in jail. She never thought that what happened to him was so important and serious. She bit her lips throughout her trip, as she never had enough time to talk to him lately and felt that this was not appropriate.

The next day the two meetings took place. Christina met Dimitri in the Arizona jail and his two friends met with Mr. Wells.

Christina was full of love and compassion for Dimitri. When they met, they both knew that they were still very much in love. Dimitri's doubts, that he could never love anyone else after Lauren, had disappeared completely. At the same time she thought that no matter how miserable he looked that day in the jail, he was the love of her life.

They went through the same dialogue that Giovanni had with him. Dimitri interrupted her many times to tell her that he was neither stubborn nor proud. He wasn't going to give up just because he did his job and everyone abandoned him. So many people had made so much more money than he did and yet they were not willing to help him and loan him what he needed at that time. Christina could not understand him and told him to stop all this nonsense. She told him that his mother was taken to the hospital from her reaction to his news and had to undergo medical treatment and be constantly sedated. Dimitri's eyes widened and his suffering was far more pronounced.

D: "Christina, I need your help. I need you to fly to Greece and meet Konstantin. He is the only one who can withdraw money from a European account that I have and he is the only one who knows that."

Christina: "Are you serious? Why does this person know things that your future wife has no idea about? Is that how you want to live your life? I trusted you with my life and you cannot trust me by telling me what is really going on here? Because I am sensing that there are many unknowns and things that you have not revealed to me! Dimitri's head was turned down when she repeatedly said, "I will not tolerate this, please tell me what is going on!"

Dimitri explained to her that he did not have liquid assets and Konstantin could help him release some of them. He begged her to trust him and do as he desired. But Christina rebelled and wanted to know more. Dimitri begged her again to trust him. After a lot of arguments, he stated that he did not have as many millions as she really thought he had. Christina became angry and asked for an explanation. Dimitri just said that his liquid assets were only some thousand dollars. Christina's eyes were wide open and she could not understand why he could not liquefy as much as he needed now to save himself from this traumatic experience. Dimitri asked for forgiveness and understanding, but to no avail.

Christina delivered a few hurtful comments about how she could have possibly trusted him and why he was deceiving her. Dimitri reiterated that he never talked about his money and wealth and everything she assumed was her own speculation. Christina burst into a temperous monologue about how she was deceived by his status and left her country to join him and then was unable to resolve a crisis because he did not have enough liquid assets. Dimitri wanted to stop the discussion as he was going back to his original point that she should visit Konstantin and everything would be OK. She burst into tears and complained why she had put her life into his hands? Since he was unable to resolve this serious crisis. Even when he tried to change the subject, she was so sorrowful that he was unsuccessful. Finally, she agreed to leave that day to go back to New York and travel to Greece and meet Konstantin in the next few days.

In the meantime, Joe and Giovanni unsuccessfully tried to convince Mr. Wells to forget the rules and the legality and go against Dimitri's wishes so they could get him out of jail. They assured him that they would keep it confidential and that was only for the benefit of their friend. Mr. Wells insisted that he needed the agreement signed by Dimitri. He could not violate his oath to Dimitri. The conversation did not become more fruitful and the two friends could not understand what was going on between Mr. Wells and Dimitri and why they had let their friend set-up this trust-like fund, which only authorized Dimitri to move funds. The only thing that Mr. Wells reiterated with pleasure was that the fund had a high enough balance to cover the bail expenses.

Joe and Giovanni gave up, as they could not understand why Dimitri would prefer being in jail instead of ordering Mr. Wells to release the money, or transfer money from his personal European accounts, which probably had more money in them compared to Mr. Wells' managed fund.

Funds and lives; stubborness for just a bail; rejection; punishment; love and humiliation.

Dimitri's mind could not stop calculating over and over again. He looked as though he was lost in space and time; always distracted, he lost the desire to walk outside with his inmates or go for lunch out of his cell. He was sick and tired of all the games and insults that his inmates graciously passed at him. He left his cell minimally and got his meal in the cell. Every time he left his cell to go out he was always attacked, but minutes later the guards would save him.

He had some people who sympathized with him but they were the weak, the ones that could not help him. Dimitri thanked them with his eyes every time they tried to offer help or their compassion. His nights were not quiet as many people made noises and provoked other inmates. Dimitri once tried to calm down someone across the hall and on the bottom floor. He cried all night and Dimitri tried to ease his pain with words. Immediately, many around him made fun of him and then Dimitri told all of them that he had nothing against them, they could go ahead and humiliate him but he would continue to comfort the desperate inmate. Almost everyone made fun of him and insulted him. To them he represented the unrealistic wealthy and hypocritical crowd. Somehow they learned that he had enough money to pay his bail but preferred to stay in jail. The majority of the inmates talked during their social time about him and they were convinced that Dimitri was a nutcase.

The day Christina decided to go to Greece to find Konstantin, she talked to Dimitri by phone and expressed again her disappointment in his behavior. She told him that his mother's mental health was deteriorating and his grandfather was still in a coma and not speaking to anyone. Dimitri felt like a knife had penetrated his heart. He was so hurt and could not understand why Joe and Giovanni could not come up with the money.

He was very sad and thought of sending a telegraph to Giovanni and Joe to beg them for another visit. He knew that if he did that they would come at once. He finally decided to do it and was somewhat relieved. Suddenly he broke into an unexpected smile, as it looked like he found the solution to his problem. Even though a bitter facial expression afterwards, showed that it was not the perfect solution.

Suddenly his mind was full of music and tunes that came and went. He thought of his early days in Astoria, the Spanish Romance, and the guitar and then looked high, outside his small window from which he could see the moon. It was a bright moon; a beautiful moon; soon after he whispered, "it is only a paper moon". He thought that this was similar to another Greek song by one of his favorite lyricists. "Paper moon! Hm... maybe that was the inspiration?" he whispered. He came up with the idea to write a limerick or a poem and have Joe sell it for a significant advance to a singer or a record producer. He was very confused, but all of a sudden thought that he should be inspired by his favorite poet and perhaps write something very good. Minutes later he penciled it on a piece of paper:

Behind every bright sun, a moon will follow
Will agitate souls when the sky will borrow
Behind every truth, wicked lies are hiding
they agitate lives and people keep fighting
Behind every single hero, a victim will appear
men baptized in blood think enemies disappear
keeping their eyes closed, accepting lies
but tears of sulfur drop from God's eyes

Who could see what fate, on his behalf, has written?
Who would give his piece to his brother to be eaten?
who would go back and who would go ahead?
who would like to loose and won't be disturbed?

Demolish my roofs, my doors and my walls
Let me share your light, and hear your calls
Let me, from your raindrops, to quench my thirst
Trumpets call for the new Jericho now to burst
Heroes and victims go, as always, together
Holding hands go forth every day and forever
A lifelong journey through tempests and tides
They soon forget that every coin has two sides

He thought that this poem may have some merit and Joe may get a favorable advance from one of the producers who had benefited a lot from them in the past. He thought that it was a great idea to write more poems. However, he was busy writing to Konstantin and some other friends. He never stopped that correspondence. Some of them got a letter almost every other day.

All and nothing; funds for many lives; the dollars, the humiliation and the cry.

The moments in jail brought back strange memories that haunted Dimitri. A cry interrupted him here and there, but he thought of more lyrics for a particular song. The next day he received the news that Joe and Giovanni would come urgently to meet him. Dimitri was happy but also worried, as he was expecting them a day later. "Finally, my friends succeeded ..." he thought, but Dimitri had a bad dream the night before and was anxious to see his friends. He had another solution in mind, besides a poem or two or a hypothetical advance from a publisher. The time came when the guard took Dimitri to the visitors' room where Joe and Giovanni were waiting for him. They were both looking at the floor; it took a while for them to break the absolute silence and whisper something. A few moments before Dimitri reached his chair; Joe lifted his eyes and saw Dimitri's eyes. Giovanni sensed that and looked at Dimitri as well.
D: "What's wrong guys?" After a long pause, "Is something wrong?" He noticed that no one was looking at him, but at the same time noticed a small case next to Giovanni. He recognized that this was his melodica. "Wow, Giovanni, you are great! You brought me my melodic," he smiled and forgot about everything else. Jail had made a simple pleasure look like an amazing luxury.
Gi: "Yes, this is for you ... your cousin thought about it...." He paused for a while and then Dimitri asked once again what was the matter?
Giovanni proceeded to the window and gave the melodica's case to the guard to pass it to him. He looked at him deep into his eyes and whispered, "I have bad news."
Dimitri immediately sensed the severity of the news and screamed, "What is it?"
Joe immediately said, "Relax Dimitri. Please it is not easy... oh God ... there is no easy way to tell you this."

Dimitri started sweating and asked again, but this time he whispered,"What is it?"
Giovanni looked at him and told him, "There was a plane crash last night, did you hear about it?"
D: "What? No, of course not, but what does that have to do with me?"
Gi: "God bless you my friend," and burst into tears... "Christina was on that plane!"
The tragedy registered now on Dimitri's face as soon as he heard Giovanni's words. His face looked like a marble statuette, which was just casted by a depressed artist to look older and in need of mercy. Three-seconds later he screamed, "No!" which was a long and loud scream while he held his hands and covered his ears at the same time. Joe and Giovanni stood up and stuck their faces to the window that was separating them. Dimitri stood holding his ears and screaming, "NO!!". The guard rushed to him and tried to calm him down, as it was obvious that he knew what was going on.
Joe and Giovanni with tears in their eyes tried to calm him down, and said that they had not recovered all the bodies yet and there could be a miracle that she had survived the accident. Dimitri was in tears and with deep sorrow asked them about the possibility of this to be probable. Joe and Giovanni stumbled about and Dimitri realized that the hope was minimal. Dimitri was carried to his cell, as he was unable to walk. The inmates realized that something is wrong with him. This time only a very few inmates made derogatory comments as everyone sensed that there was something seriously wrong with him.
Minutes later the guard opened his cell to deliver the melodica to him. Dimitri did not even look at him. He constantly faced the wall across. The guard told him that he had to go back to the visiting room, as his friends needed to see him again. Dimitri asked him to be allowed to make a telephone call as soon as possible. The guard took him to the telephone booth and Dimitri called his cousin in Astoria. Since he had been in jail he had not contacted anyone in his family. His cousin picked up the phone and asked him right away, "Why did you do this?" Dimitri asked for clarification and the cousin delivered to him an angry statement; he told him that he was such an insane person, with foolish pride for not paying the bail already. Dimitri apologetically tried to clarify that he called to learn about his fiancé's fate and what

his family knew about the accident. His cousin said fiercely that he had more serious problems to care about, as this was not the only one. Dimitri asked for clarification. His cousin told him that after getting the news, his father had a lot of wine and stood up in the Greek tavern to dance a dance of sorrow, a "zebekiko". After his first turn he had a heart attack and died on the spot! Dimitri dropped the phone from his hands. He could not believe what he had just heard. He was delirious, full of tears, and screamed so loud that the guard came and carried him back to his cell. Dimitri asked again for mercy and requested to be let out to meet Giovanni and Joe sooner than the evening visiting hours. However, this was against the rules and he knew very well that he had to wait.

In the meantime, he could not hold back his screams and tears. His inmates were disturbed and bombarded him with curses that normally no one would tolerate. Initially they made fun of him saying he cried like a woman. Later on, they threw any object that could possibly pass the iron bars, any object that could hit his body and reprimand him and make him shut up.

Dimitri was exhausted by the evening and when he met Giovanni and Joe he asked them if they knew about his father. They assured him that they found out about it later and were very sorry and tried to console him as best as they could. Dimitri a few minutes later realized that his tragedy and bad news were not over yet, but spread to every person he loved. His mother was going insane in the hospital. She lost touch with reality, not recognizing anyone of her relatives. Her sentences made no sense and she had a permanent smile on her face, not her regular smile, but a smile that underlined suffer. And his grandfather, yes his beloved grandfather in his 96th year of age was in a deep coma. He could never accept the news that Dimitri was jailed and perhaps the sum of all the disasters made him fall into this coma. Dimitri was shocked to a degree that no one could discriminate his sweat from his tears, his friends could not tell which one was which and were worried to see this aqueous layer expelled from his body. He never realized the degree of this disaster and what his own tragedy could bring on to his family.

He had touched the lives of the people he loved most in such a negative way. He realized that he had lost his fiancé and his father and was also loosing his beloved grandfather and mother. He realized that everyone else in his family was seriously angry with him including his best friends, as he heard and sensed that everyone held him responsible for all these tragedies. Why was he being so stubborn and so foolish to refuse and pay that bail? God, after all, had blessed him with such a wonderful life, full of success and awards. He had acquired recognition in his field and generous royalties for his creative work.

Dimitri had always been a giving person in the last dozen years; a dozen years of personal glory and recognition. Every one of his relatives had his support, predominantly financial support, when needed. Dimitri traveled too much around the US and Europe, and perhaps was not always next to his family, but he always contributed financially when a relative needed help. Dimitri never asked them to repay him or enforced any deadlines for the return of a loan. Many of them never did, but everyone in his family knew he was wealthy, so they did not care too much about being on time with their payments. Why would such a person be so stubborn and cheap in his personal tragedy, which became a tragedy for all of his beloved family members? In addition, Christina's family was very upset that their daughter abandoned them to follow him to the States ... and what happened at the very end? ... His request cost her her life, the life of a very beloved person within her own family. Everyone was against Dimitri and his rotten decision and pride. Even Giovanni and Joe gave up on him.

Now, he was alone in his cell crying out loud and the other inmates were getting mad at him and continuously cursing him, ordering him to shut up. But his weeping was continuous and immense. It sounded like the crying of a baby, but at the same time the crying of someone who suffered the ultimate loss in his life. He asked to see Joe and Giovanni again, but the guard told him that they had left. Dimitri didn't believe him, and begged the guard to declare that this was not true. The guard told him that he should relax since his two friends had left feeling very angry at him and probably resented him as well. The guard warned him to stop crying before the whole jail population attacked him. There was not anyone in there who did not resent him at that moment for his silly crying.

Dimitri did not listen to the curses and the loud mocking from his inmates. He was in his own zone of pain and did not listen to what was going on around him. He cried for hours. He cried until he fell to the floor exhausted. He felt powerless, unable to move his fingers. He stared at the ceiling. He was dehydrated and had no strength and power to move from that position. His mind blanked and he closed his eyes, opened them again and closed them again. He saw his grandfather walking with him, suddenly he saw and felt the kiss of his mother and the smile of his father. He imagined the embrace of his fiancée, but also her yelling at him. That scene, the same scene where she attacked him verbally ... since he was responsible and the person who she depended upon did not even have the power to help himself ... all these images came to his mind again. His mind felt static for a while. He could not think anymore, he could not feel anything anymore. He could not even feel the sensation in his feet or anything else. His prayers came to his mind and all of a sudden he started again. He started praying again with all his power and energy. He had nothing else to do other than pray; a strong and firm prayer and all of a sudden his mind was shut down again. The second movement of Beethoven's seventh played in his mind again and again, soon faded out and minutes later it started again. He saw a full symphonic orchestra in front of him, repeatedly playing that motif; again and again. When the music slowed down and became quieter he realized that his inmates were still yelling at him, but later the orchestra became loud again, so very loud that it covered their voices. He found the power to move his feet and started feeling the cold and wet floor under his body again. He immediately made a huge effort to curl up his body forming almost a circle and stop shivering. He regained his feeling but was now cold and shivering. He screamed and moved like a serpent towards the bed with squeals of pain. He tried to get onto his bed to wrap himself in his blanket. All of a sudden the guard came to his cell. He had a telegraph to deliver to him. Dimitri could not stand up but saw that the guard had dropped it inside his cell. It was not the proper time for him to throw a telegraph in his cell and Dimitri thought that someone paid the guard to have this done. He felt that the telegraph was important. He thought at once *"Thank God! You heard my prayer – it is Konstantin"*. He closed his eyes for a few seconds and tried with all of his power to crawl towards the piece of paper. A few seconds later he reached it and unfolded it with accelerated anticipation.

"Oh my God!" he screamed. He was surprised to see that it was not from Konstantin, but from Germany. He thought that it was from his dearest friend Alexander who he was friends with for the last dozen years and worked closely with for many years. To his amazement he saw that it was not from him. It was from Christina's parents. As he unfolded it, trembling from the cold he read every third word and was terrified, as he could not understand what it was about. He tried to concentrate and later found the power to read it word by word and tame his anticipation to understand it. It was a powerful statement against him, blaming him for the loss of their daughter … but not only…

"OH MY GOD!", Dimitri screamed as he read the last line that said, her doctor revealed to them that Christina had been diagnosed a few days before the accident, pregnant. Apparently she was the only one who knew this and took her secret with her. Except that her doctor knew about it and when he heard about her demise, he notified her closest relatives. Dimitri's face was numb and his body felt calcified. He did not realize that he had so much power, but an intense and prolonged primal scream was expelled from his body. The whole jail froze with that scream and everyone wondered where it came from? Almost sounded as supernatural…they did not understand how such a "human rag" screamed so loud. His cell neighbor felt that his whole body resonated with that scream. The rest of the inmates became for a moment and moved towards the iron bars to see him. The silence ended at once, since Dimitri's weeping started again. This time the weeps sounded like he was suffocating and were not consecutive. His head touched the floor while he was kneeling. All of a sudden he started talking, but no one could understand the words. Most of the inmates repeatedly cursed him out using the same curses over and over again. The whole jail was in absolute chaos. His cell neighbor from the left side put his hand through the iron bars and successfully threw his wooden dish at Dimitri's back. Dimitri perceived immediately the blow from that hard and heavy wooden dish and his weeping peeked.

"Next time you leave your cell, I will break every one of your bones, you idiot. Just shut up". His other neighbor though, to the amazement of the inmates tried to calm him down and told them, "he is already in a lot of pain, please have mercy."

Left neighbor: "What mercy? He is such a nuisance, this coward."

Right neighbor: "Oh please, there is something wrong. Please all of you give him a break!"

Left neighbor and others: "Give him a break? He should give us a break! That stupid crying cannot be tolerated anymore."

"Yes…..yes!" most of them yelled.

"If he is as rich as they say, why doesn't he save himself and get himself out of this hole?" Someone yelled. This comment made most of them laugh.

"And you guys thought of asking him for money to save you!? Hahahha," someone else said.

"Who was such an idiot to expect money from such a looser?" another one said.

"Hey idiot, if you have money, why are you weeping and kneeling down like a serpent?"

"Haha. I am one of the idiots who I thought that you could save me. Look at you now, how stupid! You can't even help yourself!"

"Yeah, look at that wealthy idiot."

Dimitri was still on his knees with his head down whispering, but no one could hear what he was saying.

"Hey you idiot, why don't you sell your house and get us out of here, we will teach you how to live life!"

His calm neighbor yelled at all of them, "Please! Don't you see that he is suffering, leave him in peace, please?"

"Shut up, you're just as stupid as he is!" the angry left neighbor replied. " He is just a criminal like you."

"I may be a criminal my friend, but he does not look like one of us," said the calm neighbor from the right.

"Haha, another wise idiot amongst us. Maybe you are also wealthy and successful like this idiot right here? That is why you ended up being his neighbor…..ha ha."

"Mind your own business mister. You can say whatever you want against me, but this man from the very first day he entered this jail, looked clean and may be a victim of some kind of misunderstanding."

"Sure…. a victim of his stupidity. He is just a moron and nothing else. But he better be a quiet moron, since we have to rest and sleep soon. You hear me, moron! Just shut up for the rest of the evening, otherwise I will break your neck the next time you are out!"

All this time Dimitri could not move, but continued to be with his head down and kneeling. He did not give any sign that he was following what was going on; It looked as if he could not hear the curses or any dialogues as he looked disconnected from his environment. All of a sudden everyone was silent again, and they could barely hear Dimitri's whispering.

His angry neighbor took his other wooden spoon and successfully threw it into Dimitri's cell, but this time he did not hit him. Without moving Dimitri continued whispering.

"What's he saying?" the angry neighbor asked.

"I think he is praying," the calm neighbor answered.

"Haha what an idiot – to whom! Haha what a superidiot! In his place I would ask to have my money at once and get out of this hell. The guy is insane to stay here. You know what? I bet he is a con artist and has nothing, not even a brain," he then reached for his wooden fork and this time successfully hit his head.

"Wow! Great shot!" the inmates from across the hall yelled. "Well, next time he is out, we will leave out the spitting and cursing and we will make him regret with our own hands the disturbance he caused!" said another one.

"You better leave him to me," yelled another inmate from upstairs. "I will teach him how to behave."

Dimitri felt the wooden spoon and moved a little bit. He burst to tears again.

"Here we go again," the angry inmate noted and immediately yelled, "SHUT UP CHICKEN!!"

"Everybody leave him alone for a moment please," his calm neighbor yelled.

"Will take care of you as well," someone else yelled at him.

"It's OK. At least I deserve it, but he does not," the calm neighbor replied.

"Yes, better be friends with him so he can pay your way out…. Hahaha," someone else yelled at him.

Dimitri crawled and moved towards his bed. With a lot of effort he successfully climbed up and fell on his back staring at the ceiling with his eyes completely red from the running tears. The recurrent Beethoven theme was there and all of a sudden he felt like he couldn't control his mind again. He saw everyone smiling at him, his grandfather, his mother, his father and Christina also who was even there, telling him not to worry. The visions continued and he crossed his hands on his chest. He saw his grandmother kneeling in front of the epitaph on Good Friday and remembered every prayer she had taught him. He tried to remember all of them, word for word, but his brain was dispersed in so many directions and he kept seeing all these vivid colors and images of his family smiling at him. Huge! Wide! Smiles! He would see Lauren Paulmerts' eyes staring at him and suddenly they would disappear and then all of a sudden he realized again, the depth of the mourning that he had been immersed in … however, it did not last. The darkness started fading away and he saw everyone smiling at him again, everyone being proud of him. His mumbling was intense and he could not feel any part of his body; he was almost in a coma. Visions flashed in front of his eyes as he was in a continuous raving and delirious state. He was physically paralyzed, but his mind was racing. He saw Lauren's eyes again and his grandfather petting his head as he used to do since he stepped foot in Astoria. But this raving and his hallucinations did not last for a long time. Dimitri soon realized that he was in bed in jail and was unable to move his feet or hands. The tears came again and again and a few minutes later he passed out from exhaustion.

He opened his eyes again, but had no idea how long he was out. An intense dehydrated feeling forced him to move and reach out for some water. He realized that it was in the middle of the night and everyone was sleeping. He realized that a glass of water was right next to him … "the guard probably placed it here", he thought. He drank the water and was immediately immersed again in a deep depression, as soon as all the sad things that happened in the last few hours came back into his mind. But all of a sudden they disappeared again. He had some remaining strength to pray and deeply prayed to God. He had hoped that it was all just a bad dream and he would wake up next to his parents, his grandmother and grandfather. He repeated again and again the prayers his grandmother had taught him.

Minutes later he opened his eyes and noticed the silence around him. His head started spinning and he heard the tempestuous pounding of the ivory keys. Melodies came the one after another. The tempest, the appasionata, the pathetique, but the disasters were not in his head. He could not understand where he got the power to recreate with such details the strikes of the ivory piano keys. He was again in a raving state, deliriously hallucinating. The old man, yes! The old man was in front of him. Ha! The old man! Yes, he was there at the bus station. Dimitri was on his way to take the bus to the countryside of Greece. People usually flocked to the bus station to wait for the bus, but it was the 1970s when no one had money for food, outside their

home, especially snacks and sweets from a bus station. Dimitri loved the sweets and picked up his favorite snack and headed to the cashier. He had to pass all these snack booths to get to him. He was on his way to pay, but wait! …, all of a sudden he came almost face to face with an old man. His eyes were fixated on Dimitri's eyes. The old man was in his early seventies and had a genuine face, a face that evoked respect. He did not wear expensive clothes but evoked class and good values. Dimitri didn't know why the old man was standing frozen in front of him, petrified, staring deep into his eyes. Indeed, he was frozen and his eyes were locked. Dimitri felt intimidated and lowered his eyes, and as he did that, he saw that the old man had a pack of biscuits in his hand… The old man was petrified in these few seconds and it was obvious that so many things were going through his mind. Dimitri proceeded since it was not his business to find out what was going on with the old man. He went to the cashier and paid. As he was walking towards the cashier he then realized that the old man was probably petrified because he was thinking of stealing the cookies. He quickly turned back and saw the old man still petrified in the same position. Then he put all the pieces together in his mind, the scene, his facial expression, his direction towards the bus and not towards the cashier and realized that the old man was frozen in place because he was embarrassed about stealing. A sudden and potent embarrassment, that a wrong decision at a single moment, could bring to the rest of the life. That fraction of time, that turned him from an honorable man into a thief. The moment that transformed a life full of fights and struggle with respect to misery and pain. His thoughts disappeared as he reached the cashier who greeted him cheerfully and Dimitri did the same. He felt the happiness of the shop owner when he got the cash from Dimitri. He felt that he had interrupted the shop owner from a series of calculations. He realized that these were calculations on how to pay rent, bills and family needs. He was assured that this was the case as the shop owner was extremely happy to have such a good customer, who left him some money, as the rest of the people in the bus station were staring at his goods but not buying them.
All of a sudden he felt compelled to buy an additional item, a pack of gums, even though Dimitri didn't liked gums. He got it and walked towards the bus booth. While he walked towards the aisle from where his bus was supposed to depart, he recognized the old man. He was sitting on a chair with

a petrified look on his face as he was gazing a borderless horizon, with his infinite abstract gaze. Next to him was a five-year old child. The child had opened the pack of biscuits and was fully concentrating on them. The child was animated and lively, evoking happiness, a happiness that stemmed from a single pack of biscuits. The old man's face was the opposite. The tragedy on his face and his gaze were reminiscent of the leading actor in de Sicca's "Bicycle Thief". He was still petrified, since moments earlier he gambled his respect for a single pack of cookies. The seventies were not easy for the Greeks and people could not spare change for snacks. However, the five-year old, possibly his grandson, was not aware of how his grandfather got the cookies. Dimitri passed by unnoticed and continued to his booth. Moments later, he tipped a twelve-year boy to deliver a paper bill to the old man. The twelve-year old did as he was instructed. He told the old man that the bill was laying next to his feet; therefore it probably fell from the old man's pocket. Dimitri could not see the facial expression of the old man. But he saw that he took the bill from the twelve-year old. He stared it for a minute or two and then he stood up. Dimitri with the class of a secret agent followed the old man. The old man went back to the snack booth and ordered a cheese pie. He gave the paper bill to the store-owner and to his amazement he did not accept the change. The storeowner scratched his head, but was radiating happiness. Dimitri hid behind a column and watched the old man returning to his grandchild with the pie in his hand. He shared it with his grandchild, while the storeowner stroked the pen on the paper with happiness for some additional calculations whistling happy tunes.

The memory passed in front of Dimitri's mind alive and colorful and his delirium continued to a tango song; the powerful and potent rhythm of tango was pounding in his head; every single cell of his being, vibrated to that intense and passionate sound ... oh the tango! How much he loved the tango! There is nothing else in the world as passionate and as complete and as multidimensional as a good Argentinean tango. The fierce and vibrant dialogue between the bandoneon and the piano, which pounded heavily; and in the background he could feel the double bass along with the vertigo that the bow of the violin created. The tango was pounding in his head over and over again and Dimitri saw the dancers move in an astonishing and delirious rhythm embraced and united like one! One flesh, but two bodies together.

The music flashed again and again in his hallucinations while the typical intense cricketing of the violin in the Nuevo Tango increased his raving state. All of a sudden he became aware that his mind was occupied by absolutely amazing music instead of being focused on his mourning. It became clear to him that he could not control his brain, which has chosen to project a couple dancing to the passionate invitation that the bandoneon and strings had irresistibly offered them. But why was the rhythm so immense and vibrant? Indeed fast-paced he was focusing on the well-shaped legs of the dancer in every ecstatic lingering of the music? And what kind of music? A real poem of unprecedent depth and beauty. Music that evoked the unprecedent passion and internal flame … ah right! Similar to the passion of a Chopin's waltz or encapsulating the power of a Beethoven symphony? "But how can this be possible?" he thought. "How can I think about Chopin's tenth waltz and the powerful feeling I had when I heard it the first time? How come I can think about the first night out with my friends in a tavern where we sneaked wine under the table? Oh and talking about a table, oh yes! All these spices and the aromas of the Christmas table when the grandfather used to put extra clove in the honey walnut cookies! And what about that pumpkin pie that joined the symphony of the Greek desserts to honor our new home and country! How nice did that platter with oranges in the middle of the desserts with cinnamon and almonds look! And of course the vanilla in the fragrant pudding what a divine thing… divine? What is divine? What is it?" Dimitri wondered. "Divine were only Lauren's eyes. But then who was there at the Gare du Nord in Paris? What a set of beautiful blue eyes. She came out of the crowd holding a boy in her right hand. Tall, slender with thick beautiful dark hair and two blue lagoons that reflected the sky; but … what sky? There was no sky. It was inside the train station, the Gare De Nord! I was many feet away, but our eyes crossed and I was overwhelmed. So much that I looked again… and she … wow she looked again. Our eyes met four times, at least, in less than a minute. But she had a child with her. He was perhaps eight, or seven? Was he her son … who knows? But I was nicely dressed that day, right after my presentation at that stupid conference. Perhaps I looked good, my jacket, my coat. I was well dressed… hm … Maybe I looked like someone she knew… maybe she was confused. But her eyes stood out so much amongst all the hundreds of people… how come? … And she looked again and again. What would I give to have this moment back! To have this moment back! REALLY! And go talk to her. Find out who she is. Maybe she was not married, may be she was accompanying her nephew? MAYBE SHE liked me? How can I find an answer to these questions? How can I turn back the clock? How can I find the lyrics to the Spanish Romance? How can I? Please, my one and only creator let me know, what is my way into this world? Why did I end up here after all I have done? And why did I have to live through this? How can I ever prove that I was right? I saw the spike; I saw the pressure build up? I did have … I did … I had … Wells wanted to give up and all these kids … why should I? Why am I here? Responsible for all these disasters my Lord? My family, my love … my unborn child, everyone I ever loved is away or suffering because of me? How could I know… why everything happened so fast? How could I ever imagine that everything would go, get lost, vanish and pass away? Why did I have to? Why did you abandon me? Why did you abandon me? Why have you abandoned me? And all this insane grief and sorrow is all over my head, all over me! What do I do? I think about an old man, a tango, a waltz and two blue eyes? And what is all that about? The music in my head? Am I a criminal for destroying everything great due to my stubbornness and stupidity and for thinking about all these wonderful things? What kind of person am I? I close my eyes in the midst of sorrow and I see paradise? Where does all the suffering and sorrow go?

What is life my Lord? What is life? How can I ever think of all these beautiful and precious things, my favorite things, when I caused death, sorrow and grief to of that magnitude? Is that part of my insanity? What is life after all? Why do I think about all these things in such time of sorrow? Is life a paradise? Is life the place for the chosen ones? Or am I going insane? Is life so sweet and great for people to return to it after they pass away? Is life a paradise? Do we return? Even when we go through pain, sorrow, grief, when we close our eyes, do we remember the happy moments? Does my fellow man who suffers, close his eyes and see the good moments? The happy moments? When our grandpa used to help me with my very first steps? When one of the dreams became reality? When our highly anticipated success becomes reality? And when we are able to kiss our love for the first time?

What is life my Lord? Is it a way to get rewarded? Do we only have one chance? Or is this the case for the ones who sin? And the others, who get granted paradise, return? Return back to life? Is there that chance? Or is there just the resurrection that I was taught? Resurrection indeed, and no matter what happens to me, I do believe in it. Do I? Would I be strong enough till the very end? Would I? Or would I be able to get out of here and live again, see the people I hurt or misjudged or I did not treat right and ask for forgiveness? Would I be able to leave this cell and restore my family's name and pride? Would I be able to see my friends, my family, my love? Would I be able to see that smile again, the smile of my mother where she holds me again after such a long absence? Isn't life so beautiful, and if you created all this beauty on earth what is heaven like? And then what are the lavender hills in Provence? Or the blossomed almond trees by the Greek coast? How can heaven be better than Ansel Adams' Rocky Mountains landscapes? Or the autumn leaves in Rhode Island? What can surpass the golden maple leaf or the pine needle and the sacred leaves of the olive tree? Perhaps the proud cypress? And how about the beautiful sea, the alpine lakes, Big Sur's cliffs or the blue and white breathtaking volcanic Santorini? Or the beautiful streets of Paris and the picturesque Salzburg? Your presence is everywhere on earth … so isn't that a heaven for humans, if and when they learn to live in peace? Oh thank you God for everything, but why? Why am I here to create all this sorrow and grief? Nobody will ever want to be near me from now on. Forgive me if I have done anything to hurt you; or hurt my fellow man. Please help me as much as you can and thank you for all your help. Please help me, please. What happened to the "Duino" poems that my Grandpa once recited to me; his words that I will make it; his persistence to never forget his words; that day in the basement of our humble house; and his statement that happiness is what follows pain; would I ever have the chance to help the man who had an injured foot? And ignored … that day, the bells tolled…"

Dimitri was so emotionally charged and got his melodica and started playing. He forgot that all his inmates were asleep. He did not even look at the time. He played the melodica in such a way that represented a sorrowful cry; he played five notes in a repetitive manner and in between a passionate crescendo with a lyrical passage. His playing was intense and powerful. Everyone was awake since the melodica was on fire expelling a powerful and intense melody.

Every single one of the inmates was dumbfounded and they all walked slowly from their beds to the iron bars as if they were hypnotized. No one found the power to yell at him and no one interrupted him. The melody was powerful and everyone felt that his soul was on fire, but he played the melody beautifully and masterfully. Dimitri, minutes later blended the Spanish Romance into the music here and there and all of a sudden everyone was holding the iron bars and staring at him. Once in a while an inmate wondered what was going on, but someone from an adjacent cell ordered him to shut up.

The melodica kept "crying" releasing powerful music, which went directly from Dimitri's soul to every wall and floor of the jail and deep into the souls of the inmates, since they felt now the tremendous pain of a human being. The place where he was condemned to remain; together with people who resented him. Dimitri did not stop for at least another twenty minutes and once he stopped three of his inmates clapped forcefully and told him to continue. Dimitri continued and five minutes later he stopped again. More of the inmates tried to encourage him to play again. The guards did not intervene and they were spectators as well. Dimitri played the Spanish Romance; after his third stop Dimitri held with his hands horizontally and wide open the iron bars and started to sing; he sang lyrics that once found in his grandfather's book, in a surprisingly loud voice. "Distressed but ordained his existence pertains, Diffused and confused his emotion refrains..." he could not remember every word and he stopped but his voice was impressive; impressive enough to pronounce the words with passion and in very powerful way that held the attention of every person in the jail. The majority of the inmates were petrified and Dimitri continued and added verses his grandfather never had. The majority of the inmates could not understand a thing, but they had tears in their eyes. His image was the image of a martyr and somehow everyone felt a deep compassion for him.

Dimitri took the melodica again and everyone applauded him. It was such a different moment for them. It was an enjoyable but unexpected evening and even the guards could not understand the power that gripped and immobilized them.

Most of them started crying and when Dimitri became exhausted and dropped the melodica from his hands everyone burst into a loud applause.

Dimitri took his pencil and a paper and started writing. Everyone encouraged him to play more, but Dimitri was passionately writing, driven by a fierce passion and an urge not to forget. All of a sudden his calm neighbor addressed everyone in jail, "I told you that this man is innocent, someone like him cannot be a criminal," … he paused and continued, "after all, do we really know what he did? What did he really do? Does anyone know?" There was a long silence. It was a long minute of silence and his calm neighbor yelled again, "This man has done nothing wrong, he does not belong here."

The hospital and the many lives; revolution and the lawyer; public info and more; the published list is too long

The morning came and there was a very strange sunlight that penetrated the windows of the jail. It had a strong character and different hue than usual. The guards came to pick up Dimitri.

"We have news for you, come outside." Dimitri was on the floor exhausted from crying. He spent his night writing, crying and praying. He never stopped and once in a while he briefly fell asleep but his eyes opened again. His eyes were red rimmed, sad, and mournful. He could not get up and the guards tried to pick him up. Dimitri asked for water and they brought him a cup. He drank it and with the help of the guards who got him up, helped him leave his cell. They took him to the office of the director, who was well groomed and shaved and wearing a suit and a tie. The director had a very clean-cut appearance for his job. He looked at Dimitri and said, "I think you will be released soon." Dimitri was so exhausted and distressed that he did not even lift his head to look at him. "I wanted to share the news with you," he said and passed him a newspaper. Dimitri did not even look at the newspaper. The director told him that he could take it and study it in his cell. Dimitri did not pay any attention to it. The director was forced to repeat himself, but since he noticed that Dimitri was almost in a coma he decided to tell him more.

"Mr. Giovas, it looks like someone in Greece claims that he has enough money to pay your bail."

For the first time Dimitri moved his eyebrows, but not his head. "Who?" he asked with a very deep and heavy voice.

"A fellow named Konstantin Politis, you should know him well."
Dimitri lifted his head and his eyes and looked at the director. "There is
something about Konstantin in the newspaper?" he asked.
Director: "Indeed, Mr. Giovas. Apparently and I suppose you know, he
works for you and manages several of your assets, which apparently can only
be released with your signature."
Dimitri lowered his head again, "But I cannot give that signature."
Director: "Apparently the newspaper speculated about that, so your fellow
colleague Konstantin broke his oath and revealed what type of organization
he was running on your behalf."
Dimitri's eyes lifted again, but now with blood running in his macular capil-
laries, as the intensity of his look was profound. "What? He would never do
that!"
Director: "Apparently the newspaper explains that as well, that is why he will
not come to you to get your signature, but is asking the public to help him
raise the hundred thousand dollars and pay the bail."
D: "What? You know what a hundred thousand dollars are for a poor country like Greece?"
Director: "Well, apparently Mr. Giovas, your friend Konstantin had his lawyer reveal to the media what was going on with your organization all these
years and the story spread to every household in Greece and somehow it looks
like the funds are already there."
The director explained to Dimitri that his friend Konstantin, after having
heard about all the disasters in Dimitri's life, broke his promise to never
reveal the foundation that Dimitri had established with him and another
childhood friend who was a lawyer. It all started several years ago when
Dimitri heard about an accident that happened to his best friend from the
neighborhood he grew up with in Greece. The kid's family had no money to
take the child to the hospital for proper surgery. Dimitri, at that time had
a job and traveled to Europe for the first time. Konstantin had been his pen
pal and they exchanged letters every week. When Dimitri heard about his
childhood friend he begged Konstantin to pay the doctors at his expense and
have the doctors pretend that the operation was part of an academic training
program, so the parents did not have to pay for it. Dimitri sent all the money
to the doctors; Konstantin was supposed to get his childhood friend the best

treatment and service and keep it as a secret. After that, when Dimitri visited Konstantin in Greece, he helped his friend buy a house, in exchange for serving as Dimitri's eyes and ears in Greece. Every problem in his old neighborhood, with his old friends, with his relatives or anyone associated with them, was reported to Dimitri by Konstantin. Konstantin admired Dimitri so much for being successful and philanthropic so he gave an oath to never reveal what was going on.

The night before Konstantin broke down in tears and went to the radio station to announce to the media in Greece that his office is nothing but a camouflaged philanthropic agency. He and his lawyer friend had a list of over two thousand anonymous donations that Dimitri made for his patriots in Greece. The list was long and it was published in the newspaper that night. Konstantin's list included anything from 50 to 100,000 drachmas. From helping the homeless, to sending Christmas gifts to the elderly and orphans, to buying food, furniture, or even financing homes to relatives, friends or many individuals unknown to Dimitri. There was the case of Dimitri's cousin who wanted to buy an apartment but never had enough money. Konstantin took on the task to find one, he paid the landlord half the total price so that the price of the house could be reduced to half. Dimitri masterfully instructed Konstantin to perform his job behind the scenes without leaving any traces behind. The owners of property got a cash bonus to lower the price and pretended that nothing was going on, or at the last moment they had a need to cash out and sell. There were cases of people who had their cars fixed for free since Konstantin took care of the garage expenses. Other cases included orphans who could not afford to go to school so Konstantin provided them with stipends in exchange of their silence. Apparently the list was too long to be published, but Konstantin was on TV hours after his radio announcement and urged everyone who benefited from his organization to chip in to help Dimitri get out of jail. He said that he broke his oath, since he learned what had happened to Dimitri in the past week. He urged everyone whose life was touched by him to contribute towards reaching the goal of raising one hundred thousand US dollars. Konstantin released the books that he had kept during the last ten years to demonstrate that Dimitri had almost spent $800,000 dollars on people in need. The television stations broadcasted and the newspapers published the bank account information where people could deposit a penny or more; and within the next few days he speculated that they would reach their goal.

Dimitri did not move while he listened to the jail director's narration. He listened looking at the floor and when he finished he returned to his cell. The next day, apparently, the international media picked up the story of this strange philanthropist. Apparently his picture was published in many newspapers throughout Europe. A viral response was initiated since the media stations got phone calls that people from small villages to big cities recognized his face. Nobody seemed to know his real name, but many swore that they had met this person. Not only did they meet him, but they also received help from him in very unexpected situations. Others narrated that he came out of the blue and offered Christmas gifts to a coal-mining city in France that had shut down the coal mines, leaving households full of unemployed people. Dimitri was dressed as a postal worker and never revealed his identity. Others narrated the story that this man approached them while they were crying by the banks of the river. Others told stories of someone who had helped them get help in a hospital when they were sick and still others spoke of a man who had presented them a gift, or heard their problems, or gave them food, or paid their bills in exchange for their silence.

The next day his friend in Europe, Alexander, made a declaration similar to Konstantin's. Alexander was the middleman between Dimitri and the poor of Europe. He had spent almost a million dollars on Dimitri's behalf in the past dozen years, to help everyone from the penniless to the ill and weak. Alexander was an alcoholic who had lost his family in an accident and met Dimitri on a bridge over the Danube in Vienna. That meeting changed his life and he promised that he would serve him till the end of his life. But he gave his word that he would never reveal anything to anyone at any time. Alexander worked for him directly.

But later that same day Mr. Wells, the manager of a fund similar to a trust fund, gave a press conference declaring that Mr. Clary Caine whom he represented was nobody else than Dimitri Giovas. Minutes later, one of the leading philanthropic organizations in New York City called Robert Palmer and released a statement saying that there was no Robert Palmer, but instead it was Dimitris Giovas.

It was the day that Giovanni also gave a press conference and explained that he and his best lawyer friend constructed these funds for Dimitri by taking advantage of every loophole in the law. Any kind of loophole they could use, they used it. They transferred the money to offshore bank accounts sheltering their anonymity and created different layers of protection for the owners, something that would be really hard for the US government to discover. They copied the same methods that trust funds and other funds with strange names used to hide money of wealthy individuals. All these funds were protected under a foreign law and their anonymity was secured; Dimitri came up with the idea of establishing these two foundations under another name and entrusting his lawyer friends to run them. The money was donated to various people and organizations in need. Dimitri's royalties fed the accounts constantly and the money was kept in trust-like funds.

Mr. Wells revealed that the balance in his fund was more than a hundred thousand dollars, but Dimitri insisted of not using the funds for his bail; as the money had already been promised to an organization that was building a hospital and immunization center in Mozambique. Every day this project was delayed the lives of thousands of children were threatened. Dimitri told Mr. Wells and Giovanni, who were loyal to him until the last moment and extremely professional, that he could not value his life more than the lives of thousands of children who had no money for food, immunizations shots or even an aspirin.

Giovanni mentioned in his interview that Dimitri never listened and refused to reduce his spendings. He was neither a good manager nor a good listener. He was only good at his work and earning money, but not good at saving it. Giovanni brought up the example that in spite of his cash flow he never fulfilled the American dream to buy a house. He was not prudent when it came to expenses and they always fought about this subject. Whenever he found out through international newspapers, about a need for help, he had Giovanni or one of his contacts either at the Caine or at the Palmer foundation follow up with the appropriate help. Giovanni did not know about the work that Konstantin and Alexander were doing in Europe. Although it seemed that Dimitri worked hard for his regular job, he was smart enough to finish his job fast and spend time reading the papers, or talking and writing to Alexander and Konstantin.

Alexander was interviewed in Europe and mentioned that he was Dimitri's right-hand man all these years in Europe, as Konstantin was in Greece and there was no foundation for him to manage, but he got the money directly from Dimitri's Swiss account, as he was the only other person who had access to it. He revealed in a moment of weakness that everyone thought that Dimitri had at least a million dollars in there, but he had way less than $10,000 dollars and declared that this was probably all the money that he had in cash. It was apparent within a few days that Dimitri did not have enough money to pay his bail. Giovanni and Joe never thought that Dimitri could be so careless, as to ignore Alexander's activity. Konstantin also knew nothing about the other foundations and it appeared that Alexander was the one who knew the most.

The Palmer foundation gave away more than a million dollars over the last seven years of its existence and almost the same was true for the Caine foundation that Mr. Wells supervised.

The news spread all over the world and the Greek bank account that Konstantin had opened received an amount of $150,000 dollars from private donations floating in through wire transactions from all over the world. Within twenty four hours, the shipping industry, big corporations, international banks and foundations donated more than ten million dollars. In France, the government opened its own account and twelve other countries followed the same example. Composers and performers around the world announced that the earnings of their performances would be donated to the Palmer or Caine foundations. Sooner or later every person who heard the story donated a penny, a sterling, a ruble, a dinare, or a yen to a similar account and for the same purpose, no matter if the funds were already sufficient.

Dimitri was aware of the news right away as the guards delivered the newspapers to him and updated him of what was going on around the globe. As soon as his inmates heard the news, they lit everything on fire to demonstrate and force the guards to open up his cell and get him out of the jail to a different section. The guards unsuccessfully tried to stop the uprising. They transferred Dimitri out with pleasure and on his way out everyone clapped for Dimitri. Dimitri who still had his immense tragedy chiseled on his face, stopped to look every single person in the circular tiers of the cells in their eyes. The inmates did not stop clapping and cheering him on. Their standing ovation was unprecedent to a person like Dimitri.

Younger: "Then it looks that the way to "Golgothas" ended for him; so how come everyone is praying for him today? Besides running to contribute money to his foundations and various accounts?"

Master: "Even though they raised more than enough money to bail him out, he did not leave the jail."

Young: "What!? Did he become insane?"

Master: "Not really! He is not insane. When the director told him that multiple installments of $100K arrived to get him out of jail, he did not sign the paper to get out. According to Arizona law he had to pay and sign a disclaimer and an additional declaration that he would behave and agree to go out under certain conditions and circumstances."

Young: "So then he was insane for not signing it and getting out of that hell?

Master: "I told you, he is not insane and I know this first hand because he writes me almost every other day! Please stop this and listen to me."

Young: "Oh no! You? Wait a second … your name is Alexander… oh is it you? Is that why you know all these details about his life?"

Master: "Listen to me. He stayed in jail all those days because he did not want anybody bothering him and this way he could lament the loss of his grandfather, the way a candle's flame is put out, who had unfortunately passed away moments before the news immersed out there. His health deteriorated quickly, as he suffered a serious stroke that almost paralyzed him. The only one left from his immediate relatives (he paused for a long time) … was his mother who was in coma, and his two brothers in NY and Greece. He did not want to be exposed to the public and the publicity that surrounded him. I won't talk about this now, but the government provided him with extra medical care and moved him to a special cell where he was confined alone, but with the proper care. The government also expedited his trial day, which is today. Everyone is praying for him as they hope that there will be some evidence in his favor during the trial and he will be declared innocent. Everyone is also praying for him today as his health has deteriorated a lot and two additional incidents were added to his drama. His beloved mother and his best pal Joe … passed away a few hours ago! Both of them… His beloved mother was on life support for the last few days … and needless to say, I think you understand. Joe was found dead after an accident at his estate in Hollywood. He had drank too much and fell fatally from the stairs. Joe, had sadly became a heavy drinker. He was together with Giovanni and I, we were the only people that Dimitri would communicate with, since the day he decided to remain in jail. Joe was like a brother to him and the news that the bells tolled for Joe were too much for Dimitri. No one really knows what happened. Joe was such a bon vivant and he fell in love so easily, but at the end he always paid dearly. He had such a strong and vibrant personality with such a sharp brain, I really cannot believe that he could ever put himself in such danger. We will all see what is going to happen today when the sun rises in Arizona. In the meantime, we can start working on the records that we need to prepare."

Young: "I feel so sorry for him ... but what makes you think that our project here is so important? Do you really think that this will ever happen?"

Master: "Listen, I am here to execute his orders. We are here to make an assessment in order to restore this church."

Young: "But this is East Germany and they don't have enough money to restore cities bombarded in the Second World War!"

Master: "I know this but Dimitri's funds will pay for it."

Young: "But this is a communist country and first of all they do not care about the churches and secondly they will not allow us to do whatever we want."

Master: "Let someone else worry about this."

Younger: "Couldn't we have chosen another church on the other side of Germany?"

Master: "This is the city where Christina and her parents are from and these are my orders, which I will execute with or without your help, and I will try to make it happen with or without the help of the government."

Younger: "Whatever you say master and I am really happy to know you and work with such an entrusted friend of Dimitri's."

Master: "I am not as important as you think; we better do the work on our own, since the city workers that we were promised are not here and are already two and a half hours late."

When the sun rose that day in Arizona, everyone could feel that it would be a steaming hot day. The court was anticipated to be full and the police had to tame the journalists who were struggling for a seat or place in and around the courtroom. The space was limited and many curious people from all over the world arrived to attend the trial and to see what would happen first hand. It was revealed that Dimitri only had $3000 dollars in his Swiss account and had spent all his big fortune helping people in every place of the world he had visited, plus other places as well. The published list of donations and the logbooks from his assistants were so extensive that every person in the world was moved and everyone was curious to know more about their fellow man. In an era where materialism was profound and everyone forgot to look after his fellow man, Dimitri's example had moved the whole world. It had awakened feelings that had been dormant for years. Every corner of the planet knew about his work, his modesty and humility, from the very poor who were unable to help him to the very wealthy and prominent. Everyone wanted to find out what would happen at this trial where a man like him was accused of destruction of a private property. At this point everyone knew that multiple accounts had accumulated major donations on his behalf. There was enough money to even cover the entire enormous damage that had been caused in the industrial plant that day. It was estimated that it was about nine million dollars. No one knew what Dimitri would eventually do; how he would face the accusation at this trial; would he sign the release for the nine million dollars that was gathered for him in bank accounts for the industrial plant damages? No one knew what the outcome would be. Unpredictable as he did not sign to pay the hundred thousand dollar bail; Very unpredictable, since everyone else would do this to leave the jail. No one knew if he would refuse to sign the allocation of the gathered funds that would enable him to return to a normal life! Also, rumor had it, that the owners of the company would not insist on such a high amount and would be willing to settle for part of the damage. However, the managing directors did not have much of a choice as they had to obey the rules and had to keep the business going. No one really knew at this point what was going to happen, but the case attracted publicity all over the world and everyone was focused on this trial and wanted to see a positive outcome for Dimitri.

The trial with no further evidence but his word; public pressure and the release.

The news that his health was deteriorating created even more sympathy. He was placed in an adjacent hall to the cells and everyone there looked after him. A lot of people believed that his depression and psychological pain had caused the deterioration of his health. However, everyone respected his privacy and some of the people who were taking care of him did everything to keep him away from the spotlight and the news stories.

On the other hand, all the people who had benefited from his gifts, money and acts wanted to meet him, embrace him, hold him and shake his hand. So many people had benefited from this previously unknown person who had been to many places, the person who happened to be around the corner, offering help here and there, wherever and whenever he could. So many people talked to the media about this strange and angelic looking face that had approached them when they were in pain, when they were crying, when they were in the hospital, when they suffered a loss. So many stories had been published in the media over the last weeks about people who had witnessed the presence of an unknown man or the presence of a donation without even knowing who deposited it for them. Many people testified that they thought that their prayers had been answered. Most of them even though they had no proof that it was him, swore that they had seen his figure days or hours before the positive outcome in their lives.

The world had never experienced a life like his. A man who had given everything he owned to his fellow man. Maybe such angels exist but they never reveal their identity... Maybe Dimitri's identity was the first to be revealed because of an incident or was it an accident? Maybe there is no such other person like him in the world! Unknown, silent, humble, giving, ready to abandon wealth to live a modest life and accept poverty, but also underestimate the moment that would reveal his poverty or wealth?

Every person in the world had his attention on the trial that was about to start on that sunny summer day where everyone suffered from the heat in the blazing sunny Arizona desert. Inside the local court room everyone had crammed in to be part of a historic trial. The judge was very respected and the chief judge of the state who had very carefully examined the case and the records of the accident. It was indeed a very puzzling case and crowds surrounded the courtroom already early in the morning. The car escorting Dimtri from the jail approached the building a few minutes after the ninth hour of that morning and the crowds fiercely applauded their hero as soon as he stepped out of the car. He was formally dressed, but everyone saw that he could hardly get out on his own. Tired and exhausted he walked slowly and smiled with tears in his eyes rolling down a very weak, bleached face, which made the thousands of people outside the courtroom cheer him on as though he was a Hollywood star. His pace was slow and he proceeded with his head lowered looking at the ground as the crowd intimidated him and perhaps he desired to avoid looking at the crowd. Some said that he did not want to show his weakness and others thought it was probably part of his low key and modest personality.

Soon everyone was in the courtroom and the crowds were silent outside, waiting to hear anything possible. The judge entered and everyone stood up politely and respectfully. Despite his long service to the community, it was the first time that Judge Collins faced a full courtroom, indeed it was overfilled with people in nicely tailored suits and ties. He started right away with the announcements and read all the appropriate documents. During the trial the industrialists and the managers of the plant recalled the events that took place and admitted that during such a procedure and mainte-nance there was no one to check the action of the engineer, who in this case was Dimitri. They testified that there was no indication of anything that went wrong, and that the factory had suffered tremendous losses from the accident and that the repairs were very costly. When Dimitri's time came to testify, the room fell absolutely silent. He used all of his force to stand up and articulate himself. He immediately went to the point telling the judge that he had to switch off the main system and the back up system in order to test their functions and that's when he saw in a nearby monitor a suspicious increase of pressure in the unit in which the toxic gases were produced. He declared that his only witness at that time was God and no one else. He knew that a local group of students were touring the facility. He did not want to endanger anyone and therefore he decided to switch everything off, which resulted in the destruction of some of the major pipes, valves, and pumps. Basically, a whole production unit ended up being highly contaminated and the total damage was enormous and surely devastating for the factory. When he did it, he was fully aware that it would be a disaster for the company, but he repeated over and over again that he chose to do that and to not endanger the health of anyone there, including the workers and visitors. He was very sad that one worker was found unconscious, but no one could tell why and what happened exactly to him, as he never recovered during these months. Dimitri was very sad and concerned about him but he stated that since it was maintenance of the central controlling panel there were no records and that he could only have God as a witness. He finished by testifying that he has nothing more to say and that he would respect any decision that the court would make.

The managing directors of the plant's company had their lawyers say that they recognized Dimitri's integrity and personality, but the damages were devastating and they needed to be paid. They emphasized that Dimitri's company did not have the money to pay the damages, nor could the insurance company cover it, as Dimitri had violated the clause that called for another person to be present to witness the sequence of the actions. Dimitri's confidence that he could deal with everything on his own had now put him in the position of being guilty and primarily for the criminal charges against the unconscious found worker. But everyone else by that time knew that he was mostly held responsible for the factory's damages.

Dimitri's defense emphasized his integrity and that he is an amazing example of an individual who would never lie. They urged to have every detail reexamined and do a detailed analysis on every part of the control panel and the case, without the consent of Dimitri, since he would never sign off on it. This was a big surprise to Dimitri, as he didn't know that his defense would propose something like that. He stood up and interrupted his lawyer telling the judge, "Your honor, for me it is enough to say that I never lied and I have God as my witness."

Appraisal, but the heavy soul.

The managing directors of the factory bit their lips as they saw that the crowds applauded him with standing ovations, which would put them in the middle of hateful comments from everywhere if Dimitri ever ended up in jail. However, they knew that Dimitri had gathered many donations, which with his blessing could pay the damages. However, the night before they argued with each other about what to do and if they should lower the requested amount. They were afraid that Dimitri would not sign to allocate these funds towards the damages. According to the Arizona law, the judge could order the liquidation of these funds gathered on Dimitri's behalf and the company would eventually get paid, but without the consent of Dimitri the public would condemn the industrialists. So during that moment the head of the board stood up, after he sensed that the trial was not under control and that no one could read Dimitri or what his actions would be, he asked his lawyers to proceed with his plan. The dumfounded lawyers turned pale and looked puzzled and then the head of the team took the podium and read a statement. It was a tribute to Dimitri's character and the company had taken the decision to withdraw the charges against him and let him decide whether he wanted to pay the company any damages. They would trust his judgment and at this point they wanted him to be free and without worries.

Everyone in the court was overcome by a delirious euphoria and the spectators including the journalists, jumped from their chairs, cheered up and applauded the decision of Mr. Blooshing. Indeed, no one could control the crowds, not even the heavy hammering by Judge Collins. Everyone embraced each other with a childish euphoria and the only ones who were still and looking down to the floor were Dimitri and the board members. Indeed everyone tried to reach Dimitri to congratulate him, but the police did a good job holding everyone back; the protagonists of the drama remained untouched and peaceful. Judge Collins' eyes were full of happiness and grace and everyone could see that he would be happy to close the case. He dismissed Dimitri and asked the lawyers on both sides to meet him afterwards.

His lawyers and everyone around him who could reach him embraced Dimitri, but he gave no signs of happiness and would not cheer up. He still looked at the floor and he accepted all the embraces but somehow his face was like Buster Keatons' without the slightest change in his expression. He confined himself into his seat and was oblivious to all the cheers and applause around him.

At least now he was free! Everyone realized that now he would go back to his old life and become part of the society again. The people did not stop cheering for him and followed him to the exit. The police and his lawyers made room for him to cross through the crowds and make his way out of the building. Dimitri lifted his head and said thank you to everyone by waving his head up and down but everyone saw that his head was also waving in a heavy way, as heavy as his steps were. He walked outside with difficulty and heavy steps with the help of the security and his lawyers; Outside the courtroom thousands of people were cheering him on and everyone wanted to embrace and hold his hand. Dimitri's facial expression was full of thankfulness and humility, but still he was not happy. He was still mourning deep inside of him and this was apparent through his body language and moves. The crowd pushed hard to come close and touch him, but his crew successfully put him into the car. The journalists pressured him for a statement in front of the cameras and the microphone, but Dimitri did not move or say a word. He was captured only whispering, *"thank you"* to everyone he crossed eyes with. His car proceeded that way surrounded by unknown citizens and admirers.

The composition is torn, the lyrics as well- May leave something later for all.

Dimitri ordered the driver to take him back to the jail, as he wanted to pick up his personal things himself. The throng of journalists and admirers followed him. He asked the manager to take him back to his original cell. Everyone was surprised to see why. As soon as he entered, his ex-inmates cheered and applauded and Dimitri simply waved his hand by turning 360 degree and waived to everyone in every tier and whispered, "see you later". Everyone was shouting now good words and words of admiration to him. They had no idea why he chose to tell them, "see you later" and some of those with life sentences told him, "Please Dimitri don't say that, you should never come back here again. Forget it!"

Dimitri waved to everyone again while with his right hand holding a bunch of papers in his left hand. His neighbor recognized that these were the papers from his time in the cell next to him and yelled to him, "Sir, please mail me a

copy of whatever you have written there. Please don't forget, I would love to hear your music again, it changed my life!"
Dimitri looked him directly in his eyes and apologized to him.
"Don't apologize, it does not matter, I will hear it one day when I get out and if it is the music or poems or even your writing, I would love to experience them again and I can wait a lifetime for this."
Dimitri looked deep into his eyes and later into the eyes of everyone else who was waiting to hear Dimitri's reply. "I would rather have no one experience this again. No one deserves to know and feel this pain again and I apologize to you, but no one deserves to hear or read this." And with a steady hand, he tore the papers into very small pieces until he could not do it anymore. Then his ex-inmate burst into tears for the torn compositions, but Dimitri could still see trust in his eyes. A trust in Dimitri's actions and a trust that he was forgiven and was allowed to do anything he wanted. Tears started running down his cheeks and he told to everyone, "I may leave something written, later, and for all of you." He did not give any more information, but he turned his back to them quietly and started walking out of the cells.

Nothing left but the love of everyone

The prisoners applauded him thinking it was the last time they would see him. Or maybe the last time they would ever see a man like him. A man who gave everything to simple and unknown people; without asking anything in return. Someone who ended up in jail, because he didn't have enough money to pay for his bail because he gave all of his fortune to the poor, to the ones in need, to the weak and to the ones in despair. A man who lost his family, friends and even his future wife and child. A man who had lost everything he loved. However, the oxymoron was that he walked out of jail, in a world full of love for him. From his first steps outside of the jail to the airport and to the plane, everyone wanted to shake his hand and hug him. Nobody knew what Dimitri was going to do now with his life, his career as an engineer and the big endowment that had been gathered on his behalf. He landed hours later in New York City's airport, where a group of journalists were waiting for him. At the airport was his right hand Alexander, who arrived from Europe. They walked to a room away from the media and a few minutes later Alexander left him alone. Dimitri did not leave the airport. The airline offered him the VIP lounge. Dimitri stayed there all night. The next day Alexander came in with a suitcase and a bag. The journalists followed him but they could not enter the lounge that the airline graciously offered to Dimitri. He had slept and spent the whole day in that room. Everyone in the media wondered what was going on, but there was no way to find out. Suddenly, in the early afternoon Dimitri walked out with his luggage and the bag that Alexander had brought.

The two LPs and the journalists back up

The journalists flocked around him. Everyone tried to extend microphone at him and Dimitri waved with his hand to stop them. He took his time to look everyone in the eyes. As he did take his time for it they stopped asking questions. The journalists suddenly became quiet as they wondered about what Dimitri would tell them and what was going on in his mind. After Dimitri looked at every single person in their eyes he told them, "Gentlemen, I thank you so much for being here. Ah shhhh… let me finish. It is my honor, in fact my great honor, to be surrounded by you, but I have a question for you and please think for a minute before you answer." He paused and continued, "Do you think that the life that I led in the past; which you all claim that you admire; gives you the idea that I want to be on your front page? I think you understand my point; you know how much I have suffered and I can only ask you for one big favor. Forget for a moment what your boss has asked you to do and what he wants from you at this moment. I would like to find peace in the near future and I can only do it with your help. I would like to stay away from the media and the microphones. If you admire me as you say that you do, respect me and leave me alone at this very moment. I respect you and your job, but there are so many celebrities out there that are far more interesting than myself." He waved his head and thanked them with passion in his voice. Everyone remained still and Dimitri quickly walked to another departure gate. The journalists did not move and then the famous photographer Petrazzeli said, "No matter how much his picture will sell for today, I won't be the one taking it." He turned his back to the others and said,

"Good day gentlemen." Half of the crowd followed him and the rest sat dumfounded in the middle of the departure hall.
"Where is he going?" "To Greece perhaps?" "Hey, leave him alone." "We can find out later," some of the journalists whispered. "Did anyone see the records that he was carrying?" "Oh, you mean the bag he was carrying?" "Yes, it was Callas", "no I saw Karajan's face," another interrupted him.
"The bag had two vinyl records, one was the "Traviata" and the other side was Beethoven's ninth," Mr. Brown told them.
"Are you sure?"
"Yes, there were only two vinyl records; the plastic bag was transparent enough."
"And now we will not find out where he is going?"
"We can't leave – we need to get the info."
"Nobody will bother him", Mr. Brown yelled at them!
"No we won't bother him, we will ask the clerks at the airport. Come on, don't be silly."
At this point Mr. Smith from the Herald, spotted Alexander walking to the exit from a departure gate so everyone ran after him, to get close to Alexander as soon as possible.
"Where is he going? Please tell us. Come on, please tell us what is going on!"Alexander tried to calm them down and thanked them for leaving him alone. He told them that tomorrow there will be an official press release announcing that Mr. Giovas will establish a foundation with whatever money was given to him and whatever royalties will come in the future. He will establish a board of directors to handle that and the rest of the charities.
The journalists bombarded him with many questions but Alexander stepped back and told them that Mr. Giovas has basically only two announcements that the new foundation will be established soon bearing the name of his grandfather and that he would oversee the board from distance via telecommunications.

Exile in Switzerland, the melon.

The next day everything was announced and the newspapers' headlines confirmed that he was headed to Switzerland where he probably planned to stay for the time being.

At the airport exit in Switzerland the press did not bother him and he left the airport without anyone bothering him other than to shake his hand silently. Konstantin was with him and escorted him to a car and they drove from Geneva to the inner part of the country.

The next days the papers printed a few paragraphs about the isolated village he chose to reside in the Alps. The people in that village recognized him right away and were pleased to see him. He knew no one in the village, but Konstantin had arranged a rental, a small and modest chalet about a mile up from the center of the village on the slope. A truly isolated place that no journalist had previously approached. They knew though that he would leave the chalet every weekend to walk to the center of the village. The peasants and the local inhabitants always greeted him with a smile, but they also respected his privacy and space. Nobody bothered him and his life was uneventful besides the constant refusal of the storeowners to accept his money. Every time he appeared on the street the local grocer handed him the best melon, which he kept for him. The rest of the citizens of the village left fresh bread and cheese at his doorstep every morning and occasionally some of them dropped off a bottle of wine and chocolate. The summer of 1981 was beautiful and still gorgeous enough for him to enjoy the beautiful nature. Konstantin and Alexander were his only visitors besides a local old lady and her daughter who helped him with the maintenance of the small chalet. The chalet was picturesque, but the fall brought the signs of a lonely and heavily cold winter.

Everyone helps as he directs via the phone; a popular name.

Everyone who was ever associated with his business was in touch with him by phone, besides Alexander who visited him every month. Konstantin was not around as frequently, but both were now working officially in the organization that he had set up with all the donations to his various accounts. He still got royalties from his intellectual property, as he used to in the past when Giovanni and Joe represented him. For some strange reason nobody knew why he kept a distance from Giovanni. He sent flowers to Joe's grave every year. He lost touch with his coworkers at the engineering firm, but was in touch with many of the employees in the new organization that bared the name of his grandfather. He was also in touch with his only brother in Greece, but he never visited Greece again. He did not go to New York either. He passed the whole year of 1982 in that small chalet and the nearby village. He was on the phone most of the day, but with a few people only. He didn't socialize and lived in exile for a long time.

Everyone was waiting for his appearance especially after the accident in India in 1984. Gas leaking from an American-owned insecticide plant in central India killed at least 410 people overnight, many as they slept, according to the official authorities. At least 12,000 were reported injured in the disaster, 2,000 of whom were hospitalized. The death toll in the city and its surroundings, about 360 miles south of the Indian capital, was expected to rise as more bodies were found but some of the critically injured had died. The authorities of India put the death toll at 500, but the news agency's figure could not be independently confirmed. An Indian environmental official, called it the "worst such disaster in Indian history." The Chief Minister of the State, where Bhopal is situated, told reporters that gas had escaped from one of three underground storage tanks at a plant in Bhopal. Everyone recognized that this was similar to the accident that Dimitri tried to prevent three years ago in Arizona. The reports were devastating as witnesses claimed thousands of people had been taken to hospitals gasping for breath, many frothing at the mouth, their eyes inflamed. The streets were littered with the corpses of dogs, cats, water buffalo, cows and birds killed by the gas, methyl isocyanate, which is widely used in the preparation of insecticides. This was the same gas that Dimitri had tried to prevent from leaking out. Doctors from neighboring towns and the Indian Army were rushed to the city of 900,000, where hospitals were said to be overflowing with the injured victims. Most of them were children and old people who were overwhelmed by the gas and suffocated according to the press reports. Even in small amounts, the gas produces heavy discharge from the eyes and is extremely irritating to the skin and most of the internal organs. Exposure can apparently lead to enough fluid accumulation that causes drowning. A spokesman of the American company said it was temporarily closing part of a nearly identical plant in the States while it investigated the Bhopal disaster. "We don't know what went wrong," the spokesman said. The managing director of the company in India, was quoted as saying that the incident occurred when a tank valve apparently malfunctioned after an increase in pressure, allowing the gas to escape into the air in a 40-minute period. It was not clear why the pressure had risen or how the leak was stopped. The environmental official said it was still unclear whether it was necessary to evacuate parts of Bhopal. The poisonous gas spread across about twenty-five square miles of the city, an area said to be populated largely by poor families. The Prime Minister Rajiv Gandhi, called the incident "horrifying," and announced the creation of a $400,000 government relief fund. Mr. Gandhi, traveling in India for the general election campaign, said that "everything possible will be done to provide relief to the sufferers," and added, "such mishaps must never be allowed to recur." The Health Minister of Madhya Pradesh State, told a reporter in Bhopal that 302 people had died in one hospital alone. The state's Chief Minister, reported that about 2,000 people overcome by the gas fumes were hospitalized. At least 10,000 others were treated for symptoms including vomiting, breathing problems and inflamed eyes. Authorities said five factory officials had been arrested and charged with criminal negligence in the disaster. Although the Company in the states reported that the managers said to have been arrested, was incorrect. The officials reportedly arrested were identified as the works manager; the production manager, and three other officials. United News of India reported the factory siren did not sound to alert the neighborhood until two hours after the leak began. It also announced that the police and doctors did not come into the area until four hours after that. The Chief Minister announced that he was ordering a shutdown of the plant and pledged not to allow it to resume production. He said the government might demand that the company compensate all the victims and their families. He also ordered schools, colleges, offices and markets closed. In a statewide radio broadcast later, he said the leak had been stopped and described the situation as "fully under control." He urged people not to spread rumors anymore. Reports from Bhopal said thousands fled the city's crowded districts as word of the leak spread. The plant was opened in 1977 and produced about 2,500 tons of pesticides based on methyl isocyanate annually. In 1978, six people were reported killed when they were exposed to phosgene gas, another lethal mixture produced in the same plant. According to a company's spokesman, the underground tank in which the leak occurred that day contained forty-five tons of methyl isocyanate in its liquid form.

The chemical is colorless, burns easily and is very volatile. The spokesman said enormous pressure had built up inside the tank, forcing a rupture of a valve and allowing the gas to pass into the air, which is exactly what Dimitri said could have happened in his case. According to a statement in Bombay, the storage tanks had special safety features. The main emergency devices, were vent scrubbers, which said were, "meant to neutralize and render the gas harmless prior to its release into the atmosphere. In the accident, the rapid pressure built up resulting in a spurt of gas running unneutralized escaped into the atmosphere," the statement described. All these similarities to Dimitri's case brought his case back into the media reports and journalists tried to approach him again after three years of silence. He never answered calls or commented on anything. He remained silent in his home in Switzerland accepting as guests only the local people, his brother's family and of course, Alexander and Konstantin.

He got an enormous amount of mail and invitations from people who had benefited from his presence in the past, but also from others who had never met him and from every neighborhood of the world. Invitations to extraordinary events, as well as humble and low-key functions were arriving daily. His name was known around the world and was not that rare anymore. Not only the Russians and Greeks had that given name, but many people baptized their children in his name in every part of the world. He knew about it through the letters of his loyal admirers, but still remained silent and distant with everyone.

Lyon Theater; never wanted the first seat.

In 1986, he was spotted in the nearby city of Lyon, where he went to attend a concert at the local concert hall with his loyal friends. As he entered to take his seat in the orchestra section, someone recognized him immediately, stood up and started applauding. The other attendees recognized him too and did the same. All of a sudden the whole theater gave him the most forceful standing ovation that an orchestra could only dream of. Dimitri was the only one without a jacket, as he was wearing a blue sweater and a white shirt. He had a humble outfit and he stood out at the back of the parquet. Immediately, a prominent gentleman in the front seats stood up and begged him to take his seat, so Dimitri had a better view and could enjoy the concert more. As he told the newspapers later Dimitri whispered into his ear that his whole life was a manifestation that he never wanted to have the first seat. He thanked him immensely as the gentleman insisted and explained how much of a pleasure this would give him, but Dimitri gave him a warm hug and took his original seat. Every musician who was already on the stage, as they were waiting for the conductor to appear, noticed this. The newspapers wrote the next day that no other orchestra had ever performed the 3rd of Brahms with the articulation and passion that the orchestra in Lyon did that day.

Concert for the prisoners

The next year, Dimitri was again in the news, for the first time since his arrival in Switzerland. He boarded on a plane to visit the States, but not to New York City. He went to the prison camp in Arizona. Alexander and Giovanni had arranged for a full symphony orchestra and choir to fly to Arizona and give a concert for the prisoners. Everyone was stunned by this action and the orchestra performed Beethoven's Ninth. It was a night full of stars. The orchestra gave a performance of class and the sound of the choir seemed to extend to the infinite and cover the vast desert with a sacred work's sounds. The sky was clear and there was not a drop of rain, but every prisoner had wet eyes. At the end everyone stood up and would not stop applauding. This continued for minutes and it was almost more than fifteen minutes that no one would stop, and no one would seemed to be tired from standing and clapping with full force. Dimitri who was just a silent spectator got up on stage and pulled the piano in front of the orchestra and performed Chopin's third waltz. Everyone was silent at once as a single instrument, without any sound amplification, played the composition. Everyone could hear the voices of the night, earth, desert and predominantly the beauty of Dimitri's performance. All his time in exile he learned how to play the piano; he played the piano for hours and hours relentlessly and became a good pianist. At the end of the piece everyone had even more tears in their eyes and asked for another encore. Dimitri ordered the orchestra to put away the music sheets and play something very unusual, Maurice Zarre's music from "Ishadora" and then there was another encore, a rhythmic piece from

"The Leopard" by Nino Rota. At the end of the piece the prisoners saw that Dimitri was heading out to the jeep that initially brought him from the airport. Hours later, early in the morning he was flying from Arizona to New York and subsequently to Switzerland, without leaving the airport grounds to see the neighborhood where he used to live and the people that used to love him.

When he arrived in Switzerland and after he picked up his luggage he noticed a group of what seemed to be college students who were probably visiting Switzerland, most likely on a holiday. Dimitri stopped suddenly as his eyes followed the tall athletic girl who led the other two of her female friends towards the exit. Dimitri looked at her, as if he knew her from the past. As she was leading her friends to the exit, she noticed Dimitri's eyes and smiled at him. He stepped ahead to follow them; they turned right towards a corridor towards the exit. Dimitri did not take his eyes off her and followed them to the corridor. As he turned into the corridor he could see the tall athletic girl fixing her hair in front of the mirror, which was at the end of that corridor and next to the exit door. Dimitri could see her eyes in the mirror as he approached and broke into a smile. The girl was almost done with her hair and turned left towards the exit that led to the taxis. Dimitri's steps became faster and he was a few feet away from the mirror. He took a brief look in the mirror and tried to turn left but something stopped him. He turned back, and looked in the mirror again. His smile disappeared and he took the exit on the right, which led him to the airport's parking lot.

Visits, technology, email, a legend; Orson on the turntable and the visit of a nephew.

He went directly back to his personal exile high in the Alps. The years that followed were the same as before and he got more frequent visits from his nephew, his brother's son, since he was now an adult man. His nephew adored him and the feelings were mutual.

His nephew introduced him to new technology such as fax machines and slowly the powerful computers. His visits were frequent and there was a similar relationship to the one that Dimitri had with his grandfather. With the only difference that they argued more about philosophical issues and preferences, since his nephew's generation was a far more spoiled, according to Dimitri.

One night before Christmas, in the early nineties his nephew decided to pay him a surprise visit. He rang the bell while waiting to see his uncle's surprised face at the door. He rang the bell again but there was no response. To his surprise, he realized that the door was unlocked so he entered into the living room. He sensed that his uncle was inside as the turntable played music. He saw the face of Orson Wells on the cover and realized that the LP had only two songs; therefore his uncle who had turned on the record player should not be far away. The next second he heard his welcome, but his voice did not sound surprised. He dropped the Orson Wells LP cover and embraced his uncle.

"Who told you that I would be here?"

"Nobody, but I sensed that you were coming."

"Nonsense, my father told you?"

"No, not at all, he didn't."

"Really then who? No one else knows besides him – oh my Mom?"

"Nobody."

"Then how did you find out?"

"Another mystery for you to solve, young man."

"Is it really true that you are out and about and you follow people?"

"Who said this?"

"Lots of people have said so in the last few years. Rumor has it that you transform yourself into a long-haired hippy or add a mustache and wear hats and you go out and about unrecognized?"

"Nah – not that I know of, nonsense, but instead of bothering me with that, tell me why have you decided to spend Christmas with me? Usually you come for the New Year's celebration... as you know I prefer to have visitors at that time."

"I thought that I should stay longer this time as I am done with the University and have more time, will I bother you?"

"No! Not at all."

"Well it looks like you had plans, let me know if I am interfering with anything that you had in mind."

"No son, no worries, I can switch things around."

"But you look like my unannounced visit is keeping you from something?"

"No, not really. You know I am working on a new project and I want to stay focused, as I want to finish some manuscripts for it."

"Everyone believes that in the last ten years or so you have been working on a few theories and mathematical models, but why don't you ever publish them? Everyone is eager to learn what is on your mind these days."

"You think so?"

"I know so! People know that you are an engineering genius and you have time to work on new theories, models and so many other things. Haven't you done that for the past decade or more now?"

"Oh, I suppose so. But why don't you have a seat and tell me about yourself and your school and your girlfriends and something more pleasant."

"I am glad you find these things pleasant, because you should leave this exile and return to life and to the people who miss you and don't want to see you living like a hermit up in these mountains anymore."

"What do they know?"

"Oh again wise man! You mourned enough for all the unjustices and shame that you suffered, so please return to New York or to Greece or to wherever else you want to go, but leave this exile!"

"To New York? Is that where you plan to go for your graduate work after college?"

"Yes, I am considering that as I want to leave Greece and go to New York, but you are still avoiding answering my question."

"Oh yes, the question... But can you tell me about a great movie that you have seen lately? I love the fact that I can watch all these movies up here in my exile, as you call it. You know I have the time for this now and with all these modern machines, I can really enjoy the high fidelity."

"You call this high fidelity? You are still behind in the times and that is part of the reason I am here. Sooner or later I will install a new communication system that will let you communicate in a more efficient and faster way with everyone in the world."

"Really? You know, I am not that interested in that at the moment. Why don't you tell me about the movies?"

"Ah, I am telling you about a revolution and you are still disinterested?"
"Of course I am interested, but I am not looking for revolutions at this time
and I am not sure what revolution your generation can bring to this world,
but have no problem accepting your word."
"Hm.. I see a doubt and you doubt again! ...Oh always so negative, why are
you so confrontational today? Aren't you happy that I am here?"
"Oh yes! Yes of course! I am very happy my little rebel, of course."
"Right, but maybe you should watch fewer movies and go out into the world
that you are avoiding."
"Listen, I experienced a lot of pain out there young man, and I need to stay
here for the time being. I am in touch with my people every day, as you
know."
"In touch? Everything is relative, but you lost your "touch"... you don't
touch as many people nowadays as you used to, when you were down ... out
there, in the real world and in their lives."
"Hmm... you think so?"
"I think so. Yes and you are getting older and you should enjoy life and com-
panionship more and more as ...""
"As...?"
"Well, you better tell me about the theories that you are working on and all
these new models."
"Not the right time, son."
"Oh again that phrase, "not the right time," when is the right time for you?"
"Ha ha. I used to ask my Grandpa that all the time ..." Dimitri whispered:
"but with more reverence and respect ... oh the new generation."
"Well yes, the new generation has ideas and you know very well that when
you are young you have the best ideas?"
"Really?"
"Sure."
"That is not true for Edison or Beethoven or many of the greatest people who
have lived on this planet."
"Well, we can always argue about this."
"No worries we won't, just accept it."
"Confrontational again? Why do you think Beethoven had the best ideas
later in life, because of his Ninth, which is your favorite?"

"Not only. Can you recall Dvorak's ninth? Sure you can, how about Schubert's unfinished? Or Tchaikovski's Pathetique, the sixth?
"I think I can."
"Well, can you recall their second symphony?"
"… (pause) … are you trying to tell me that you have better ideas now? Then why don't you publish them?"
"Not the right time."
"Oh not that again! Ok, let me change the subject before we go in circles; the same circles over and over again."
"Well great!"
"Talking about Beethoven and since you like music and the movies, I saw "Amadeus" the movie."
How did you like it?"
"Well, … hard to say … you know I hated the fact that my favorite composer is portrayed as an immature, childish person with an idiotic laugh. Mozart was the greatest musical genius."
"Maybe, way after Beethoven."
"Here you go again! You try to confront me and argue again. Well do you account that he did not live long enough to have his "best ideas"… in his "late youth?" ha ha if I may say!"
"So you thought that this childish and psychotic laughter was idiotic, and you did not like it?"
"You are right! Absolutely unnecessary and wrong! Like he was on drugs!"
"Well son, the film is a study on one of the most recognized geniuses to have ever lived on this planet. Spontaneous, sometimes, but vivacious and intelligent, moving with a relatively fast tempo and brio; the main character is approached indeed in an unusual way by the writer or director. There is a constant laughter, which produces a ridiculous overtone and makes Mozart look like he was under the influence of drugs, according to some people like you. He looks like he can never be serious … or "normal". The character could be very unsympathetic to the serious admirers of bombastic and classic expression. The creators of this film could be geniuses, as well, since they demonstrate that a true genius can never be understood by perhaps a "normal" person. Indeed all these normal people never understood his real creative soul so how can a genius ever be understood? Why such a genius was so

poor?? Perhaps take it as the intention of the director to show that if Mozart ever lived again he would again be poor and misunderstood! Don't you think that when the director chooses to show you Antonio Salieri, the person who supposedly killed him in the play, in the very final scene in the middle of the madhouse when he's declaring loudly "look around, whatever you see is mediocracy...plenty of mediocracy, everywhere mediocracy"...that perhaps that mediocracy misunderstood Mozart and kept him starving and actually killed him at the end. This could be the reason why you see an obnoxious and a somewhat incomprehensive character. The creator of this film took the risk of making him look bizarre and to differentiate him from the norm. And if you think Mozart's wit and genius was appreciated at that time, then you belong to the majority of the people who killed him with their selfishness and ignorance. Dimitri pronounced the last sentence with intensity and then whispered: "Bothered by his "laughter" ha... how can a genius ever be understood?"

"Wow, you are so confrontational today? What is wrong with you? Do you want me to leave you alone? I adore Mozart and you are telling me that I am like the ones who killed them? I wish I was Austrian and lived in his times."

"Well you are Greek and live now, and you know the famous Greek painter who said that in Greece mediocrity governs and very few Greeks recognized Maria Callas while she was championing and reviving the opera; in every corner and stage of this planet! Well the same story again. Well not long enough, maybe a hundred years from now the Greeks will build a museum in her memory but not now, not you, right? Or are you working on that project?"

"Do you want me to leave you alone for Christmas? Are you really bothered by my presence here?"

"Listen, I am trying to finish a project here and it will be more pleasant for you to go to Verbier, nearby, where I have already arranged a package for you. A package for four days including everything; a nice hotel, meals, a lift ticket and of course entry to the nightclub, where you can mingle with your future fellow New Yorkers?"

"Wait, but you had no idea that I was coming here! Why did you purchase this for me?"

"Well, the best ideas come with age, my friend. Well, listen, this will be better since I need to concentrate here to finish something and then you can work on whatever technical update you want to do, while I have others around to argue with over New Year's!"

"OK impossible man, you convinced me, but you know that in the very end I admire you."

"Well, I do to."

The night ended with the two relatives enjoying Wilhelm Kempff's interpretations of the late Beethoven sonatas.

Epilogue; love – family – circus; The sharp pain from the third act; disappearing in light!

And the years passed by, as usual, after summer came winter and Dimitri never left his chalet to return to the outside world. He never replied to invitations in his honor to receive awards and honorary degrees or to wine and dine with celebrities. The last time he was seen in public was the night of the outdoor concert at the jail in 1987. In the mid-nineties, he eventually acquired the familiarity of the internet and he directed and communicated with his friends via email. Not that many people knew about his messages and nothing extraordinary happened with his foundation, apart from his regular contributions to charities and organizations. However, rumor had it that he transformed himself and visited constantly different places unrecognized. The media left him alone and respected his wish, so there had been no published pictures of him since 1987. However, many people in the meantime declared that they saw him, or at least someone like him who came across their path but no one could prove his identity. His organization firmly denied that he ever left his place in Switzerland. The peasants around his chalet always brought him bread, fruits, cheese, wine and chocolate. He had plenty of mountains and meadows around fim for hiking and breathing fresh air, and every New Year's and every summer he had visitors from his extended family. Alexander and Konstantin were regular visitors, but they were of advanced age as well and as the years went by they would visit him less frequently.

On Thanksgiving of 2007, he wrote to his nephew requesting him to take off from work during the next year and come up to his place to help him out. He did not write an email but wrote a hand-written letter. His nephew understood the severity and replied that this would be really difficult for him as he was part of corporate America and could not take such a long break. Indeed it was not easy to find such a chunk of time or to get a leave of absence. Dimitri wrote back and explained to him that it would be the best gift for his 70th birthday and he would personally negotiate his leave of absence with his bosses and corporation. He asked him to fully trust him and skip his visit this year and instead visit him between Thanksgiving and Christmas of next year but in the mean time to be prepared to stay for some time, which he would define to him and his corporation in more detail later. So towards the end of 2008 his nephew one day appeared in front of the chalet's door. The snow came early that year and the landscape was covered with a heavy blanket of snow, as pure and white as a bleached white cloth. The door was again open and he heard that his uncle had the radio on loud. It was not necessary for him to ring the bell or knock at the door so he entered into the living room. He realized that it was not just any radio station but that his uncle was listening to the Minnesota public radio via the web. He was taking a shower and that is why the volume was so high. Dimitri's nephew stepped in front of the monitor to lower the volume and when he did so his uncle's voice came like a thunder from the shower

"Why did you do this? Right at the moment he was going to conclude his joke?"

With a deep sigh his nephew said, "OK, OK, no worries here is your hero again."

"But I missed the joke now!"

"Don't they podcast it? Why are you such a pain?"

"I don't do that podcasting and blah blah I am not an mp3 generation kid as you know, I still order LP's from the web."

"OK! OK thank you for the welcome. I will wait here till you are ready … yeah from the web tha blah blah web," concluded whispering.

Dimitri came out drying his thick all-white hair with a towel and hugged his nephew.

"Aren't you tired of listening to this guy year after year?"

"What are you talking about? This is the sole reason to have a computer, besides the email. I listen to my favorite radio shows."

"I believe you don't know about satellite radio?"

"Why should I know about it? What I have is the best!"

"Oh! So not better or just good…. but the best! Hm… this guy on the radio keeps repeating himself, isn't he? Why are you addicted to such a show? Well, I guess it is for old timers like you?"

"You never paid attention to it son; that is why it looks that way to you. It repeats itself as much as a fugue from JS Bach that repeats itself and makes you addicted; you are waiting for the next variation and you know very well that only one note will change, but this note gives it another meaning, delivers another message, another dimension, another flavor and the story goes on and where does the music go when it stops? Nowhere and everywhere? It is in your mind playing again and again. You see son, music is the most divine "creature" of humankind. That is why Beethoven, the best ever of all the musicians, seems like a God. How can you capture music? With what means and how would you measure its dimensions? It does not have dimensions for physicists like me."

"Oh, there you go again with your philosophies and your Beethoven and all that nonsense."

"What? You still believe that Mozart could measure up to him?"

"Or better! OK…OK I am just kidding. OK, it was just a joke."

"Well you see my son, Beethoven is not only responsible for authoring the old and new testament of contemporary music, but he made the impossible reality."

"Wait I am loosing you again, does he share credit for the Bible in your opinion and what is the other revelation about the impossible?"

"The old testament of music is his thirty-two sonatas for piano and the new is his nine, unfortunately not ten, symphonies that he left behind."

"Really? But you do understand that this is your opinion?"

"Sure I do."

"OK, then."

"Yes, but you know son, in your new beloved hometown, every year the New York Times has your beloved New Yorkers vote on the best piece of music ever written and every single year your favorite New Yorkers vote for Beethoven's Ninth."

"Oh really!"

"Well, not only that, but four or more of his other compositions are also in the top ten of that list! And all this where? In the most decadent and outrageous ... and whatever else you can call this city."

"And what is the impossible that became reality? Are you alluding to the fact that he was deaf or the 10th? Probably not because he never finished it"

"He didn't have to."

"Why?"

"Well, the Ninth was too perfect."

"In your opinion?"

"And don't forget the New Yorkers!"

"Right? You are always right I guess."

"Well, the impossible was to compose the best song ever, based on lyrics in the most difficult and harsh language of the world."

"Oh I see! You mean the ode to the joy?"

"Indeed."

"Yes, I suppose that this is something; a real achievement."

"You are getting better."

"Sometimes I wonder if your grandfather was as bad as you? Worse? or better!"

"Oh he was far better, as he was more original and less educated."

"Not hard to disagree with you on that."

They both laughed and tapped each other on their shoulders as they proceeded to the table to have a glass of wine.

"So what is that all about? Why am I here and why could you not explain it to me?"

"Not the right time, son."

"Ah. . . I see, again, the pattern has not changed."

"But ... oh well, this time you will not have to wait long."

"And how long is 'not long'"?

"A couple of days or more, it really depends on you."

"On me? How come on me?"

"Well listen, I have something here for you to read. I assume it will take you some time to do so."

He stood up and took a few steps to his study desk. He returned with three packs of paper, bound together.

"Here they are. Three of them."

"What are these?"

"Take a look."

Silent and reluctant for few seconds he looked his uncle deep in his eyes.

"Are these the manuscripts that you were working on the past twenty or so years?"

"Hmmm…more or less."

"Are these patents to be? Or new theories? Review articles? Or what?"

"Oh I forgot! You belong to the generation that does not like to read, sorry. Shall I rather give you the message in twenty-five words or twenty-five seconds or perhaps give you the executive summary?"

"Come on, of course I read, you know I read all the time."

"All right then, I will post them on the web, so you can read them."

"No, come on. I don't mean that way … but can't you tell me what they are about?"

"Mr. high-end executive, don't you realize that the world out there is in deep trouble because people want the story in one serving, and it has to be fast and not diluted with nonsense which old timers like me call details?"

"OK! OK! I would rather have no more preaching here. What am I supposed to do with them?"

Dimitri's face became angry immediately.

"Oh sorry! Of course, of course I will read them, I don't mean that … but what will happen afterwards? I mean, I am not an engineer or physicist and will not understand your high-end logic and conclusions."

Dimitri's face was angry, but also pitiful.

"Mr. New Yorker, you have not even looked at the front page and you have already concluded that this is not for you?"

"What do you know about New York when you let yourself rot in this mountain and in isolation?"

"You know son, I have lived as much as you have lived in New York, this center of the world. These mountains have a lot to teach you, which you can never learn in the streets of New York."

"You know things have changed since the last time you were there, maybe you should join me and see what it's like nowadays?"

"Sure, I should really make that trip with you. But what is there to see? To walk around the farmer's market at Union Square and see an old lady offer berries to people and encourage them to taste them and have them buy her berries? You know, that old lady's wrinkled palms are full of wholesome fresh berries and the young man on her right doesn't take one, because he is afraid that she has not washed her hands. The lady on her left does not taste them because she is afraid that they are not washed. And the young mother behind her does not allow her child to go and get them, because she is afraid that the berries have been treated with pesticides. You may want to come with me to a place where the old lady might get squeezed or run over by children who have never seen such a nutritious food for days. When I refer to food, I am not talking about berries that have flavor, aroma, color, pleasant taste and precious nutrition with their vitamins and antioxidants, but insects, grass and uncooked roots. So, please do not forget whom you talk to and show the proper respect."

His nephew lowered his head as the whole drama of his uncle's life ran through his mind again. He swallowed hard and asked his uncle with reverence and fear.

"So,... have you been to Union Square lately?"

"That's beside the point my dear. The point here is to teach you to start reading again, perhaps the way that another generation used to."

"Uncle, you know, I read at work everyday."

"Sure you do! But how many things stay with you at the very end? How much pleasure is there for you? How do all these things that you read, help you understand that there is no more powerful and potent start than the explosive beginning of Prokoviev's "Romeo and Juliette" and no better end than Tchaikovsky's end of the Pathetique? The end that resembles and surpasses the way that a candle disappears after the last molecule of wax is burnt and becomes air."

"What do you mean? I don't understand your point?"

"And that is why you will die happy! Along with the majority out there."

"OK, look I will read them with pleasure of course. I just wanted to have an idea, as I am afraid that you are way too advanced of a scientist for me."

"They are deeply scientific …indeed … but in a language that you understand."

As he said this, he stood up and left the room while his nephew opened the first page of the first one and read "Love". He did the same for the second and he read "Family" and then he rushed to the third one and he read "Circus". He was so puzzled that he could not hide his bewilderment, so he asked his uncle in a loud voice, who had walked to the other end of the living room.

"Are these your diaries?"

"No they are not."

He turned to face his nephew.

"What are they then?" he sensed that his uncle was getting angry again and continued.

"Of course I will read them, but I just thought that if they were your diaries everyone out there would love to read them. You had such an interesting life and experience after all and I was hoping that you could share it with everyone one day."

"Well, I think whatever happened to me and my life is already written out there and not interesting to the people anymore."

"But then … is this what you have been writing all this time up here?"

"Indeed."

"They look like three novels to me."

"And they are. That is why you are here, as I want you to read them and then take them down to your world and find someone to publish them for me."

"But … all these years you were writing novels and not patents or theories?"

"Read them and when you finish we can talk about them."

"And what is with that title '*Circus*'? I understand '*Love*' and '*Family*' but '*Circus*'?"

"Will you ever change? You will find out by reading and studying and not by eliminating important details and losing the essence of things?"

"Sure. OK, I profusely apologize."

The next few days Dimitri did not talk to his nephew and pretended that he was busy with something very important. He let him alone, to fully absorb the three novels. He told him that he should not talk to him until he finishes all of them and in the right order.

Seven days later and after some breaks to talk on the phone, surf the internet or rest, his nephew knocked on his door in the study room, and announced to him that he had finished reading the novels.

Dimitri interrupted him promptly and told him that he did not want to hear his opinion about them and begged him to ask only one question if he had one. He reiterated that he would only answer one.

His nephew took a deep breath and started thinking about what that question could be. Dimitri could tell from his eyes that he had many questions, and it was hard for him to come up with only one. He thought for about five minutes and said:

"OK, I can see why you wanted to write about "Love" and "Family", but why "Circus"? I don't really understand … why did you choose this …? Why did it have to be a Circus?"

Dimitri took a deep breath and answered him:

"And what should I have named it "Society"? It is an allegory and since I promised to answer one question I will give you the key tomorrow. I want you to really understand the message behind it. I will leave a written note for you at the table after my breakfast. Good night for now, as you seem exhausted and I am also really exhausted and have to rest."

His nephew accepted that happily as he was really exhausted and he went upstairs to sleep.

He knew that he would sleep really well and deep, as he was exhausted and the warmth of the room was calming and soothing, in contrast to the heavy snowfall outside. As he fell on to bed and covered himself with a heavy blanket, his eyes opened. He thought of a paragraph or two from his uncle's books and stood up to pray. That was something he used to do every day as a child as his parents educated him. Something that became a habit, but faded as he entered adulthood and the years went by. Sometimes he didn't pray because he was tired or because he happened to get home late after a night out in clubs or sometimes because he did not want to embarrass himself for such an act in front of his girlfriend. This time he did it with a strong desire and despite being so tired.

After he finished praying, he fell in bed again totally exhausted. He was sure that he would sleep at once but he couldn't. He saw the snow through the window and thought that he should get up again to lower the blinds, as the snow would reflect the morning sunlight into his room in an intense way and wake him up early.

He got under the blanket for a third time and opened his eyes again, but this time because he was thinking about his uncle's books. Although he was exhausted his mind kept spinning about the novels and the true meaning of the last one. All of a sudden he realized that the more he thought about it the more he uncovered about the meaning of the last story. Hours passed like this and he could not sleep. He felt like the first sunlight of the morning would be in his room soon. Hours later he woke up and realized that it was late in the morning. He felt exhausted and tired and as he got up he could hear that his uncle was downstairs listening to dramatic music.

As he stepped out of the room he saw him stepping out of the house. He walked downstairs and noticed that he had just placed a vinyl record on the turntable. As he lifted the cover to see what that deep melodic piece was, he saw the portrait of Maria Callas and realized that this was a recording of the Traviata. He initially thought that the music did not sound the way he remembered it, especially the overture. He lifted his eyes to view the portrait of the great soprano on the wall. Next to it was Karajan's portrait and in between Beethoven's sculptured head. Then to the right were, Disney's portrait and movie posters of Visconti's "Leopard", another poster from a Felini film, The Umbrellas of Cherbourg and in between the poster of "A man and a woman". He looked at the walls more carefully to see pictures of the Golden Gate, the Madeleine, the Acropolis and Santorini, a couple dancing the tango, some belle époque vintage posters and finally Manhattan. Suddenly he turned left and then right and he saw family portraits and realized that he understood more and more about the novels. The trapeze photo, the wine drawing, a music partiture, they all looked familiar, but all of a sudden he felt very sentimental and a sensation like a knife penetrating his chest, again and again. It was toward the ending of the Traviata's third act overture where the strings play a funny role in the plot proclaiming the tragedy. "A tragedy?" he thought and paused from any thought for a second and approached the table where his uncle had just had his breakfast. He saw a note for him and a stack of papers, which was the key to understanding the "Circus". Dimitri skimmed through it quickly and again looked at the family pictures and portraits hanging on the wall. "Oh my God!" he howled at once and thought for another minute till his thoughts were interrupted by his uncle who opened the door.

"Hey, you are finally up! I am ready to go son and I don't have time to waste, so please stay here until I call you. And remember your job is to take these books and try to publish them in your favorite city. I am sure you will make it happen, but wait here till you hear from me directly."

"What do you mean and where are you going?"

"You know my answer son. Not the right time for you to know. Trust me" ...

"You read my little note I see."

"Yes I did."

"So, does it make sense?"

"I am still thinking about this poem with the 32 verses and all these verbs in Circus... pertained and repented and obsessed and... I still need to decode it. "

"I am sure you will one day, but please stay here till I tell you to leave."

"But what do you mean? Are you going out there? Again? After such a long time?"

Dimitri said nothing, hugged his nephew and turned his back to him, ready to leave,

"without a wig or beard or hat? With your white hair and wrinkled face?"

"Well son, the last time they saw me was a long time ago so no one will ever recognize me. No one even cares about me. Very few remember me and very few have a desire to see me. It is time for me to go out there again, for a second time," he smiled while he turned and opened the door, which allowed the ample light to get in and exited with a quiet and rather fast pace for a seventy year old man. He was still in good shape and he started walking towards the village. His boots left deep imprints in the thick blanket of snow.

Dimitri's nephew went to the window. He watched him walk towards the village; he kept watching his back, as he was leaving the chalet behind. There was so much snow everywhere that he had to squint, his eyes blinked all the time, as the snow reflected so much light. He closed his eyes from the glare and looked down to glance again at the note that his uncle had left him and moments later he watched his uncle's silhouette as it became more and more distant. He reminded him of Chaplin who walked away from the camera towards the vast landscape during the final credits of his movies. Walking alone becoming smaller and smaller, more and more distant. And the landscape was vast, full of snow. His head was spinning as he finished the last lines of his uncle's note, he sighed and then shouted again "Oh my …" and looked once again at his uncle who was disappearing in the strong glare of the snow even though white clouds were everywhere, covering most of the sky. He looked at the note again and tried to see him one last time despite the glare and sighed!

Oh! Please God bless, oh my…!

All of a sudden, fast, but why?

White clouds cover the sky.

The sun is now out of sight.

How could it be so bright?

Light! Pure ample light!

THANKS to:

All the people who helped realize this dream; this work would never have been possible without the help, encouragement and work that I have received from all of you, you know it or not.

Also my sincere appreciation to the editors that worked in the manuscript: Ms. Joan Osterwalder and Ms. Jo Buffolino.

Extreme THANKS to Mrs Julie Chirdaris for her additional editions, valuable moral support and precious passionate encouragement. Thanks also to Jill, Stathis, Nik, Kok-Hwa for giving me additional power!

Thank you to Mr. George Stephanopoulos for all his work, help, advice and friendship. Special thanks to Amazon and everyone who worked on this project. So many more thanks to give (another 100 to):

1. Grandmother Maria
2. Grandparents (Vasilis,
3. Apostolos
4. Chrissa)
5. Father
6. Mother
7. Brother
8. Aunt Kaliopi
9. Uncle Vasilis
10. Uncle Angellos
11. Angel
12. Garisson Keillor
13. Ludwig van Beethoven
14. Anonymous Composer of Spanish Romance
15. Sergei Prokoviev
16. Piotr I Tchaikovsky
17. Giuseppe Verdi
18. Frederick Chopin
19. Dimitri Shostakovich

20. Johan S Bach
21. Wolfgang A Mozart
22. Johan Strauss Jr
23. Gustav Mahler
24. Isaac Albeniz
25. Francisco Tarrega
26. Nino Rota
27. Michel Legrand
28. Francis Lai
29. Ennio Morricone
30. Henri Mancini
31. Nicola Piovani
32. Maurice Zarre
33. Astor Piazzola
34. Mariano Morres
35. Carlos Gardel
36. Peter Ludwig
37. Luiz Bonfa
38. Manos Hadjidakis
39. Vasilis Tsitsanis
40. George Polychroniadis
41. Apostolos Kaldaras
42. Paul Mauriat
43. The 4 evangelists Mathew
44. Mark
45. Luke
46. John
47. author of the book of Job
48. Rainer Maria Rilke
49. Socrates
50. Aristophanes
51. Euripedes
52. Sophocles
53. Aeschylus
54. Nikos Gkatsos

55. Agathi Dimitrouka
56. Leon Tolstoi
57. Fiodr Dostoyevski
58. R Kipling
59. Victor Hugo
60. Ernest Hemingway
61. John Steinbeck
62. Gabriel Garcia Marques
63. Charles Dickens
64. Jules Verne
65. Alexander Dumas
66. Frank Capra
67. Walt Disney
68. Orson Wells
69. Guissiepe Tornatore
70. Claude Lelouch
71. Charlie Chaplin
72. Jacques Demy
73. FF Copola
74. Luchino Visconti
75. Peter Shaffer
76. Alec Baldwin
77. Michael Douglas
78. Robert Redford
79. Alain Delon
80. Marcello Mastroianni
81. Andre Segovia
82. Wilhelm Kempff
83. Maria Kallas
84. Herbert von Karajan
85. Sexteto Mayor Argentinean tango players
86. Leonardo Da Vinci
87. Pierre-August Renoir
88. Yiannis Tsarouhis
89. Jules Bastien Lepage

90. Photographer of Dresden's destruction
91. Johan Strauss the architect
92. Senator J William Fulbright
93. Dr. SM Constantinides
94. Brita Schulze
95. Magda Eisinger
96. My friends at FT
97. Simone
98. Jill Richardson
99. Martina
100. SR

9640290R0

Made in the USA
Lexington, KY
15 May 2011